No Less in Blood

NO LESS IN BLOOD

D. M. PIRRONE

FIVE STAR
A part of Gale, Cengage Learning

GALE
CENGAGE Learning™

Detroit • New York • San Francisco • New Haven, Conn • Waterville, Maine • London

GALE
CENGAGE Learning™

LIBRARY OF CONGRESS CATALOGING-IN-PUBLICATION DATA

Pirrone, D. M.
　No less in blood / D.M. Pirrone. — 1st ed.
　　p. cm.
　ISBN-13: 978-1-59414-927-6
　ISBN-10: 1-59414-927-5
　1. Adoptees—Fiction. 2. Family secrets—Fiction. 3. Inheritance and succession—Fiction. 4. Murder—Fiction. 5. Chicago (Ill.)—Fiction. 6. Minnesota—Fiction. I. Title.
　PS3616.I76N6 2011
　813'.6—dc22　　　　　　　　　　　　　　　　2010043352

First Edition. First Printing: February 2011.
Published in 2011 in conjunction with Tekno Books and Ed Gorman.

To Mom and Dad, who always encouraged my way with words.

ACKNOWLEDGMENTS

I owe debts of gratitude to many people in the making of this book. First, to two authors whose books on Chicago history informed my creation of the city Mary Anne Schlegel found in 1893: *City of the Century,* by Donald L. Miller, and *Devil in the White City,* by Erik Larson. Both of these works helped me make the Chicago of the past as real as the city I live in today.

I am also indebted to the late Hugh Holton, who allowed me to buttonhole him at a mystery convention and ask how a Chicago cop would handle pursuit of a murder suspect into another state. Helene Trapper, LCSW, helped me work through such knotty issues as adoption law and custody matters; thanks, Helene, for letting me pick your brain. John Ruemmler and my classmates at the Maui Writers' Retreat gave me invaluable feedback on earlier drafts of this work. My eagle-eyed editor, Deni Dietz, did her usual excellent job; any errors that may remain are my fault. Thanks also to Roz Greenberg at Tekno Books for giving this book its chance.

My brother and sister-in-law, Kevin and Cheryl Piron, took me on sightseeing trips around Hibbing, Minnesota, and other small towns in the Iron Range. Birch Falls is my own invention, but it has its genesis in several real and delightful places. (And yes, the food at Valentini's really is that good.)

Finally, a heartfelt thanks to my husband Steve, who took point with our boys so I could have time to write . . . and who loved this book as a work-in-progress, but was also honest enough to say so when something didn't work. You always tell it to me straight, love—no words are adequate for how much that means to me.

CHAPTER ONE

All he'd wanted to know was where to find Linnet. A father wanting to see his daughter—what was wrong with that? Nothing. Not a goddamned thing.

Luke glared at the crumpled body by the base of the swing set. "Why didn't you just tell me? You always do this, Grace. The simplest little thing I want, and you won't give it to me. You are *so* goddamned stupid . . ."

He clenched his fists to stop their shaking. Talking to a corpse. He was losing it for sure. Bark crunched under his sneakers as he turned away from the body. He propped himself against the swing set with one arm and gulped the cold night air. It smelled of wet leaves and mud, plus a hint of exhaust. Drizzle stung his face. The swish of traffic echoed across the playground, unnaturally loud.

He snagged a Marlboro from the half-empty pack in his jacket and lit it on the third try. The flame warmed his fingers, which were stiffening in the chill. Lungs full of nicotine, he leaned against the cold metal of the swing set frame and considered his next move. In this part of town, the few night owls who might be lurking weren't likely to be chummy with cops. Grace worked the five-to-one shift; this late, no one much was around. *Used to work,* he corrected himself, and choked down a nervous laugh.

She should have given him another chance. She should have known he meant it this time when he said things would be different. She should have let him explain. And she sure as hell

9

shouldn't have had those papers served in front of every waitress in the goddamned diner. He'd wanted to belt her one right there. But they'd all come up close around her, the women in their red aprons and sneakers, daring him to throw a punch or even say a nasty word. So he'd tossed the divorce papers on the floor and taken off. Walked around the block, then doubled back to linger over two cups of coffee and a donut in the Golden Apple across the street. Its front window gave him a clear view of the diner where Grace worked.

When the frizz-haired waitress with a nose stud gave him funny looks, he'd left the Apple and stationed himself in the entryway of a nearby funeral home. He'd watched Grace leave the S & G, without her usual escort, just after the bells of St. Alphonsus Church struck ten. He'd given her half a block's head start, then slipped out of the alcove and followed her.

She moved fast, constantly glancing back as if expecting to spot him. The throngs of twenty-somethings who nightly flooded Lincoln Park West in search of trendy cafés and bars made great camouflage, but also slowed him down. He almost lost her twice, until they reached residential streets and the crowds thinned out. Grace had begun to relax by then, only occasionally looking over her shoulder. When she cut across the park, he'd grabbed his chance.

Only it all went wrong.

He paced across the park as he smoked. If she'd just told him where Linnet was, he wouldn't have had to hit her. Time was, she'd known better than to make him angry. A few months without a strong hand had made her cocky—or crazy. Shouting at him, calling him names, fighting and screaming loud enough to wake the whole street—what else could he have done but shut her up the only way she understood?

Streetlights glowed through the drizzle, illuminating the spot where Grace's head had struck the swing set frame. Any decent lawyer would plead this out as second-degree manslaughter. He'd have gone for that, if he'd ever finished law school. But time inside wasn't an option for a man with a family. He had people to see, papers to file, lawyers to talk to. And a kid to find. Linnet came first. Without her, all his plans were nothing.

He took a last drag on his cigarette, stubbed it out and stuck the butt in his pocket. Then he went through Grace's purse and clothes. One coat pocket lay trapped beneath her hip. He breathed deep to steady himself and then turned her over. After a few minutes he sat back on his heels and swore. Nothing. Not a goddamned thing to tell him where Linnet might be. His fury vanished in a wave of queasiness as he met Grace's sightless, upward stare. He half-expected her to blink away the raindrops.

He stuffed his pockets with Grace's battered wallet and what little else he'd found in her coat: an "L" card, her Minnesota driver's license, a Walgreen's receipt, a plastic gum-machine bubble with a cheap child's ring inside. Then he strode out of the park, in the direction Grace had been going. Linnet was somewhere in this city. He'd find her no matter what it took.

Rachel couldn't breathe. A smothering warmth covered her nose and mouth. She flailed her arms and sucked in a mouthful of hair. Her hand struck something soft. She shoved it away.

A yowl and a thump accompanied the return of oxygen. She breathed deep, sat up and glared at the fat gray tabby by the couch. "Dammit, Quincy, how many times have I told you not to sit on my face?!"

Peter Quince glared back. His attempt at outraged feline dignity made him look like a petulant, furry football.

On any other night, she'd have found it hilarious.

She leaned down and dragged him into her lap. He filled it to overflowing. His warm, soft weight and the scent of clean cat fur made up somewhat for the pounding headache she'd given herself, part red wine and part the aftermath of crying into the sofa pillow. "One of these days you're going to kill me. Then who's going to feed you, Bonehead? You'd starve to death. You're afraid of ants, for Chrissake." She scratched under his chin. His grumbles turned to purring.

"God, you're easy to please." She leaned back against the cushions and closed her eyes. One hand kept scratching. The other gently massaged her throbbing, overstuffed sinuses. "One of many reasons why cats are better than men."

The grandfather clock in the corner chimed twice. Two A.M. Her inadvertent nap on the couch had given her a killer crick in the neck without doing a thing to soothe her headache or the gritty feeling in her eyes. She looked down at Quincy, who had drifted into blissful kitty half-sleep. "Can I be you, fuzzball? Just for a few days? Hell, just for the next few hours. No worries. Nothing in your little head except food and sleep."

A purr was his reply. She switched to long strokes across the top of his head. Cat hair fluttered upward. She watched it float down, willing herself not to recall the earlier part of the evening. It worked for maybe three minutes.

She got up, dislodging Quincy, and grabbed her empty wine glass off the coffee table. "More cabernet," she said, in reply to his cranky glare. Moving stiffly, she stumbled toward the kitchen. The half-full bottle of Yellowtail was right where she'd left it a few hours ago, between the fruit bowl and the espresso machine on her postage stamp–sized excuse for a kitchen counter. A lump rose in her throat. Nick had bought her that espresso machine. Eight months back, when he'd been working extra hours and she hadn't, and he'd wanted to make up to her for "being such a lousy boyfriend."

She grabbed the wine and poured herself a generous slug. The bite of it on her tongue distracted her thoughts for all of half a second. *Hooray.*

For the first time in a year of serious dating, Nick hadn't brought wine for dinner. He prided himself on his knowledge of wines and loved to surprise her with new vintages—generally more expensive ones than she could afford to indulge in. But for this, their first real date after weeks of grinding overtime finishing up the rule books and cover art for the latest *Star Empires* game release, no vino. Just a limp smile and a hurried sorry-I-didn't-have-time-to-pick-anything-up.

"I should have seen it coming when he didn't even flinch at the Yellowtail," she told Quincy, who'd followed her into the kitchen and was twining himself around her legs. "I toast our anniversary, and he comes back with, 'Honey, I'd like to talk about that.' He has *never* called me honey."

Quince butted her knee. As low as she felt, she couldn't help smiling a little.

"Yeah, right. You men are all alike. You just want one thing from a girl—" Her voice caught and her grip tightened on the stem of her wine glass. "And then you get bored. Or something. Been there, had that, want something different. Something not short and dumpy and plain-brown-bag. Or maybe I got too 'high-maintenance' for him, along with not being hot enough. I don't know." She gulped wine. "Oh, but he's not dumping me. He just wants to see other people. Like the new girl in the Art Department. Carol. With tits, but no ass. And height. And California surfer-chick hair." She forced a laugh that hovered close to tears. "Burnt Honey Blonde. Or some other stupid food name. Saffron Sunshine? Lemon Luscious? Color Me Chamomile?"

Why hadn't she said any of this while Nick was here? But no, she'd sat there silent on the couch, a cracker spread with homemade roasted red pepper dip forgotten in her hand, while he rolled out his spiel. Gender-adapted from a back issue of *Cosmo*, no doubt. "Nothing's over, sweetheart. Not unless you want it to be. I just . . . well, I thought we both needed some space. To loosen up, expand our options. I mean, it's not like we made any promises, right?"

"Not unless you count sleeping together since April." The cracker had snapped in two, the halves tumbling to her lap. Spread side down, of course.

"I'll get a towel," Nick had said, pushing himself away from the arm of the easy chair. First no wine, then he couldn't be bothered to sit down properly. How stupid was she, not to have seen it coming?

"No—" She'd heard her voice crack, and despised herself for it. "Don't put yourself out." Sudden anger—at herself for being so damned vulnerable, at him for causing it—gave her a flash of courage. She'd stood up, yanked Nick's bomber jacket off the coat rack and thrown it at him. "Unless it's the hell out of here. Permanently."

She bent and rubbed Quincy's ears with a half-hearted chuckle as she recalled Nick's parting expression. Wide-eyed as a dead trout. He hadn't expected that shot of backbone, either.

Wine in hand, she slouched toward the dining room. The cream sauce she'd intended to pour on the steaks au poivre had turned to beige paste, and the steaks were dotted with congealed fat. The steamed vegetables had long since wilted. At least the chocolate mousse had stayed safely chilled in the refrigerator. She set down her wine on one end of the sideboard. In a flurry of activity, she scooped up silverware, stacked and put away the unused plates and scraped the spoiled dinner into the garbage. Here, at least, was one mess she could control.

She ran out of steam before the final washing-up, though she did manage to rinse off the largest food clumps before giving in to a sudden craving for chocolate. A cereal bowl held almost two-thirds of the mousse. She carted bowl and spoon back to the sofa. Chocolate was better than more wine, which only made her headache worse. Quince wandered over for a sniff, then turned up his nose. "You don't know what you're missing," she mumbled through the first bittersweet mouthful. The taste distracted her from more serious thoughts. She ate the mousse slowly, then wiped bowl and spoon clean with a finger and licked it. No good. The thoughts were still there.

"Fine," she muttered as she went to dump the dishes on top of the rest in the kitchen sink. "Let's sum things up. What Has Rachel Connolly Done With Her Life? Not much. A dead-end job for a teensy game publisher, no progress on the novel for— what is it now, two years?—and no significant other in sight. Anymore. Plus I really hate this apartment, and I have a major head cold coming on. How'm I doing so far, Quincy?"

She wrenched on the hot water, then leaned against the sink and rested her head in her hands. Her temples throbbed against her fingers. *I want to call Mom. I wish to God I could.*

The driver had been too drunk to see the stop sign, or the slight, sixtyish woman in the dark wool coat walking home from early evening Mass. He—or she—hadn't even stopped to see what he'd hit. A neighbor had heard the screech of brakes, followed by burning rubber, and rushed outside to see what was going on. Too late to do anything except call 911 for a woman already dead. "At least she didn't suffer," people kept telling Rachel at the funeral. As if that mattered.

Nick had been wonderful then. He'd cooked her meals, endured her rambling phone calls late at night when the loneliness hit hardest, listened to her rant about the hideous unfairness of a universe where such bad things happened to good people. At least he'd waited for her to get over the worst of that loss before handing her another one. He'd always been outwardly considerate. *I bet his mother never had to nag him about writing thank-you notes.*

Mom hadn't liked him, which should have warned her.

Anyone else with such impeccable manners would have won over Mary Connolly long ago. She wondered what Dad would have thought. The same as Mom, probably, though too tactful to say it. He'd always been one to let her make her own mistakes. Mom had been the rescuer, voicing her opinions emphatically and often. She certainly had about Nick; they'd fought about him more than once.

A hysterical chuckle escaped her as she turned and leaned her back against the counter's edge. "You were right, Mom," she said to the room at large. "Got any other useful advice from beyond?"

No one answered. No one would. She felt lost, bewildered. Suddenly she was fifteen again, groping for some sense of back-to-normal after Dad's heart attack. He'd been puttering over coffee in the morning, dead at work before lunchtime. Back then, she and Mom had propped each other up to get through the days. Who was there to do that for her now?

She wandered out of the kitchen toward the second bedroom. Too cramped to sleep in, it served as a study, even though she'd had to shoehorn in the heavy mahogany desk and bookshelves. Family heirlooms, dating from her first year in high school. She touched the smooth wood. They'd made an expedition of it, she and Dad—a treasure hunt for just the right furniture to celebrate her freshman-hood.

The computer, its screen dark, took up half the desk space. The rest held a paperback *Webster's Dictionary* and a thesaurus, a hardback titled *Mining Towns of Northern Minnesota* and scattered pages from three different drafts of her novel-in-progress.

She picked up the first page and read a few lines by rote, not really comprehending. *Winters came hard to the Range. The winter of 1940 came harder than most, though Adele didn't learn the reason until much, much later.* She pulled out her swivel chair and sat down. The page drifted to her lap as she gave herself up to memory.

A comment of Mom's had sparked her interest, over dinner on a cold February night. "Horrible weather," Mom had said—the opening line to their customary mutual kvetch about Chicago winters. "Three weeks in the low teens, and no end in sight. I should move to Florida."

"Which is hot and sticky and full of bugs the size of soup spoons." Rachel smiled and snagged another corn muffin. "You'd take the cold and snow any day over that. Admit it."

A chuckle from Mom. "Guilty. Though on days like this, with a minus-seventeen wind chill, I'm tempted."

"You and me both. When it gets cold enough to make *me* wear gloves, you know it's bad. I'd almost prefer the bugs."

"How you can stand freezing your fingers like that, I'll never know." Without waiting to be asked, Mom passed her the butter. "I think your mother came from northern Minnesota. Maybe she passed on a genetic tolerance for cold."

An offhand remark about Rachel's background, soon lost in the rest of their rambling conversation over spicy chili and salad. It had made Rachel curious enough to do some reading on the region, which had led her to set a story in the rough-and-ready mining towns of Minnesota's Iron Range. The fleeting sense she had of telling her birth mother's tale soon vanished in the labors of creating her fictional heroine, and she'd given the real woman barely another thought.

In the months since the accident, though, such thoughts hadn't left her in peace. They cropped up whenever her guard was down: dozing on the couch with Quincy, waking to a half-empty bed and the sound of Nick in the bathroom. Or worse, when she woke alone in the small hours, her mind racing with things left unsaid and undone.

Sorry-for-yourself doesn't get the dinner made. She could hear

Mom say it, the way she had a thousand times while Rachel was growing up. *You have five minutes to sit and stew, lovey. Then you need to get on with things.*

"Get on with what?" she muttered. "Booting Nick out of my life? Finding someone else? Finishing my novel? Moving out of this apartment?" She buried her fingers in her hair. "I can't even dredge up the energy to do my damned dishes. What do you want from me?"

She slumped backward in the swivel chair. It turned a few inches with a protesting creak, and she found herself staring at the top right-hand drawer of her desk.

She reached out and slowly opened it, knowing what she would see: an Information Exchange Authorization form from the Illinois Adoption Registry.

She took the form out and stared at it. Nick had suggested she get it, back when she'd felt the first stirrings of a need to know. He'd made it sound so easy, so rational. "You're curious. Who wouldn't be? Hook up with the registry and tell them you want contact. If your mother does too, they'll have her on file. Name, address, whatever. They'll tell you what you need to know, and you take it from there."

"And if she doesn't want to see me? Or if they don't tell me a damned thing?" There she went again, assuming the worst-case scenario. If there were prizes for that, she'd win a Pulitzer.

"Then it didn't work. But at least you gave it a shot. Anything's better than just sitting around agonizing, right?"

It had struck her, then, that Mom would have agreed. So she'd sent away for the form, and then sat on it for nearly three months. Didn't even have the gumption to fill it out.

She was so tired of being afraid. Of little things, stupid things, like calling people she didn't know well. Or driving the S-curve along South Lake Shore Drive. Or forcing her jerk boyfriend to admit he was dumping her. *Hey, at least I managed that. Sort of.*

She rooted in the drawer for a pen. Then she wrote, fast, before she could change her mind.

The new-car smell had given Linnet a terrible headache. She couldn't sleep, though she'd been trying since they'd passed Milwaukee. She squeezed her limp stuffed rabbit tighter, nearly strangling it. The worn fabric smelled like wet cardboard. The familiar scent should have calmed her. But there was no comfort in the toy, nor in anything else she could think of. Back when she was eight, Ears had held enough magic to drive the demons away. Now she was twelve, old enough to know better. *It's a stupid stuffed animal. It can't fix anything. Only a stupid little kid would think it could.*

Her eyes felt hot, and for a moment she wanted to throw Ears across the car—but then Ruth would know she was awake, and would insist on talking. She didn't want to talk right now. She didn't want to hear Ruth's too-cheerful voice telling her that everything was going to be just-fine-don't-you-worry, when underneath she could hear that everything was not going to be fine. She wanted Mama, and a home for them someplace other than at the women's shelter Ruth ran. Someplace where she could have her own room.

Someplace where her father wouldn't find them.

The dark, the cold, the strangeness of hurrying down the street with Mama in the middle of the night—she remembered that most clearly from the first time they'd left, four years ago. They'd taken the bus for hours. She'd fallen asleep holding Ears, lulled by the dull rumble of the motor. Ears was new then, her Easter Bunny present—though it really came from Mama. *Dad started yelling and wouldn't stop. Quit spending money on stupid shit, he said. You're too stupid to live, you dumbfuck whore.* When the beating began, she'd hidden under her bed with her face pressed against Ears' soft belly. She hadn't dared come out, even after the slam of the front door and a long silence told her that her father was gone.

They passed a highway sign. Linnet read it in the glow of the headlights: Minneapolis 70, Duluth 207. They were headed beyond Duluth, to a town called Birch Falls where her grandfather lived. She'd seen a picture of him once: tall and bony, with a face that looked as if it didn't know how to smile.

Linnet wondered how he'd look when she and Ruth showed up on his doorstep.

They turned off the highway and pulled into a filling station. Linnet closed her eyes as Ruth killed the engine.

"Linnie?" Ruth turned around with a rustle of fabric. After several seconds, Linnet heard the car door open and shut.

She risked a quick peek out the window. Ruth was filling the gas tank. Then she'd go inside to pay, buy a twenty-ounce Coke for herself and some fruit juice for Linnet. After that, they'd be on the road again, bound for northern Minnesota and her new home with a stranger who happened to be family.

She wanted to bolt from the car, run off into the dark and hide until someone came by who would give her a lift back to Chicago. As soon as she got back to the city, she'd find Mama. *I couldn't go away without you,* she'd say. Then Mama would hold her close and tell Linnet she loved her. She'd say how glad she was that Linnet had come back, even though Linnet had disobeyed her.

She remembered her mother's voice, crackling through static over the phone. "I love you, little bird. You remember that, okay? Go with Ruth; I'll see you soon."

Linnet didn't want to wait for soon. She wanted Mama now, right here. She had to get out of this car. She had to get out this second, get herself home before it was too late.

She didn't move. Instead, she hid her face against Ears and cried.

CHAPTER TWO

A brown manila folder landed with a slap in the only clear space on Detective James Florian's desk. The sudden sound made Florian slosh lukewarm coffee over his fingers.

"Morning, Flo. Special delivery," came the snide voice of his lieutenant. "You don't have to thank me. This time."

That's Florian, he wanted to say, but didn't. Letting Lieutenant Commander Mitchell know how much he hated being called Flo would only encourage the man to do it more often. Instead, he put down his coffee cup and picked up the folder, swinging his long legs from the desktop to the linoleum floor. His heels just missed the top corner of a stack of forms in a rainbow of colors: pink, yellow, mint green, baby blue. Around him, ringing phones and hurried footsteps blended with the screech and slam of filing cabinet drawers being opened and shut. Voices rose over the background noise: "District Twenty-Three." ". . . description of the car, ma'am?" ". . . Montrose and Winchester, first floor . . ." "Weston. What've you got?"

The folder felt far too light for his liking. Not surprising for a Jane Doe homicide on a quiet Lakeview street. He and his partner, Maggie Harper, had caught the case late last night. Inside the folder were the crime-scene photos he'd expected, as well as a copy of the ME's preliminary report. The pictures showed a huddled shape at the base of a swing set, then a close-up view of the victim's head. High and to one side, something a tad thicker than the business end of a baseball bat

21

had crushed the skull like an eggshell. He glanced at the report and wasn't surprised to read that the probable cause of the fatal injury was the swing set frame. Traces of blood and hair on it matched the anonymous victim's. Identification would have to wait. The mugger—or whoever—had picked Jane Doe's purse and pockets clean.

She'd been wearing a waitress' uniform, a pair of worn sneakers, and a tan raincoat with a torn lining and a shiny patch on the right shoulder, most likely worn down by her handbag. The bag was black vinyl mock-leather, the zipper handle a stub. He looked back at the snapshots, trying to fix the victim's face in his memory. Regular features, good bones—alive, she'd probably been pretty. That thought saddened him for no good reason.

He pushed himself out of his chair and ambled toward the coffee room for a refill. Once he had an ID, he could start rooting around in the victim's life for plausible culprits. Assuming this wasn't a random mugging gone worse than its perpetrator intended—though it would've taken one pissed-off mugger to shove her into the swing set that hard. The neighbors he and Maggie had roused had been asleep or oblivious, or had figured someone else's trouble wasn't any of their business. Learning anything useful meant a chat with the night owls among the local street people. He'd start there, let Maggie nag Forensics for a complete report. Persistent as a terrier digging for a bone, Mags could get what they needed faster than any other cop he'd ever worked with. He grinned, imagining the chief med examiner's reaction. *"Jesus God, it's Harper again—give her what she wants and get her the hell out of my hair!"*

He filled his cup, sipped and made a face. The coffee had been sitting on the hot burner awhile. It looked like tar and tasted worse. As a kid, he'd once tried to eat a piece of tree bark on a dare. That taste came back to him now, making him smile in spite of the insult just done to his tongue. He leaned against the counter, cradling the cup in both hands to warm his fingers. They always felt cold from October to May, no matter the interior temperature. Pianist's fingers, his ex-fiancée had called them. She'd thought it a terrible shame that he'd never learned to play.

He ran one warmed hand through his thinning dark hair, then fingered the rough lump on the bridge of his nose. It was a nervous habit he'd developed years ago, after an angry drunk in a brawl had bounced his rookie-cop head off the edge of a table. Afterward, sympathetic friends told him the ill-healed break gave his face character. Ruthie used to say he reminded her of granite: solid, strong, able to withstand anything life threw at him. Later, she'd used different words: unyielding, immovable, rigid. Sometimes he still wondered if she was right—if he really was the kind of guy who'd rather be dead than wrong.

He walked back to his desk and dialed the medical examiner's office, sipping coffee while the line rang. They wouldn't have a definite ID yet; right now, all he wanted was a decent guess as to when he might get that information. Jane Doe's uniform was the kind they wore at most diners; he could think of at least three within easy walking distance of where she'd been found. Nothing said she'd worked in the neighborhood—she could've gotten jumped on her way from a bus or L stop—but it was a place to start. He might even pick up a decent cup of coffee.

A voice came on the line. Florian made the appropriate noises to get the call transferred higher up the food chain. Phone to his ear, he picked up the close-up. The dead woman reminded him a little of Ruthie, though his ex never would have worn her fine hair that long. The thick braid lay across the woman's throat, dark as a gash against her pale skin. A twinge of revulsion passed through him. Suddenly, he wanted very much to find her killer.

★ ★ ★ ★ ★

The light pole felt cold against Luke's back, even through his heavy wool jacket. He ignored the chill as best he could, his eyes on the playground across the street. Children in bright-colored coats bobbed across the asphalt, swarming over the swing set and jungle gyms. Luke envied them. He'd never been that carefree. Early on, he'd learned there were two kinds of people in the world: those who did and those who got done to. By the time he turned eight, he'd known which kind he had to be. He wanted things to be different for Linnet, and now maybe he could make that happen. If he found her in time.

He spat sideways into a puddle to get the sour taste of failure out of his mouth. This was the fifth schoolyard he'd been to, showing Linnet's picture around, and once again he'd come up empty. None of the children recognized her, or remembered seeing her pass by.

It had seemed like such a simple way to narrow down the possibilities. He was sure Grace had holed up in a women's shelter, just like the last time she'd left. He'd ruled out anyplace close to where she worked. He'd tracked her down that way before, and Grace learned fast. Shelters near grade schools seemed like a good bet. Being able to walk to school would make things easier for Linnet, and there weren't an impossible number to check out. All he needed was one kid who knew Linnet to set him on the right track. Then he could check the nearest shelter, make sure she was there, and bust her out. The shelter workers might assume she'd run away. It happened. If not, he knew how to disappear. Linnie would be scared, of course, but not for long. And once they got what was coming to her, he'd make up for everything.

That was the reason their lives had gone so wrong, he thought as he dug out a cigarette and lit it. Money. They'd never had enough. He'd grown up poor and hated it. As soon as he could, he got out to make something of himself. Brains and a scholarship landed him in pre-law, but he lost a coveted law school slot to some bitch who fit the quota. So he took time off, worked every job he could get, and earned his way onto campus.

Down the street, a cop car turned the corner. He tensed as he watched it crawl by. Through the passenger-side window, he could make out the cop riding shotgun—hard-faced, black, female. And definitely giving him The Stare. The car kept moving, so he stayed put. He watched it vanish down the street, then dragged on his cigarette.

His first year of law school wasn't anything like the idyllic crap they showed in those yuppie-fied college brochures. He'd worked like a dog, wearing himself down with classes and a part-time job, making barely enough to cover his expenses and getting five hours' sleep a night. After awhile he started needing a couple of beers to unwind, then a couple more, then some harder poisons with his buddies at local bars. Before the year was out, he needed a shot or two before breakfast just to face the day. Unfortunately, slowing down wasn't an option. He needed every penny just to keep a roof over his head and the bursar's office quiet.

All his striving had come to nothing. Dazed from drink and exhaustion, he'd tanked his final exams. His work had been slipping for awhile, but the test results killed him. He'd stumbled down to his mailbox the day after and found a stiff note from the dean advising him not to return the following semester. Fees paid in advance would be refunded, and best of luck in future endeavors. Funny, now he couldn't even recall the man's name.

He flipped the cigarette butt into a nearby puddle. The action earned him a scowl from a pretty-faced young man, decked out in leather and walking a dog that looked too small to be alive.

"There's an ordinance against littering, you know," Pretty-boy said. The dog yapped.

They sounded so alike, it made Luke snicker. Whiny voices straight through the nose. Probably homos, given this part of town.

The laugh got Pretty-boy's back up. He jerked his head toward the cigarette butt. "Pick that up. Were you raised in a barn?"

"Fuck you," Luke said. "Oh, wait, I bet you already do that."

"Look, you son of a bitch—"

The stupid fuck actually took a step toward him. Trying to intimidate him. As if he had a prayer of it, with that face and that voice and those clothes. And the damned dog, which chose that moment to lunge toward Luke's ankle. Luke raised his foot to punt the little rat-bait across the street.

Pretty-boy snatched the dog off the sidewalk and backed away. "Don't you touch him, you bastard!"

That's right, Luke thought. *Back off before you and your rodent get hurt.* He felt powerful, energized. "You want my litter?" He kicked the butt and a slosh of dirty water toward them. "Here you go, faggot!"

With a muttered curse, Pretty-boy took himself and his dog down the street. Fast. Luke lit a second cigarette and blew a cloud of smoke after them. He felt on top of the world. Then he glanced back at the playground and saw a teacher's aide striding toward him. Scrawny Puerto Rican, bad haircut. Looking at him like he had *child molester* tattooed across his forehead. Time to move along.

He pushed away from the light pole and ambled down the block. *Nothing to see here, ma'am. Just a guy enjoying a walk and a smoke, and none of your fucking business.*

What *had* that dean's name been? Bristow, that was it. Seymour Bristow, a cramped scrawl across the bottom of the paper.

Real faggot name. He'd torn the letter into fragments and flushed them down the john, then poured every drop of liquor in the apartment down his throat. A couple of days later, he'd crawled out of bed, gone down to the Greyhound station, and bought a bus ticket for Minneapolis. One of his drinking buddies knew a guy there who might be able to give him a job—and if not, Minnesota had a generous dole with no prior-residency bullshit.

He landed the job—tending bar, irony of ironies, though he knew better than to drink from the house stores. It paid enough for a small apartment in a scruffy neighborhood, plus utilities and groceries if he watched the nickels. For a while he couldn't even afford a used car. He hated it all the more because he couldn't figure a way out. When he met Grace, he hoped sharing his life with someone would make it better—but all it did was turn up the pressure. He wanted to earn enough so she could stay home, to make the apartment nice and cook decent meals and keep his shirts clean. Instead, they ate leftovers from the diner where Grace worked, or slapped-together meals like tuna casserole. Half the time Grace wasn't even home to eat with him. She'd leave a scrawled note with a heart on it and some frozen muck for reheating.

And then she'd started on him about spending his hard-earned money on an occasional fifth of decent Scotch, or a few six-packs of beer that didn't taste like old dishwater—as if he wasn't entitled to what few pleasures he could afford. He hadn't meant to hurt her, but the nagging drove him crazy. He was always sorry later, and if Grace had shown him even a scrap of understanding, he'd have stopped it cold. But she hadn't. Too late, he began to realize he'd married a stupid, selfish bitch. And he was stuck with her. Divorce wasn't in the cards—when he made a commitment, he kept to it. Plus, it wasn't all bad. Sometimes, when Grace behaved, he could almost believe they were a happily married couple.

He reached the far end of the school building. Its brick bulk shielded him from the playground. He counted to a hundred in his head. The cigarette was gone by the time he finished. He tossed the butt off the curb and pondered. Sneak back the way he'd come and hope the aide wasn't looking, or go all the way around to buy extra time out of sight? More time meant better odds that the Dragon Lady would've lowered her guard. It also meant recess might be over.

He glanced around the deserted street, then turned the corner. A driveway beckoned partway down. He could sneak around the other side of the playground through the school parking lot. He ran toward the drive, thoughts pounding in his brain, matching the rhythm of his shoes on the pavement.

Everything had fallen apart when Linnet came along. Luke loved her more than he ever thought he could love anything. He wanted to buy her every toy he saw, dress her in clothes that showed off how pretty she was, give her a perfect life from the first day of her existence. But he couldn't do it. On what he made, he couldn't even come close. Grace had cut back to occasional part-time shifts and was home more, but the baby took up all her time, and the rest of their everyday life went even further to hell. He hadn't realized how much they needed her paychecks, and the knowledge galled him. No surprise he'd hit the bottle harder just to cope with the extra stress. And then Grace started getting seriously weird on him, hardly ever leaving him alone with Linnie. Like he was some lush who'd drop his kid on her head without noticing, or the kind of bastard who'd beat up his baby for crying.

He reached the driveway and slowed to ease the stitch building in his side. He bent over to stretch out the kinks, breathing hard. "Happy now, Grace?" he muttered between gasps. "Happy to see me out here, wheezing like a dog and freezing my ass off?

I bet you are. I bet you're laughing. Well, you won't be laughing when I find her."

Grace had made Linnie afraid of him. He'd never forgive her for that. It hurt so much to see his daughter cringe from him, like she was expecting a slap even though he'd never raised a hand to her. He heard her crying sometimes, after he and Grace had been having it out, and it made him want to hurt Grace even more because she'd made him frighten his kid. He headed out to the bar whenever that feeling came over him, afraid that otherwise he might lose control and kill her.

He reached the corner of the school building and leaned against it, neck craned to watch the children. Cold seeped through him from the rough yellow brick. A small knot of girls with a jump rope drifted his way. In their midst was a thin blonde, moving like a leaf in the wind, pale honey braids bobbing on the shoulders of her violet parka.

Luke gripped the wall, every muscle taut. Then the girl took her place between the rope-turners, and he choked back the name he was about to call. The child was a stranger.

Rage made him pound the wall. It wasn't fair, damn it! After all he'd done to find his kid, it plain wasn't *fair*. He'd gotten the letter meant for Grace, hadn't he? Five whole months after she and Linnet had vanished. That kind of luck almost never came his way. Didn't it mean something that it finally had? Didn't it?

He stuck his unbruised hand in his jacket. The contents of the inside pocket made a reassuring bulge against the soft cloth. He retreated a few yards down the wall, then took out the thick letter with the Duluth postmark. The return address read *Thompson and Bizal, Attorneys at Law.*

He didn't even need to take the letter out anymore. He'd memorized the part that mattered.

As a direct descendant of William Henry Schlegel, named in the last will and testament of Andrew Jackson Schlegel dated

*September 3, 1904, you and any dependent children may be
entitled to a share of the bequest made by said Andrew Jackson
Schlegel to the heirs and assigns of said William Henry Schlegel, to be disbursed one hundred years after the date of said
Andrew Jackson Schlegel's death, which occurred on October
30, 1907. Please contact this office within ninety days of the
disbursement date, October 30, 2007, with adequate proof of
identity. Failure to do so will be taken as a waiver of your
claim . . .*

One point five million dollars, the letter said. He didn't think
Grace had much family; she never talked about them, and had
run to shelters instead of relatives each time she took off. How
many other claimants could there be? Surely not so many that
he couldn't take home a sizable chunk of that one point five mil
for his wife and daughter. Enough to buy a house in a decent
part of town. Enough to put him back in law school—this time
without the money troubles and exhaustion, so he'd make a go
of it. Enough so he wouldn't need to drink any more. They
could have had a perfect life, if only Grace had understood.

It was down to Linnet and him now, provided he found her
before the ninety days ran out.

He tucked the letter away and strode back the way he'd come.
The schoolyard tactic was a bust. Bus and L routes might work,
starting with whichever one Grace had been heading for that
night. Home shouldn't be too far from a bus or train stop. Once
he figured out the likeliest possibilities, he'd pick one and stake
it out for a day. And keep trying until he found Linnet.

He refused to contemplate how long it might take. He didn't
have any quicker options. He'd just have to trust that the fates
that ruled his misbegotten life weren't pulling one more trick
from their bag, dangling a fortune in front of him only to have a
stubborn dead woman yank it away.

Chapter Three

The letter from the Department of Public Health arrived in Rachel's mailbox the day before Halloween, buried amid junk flyers, bills and expiring subscription notices. For a moment, she stopped breathing. Then she carried the letter upstairs, curled up on the couch and looked at it awhile.

Quince ambled over with an inquiring remark. "It's not edible," she told him. There couldn't be much inside the slim envelope—a single sheet at most. She felt light-headed. Who was she kidding? There was *everything* inside. She traced the envelope with one finger, then flipped it and traced the flap. Picking up on her mood, Quincy offered comfort: a head-butt to her knees. She looked down at him.

"I don't know what to do." This was insane—asking a cat for advice. Even more insane, half-expecting an answer. *Open it, Wimp Girl. Go on, do it.*

The cushion gave as Quincy jumped up beside her. He sniffed a corner of the envelope, then rubbed his cheek against it. A nervous chuckle escaped her. "All right. If you say so." *If it all goes wrong, I can blame Bonehead. Yeah, that'll work.*

The envelope held a cover letter and an Information Exchange Authorization form. She skimmed the letter—standard bureaucratic boilerplate—then set it aside and read the form.

I, Minna McGrath, state that I am the person who completed the Registration Identification; that I am of the age of sixty years; that I hereby authorize the Department of Public Health to give to my child the necessary information so I can be contacted; that I am fully aware that I can only be supplied with the name and last known address of my child if such person has duly executed an Information Exchange Authorization which has not been revoked; that I can be contacted by writing c/o Rose Mulvihill, Mulvihill Galleries, 3316 North Center Street, St. Paul, Minnesota, 55746. Dated this 10th day of March, 1999.

Rachel gulped air. Eight years. That long, her birth mother had been waiting for her. She stared at the right-hand signature—bold and sharp, slanting upward and to the right, as if its author were left-handed. Like her. The witness signature to the left read *Rose Mulvihill* in swooping, rounded letters. Interesting that Minna McGrath had arranged for contact through a business address. *Probably didn't want me turning up on her doorstep without some warning.*

She sat for a long time with the form on her lap. Quincy butted her hand. She scratched him gently. "Minna McGrath," she murmured. The name sounded strange in her ears. Scots, or Scots-Irish. Not too different from the Connollys. Or maybe McGrath was a married name, and Minna's ancestry was something else entirely. *My ancestry.* The thought prompted an odd shiver, half excitement and half unease.

She looked back at the name. *Minna. Does she have a family? Children? Do they have any idea I exist? How many lives will I disrupt if I track her down?*

The date leaped out at her from the sea of black type. *Does she still want to see me? After all this time, does she think I don't care?*

She stood up, the form dangling between her fingers, and began to pace. Right now she needed logic, not phantom fears.

Her appearance even at this late date shouldn't be a total disaster, or Minna wouldn't have filed that form. As for how Minna felt, it said something that she hadn't revoked the IEA after so long with no response. Didn't it?

She halted in the middle of the living room. Irrelevant sights and sounds suddenly took on enormous importance: the sofa and easy chair's navy-and-white stripes, the jewel-like colors of the rug against the scuffed brown floorboards, the hot-metal smell of a forgotten teakettle boiling dry. She knew she should rescue it, but stayed rooted to the floor.

A framed snapshot on the coffee table caught her attention. She and Mom had sat for it a few months before the accident. Though part of her recognized it as fantasy, her mother's bright smile seemed to tell her to go ahead.

She knelt by the table, getting eye-to-eye with the photo. She'd never paid much mind until now to just how different she and Mom looked. Tall and rangy even seated in a chair, auburn hair going lighter as it grayed, blue eyes so bright you could spot their color from across a room—that was Mom. Rachel, standing behind her, looked short and dark and could stand to lose ten pounds. The picture at least brought out the reddish highlights in her hair. Would she look like Minna at all, when she found her?

She replaced the form in the envelope, went to the kitchen and shut off the burner. With an oven mitt dug out of an overcrowded drawer, she moved the hot kettle off the glowing ring. The prudent thing to do was write to Minna, but she swiftly discarded that notion. Sometimes people changed their minds when a dream threatened to turn real. She couldn't face that. Better to take a different kind of risk, for once in her life to grab for something that mattered. Where had the prudent approach ever gotten her? A teensy apartment, a so-so job and a smattering of friends whose lives only lightly touched hers. This chance meant too much. She couldn't let it slip away.

She licked a finger and then touched the kettle. Stinging pain made her snatch her hand back, hissing through her teeth. Still too hot to dump in the sink. She leaned against the counter, shaking her hand while she worked out details. Early November was a rotten time for a road trip, but it would have to do. Clementine, bless her, would give her time off like a shot once Rachel told her the reason. She could be on the road by the end of the week.

She sucked on her finger, which still hurt. What if it snowed? They probably got snow in November up there. What if her aging Corolla broke down? Should she join Triple A? What if it broke down in the middle of nowhere—like northern Wisconsin, where she'd gone on a disastrous camping trip once? A region of towns so small they could barely fill a high-school auditorium, scattered across miles of empty woods and open land. Who would help her if she broke down out there in a snowstorm? Or what if she made it to St. Paul just fine, but Minna turned her away?

What if she doesn't turn me away?

Exhilaration swept through her. Quincy stalked into the room, aiming for his food dish. She scooped him up and nuzzled his fat neck, then laughed at his pouting face. "I'm going to do it," she said, giddy with her own daring. "I'm going up there. To meet her." She paused, then said the rest just to hear it out loud. To hear it given weight, shape, reality. "I'm going to meet my mother."

Breakfast was oatmeal again, with lumps. Linnet had never liked oatmeal. After a solid week of it, she'd begun to hate it. No flavors, either, like blueberry or apple cinnamon. Her grandfather made the old-fashioned kind out of the red-and-blue canister that you had to cook in a pot before eating it.

The first few mornings, he'd tried to talk to her while the cereal bubbled. She could tell he wasn't used to kids. He'd say things like, "Thought I'd finish winterizing the gardens today. Get that done before the snow flies," and, "You keep your bed made and the room neat. Hear?" He didn't talk to her the way Mama did. They used to make up secret lives for the people they passed in the street. Linnet couldn't imagine doing that with this strange, near-silent old man. He'd just grunt at her, or say nothing at all.

The thick silence magnified ordinary sounds: the clink of spoons against bowls, the ticking of the kitchen clock, the slight slurping noise as the old man sipped his coffee. Linnet could feel him looking at her. Probably wondering why she wasn't eating. She hastily shoved a spoonful of oatmeal into her mouth. It didn't taste quite as awful as the last three had. Maybe she was getting used to it.

Even the sunlight didn't care much for this place. Weak and watery, it snuck in under the blind that covered the window over the sink. There was just enough of it to strike a glint from the refrigerator door handle and raise a faint glow from the paler squares of what must have been black-and-white linoleum. The Formica-topped table where they sat filled a whole corner of the tiny room. Linnet could feel a draft at her back from the open door to the hallway. She shifted in her chair. The flattened, brown cushion held hardened lumps the size of skipping stones. She wondered if she'd end up with bruises on her legs, like in *The Princess and the Pea*.

At least he hadn't made her start school yet. She didn't want to ask why. He'd be busy around the big house all day, leaving her free to explore. Schlegel House was the one bright spot in her dreary existence: a historic mansion, once the home of the rich mine owner whose money had built Birch Falls, now a site for summer visitors to the Iron Range. Her grandfather was its caretaker.

A lump dug into her right thigh. As she squirmed away from it, the chair creaked. The old man looked up. She dipped up another spoonful of oatmeal. A faint slurp and a swallow told her that her grandfather had gone back to his coffee. She was safe.

She'd used to dream of having a big house with a bedroom that could hold all the books she ever wanted. Schlegel House had enough bedrooms to let her choose a new one almost every night—if she were allowed to sleep in them, which she wasn't. The old man had explained that the house wasn't theirs; it belonged to the Schlegel Trust. She could wander through it whenever it was closed to the public, as long as she didn't disturb anything. Other than that, she was to keep to the caretaker's cottage at the bottom of the back garden. Linnet had absorbed this silently, responded, "Yes, sir" when asked if she understood, and immediately resolved to explore Schlegel House from basement to attic. She wouldn't hurt anything, and surely there was no harm in pretending the mansion was hers, just for a little while.

Just until Mama comes for me.

She held that consoling thought close, like a blanket. Lately, she'd had trouble making herself believe it. A whole week without a letter or phone call. At first, she'd slept in her coat in case Mama turned up in the middle of the night. She gave that up after a few days, but kept her suitcase packed. Rearranging everything after dressing each morning was a pain, but she wanted to be prepared in case they had to leave in a hurry. She could think of only one good reason for her mother's silence: to keep her father from tracking her here.

That would explain why Ruth had been so upset, and why she'd told Linnet that story about Mama spending the night with a sick friend. As if Mama's voice on the phone wouldn't have told her things were a lot more wrong than that. Ruth was a rotten liar. She smiled too wide and her voice got a funny singsong edge. She'd been in a big hurry to leave, rushing Linnet through dinner as if their lives depended on hitting the road before seven. She hadn't lost the nerved-up set to her shoulders until they were well past Milwaukee. Nor had she told Linnet any of the truth, even after Linnet said she didn't believe the sick-friend bit. All Linnet could get out of her was their destination, and that Mama had told Ruth to bring her.

It had to be her father. Nothing else made sense.

Suddenly she didn't want to sit in the silent, cheerless kitchen. Softly, she asked to be excused. At her grandfather's grunt of assent, she slid out of her chair and darted from the room.

The small study where she slept was just to the left of the shoebox-sized parlor. Her coat lay across the foot of her mattress, a bright purple splash against the beige-and-brown striped blanket. The place didn't look like a bedroom, which made her glad and sorry at the same time. As long as she was here, it would have been nice to sleep in more homey-looking surroundings. On the other hand, a proper bedroom full of pretty things would have been a sure sign that her grandfather's cottage was home now. That was the last thing she wanted.

She shrugged into her coat, then returned to the kitchen. "Can I go out?"

The old man nodded. "Don't go far. And watch the flower beds."

"Yessir."

A path led from the front door up a gentle slope toward Schlegel House. A little way from the cottage, where its scant yard gave way to the manse gardens, smaller paths broke off from the main walkway and wandered past sculpted bushes and beds of flowers. The beds were bare earth now, spread with mulch the old man had laid down a couple of days ago. The tops of the markers protruding through the mulch told Linnet what the flowers were: daffodils, hyacinths, primroses, narcissi. And rose bushes, snugged away for the winter under Styrofoam cylinders. She caught herself wondering how the flowerbeds would look in spring, with everything in bloom. Of course, she'd be back in Chicago long before spring came.

She looked at her watch. Her grandfather should be hard at work soon, and he never locked the doors while he was on the job. Today she'd check out the attic. There must be loads of stuff up there. The public library wouldn't be open yet. A walk would have to do.

She strode uphill past the mansion; then, after a last look at it, headed toward town.

The dregs of his coffee were going cold. Jackson Schlegel swirled them in his cup, his mind on the girl who'd just left. The poor child was afraid of him, and no wonder. He'd never learned how to talk to children—not even his daughter, whom he'd raised alone after his wife died. Now the raising of Grace's girl had fallen to him, and he felt desperately unequal to the task.

Linnet clearly regarded her stay as temporary, and he felt reluctant to tell her otherwise until he knew for certain what had happened to Grace. At the moment, he knew only what the woman from the shelter had told him, over strong black coffee after they'd packed Linnet off to sleep.

"Luke tracked her down again," Ruth had said. "Turned up at the diner where she works, complete with half a dozen long-stemmed red roses. 'Come home darling, I'll never hit you again, this time I mean it.' Roses! He asked if he could walk her home and stay the night. Of course she said no. He was there every day for a week. Waiting for her to come have a friendly cup of coffee with him. She laughed about it at first, in a whistling-past-the-graveyard kind of way; told me she'd found more roundabout routes from the S & G to Sally's Place than she ever knew existed."

She'd spoken so softly, he'd had to lean forward to hear her. "After the first three days, he got sullen. Told her he didn't have all the time in the world, and she better stop wasting it. Grace didn't know what he meant. He dropped that pearl of wisdom on Day Five. Then he started asking where Linnet was—did Grace ever bring her to work, where did she go to school. That Monday morning, Grace got the divorce papers from her lawyer. She was going to give them to Luke if he showed. She was afraid of what he might do, so she told me to bring Linnet to you as soon as I could. 'Just in case,' she said."

She'd taken a giant gulp of coffee then, as if belting a shot of whiskey. "Grace called me just after six. She'd served him with the papers. He threw them at her and left. She told me to take Linnie, said she'd call me when she got home. I never heard from her." A two-handed grip on the mug this time, her voice cracking. "I hope to God I'm wrong, and she just hasn't had a chance to call. Or she changed her mind, though I can't think why she would . . ."

He'd offered her his own bed for a few hours, before she set off on the long return trip. The three of them had shared an awkward lunch, with Linnet too cowed to ask questions. Ruth told her Grace would be in touch when she could, but Jackson could see his granddaughter didn't believe her. After Ruth left, Linnet had shut herself up in the study, which he'd turned into a makeshift bedroom upon their unexpected arrival. When he'd gone to tell her he'd be working in the manse for the afternoon, silence was the only response.

He finished his coffee, then carried the mug and other breakfast dishes to the sink. Time he fixed the chips in the porcelain. Maybe he should put up some curtains, something bright. After several days of Linnet's silent scrutiny, he'd begun to see his home through her eyes. No wonder Grace had left. Between this place and him, there hadn't been much reason to stick around. And she'd never cared for Schlegel House the way he did.

He drowned the dirty dishes in hot water, then squirted Palmolive into the sink. The clean scent of it briefly lifted his spirits. He picked up the scrubber sponge, then wrinkled his nose and set it down. It smelled of old eggs and boiled vegetables, and its rough layer was coming off in patches. He bent down, ignoring the twinge of a chronically stiff back, and took a new sponge from the metal basket mounted just inside the door.

Grace had found the basket funny. "Organizing under the sink! What's next, Dad—rearranging all the food in alphabetical order?"

No respect, that had been Grace's trouble. Not for him, not for their home, not for her roots. She'd wanted bright lights and busy streets, away from all reminders of what their family had once been. The manse to her was a relic, Birch Falls the next best thing to prison. He still didn't understand how she could turn her back on the place her own kin had made from nothing. To him, this place was everything. He felt privileged to care for the house his namesake had built, in the town that owed its life to the Schlegel fortune. So what if the iron mine had been tapped out for almost thirty years? That didn't alter the plain fact that a man with his name had created Birch Falls. An entire town, where once there had been only rocky soil and scrub pines. That was a thing to be proud of. But he'd never made Grace see it.

"We don't even live in that house," she'd said once. "If you spent a night there and the Trust got to hear of it, they'd fire you, and your family name wouldn't do you a damned bit of good. It never has! Who cares how much money Great-Great

Uncle Andy had, if we can't get any of it to live decently with? Who cares about goddamned Schlegel House, when all we're fit for is to clean up after the summer visitors tromp through? Who cares?!"

So Grace had gone, seeking a life somewhere more exciting than what she called "this one-stoplight mudhole." From what Ruth had said, he guessed she'd found it. He'd learned of her marriage in a stiff note, most remarkable for what it didn't say. No church, apparently no reception, no details and no invitation. Just bare notice of the event: *I will be Mrs. Luke Chapman two weeks from today. He has a good job. We're happy together. Grace.*

He scrubbed Linnet's cereal bowl, working slowly to dislodge every last bit of oatmeal. Even considering the terms on which he and Grace had parted, that poor excuse for a letter had seemed strange. Stranger still that Grace never brought Luke to visit, or Linnet. A homemade birth announcement typed on a three-by-five card, plus an overexposed Polaroid of the baby on Grace's lap, was all the word he'd gotten of his granddaughter's entry into the world. The sparseness of contact made him uneasy, but he found ways to explain it: fear of rejection, desire to make a complete break from Birch Falls, embarrassment if her new life hadn't turned out all roses. The last guess was the right one, though he'd never dreamed to what extent.

He squeezed out the sponge. The warm water ran over his hand. *I should have gone to her. Or at least written, so she'd know I gave a damn. But I left her alone with that bastard, told myself she wanted it that way. And now it's too late.*

He rinsed the bowl, dried it with meticulous care and placed it in the drainer. Grace always left wet dishes out overnight, a sloppy habit. He couldn't afford to be sloppy. Laziness at home would become laziness on the job. Schlegel House deserved better. It belonged to him in a way he'd never been able to explain to another living soul. He knew the manse and it knew him, inside and out.

Grace would have laughed at such a notion. He wondered if Linnet would.

He washed and rinsed his own bowl, then scoured their spoons. He could tell his granddaughter loved the house. He'd taken her through it a few days after her arrival, and for awhile she'd forgotten to be wary of him. She'd even worked up the nerve to ask a question or two. Her tentative interest vanished the minute he laid down the rules, of course. But he knew she was slinking around, whenever she thought he was working safely out of earshot.

A single swipe with the sponge took care of his coffee mug. Linnet's juice glass needed painstaking attention; orange pulp stuck to it as if glued there. He scraped at the pulp flecks, alternating between sponge and thumbnail. So far, Linnet herself had been no easier to deal with. She'd barely said ten words to him in a day, except on the rare occasions when she asked him about the manse. Her face had a kind of hunger to it then. He knew that look. He wore it every day, when he first stepped outside and looked up the hill. They had something in common, he and Linnet. That was a start.

Dishes finished and put away, he left the kitchen and took his heavy coat from the front closet. The bottom button had long ago cracked in half, and a coffee stain he'd never managed to get rid of showed dark brown on the worn, tan lapel. He hadn't noticed until Linnet came just how shabby so many of his possessions were. Clean and neat, but shabby. For a moment, he saw himself as she must: a skinny old man with thinning hair and taped-up spectacles, shuffling around in mended sweaters and paint-stained pants. In the cottage, he tended not to notice his surroundings. He just ate and slept there. Schlegel House was the place on which he lavished his attentions. Nothing in it was allowed to get shabby or timeworn. The Trust provided generously for refurbishments, though he would have paid out of his own pocket if necessary.

He pushed up his glasses, which were sliding down his nose. A rough edge of tape caught his finger. He pressed it flat. Maybe he should ask for a small raise, especially with Linnet to consider. His salary hadn't changed in years. Of course, if the letter he'd received just a month ago lived up to its promise, he'd never need wages again.

Paper crinkled as he shrugged into his coat. He drew the letter from one pocket and read the return address: *Thompson and Bizal, Attorneys at Law, Duluth, Minnesota.* The Schlegel family firm. Seeing those names had spooked him, until he read the letter and realized his place was safe. For good.

He hadn't cared much about the money at first. He'd thought of buying a new coat, and perhaps some top-quality tools. Linnet's appearance changed things. Her share as well as his would make quite a sum—perhaps enough to buy Schlegel House from the Trust. Enough that they wouldn't need paying summer visitors. Enough to make it their home.

He checked the other pocket for his keys to the cottage and the manse, then stepped out the front door and locked it behind him. The air felt crisp, like a ripe apple. It smelled of pine and chimney smoke. He shot the deadbolt, then looked up the hill as always before going on. The manse needed touching up. Minnesota winters were hard on paint. Despite the weathered spots, the house was beautiful. Sunlight glanced off the eaves and the shingled roof. The shadows of branches fell like dark lace over the wide expanse of cream-colored clapboard.

It surprised him, how much he wanted to own Schlegel House. Despite his attachment to it, he'd never thought of the place in that way before. Now that such a wild possibility seemed attainable, he couldn't stop thinking about it. The more he thought, the more it appealed to him. The manse was already his in the way that counted—why shouldn't it be his legally as well? The Schlegel Trust hadn't found any direct heirs in a hundred years. So why shouldn't the house fall to him, as the senior living family member? Why shouldn't Jackson Schlegel call it home?

He walked uphill and around to the front to look at the gingerbread edging that overhung the wraparound porch. If Linnet's ne'er-do-well father showed his face in Birch Falls, Jackson would do whatever it took to keep him away from her. She was the key to his hopes, his reward for years of patient service. And maybe his chance to redeem the mess he'd made of things with Grace. He'd raise Linnet right, give her the attention he'd never managed to give his daughter, teach her everything Grace had never cared to learn. He certainly wouldn't send the child off with a thug who was her father through an accident of biology, who'd surely harmed Grace and might even have killed her. He'd kill Luke Chapman himself first.

The woodwork glowed golden-brown where the morning light struck it. Jackson was proud of that paint job, especially after the time he'd had convincing the Trust that the contrasting color was appropriate to the period. They should have learned to trust his judgment by now. He knew what Schlegel House needed.

He fished the manse keys out of his pocket and let himself in, then ambled down the long hallway to open the back door for Linnet. She'd come before too long.

Sure enough, the back door was open. Linnet stopped just inside and listened. Faint music sounded beneath the floorboards: piano, something classical. The old man was working in the basement. She could roam upstairs to her heart's content.

A quick jaunt up the steep back staircase brought her to the second-floor hallway, where she paused. The attic steps led up from the schoolroom, if she remembered correctly—the first door to her right, across from the maid's quarters. Next to the schoolroom was the bedroom that had belonged to Mary Anne Schlegel, only daughter of Andrew Jackson Schlegel, who'd built this grand house.

The daughter who'd disappeared.

Linnet walked down the hall, hesitated by the schoolroom door and then went on. She'd been in Mary Anne's room several times, but it hadn't lost its fascination. Mary Anne was just a few years older than Linnet when she ran off. According to Grandfather, no one had ever found any trace of her.

The room looked as it must have on the last night Mary Anne had spent in it. Her father had refused to alter it during his lifetime, and had ordered the Schlegel Trust not to change anything afterward. A lace-trimmed coverlet, white silk spattered with tiny roses, draped the four-poster bed. Across from it sat a writing desk and matching chair, painted white and trimmed in gold. The deep-rose background of the patterned carpet matched the curtains that framed the wide window seat and its velvet upholstery. The night table near the bedstead held a few old books and a lace-edged handkerchief. Near the head of the bed, a door with a cut-glass handle led to a small dressing room.

Linnet curled up in the window seat, which offered an excellent view of the side garden. A tree that her grandfather called flowering dogwood raised delicate, bare branches toward Linnet's perch. In spring, Mary Anne Schlegel must have looked straight down into a mass of lavender blossoms. What was it like to wake up in this rose-bower of a room every morning, with a maid to bring you tea and toast, beautiful dresses to wear and more books in the schoolroom than Linnet had ever dreamed of possessing? To look out across trees and grass and flowers of a dozen different colors and know that they were yours to gaze at or smell or decorate your room with? To have so much that no one could take away from you?

Her gaze drifted to the portrait on the opposite wall. Mary Anne was seated at her writing desk, pointed chin propped on one slender hand. The other hand held up a white rose, at which she was smiling as if she and the flower shared a secret. She wore a cream-colored lace dress; a single, flyaway lock of dark hair brushed her shoulder. Only her eyes didn't fit with the rest of the picture. They reminded Linnet of a look she'd seen on her mother's face, the one time she'd asked what would happen if her father tried to take her away. "He won't," Mama had said, in a hard voice that told Linnet the subject was best dropped. She wasn't sure, afterward, if what she'd seen in her mother's face was anger or fear.

She stood up, suddenly restless. She couldn't be sure how long her grandfather would stay in the cellar. If she wanted a good look around the attic, she'd best get going.

The floorboards creaked as she crossed the schoolroom toward the attic door. She took the shallow steps two at a time, dropping to one when the staircase curved sharply. Ahead of her surely lay a morning's worth of happy rummaging, and she was eager to get started.

Instead of the huge, drafty, unfinished chamber she'd expected, the staircase gave onto a small, sparsely furnished room. It held a heavy table with a single long drawer, a straight-backed chair, and a shelf full of narrow leather-bound books. She opened one and saw columns of figures written in faded ink. Some were dates: 1877, 1878, 1879. The others she couldn't guess at. Disappointed, she looked around and spotted a door in the far wall.

Opening it raised a puff of dust. She sneezed, then fumbled

in her pocket for a Kleenex as she drank in the sight before her. *This* was a proper attic.

Mismatched pieces of furniture crowded the vast room: standing lamps with brass curlicues jutting from their tops, wooden chair-frames carved like vines, a rolltop desk, a glass-fronted cabinet brimming with china, a bedstead whose twisted columns reminded her of soft-serve ice cream. Rolled-up carpets with dusty fringes leaned against the walls next to stacks of heavy picture frames. Some had pictures in them; others were empty. She saw a headless dummy shaped like a woman from neck to hips, wearing a old-fashioned dark green dress. Near it stood an ancient sewing machine attached to a wrought-iron table. Huge trunks with curved tops sat amid a sea of boxes, some of which rose in pillars halfway to the slanting ceiling.

She started toward the nearest box pile, then stopped. There was so much! Of course, a lot of it might be boring ordinary things, like shoes and coats and old tablecloths. The storage lockers in their last apartment in Minneapolis had been full of that kind of stuff. She was hoping for something more interesting: books, dresses, old toys, costume jewelry, maybe even old letters. Something she could build a secret life around, to share with Mama when she came.

She walked to a clear space in the center of the attic, closed her eyes and turned slowly in circles, muttering under her breath. "Round and round and round she goes, and where she stops . . . nobody knows!"

Her eyes flew open. Ahead of her stood a small trunk, apple-green, with tarnished brass edging. She knelt down beside it and discovered that it was unlocked. The magic was working. Inside the trunk lay two piles of neatly folded clothes, a piece of half-finished embroidery, a stack of yellowed sheet music, a threadbare stuffed rabbit in striped trousers and a long coat, and several hardbound books.

She scooped the books into her lap and read their titles aloud. "*Poems,* Alfred Lord Tennyson. *McGuffey Reader. Romeo and Juliet. Jane Eyre. The Rose and the Ring*—hey, I read that last summer." She flipped open the cover, and was only half surprised to see *Mary Anne Schlegel* written on the flyleaf.

She set *The Rose and the Ring* aside and returned to her sorting. "*Etiquette for Young Ladies.* Yuck. *Great Expectations. Sense and Sensibility. Holy Bible.*" The final book, bound in dark red leather, had no title. Linnet opened it. The flyleaf read *Mary Anne Schlegel. May 10, 1892.* On the inside cover opposite was a sketch of a teenage boy, with mussed hair and a pencil stuck behind one ear. She wondered who he was. Not Mary Anne, that was for sure.

She flipped through several pages, all of them covered with cramped handwriting. The light was too dim to read easily. After a few minutes of trying, she set the red book on top of *The Rose and the Ring,* replaced the others in the trunk and closed it. She took the two volumes back to the anteroom, where the light was better. The window seat in Mary Anne's bedroom would be more comfortable, but she felt too impatient to wait. Besides, her grandfather might come up there. Taking an old book out of a trunk surely wasn't hurting anything, but he might not see it like that.

She hitched herself up on one end of the table, opened the red book and began to read.

CHAPTER FOUR

14 June, 1892

It is hotter today than it has any right to be, considering how northerly this state lies. They say Minnesota has ten thousand lakes; what I wouldn't give to be on the shores of one now, all decked out in a bathing dress and ready to throw myself in! Now there's a fine thing to waste precious journal space on— the weather, as if I were writing a letter to an elderly maiden aunt. I haven't any such relative, thankfully. There's only Father and Uncle William on the Schlegel side, and Mother was an only child. Like I might as well be.

I miss Jonas. I wish he hadn't gone. Though I'm beginning to understand why he had to.

A rush of wings, a dark flutter against that too-blue sky . . . one of my blackbirds just left the nest. A family of them took up residence this spring in the dogwood by my window. I've been watching the young ones fly off since yesterday. When, oh when will it be my turn?

A few more months at most, please God. Bless Mother for helping with the money. I could never have done it on the pitiful allowance Father gives me.

When I told him I wanted to write, he laughed at me—the way he did when I was six, and I said I meant never to get married because I didn't want to leave home. Did I ever say that? At the present moment, I would give all I possess to run away. From this house, from this tiny town where everyone knows exactly who I am and exactly who I should be. If I were to take a notion to go dancing in my nightgown some fine summer evening, the very next day all of Birch Falls would be gossiping about poor Mary Anne Schlegel's lunatic fit; so sad for the family, never would have thought it of such respectable people. Never mind that Father didn't grow up with money, any more than the greenest boy in the mine. To hear him tell it, he and Uncle William were poor as dirt until they went out into the world and made something of themselves. As I want to do, only I can't make Father see it. Damn him for a stubborn old man!

Tsk, tsk. Cursing, even on paper—and my revered parent, at that. If I were a normal girl, I'd be ashamed. But I'm not. Ashamed, that is—or normal. At least not to Father's way of thinking. Normal is applying myself to French and drawing while placidly waiting for him to find me a suitable husband— like a minor character in a Jane Austen novel, buried in the English countryside in eighteen-oh-something, instead of in America eight years shy of a new century. What a ring that has. A new century. I intend to be part of it, with or without Father's consent. Pigheaded old goat.

Mother puts it more kindly. "He's used to having his own way," she says. As if that's an excuse! She told me once I should be grateful for such spirit; without it, Father would have stayed poor and struggling all his life, and then where should we be? Free, I always want to answer. Sometimes I have to bite my tongue until it hurts.

Mother encourages me, though, in her own way. My little scribblings wouldn't be worth much without her critical eye. She must have been an excellent governess before she married. I think she misses teaching, though she would never tell Father so. Not after the ten days of frigid silence he inflicted on her for daring to suggest giving art lessons to some of the local children.

Poor Mother. Father's expectations trap her, too.

I won't be trapped any longer. I should hear something by autumn; come next spring, this house will see the last of me. I hardly know how I shall wait. Patience has never been my strong suit. Unfortunately, I take after Father that way . . .

A droplet of sweat splashed on the page. Mary Anne puffed her bangs out of her eyes for what felt like the hundredth time, then put down her pen and leaned back against the rough bole of the birch tree. It was too hot to write anymore. She closed her eyes, daydreaming of a cool sponge bath and a tall glass of lemonade. The slight breeze she'd come outside chasing had long since died. It might be marginally cooler in the house by now.

The manor, freshly painted after the spring storms, glowed in the sunlight. Mary Anne squinted at it. The house sat on top of the hill like a crown, its bulk a monument to fierce paternal pride.

She turned away from it toward the more restful sight of the gardens. Swift to take advantage of the short northern spring, bright blossoms ran riot across the flowerbeds: purple hyacinths, daffodils, narcissi and multicolored tulips nodding over patches of white alyssum and deep blue forget-me-nots. A little way off she saw Rhys Powell, crouched on one knee, carefully edging around a stand of pink-throated day lilies. His shirt clung in wet patches to his back. He was too far away to call out to—not that she should, she supposed, with him so recently hired on as junior gardener. *And to think that just two weeks ago, Rhys and I stood next to each other waiting to receive our diplomas. We joked about spending another summer lazing by the fishing hole. Now Father pays him to weed our gardens, and I feel strange about even saying hello.*

She looked away from Rhys, westward toward town. The gradual rise of the ground blocked her view of the buildings that she knew lay a few miles off. Another half-mile beyond them lay the headworks of Hadleigh Mine. Her father had rescued it from the verge of bankruptcy almost twenty years ago. Together with a sizable stake in the Great Northern Railway Company, the mine had put the Schlegels and Birch Falls on the map.

Mary Anne hated the place. Father had taken her down the mine once, after a fit of sulks at being denied a new dress for the annual Easter picnic. "It's time you saw for yourself where your pretty clothes come from," he'd snapped, his harsh tone startling her as much as the force with which he'd hauled her into the carriage. The rattling of the elevator cage sounded like bones; she imagined men frozen to death in the chill blackness of the mineshaft. Halfway down to the first level, she could sense the huge stone walls caving toward her. The cold, thick dark grew fingers that reached for her throat. Stillness alone could save her; if she moved, she would die.

Terror held her rooted to the car when they reached the bottom. His hands burning against her freezing skin, Father pried each finger from its stranglehold on the car rail. Then he dragged her, stiff and shrieking, into the dim chamber where the miners picked up their supplies. Only when she began gasping for air did he realize something more was wrong than a child's tantrum. For weeks afterward she dreamed of being buried alive, smothered under miles of granite.

She still avoided the headworks on her daily walks; the sight of the giant pulley-wheel that hauled the cages up and down made her throat feel tight. Rhys's two older brothers worked down the mine. She wondered how they kept from going mad. Suddenly, she felt glad Rhys was a gardener. She liked to think of him tending to living things, in the fresh air and light.

The clink of ice interrupted her thoughts. She looked up to see her mother standing nearby, holding two glasses of lemonade.

"Thirsty work." Mother nodded toward the book that lay open on Mary Anne's lap. The heat was making her hair curl; small frizzy wisps marred its customary smoothness. Mary Anne accepted the lemonade, taking momentary comfort in a familiar pang of daughterly jealousy. *I wish I had lovely copper hair like that, not this dull dark brown stuff. Reddish tinges in the right light hardly count. And mine curls even worse than hers. Blast this heat!*

As if reading her mind, Mother reached out and smoothed her hair. "You look like—"

"—A wild pony, I know." Mary Anne laughed. "It's the damp. I could live with our summers, if they were only dry. On days like today, one could take a fistful of air and wring it out. Why do we live here?"

"A storm might break this heat . . ." Mother trailed off, her eyes fixed on a stand of clouds that hovered in the distance. She looked troubled by more than the weather.

Before Mary Anne could make up her mind to ask, her mother turned to her with a determinedly cheerful smile. "A new story?"

"Just ramblings." Mary Anne closed the book. "Mostly about the heat. My brain feels stifled today." She took a sip of lemonade and continued, carefully not looking at her mother. "I sent a few stories to Minneapolis last Friday. To Mr. DuFresne, at Northern Lights Books. The ones you said were best."

There was a long silence. Mary Anne snuck a glance at her mother, who sat with her own glass of lemonade resting on her lap. "I wanted to speak to you about that," she said slowly. "This may not be the best way—"

Mary Anne sat up straight, setting her glass down hard. "You told me yourself they might be good enough to publish. Did you think I'd keep them in the back of my stationery drawer forever? I want to go to college, Mother. See the world. Be a real writer. How can I do that if I don't first prove to Father that my writing is worth something? Or do you think I should stay home and be a good girl, too?"

"I do not." Mother emphasized each word. "But there are ways to manage your father and ways not to. Going behind his back like this—"

"How is it going behind his back? He never told me not to write to publishers!" At her mother's look, she scowled and slumped against the tree trunk. "He already thinks my writing is a ridiculous notion. Maybe Mr. DuFresne's approval will convince him otherwise."

"You are your father's daughter." Mother picked up the lemonade and held it out to her.

She turned just enough to take it. "Why did you marry Father?"

"Because I loved him. Someday, you'll understand what that means."

"I hope not, not if it means I can't be who I—" Too late, she realized what she had almost said. "I'm sorry," she murmured into her drink. "I've no right to say—"

"No. You haven't."

She'd heard that edge in Mother's voice once before: when dismissing Jenny Llewellyn, the kitchen girl they'd caught stealing. Mary Anne kept her eyes on her lemonade. An ice chip the size of her thumbnail floated in the pale yellow liquid. She could hear the grass baking in the awful silence.

"Do you think I gave up so much?" Mother asked, more gently.

Mary Anne clenched her hands around the glass. "You were a teacher, and you loved it, and he won't let you do it anymore. Not at the town school, not at home, not even for no money. Those art lessons—Father acted like you'd suggested setting the house afire. He doesn't mind it when you put money in the church collection plate, or bring food baskets to the cottages when one of the miners gets laid up. Why should it make a difference when it's your learning you want to give away? Doesn't he care that a whole part of you is just lying there unused? And you let it lie, because it's not worth upsetting Father to have your own way a little! Why? Why does it always have to be his way?"

Mother wiped beads of moisture from the rim of her own glass. "I'm not sure I know how to tell you. Except to say that I knew what your father was like before I married him, and we took each other for better or for worse. If that means I've given up some things, I've gotten others in return." She blotted her damp hand on the underside of her skirt, then gave Mary Anne a small, warm smile. "Like you. So don't waste your sorrows over me, love. Think about what you want to do. And then come and talk to me, before you run your head straight into a wall."

"Like Father would."

"He loves you very much, you know. Nothing would please him more than to see you happy." Mother sipped her lemonade. "We'll simply have to make him understand what that really means."

"And if we can't?" Mary Anne stood and paced away from the birch. A faraway whistle echoed through the air—the train leaving Birch Falls, bound southward for Duluth and the Twin Cities. *And after that Milwaukee, and Chicago . . .*

A hand dropped lightly on her shoulder. "Let's not borrow trouble," Mother murmured. As clearly as if she'd voiced them, Mary Anne heard the unspoken words: *Not yet.*

She rested her cheek against her mother's fingers as the sound of the train faded.

Julia Schlegel watched Mary Anne head toward the house, pale blue skirt hitched knee-high as she strode up the gentle rise.

She could move with a lady's grace when she chose, but lately she made a point of choosing otherwise. Andrew had already spoken to Julia about her twice; she knew he was fast losing patience with a daughter he no longer understood. Somehow she had to make Mary Anne behave, before that child or her father precipitated a crisis neither was prepared for.

Part of it was the end of school, of course. Mary Anne would have a governess in the fall, to give her the finishing that the town school couldn't. Home teaching meant that much less contact with the world outside . . . narrow though that world was, as Mary Anne herself had complained on more than one occasion.

Julia had chosen the governess with care, determined that her daughter should receive the finest possible polishing—and a bit more. Miss Hanley would foster Mary Anne's writing discreetly, taking up where Julia had left off. Between them, they should manage to tamp down Mary Anne's rebellious instincts long enough to change Andrew's mind.

She refused to think of what might happen if they couldn't.

She wandered up the hill and past the house, letting her feet take her where they would. Unbidden, images of her stepson Jonas came to mind. A shy, serious thirteen-year-old, showing her his sketchbook soon after she first came; white-faced but tearless at his mother's funeral, not quite a year later; drawing his mother's face in charcoal with furious concentration when he was meant to be working out sums; thanking her awkwardly for an eighteenth birthday gift of fine pastels, in the wake of sour comments from Andrew about wasting his time with "that girls' nonsense." And finally the memory she'd been avoiding— Jonas on the threshold of her dressing room at an hour shy of midnight, suitcase in hand, saying goodbye.

"But the train doesn't leave until tomorrow afternoon," she'd said stupidly, twisting her hands around her hairbrush.

"I'll have plenty of good sketching time, then." He made an attempt at a smile. Then, flexing taut fingers around the suitcase handle: "I'm sorry, Julia. I know you tried. But Father won't hear reason, and I won't bury my soul learning to be a businessman. So there's nothing else to be done."

Half a dozen responses flashed through her mind, all considered and discarded in an eyeblink. They hadn't worked before; they wouldn't now. "Mary Anne will miss you," she said finally. How weak that sounded—as if she herself didn't care whether he stayed or went. As if his little half-sister was the only member of the family who mattered. *Please don't go,* she wanted to say. *I'll have no one to talk to.* But that was foolish. She had Andrew. *Who's near fifty to your thirty,* whispered a treacherous voice in her mind. *And rarely lets you forget his greater age and wisdom.*

Jonas looked at the floor, then back at her. "I'll never forget you."

The look in his eyes froze the words of protest in her throat. Then he was gone, and she could breathe again. Could convince herself that the intensity of that last look was an illusion brought on by the lateness of the hour and the unreality of the situation. Throughout her solitary breakfast the next morning, she'd half-expected him to bound in as he always did, sketchbook under his arm, and snatch up a slice of toast before departing. Blessedly normal, showing her a son's careless affection, the same old Jonas. She had not wanted to believe he was gone. Still less had she wanted to acknowledge how much it mattered.

Andrew had grumbled at lunch about his son's absence. "Out drawing pretty pictures again, I suppose. I won't have it, Julia. You tell him so." Not until Jonas failed to turn up for supper did Andrew realize the truth. She had meant to tell him earlier, but the words wouldn't come.

He made her pay for it with a week of frosty silence, occasionally broken with a look of bewildered hurt when he thought her attention was elsewhere. In spite of herself, her heart went out to him. All his love for Jonas couldn't help him understand the boy, and he took his son's defection as a rejection of everything he had achieved. Her own part in the incident, he saw as another betrayal—she should have stopped Jonas, or at least warned Andrew of his intentions. She'd never been able to tell him all her reasons for letting Jonas go.

She lengthened her stride as the ground rose gently beneath her. Drought-withered grass crunched beneath her boots. She could smell the heat: brown-black and sharp, like overdone piecrust. On a day like this, she almost envied the miners. At least it was cool down there.

Poor Jonas. Andrew had written him out of his will, never mentioning his name in the eleven years since his departure. Instead, he had transferred all his hopes to Mary Anne. More than once, he'd confided his dreams for their daughter to Julia in the quiet darkness before sleep.

The creak of mattress springs rousing her from a half-doze; cotton rustling as Andrew turned over and trapped his nightshirt around his long legs. Suppressing a sigh, willing him to say his piece quickly and let her drop off. "We'll go to Minneapolis in a year or two, spend the summer." Hushed excitement in his voice, like a boy listing Christmas presents he wanted. "Make sure Mary Anne meets some dependable young men. Good stock. She'll need the right husband to keep the mine profitable." Dry warmth against her hand as he enfolded it in his own. "With good management and a little luck, our grandsons will have a solid business to inherit long after we're gone. And a family name that means something." His palm against her hair, a puff of breath that smelled faintly of cherry tobacco. "You and our Mary are all that matter to me. You know that, don't you, my dear?"

He had never bothered to ask Mary Anne's opinion, or hers. Brief anger carried her swiftly to the top of the slope. *Once again, the rest of us must bend to his will. Andrew proposes, and we dispose. It would serve him right if Mary Anne ran off!*

A fat gray squirrel barely missed her foot in a mad dash for the nearest birch trunk. She watched it scurry higher, scolding all the way. *Interloper!* it said. *Get away from my trees!* "You and half the town," she told it. "You'd love me to go away, even after all this time. But I won't."

The squirrel chittered. Something small and hard struck the bridge of her nose and then dropped to the dirt a finger's width from her shoe. An infant pinecone, brown-gold against the scattered dry pine needles and curling bits of birch bark.

She kicked the pinecone aside before walking on. She didn't want another fracturing of her small family. She'd sacrificed too much for it, stifling her own wants and sometimes her very self to keep the peace. To lose her stepson had been bad enough, even though the gossips had eventually gone silent. She wasn't sure she could bear losing her daughter.

Looking up, she was startled to realize how far from the house she'd come. Another thirty minutes' walk would bring the head-works into view. Andrew would be there now, going over accounts, talking to the foreman about increasing output to take advantage of the recent rise in the price of iron ore. Everyday, ordinary things, as if their life could never change.

Suddenly she wanted to see him. To watch him at work, share a smile, talk a little about nothing in particular. She picked up her pace, then stopped as good sense reasserted itself. Her blouse was clinging to her back, her hair was a fright, the hem of her skirt was dark with dust. Mrs. Andrew Jackson Schlegel couldn't possibly turn up in public looking like that. The town would live on it for days.

Wearily, she turned and began the long walk homeward.

As the foreman left the small office, Andrew turned back to the open ledger on his desk. He would have to hire more hands if he wanted to increase output; the men were already working as much as they could without cutting dangerous corners. Some owners might go that route; not him. He knew the consequences too well.

The extra salaries might be a problem until the larger ore shipments reached the buyers. He would have to balance how many more miners he needed against the number he could afford to pay. Even if the family had to give up their Sunday roasts for a month, he couldn't let this opportunity slip by. More money for the iron now meant that much more for Mary Anne and her children one day. Enough that she need never fear losing it, no matter what.

His gaze wandered to a gilt-framed photograph that stood nearby. Mary Anne had posed for it last year, on her fifteenth birthday. She sat at her writing-table, wearing a lace dress and holding a white rose. For this year's birthday, he'd commissioned a portrait artist to paint the photo. It had seemed a wonderful idea at the time. Now he wasn't so sure. He wasn't sure of anything these days when it came to Mary Anne.

He scowled at the photograph, more in puzzlement than in anger. *My little girl. Sometimes it seems she's disappeared. Left an angry stranger to take her place. Do they all get like this when they grow up?*

He flipped a page and skimmed the first column of figures, a task that took only half his attention. The rest remained on the mystery of his daughter. Sour enough to curdle milk lately, that girl. He'd expected Julia to manage her better, but she'd grown worse over the spring, especially since he'd dismissed her skylarking plans for an author's career. He'd wounded her pride, he supposed. Part of him regretted that, but what was a loving father to do when confronted with his offspring's utter lack of sense?

He would be grateful when she came out of her sulks. The child had scarcely said a word at dinner last night—just sat there, sullen as a wet cat, pushing chicken and potatoes around her plate. "Blast it, girl, eat something," he'd snapped finally. "Mrs. Tomczack makes us a fine meal, and you treat it like dog scraps. I won't have it."

"I'm not hungry." Her muttered reply came with an insolent glare. "May I be excused?"

"I saw the loveliest dress in the new Ward's catalog yesterday—" Julia's voice, strained with the effort at normality. She might as well have tried to dam a creek with a broom straw.

He'd have let the child go if it hadn't been for that look. What decent father would tolerate open defiance? "You may not be excused. You may eat your dinner. Every morsel. And then you may apologize to Mrs. Tomczack for treating the result of her hard work with such contempt. Do you understand me, girl?"

Utter stillness. He counted five heartbeats before it broke. Mary Anne's knife and fork clattered to her plate. Wood screeched as she threw her chair backward and stormed out.

He rose to go after her. Julia's voice, shaking, stopped him. "Please, Andrew. Let her go. I'll speak to her."

He sat back down and cut a bite of chicken breast. It tasted like paper. "See that you do."

His eyes ached. Too many figures, too little light left in the day. He closed his eyes and rubbed them, then blinked until the nagging ache subsided. He shouldn't blame Julia for Mary Anne. She was doing her best. Girls were difficult. Unfortunately, Mary Anne seemed to have inherited his stubborn streak. Too bad she wasn't a boy. She'd have made a formidable businessman.

He picked up the other photograph on his desk, a daguerreo-type of himself and his brother William. He had been eighteen then, William just past nineteen. They'd hiked to Chicago from the little prairie town of Long View, two blocks of weathered storefronts surrounded by cornfields. Too small a place to contain William's ambition—or his own. Back then he'd been happy to follow where William led. He'd done it most of his life. Blind fool.

He remembered the mud sucking at his shoes like a live thing, all the way down the last few miles of road. The spring breeze smelled of it, heavy and wet. Breathing too deep made his tongue taste like old fish. The city itself was a smudge on the horizon, a dirty thumbprint against the pale blue sky.

He'd told himself it was just fatigue that made his steps lag, but William knew better. "Hurry up," his brother said over his shoulder, while Andrew stood a couple of yards back and rubbed his aching calves. "We'll be there in another mile." William folded his arms, suddenly turning scornful. "Or would you rather walk all the way home?"

He'd made the mistake of being honest then. "I don't know. I'm just not sure—"

"You want to be a dirt farmer all your life?" William strode toward him, scowling. "Thought you had *some* guts. Guess I was wrong." He dug in his trouser pocket, brought out their slim cash stake and peeled off two dollar bills. "Here. This'll get you safe back to nowhere. I'm going where I can make something of myself." He dropped the bills in a puddle, then stalked off toward the blotch on the skyline.

Much later, Andrew cursed the pride that had made him follow. No guts? Dirt farmer? He'd show William who the greenhorn farmer boy was. He hurried along as fast as the mud would let him, ignoring the cold wet that seeped through a crack in one boot-sole. He caught up eventually, and they walked side by side awhile in angry silence. Then William shot him a sideways look, grim mouth relaxing into a smile. Andrew grinned back, caught as always by his brother's sudden shift from temper to enthusiasm.

"Just you follow me, boy." William threw an arm around Andrew's shoulders. "We'll be rich enough to own Long View and every farm around it before we're five years older!"

At Chicago's western edge, rough planks covered the mud. The sodden wood gave underfoot, and greenish-black ooze glimmered through the cracks. It smelled like a privy, overlaid with fish and damp. Andrew breathed through his mouth and tried not to gag. William strode on, looking at everything, his face alive with excitement.

Near a signpost labeled "Kinzie Street," two men had set up a camera. The barker, a rope-thin Irishman, hawked their services in a lilting voice: "The picture of a lifetime! Memorialize your first steps on the soil of Chicago, soon to be the leading city in these United States!" He spotted them lingering and strolled toward them. "You gentlemen'll be wanting a photo, I'm sure. A memento of who you used to be, before you made your fortunes—which you will, or my name's not Pat Grady. How about it?"

William's hand was already in his pocket. "How much?"

Grady quoted a price that made Andrew's stomach drop, then flashed them a crooked grin. "And worth every penny. What do you say?"

Before Andrew could manage a word, William clapped him on the shoulder and hauled him over. "We haven't the money to spare," he hissed in William's ear, stumbling over his own feet in the wake of his brother's exuberance.

William laughed. "You heard the man, Andy—there's a fortune out there with our name on it! Didn't I tell you? You can turn your hand to anything here and make a go of it!"

He remembered squinting in the sunlight, gritting his teeth against a coughing fit when a puff of wind made the privy smell overpowering. The exorbitant price they'd paid for two copies would have bought them at least one night in a decent hotel, though William had scoffed when he pointed that out. In the end, he was glad they'd done it. The picture was a talisman of sorts, a reminder of how far he'd come. And of how he'd managed it—by trusting himself and no one else. No one else ever again.

His grip tightened on the picture frame. He wondered if William still had his copy, and if he ever looked at it. *Buried it in a drawer, most likely, to be taken out whenever he needs to stoke his envy. As well as he's done for himself, he still can't stand it that the younger brother he ruined ended up doing better.*

The gangling youth of the photo had long since vanished, but Andrew flattered himself that his shoulders were still as broad and his hands as strong. The thick dark hair was streaked with gray now, the clean-shaven face ornamented with a glossy mustache. Tastefully styled, none of your exaggerated handlebars or waxed tips. He was a solid citizen, not a dandy. Still, he couldn't help being proud of it. There had been a time, in his mid-teens, when he'd despaired of ever growing one.

Jonas had looked much the same—long-boned and knobby-wristed, with a face as smooth as a girl's. He had his mother's eyes, though—misty gray, as if clouded with dreams. Andrew brushed a thumb across his younger, sepia-toned face. He wondered what his son looked like now . . . any meat on his bones, anything in his head that Andrew had tried to put there.

He set the photo down. It was no good missing Jonas. The boy had made his choice years ago. Better to focus on the here and now than to waste time with useless regrets.

He turned back to the ledger. Work would banish this

sentimental foolishness. "That's your solution to everything," Julia had once accused him, after a blistering argument between he and Jonas not long before the boy left. "You bury your head in your books and balance sheets, and you don't come out again until it's safe. Until we've given up. You're a coward, Andrew Schlegel—afraid to listen to people, because then you might have to change your opinion. And God forbid you should ever be guilty of that!"

He turned another page without seeing it. Funny, how harsh words could stick in your mind. Until two minutes ago, he'd forgotten that conversation—if it even deserved the name. He had responded, he recalled, by telling Julia not to be hysterical, then saying he was going to his study and did not wish to be disturbed. He no longer remembered what she'd shouted after him as he strode down the stairs. Now he wondered if Julia was right.

I know what's best for Mary Anne. Julia would surely agree with that. But I suppose it can't hurt to treat her odd notions with a little more respect.

He closed the ledger and took out a sheet of stationery. Mc-Cann's Booksellers in St. Paul ought to have some new novels by now; he would ask for a list and let Mary Anne choose one. She loved a good novel. Perhaps they could read one together and discuss it, the way they'd done this past winter. He missed those conversations.

He picked up his pen and began to write.

CHAPTER FIVE

"So . . ." Clementine Turner-Chiu sawed her shredded pork burrito in half with a dinky plastic knife. "Are you excited?"

Rachel dipped a tortilla chip into the bowl of pico de gallo. " 'Excited' is an understatement."

They shared a small table in a corner of La Cucina, where the chile-green hot sauce could blister your tongue and the burritos were as big as your head. Bright serapes covered the walls, and a tinny radio played salsa tunes from somewhere back in the kitchen.

Rachel crunched the chip while eying her own burrito. Carne asada—shredded steak, instead of her usual chicken. She'd felt hungry when they walked in, but now she wondered if she could eat it. Her upcoming journey to Minnesota was playing havoc with her appetite. "It's been such a roller-coaster, Clemmie. I'm excited, I'm terrified, I'm wondering if this whole idea is insane. But I can't imagine not doing it. I have to go there and meet her. Isn't that weird?" She picked up a burrito half. "I mean, I've never been bothered by this kind of thing. Not even after Dad died. Who am I, where did I come from, where's my real family . . . it seemed so, I don't know, self-indulgent. I have a real family. They're the ones who raised me. Why would I need another one?" She drizzled hot sauce over the burrito. "It snuck up on me."

"Because of your mom."

"Yeah."

Clementine tucked blonde hair behind one ear. Her open, friendly face held a quizzical look. "Did you think it would bother her if you looked for your birth mother?"

Rachel contemplated her burrito. Scraps of iceberg lettuce showed pale against the rich brown of the meat. "I didn't see it like that. I just—I had a mom already. I never questioned that she and Dad were my family. Only now they're gone. All I have left in the world is a fat, cranky cat. Some family life, huh?"

Clementine touched her arm. "We'll take good care of Quincy while you're gone. Roger said he'd come over with me—he wants to torture the poor baby with beads on a string."

Rachel laughed. "Good. Quincy needs the exercise." The enormity of it hit her, and a thrill shot down her spine. "This time tomorrow, I'll be on the road. I can't believe it." Suddenly she felt hungry again. She bit into the burrito with relish.

Clementine picked up her Coke and swirled her straw around in it. "Were you ever angry at her? At your birth mom, for giving you up?"

"I hardly thought about her. Except when I was pissed at Mom for making me clean my room." She noticed her friend's stillness, and the grin left her face. "What?"

"We're thinking of adopting. Roger and I." Clementine set the Coke down and rested her chin on her hands. "We've been looking at China—his family's from Sichuan, so we're hoping that'll cut some extra ice with the folks who make decisions there. I just . . . I wonder sometimes how to handle it. Especially since our daughter won't look a thing like this Iowa farm girl."

Rachel put down her food and leaned toward her. "Hey. Just be a good mom. Deal with everything else as it comes up. You won't know what it's going to be until it does."

"That's what they said at the counseling group. I guess I just needed to hear it from someone who's lived it." She ate a bite of burrito, then grinned at Rachel. "Tell me how it goes, okay?

I'm nosy. I want to know every single thing."

Lincoln and Southport lay considerably west of the lakeshore, but the wind still cut like a cold knife. Florian pulled his coat collar tighter around his throat and strode faster toward the S & G Diner.

The neighborhood canvass had been little help in identifying Jane Doe. Only one person in the vicinity of Mountjoy Park admitted to having seen or heard anything. Tin-Can Jake, on his nightly garbage-picking rounds, recalled hearing raised voices and then screams from the right direction at about half-past one. Jake couldn't tell what the shouting match was about, and it was none of his business. His business was picking cans so he could keep a roof over his head and a little something on his hot plate. Not nosing into other folks' doings, no sir.

Fingerprints had turned up nothing; Jane Doe wasn't in the system. And without some notion of who she might be, Florian couldn't track down her dental records to confirm her identity.

So he'd spent most of the afternoon checking out diners and greasy spoons: every place where the waitresses wore the right kind of uniform, within reasonable walking distance of Mountjoy Park and the nearest L and bus stops. Jane Doe had been going somewhere, and they'd found no car key. It might have been swiped along with her wallet and license, but he was betting she took public transport. After four lousy cups of coffee at as many diners, plus a basket of limp fries, a pizza puff and a surprisingly good cheddar burger, his stomach was regretting his choice of tactics. The S & G was next on the diner list. He hoped for decent coffee this time.

He walked in and stood by the "Please Wait To Be Seated" sign, cheeks and hands tingling in the warmth. The clink of flatware on china mingled with the muted conversations of scattered customers and a Top-Forty pop station played at mercifully low volume. Nice little place: sparkling clean, lots of frosted glass and blond wood. He smelled beef gravy and cherry pie. Maybe he could just loiter here and inhale while he showed Jane Doe's photo around. No risk there if the food didn't live up to its odors.

"Smoking or non?" said a nasal voice to his left. Its owner, middle-aged, with bright red hair out of a bottle, bore down on him with menu in hand. Her uniform matched Jane Doe's: brick-red apron and skirt, red-and-white striped shirt.

He nodded at her and pulled the photo out of his coat pocket. Not for the first time, he wished he had something other than the crime-scene shot. Hopefully, this woman wouldn't go all rubber-kneed at the sight of it. "Sorry, ma'am, but I'm here on business. Ever seen her before?"

The woman took the photo, then blanched. "My God, that's Grace. Oh, dear God." She groped for the nearest chair. He nudged one into her path. As she sat down, she glanced toward the dining room. "Ellen?" Her voice shook slightly. "Come here a minute, would you?"

A tall black woman, her ponytail wrapped in a bright purple scrunchie, looked up from a table halfway down the room. With a smile and a brief word to the customers whose order she was taking, she put away her pad and pen and walked to the front of the diner. Florian watched her expression change from curiosity to concern as she got a good look at her co-worker's face. "What is it, Connie? Is it Grace? Is she all right?"

"I'm afraid not," Florian said gently, as Connie handed Ellen the photo. Ellen glanced at it, then flinched away.

"That's Grace," she said after a moment of silence. Her face stony, she handed the photo back to Florian. "I hope you get that bastard. I hope you get him good."

"You have someone in mind?"

Her answer was a single, sharp nod. He gestured toward a

chair. "Tell me about him."

As Ellen sat, Florian pulled out another chair and sat down across from her. "I don't know his name," she said, while he brought out his notepad and flipped it open. "But he was here every day since last Monday. Came in right after our shift started and stayed till closing. Grace was scared of him. I could tell."

"Tell me a little about Grace; we'll come back to the mystery man. Grace what?"

"Chapman. Grace Chapman." Ellen moistened her lips. "She hadn't been here long; she just finished her three-month a few weeks ago. We made her lunch to celebrate. On the house."

"She hadn't been at the S & G long, or hadn't been in the city?"

"In Chicago. She came here from somewhere else—Michigan, Wisconsin, somewhere like that. Some state close by. She told me once, but I don't remember." She straightened and looked at him. "She was living at Sally's Place—that's a shelter, right off Montrose by the Ravenswood line. Gives you an idea why she came here. She didn't say much about it, but she was running." She glanced down at her hands. "My older sister married a crackhead. She ran. Till he caught up with her."

"Grace was running from our mystery man?"

She nodded. "He sat in that booth over there. Six days straight. Had himself a meal, then drank coffee for the rest of the shift. Kept trying to make Grace come over and talk to him. Offered to buy her dinner, told her how tired she looked and to take a load off. How she needed someone to take care of her. Him, I guess. He even brought her flowers, that first day. She wouldn't take them." She paused. "He watched every move she made, like she was some toy he was deciding whether or not to keep. She started off trying to pretend he wasn't there, but after a couple days she got that look—like she was expecting something bad to happen, only maybe it wouldn't if she pretended hard enough."

"She did talk to him eventually?"

"The fourth day. He was getting nasty by then. I guess she was afraid he'd make a scene. So she sat with him for a little bit. Wouldn't touch the coffee he bought her, though." A bitter half-smile crossed her face. "He made a big deal out of paying for it. Told her he'd always wanted to buy her things, and this was just the beginning. A lousy buck fifty, and he acted like it was diamonds or something."

"Did you hear what they talked about?"

Headshake. "He did most of the talking. Kept his voice low, so it'd be nice and private. Once, while I was taking an order two booths down, I saw him try to take her hand. She moved it away, and he grabbed her wrist. Hard. He let her go after a minute; I guess he'd made his point. After that, she kept her hands in her lap."

"Did she tell you anything about him?"

"I think she was scared to with him watching. The first night, when we started to close up, he said he'd wait for her outside. She told him no thanks, she was going home with a friend. Then, in the ladies' room, she asked if I'd walk with her to the bus stop. He didn't follow us that night—just said, 'Good night, Gracie,' with a big laugh."

"He followed you other nights?"

"The third night, he followed us for about half a block. Made the same bad joke before he took off. After that, we took different routes. Grace figured he'd be waiting for her if he knew for sure where she was going. He followed us for a couple of blocks on Friday night, but not the night after. No 'good night Gracie' Friday night, either. I guess that should have told us something."

Her voice dropped a fraction. "We neither of us work Sundays, and that Monday I was out sick. Grace didn't show at five on Tuesday, and neither did what's-his-name. Connie was worried; after she told me what happened Monday, I knew why. Grace gave him some papers, legal-looking stuff. He got mad and walked out. He didn't come back; Grace must've thought he'd gone." She clenched a fist against the tabletop.

He asked her a few more routine questions and then thanked her. Slow as an old woman, she stood up and headed toward the kitchen with her orders.

"Will you need to talk to anyone else, Detective?" Connie asked.

"Just you, if you don't mind. I'd like to hear what happened Monday."

She tucked a loose strand of hair behind one ear. "Grace got here about fifteen minutes early. She kept watching the door, waiting for him. He turned up about half an hour later. The minute she spotted him, she ducked into the closet and came out with some folded-up papers. She gave them to me and asked would I give them to him. I'm divorced; I know what the paperwork looks like. I tried to hand them over. He wouldn't take them."

"Did she say anything?"

"Not a word. They just stared at each other. We were all watching by then. We knew something was going to happen.

"When Grace didn't back down, he finally took the papers and glanced at them. He didn't much care for what he read. He threw them at her, called her and me bitches and several other things I won't repeat. He'd have hit her if we all hadn't gathered around; I could see it in his face. Then he called us all effing you-can-guesses and left."

"What did Grace do?"

"Put the papers back in her purse. From the way she looked, she needed a strong cup of coffee and a good long talk. But she said she was fine. I let it go. I didn't want to push." Connie paused. "She seemed to get better during her shift—not relaxed, but calm enough to handle full plates and cups. I offered to walk her to the bus, but she said no, she was tired of running scared. She had a look—like she'd said *no more* down to her bones, you know? We hadn't seen him for hours by then, anyway." Tears began to well up; Connie shut her eyes. "That poor little girl. Lord knows what'll happen to her now."

He sat up straighter. "Little girl?"

"Grace's daughter. Linnet. Cute little thing, about twelve; Grace had a picture in her wallet. I told her she could bring Linnet by one day for a free dessert, but she never did." She pulled a Kleenex from her pocket and dabbed her face. "That poor child. I hope to God that man isn't her father."

Florian echoed that sentiment over a decent cup of coffee and a slice of fresh-baked cherry pie, both pressed on him by Connie. She hadn't heard Grace's conversation with the mystery man either, nor did she know whether Chapman was a married or a maiden name. So now he had a likely perp, whose surname might or might not be Chapman, possibly residing somewhere within the greater Chicago area. Or long gone, back to wherever he and Grace had come from.

Neither waitress had seen the suspect with a car, or had any idea how close to the diner he might have holed up. Both eagerly agreed to work with a sketch artist at the station the next morning, to help separate Mr. Whoever from the general population of just-over-six-foot white guys with light brown short hair, greenish eyes and no facial hair or distinguishing marks. Meanwhile, Florian had another lead to follow.

Ellen had said Sally's Place was near the Montrose L. He turned up his collar again and headed back out into the bitter wind.

Luke was getting tired of playing spy. Unfortunately, he hadn't thought up a better tactic. He could hardly walk into every women's shelter in town, demanding to know if any of them had his kid. Not that they'd tell him.

Sally's Place was the name of this one, or so said the little brass plaque by the entrance. From the bus stop where he loitered across the street, he couldn't tell what the place was. All he could see was a long expanse of glass, backed by dark wooden shutters. If he hadn't found it in the phone book, he never would have guessed it was here. He wondered who Sally was and how badly she'd screwed over her old man before running off.

He'd gotten here at nine-thirty that morning, too late to catch Linnet going to school. Too much Scotch always made him oversleep. Four aspirins, washed down with a cup of thin coffee from the nearby Seven-Eleven, had mostly gotten rid of his headache by lunchtime. He hadn't seen Linnet then, either. But at least he knew he was on the right track.

She hadn't been on the playground at St. Teresa's when he'd walked down that way to catch lunchtime recess. Most of the bigger kids had learned to be wary of strangers, and the little kids didn't know who Linnet was. Finally, a skinny redhead whose arms hung out of his jacket sleeves had sidled up and bummed a smoke. He and Linnet were in the same math class. The redhead didn't like her because she was smarter than him. Luke gave him the rest of the pack by way of thanks, then went back to Sally's Place. The smoking section of a diner around the corner gave a clear view of Montrose Avenue. He decided to wait there until Linnet came along.

He'd waited for hours, reading papers, chain-smoking and swilling coffee. After awhile, the beefy black waitress had started dropping increasingly blatant hints to pay up and move on. She left him alone after he flashed a twenty at her: "Keep your mouth shut and you get this. Throw me out and I'll sue this place for harassment. Got it?"

By five, he was telling himself Linnet might have gone home with a friend, or maybe she had some after-school thing like choir practice. Now, after forty minutes' wait for a bus he had no intention of taking, he was sure she hadn't been to school. Was she even still at Sally's Place, or had Grace somehow arranged to spirit her away?

Traffic whizzed by on Montrose, including a westbound bus. An old brown Chevy pulled around the corner onto Winchester and drove slowly down the one-way street, looking for parking. Luke grinned at the departing car. Poor bastard—he'd be looking a long time before he found a space for that boat.

The Chevy pulled out of sight. Luke turned his attention back to the building, hoping against hope that someone might come out with Linnet in tow. If she'd already left the shelter, he was sunk. He had no way of knowing which idiot bleeding-heart might have taken her in, or where they might have gone. His only hope lay in spotting Linnet tonight. Then he could follow and get her away later.

He opened a fresh pack of cigarettes, stuck one between his lips and lit it. That shook off boredom for maybe a minute. With an eye on the shelter entrance, he watched cars and people go by. A fat woman in a brown cloth coat strolled out of a bakery halfway down the block, chomping on a donut. Two skinny Latino kids whizzed by on bikes. A cab going a good twenty above the speed limit veered around a slower-moving white hatchback, blasting its horn. A lanky man in a trench coat, shoulders hunched against the cold, headed down the street toward Sally's Place.

Luke straightened as the man stopped in front of the shelter. After a few minutes, the man opened the door and disappeared inside.

Cop? Luke took a long drag on his cigarette. After two more, the jolt of adrenaline began to subside. Maybe not. Could be a private dick, or somebody's brother. Or could be a thousand reasons a cop'd come to a place like this that had nothing to do with him.

He distracted himself by looking at nearby parked cars. *That Camry's seen better days. Look at that rust. What the hell is that little one—a Fiesta? Nice new Prizm. Wonder how long before some kid scratches it up—*

He froze, cigarette halfway to his mouth. A stuffed rabbit lay across the top of the Prizm's back seat. He wandered over for a closer look.

He knew that loved-to-threads toy as well as his favorite brand of smokes. Linnie's rabbit. The one he'd hit Grace for buying because she stole his liquor money to pay for it.

Common sense stifled his first impulse, to confront the owner. She—he'd bet anything it was a woman—would know who he was the second he said Linnet's name, and would likely go straight to the cops. Unless he dealt with her first, which he shied away from doing. He wasn't a killer. Grace was an accident. Some kind of con, then—but what? People who worked in places like Sally's saw too much to make easy marks. A workable con meant planning, which would eat up time he didn't have. No good.

He thought next of tailing her, but how? Hail a convenient cab and order it to "follow that car"? Hunt down a rental he couldn't afford and hope to hell the Prizm was here when he came back? Tail it in a fucking bus? The license number wouldn't help him, either. At the moment, tracing the owner's address that way was beyond his capabilities. He prowled around the car, smoking in short, frustrated bursts.

Something white on the dashboard caught his eye. Letters, stamped and addressed and ready for the mailbox. For once in his rotten life, something was working his way. He tilted his head and squinted through the windshield at the name and return address. Ruth N. Mason, 5020 W. Albany.

Albany lay pretty far west of here, if he remembered his city geography right. He looked down the street and spotted a westbound bus just two blocks away. At the first gap in traffic, he sprinted across to the bus stop.

CHAPTER SIX

They'd gone to some trouble to make Sally's Place look like home, from the overstuffed sofa and chairs to the copious potted plants and artwork on the walls. Prints and watercolors, mostly, of wildflowers and birds and other soothing subjects. Interspersed among them were children's drawings in bright colors. Florian walked over for a closer look at one, a scraggly rainbow that must have used half the hues in the classic 64-Crayola box. Two figures stood under the rainbow, which was raining colors down on them. The adult figure, clearly Mommy, looked up at the rainbow with a bright yellow tear on her cheek. The child figure was dancing amid a shower of green, blue and orange droplets.

"Kenny Jones drew that one," said a familiar voice behind him. "The first with any colors except black and brown. He'll be six next week."

His gut clenched. Not a scrap of warmth in her tone—only a dead flatness that told him how hard she was controlling her feelings. What they were, he could only guess. Anger? Sadness? An echo of love?

He turned to face her. A thousand words churned through his brain. The one that came out was her name. "Ruthie."

A shadow he couldn't define crossed her face. Once upon a time, he'd been able to read this woman as easily as a road sign. "Sophie said you were here about Grace." Still controlled, smooth and cool as the keys of the upright piano he'd never

78

learned to play.

"You still have the Baldwin?" he heard himself ask.

A flicker of surprise, then a brief twitch that might have been a smile. "You ever figure out how to play something besides 'Chopsticks'?"

"Not yet."

The glimmer of humor vanished as quickly as it had come. Another woman might have flinched as she asked the next question, but Ruthie never backed away from anything. "Is Grace dead?"

One word, all he could manage. "Yeah."

She closed her eyes and bowed her head. Light glinted from her tortoiseshell glasses. One hand came up to worry the nape of her neck. She'd chopped her hair off sometime in the past two years; dark curls feathered her earlobes. He remembered those curls brushing her shoulders, freshly washed and gleaming, begging to be touched.

"I, uh—" He cleared his throat. "I need to ask you a few questions. Here if you want, or somewhere more private."

"Business as usual." Behind the lenses, her eyes shimmered. "You make an effort for the dead ones."

He told himself her cold anger wasn't directed at him this time. He just happened to be a convenient target. It didn't help much, but at least he managed not to snap back at her. Silently, he followed her past a closed office and a bathroom to a cheerful, cozy kitchen. A half-full pot of coffee steamed on one counter. "Nice. When did you quit New Life?"

"When Sally Crane and I scrounged enough money to open this place. Never an empty room. Extra cups in the cabinet." She gestured with her head toward the right one, then lifted her own mug from a row of hooks near the coffeemaker and filled it. He watched her doctor it as he poured his own: teaspoon of sugar, slug of cream. Her spoon stayed in the mug. He still

79

wondered how she avoided poking herself with it when she drank.

Instead of joining him at the table, she leaned against the counter. Silence fell. He watched her stare into her coffee as he tried to frame his opening question.

"Chapman," he said finally. "I'm assuming that's his name. Couple of people at the S & G told me a guy was stalking Grace. Did he turn up here?"

"I never saw him. Grace didn't, either; she'd have said." She blew on her coffee. "His first name's Luke. I'm not surprised he tracked her down through work; he'd done it before. He followed her from the Twin Cities to Milwaukee a few years back. Her first few weeks here, she was terrified he'd find her again. She never really lost that fear. Most of them don't." A cautious sip, then a glance as cutting as a knife blade. "But you know that."

He counted to five, willing himself to let it go. "Were they married, or just together?"

"For better or worse, till death do us part." Her brief smile had no mirth in it. "She was going to pick a new surname after the divorce came through. She wasn't on good terms with her family, so she didn't want her maiden name. She never told me what it was, or what the problems were. Grace didn't talk much about her past."

She spoke Grace's name as if it meant more to her than a client usually did. He felt chilled, though the kitchen was plenty warm. Emily Leavitt all over again. A dead woman and a perp he couldn't touch. And Ruthie ripped to pieces over it. His hands tightened on his mug. "Do you have any idea where I might find this guy Chapman—where he might be staying, where he might show up? Did Grace tell you anything?"

"She didn't know. I only wish I did." After a small silence, she continued. "This one bothers you, doesn't it?"

"What makes you think Emily Leavitt didn't?"

He felt a small, mean gladness when she looked away. *It bothers me because of you,* he wanted to say. Would she believe him if he told her?

He didn't want to find out. He sipped coffee, then set down his mug as an idea occurred to him. "Chapman might come looking for his daughter, assuming he traced them to the shelter. She is his—the little girl?"

"Unfortunately." Another silence stretched between them. She took the spoon out of her coffee, shook droplets from it, snagged a paper towel from a nearby dispenser and carefully wiped the spoon with it.

He didn't want to ask it, but he had to. "Is she here?"

She looked at him. "Please don't expect me to answer that. She's safe. That's all you need to know."

Irritation boiled up. "I'm not the enemy, Ruthie, all right? If Luke Chapman killed Grace, they're not going to give him the kid. So why—"

"You don't know that. And what if he did it, but you can't prove it in court? Then there's no blot on his record. Abusing his wife doesn't count, if he never hit his child. They'd fall all over themselves to give Daddy custody, rather than take on another ward of the state." She thumped her mug on the counter and crossed her arms. "You know how it works. Don't pretend you don't."

Hearing the strain beneath her anger, his own vanished. He felt horribly tired. "I just want to do my job. Can we have a truce?"

Her shoulders slumped, as if fatigue was hitting her, too. "I didn't know this was a war," she murmured, but her tone had lost its sting.

He took refuge in professionalism. "I'll send a couple of guys around, if that's okay. Chapman likely doesn't know his

81

daughter's gone. If he shows up, they'll take care of him."

"Thanks."

He couldn't think of anything more to ask, and didn't want to stay. He carried his mug to the sink, dumped it, and filled it with water. Ruthie was close enough to touch. Not daring to look at her, he wrenched off the tap and walked out.

The West Albany address was a courtyard building, three stories with a security fence and a phone pad next to the front gate. Not an easy place to slip into, unless Ruth Mason had careless neighbors. He walked around back to the parking lot, but saw no red Prizm. He had no idea when Mason left work; it might be anywhere from half an hour to half the night before she showed up.

He returned to the front entrance and found Mason on the phone list: 3E, third floor east. He spent a minute working out which direction east was, then went back to the parking lot.

The back door was triple-locked, with two deadbolts. He could kick it in or smash the glass, but the noise would attract attention. If Linnie were in there, would she open the door if he knocked? What if he buzzed from the front and told her it was Daddy? Or had Grace and this Mason bitch made her too afraid of him?

It was worth a shot. He strode to the front gate and punched Ruth Mason's number.

Nothing. Either Linnet wasn't answering or she wasn't there. But she had to be there. Otherwise he was back to the beginning, with time running out. He glanced around. Except for a dog walker on the opposite side, the street was deserted.

He punched every number in turn and crossed his fingers. Maybe somebody'd ordered a pizza.

Once again, luck was with him. The buzzer went off. Luke

opened the gate and headed toward the east wing.

The Dominicks was crowded, as usual between six and eight on weekday evenings. Ruth maneuvered her cart between a half-full one abandoned in the middle of the cereal aisle and a pre-holiday display of canned pumpkin. Miraculously, she managed not to knock over any cans or scrape her fingers. She ought to go home, put her feet up for an hour and come back to shop when it was less of a madhouse. But she always shopped for groceries on the way home from work—and after Jamie's visit, she needed the distraction.

She aimed for the meat section, mentally listing ingredients. Stew beef, green peppers, onions. Goulash would be nice for tomorrow night, which was supposed to turn even colder.

Jamie had given her the recipe, a marked improvement over the old chestnut from *The Joy of Cooking*. "Hot paprika, that's the secret. The mild stuff all by itself gets boring. When it's thirty degrees and whipping sleet out there, you want something with zip to it." He'd shown her another kind of zip shortly afterward, surprising her with his energy. After twelve straight hours dealing with the city's roughest edges, the first thing she generally wanted was a shower and some sleep—but not that night. He'd always been able to rouse her, one way or another.

Stew beef was on sale. She bought two pounds and turned her squeaking cart toward the produce department. "There's a cop out front," Sophie the admin assistant had told her, looking ready to cry. "It's about Grace. He wants to talk to you." To the person in charge, actually. He hadn't expected her; she could tell from the taut blankness on his face when he turned around. She should have expected him, given that Sally's Place was in his precinct. Sooner or later, their paths were bound to cross. Only, God, why like this?

Green peppers were on special for a dollar each. She sorted

through the pile, unearthed two that weren't too wrinkled, and went searching for a plastic baggie. A tall man with dark hair and a paunch was ripping bag after bag from the nearest dispenser. She counted five before he finally stepped away, leaving his cart in the middle of the aisle. Jamie would have moved it, manufacturing a cart crash to get the man's attention. Then a shrug and a clumsy-me smile: "It was in the way. Sorry."

He'd lost weight, she'd noticed. He also needed a haircut. She didn't want to think about the shadows in his eyes. Something had left him when she did—a little of his cop arrogance, maybe. If it was more than that, she didn't want to know. Not yet. Maybe not ever.

Shopping finished, she turned toward the checkout. Chilly tendrils of outside air reached halfway down the line as the automatic doors swung open. She wondered how cold it was in Birch Falls, and if Linnet had yet realized that the little town was home.

She'd sent the letter that morning, the one she'd hoped not to have to write. She'd thought of calling, but quailed at the idea of saying out loud the words Linnet had to hear. How do you tell a twelve-year-old her mother is dead, probably at her father's hands?

At least he wasn't likely to find her. That last day, Grace had said Linnet would be safe up north. If Grace thought Birch Falls was a safe haven, then Luke Chapman likely didn't know the place existed. *And neither will anyone else. Fair warning, Jamie.*

She moved closer to the register, steering the cart one-handed while she dug out her checkbook. Home with the groceries, a simple supper, then a couple of hours with a pot of tea and the new Amy Tan book. After today, she needed a quiet night.

The security gate had made the landlord careless. The cheap lock on the downstairs front door was easy to jimmy with the edge of Grace's driver's license. The apartment door gave him even less trouble. Luke maneuvered his arm through the opening, unhooked the chain and stepped inside.

The place was dead quiet. He pictured Linnet sitting still and small in the center of her bed, face hidden against her drawn-up knees, trying not to make noise breathing. He called her name softly. Only silence answered.

Front room, dining room, bathroom, bedroom. Linnie wasn't here. He prowled back through the apartment, shouting her name even though he knew it was useless. God damn Grace. And her bitch friend. And every woman he'd ever met, or ever would.

He stopped in the middle of the bedroom, seething with the desire to smash it to pieces. He'd take that stupid little crystal bird off the dresser, hurl it dead center and shatter the oval mirror. Then the few makeup and perfume bottles. After that, he'd toss over the bookcase. Flimsy glued-together stuff. Ought to break easy. He'd gouge the furniture he couldn't splinter, slash jagged bright lines in the smooth, dark finish. A kitchen knife would do it. And those scarves over the closet doorknob—he'd cut them into a hundred colored scraps and scatter them across the bed. Let this bitch know she shouldn't have messed with him.

Instead, he jammed his hands in his pockets. Breathing deeply, he tried to think things out.

The Mason bitch must have taken Linnie somewhere. He riffled through the papers on her desk, then searched each drawer. There had to be something: a phone number, an address. Grace hadn't known how things would go down. She'd have expected to join Linnie, or at least be in touch.

The desk yielded nothing. He moved on to the dresser, the nighttable, the closet. In the back corner of it, half-hidden by a black cloth coat, he found a familiar suitcase, pale blue with brass trim. A tiny key hung by a beaded chain next to the broken lock.

He pulled the suitcase out and jiggled it open. On the top lay a flowered dress with a lacy collar, the one Grace used to wear to church. He shook out the dress, then dug in its pockets.

His hand closed over Grace's rosary: ice-blue and ivory beads, ending in an ivory cross half the length of his pinkie finger. He flung it away and dumped out the suitcase on the bed. Clothing, underwear, nightgown, makeup bag, sandals, low-heeled pumps, strand of pearls, two paperbacks. He swore, then went quiet as a deadbolt shot back.

He heard the thump of grocery bags being set down, and thought of sneaking out the front way while Ruth Mason unpacked them. Then he heard footsteps coming toward the bedroom.

She stepped into the room, stared wide-eyed at him, and turned to dash for the kitchen. Before she could take a step, he was across the floor and on her. A swift uppercut to the jaw and she sagged to the floorboards, out cold.

He scrabbled through the pile on the bed, cursing his rotten luck. She'd gotten a decent look at him, and he'd probably left forensic evidence all over the place. He never should have come here. He had to find something in that goddamned suitcase and then run like hell after Linnet. The sooner he left Chicago, the better.

There was nothing in the pockets or the lining pouches. He stalked to the kitchen and rifled through Mason's purse. Old credit card bill, ATM receipts, new twenty, packet of Kleenex, comb, bottle of Advil, Greyhound bus ticket.

He pocketed the twenty and opened the top flap of the ticket holder. One way, Chicago to Birch Falls, Minnesota. Purchased the day after he'd followed Grace to Mountjoy Park.

Luke stuffed the ticket in his back pocket and ran.

CHAPTER SEVEN

Mulvihill Galleries lay half a block past the busy intersection of Center and Third Streets. Cold even inside her heavy wool duffel coat, Rachel glanced up at the enclosed bridges between the tall office buildings and reflected on how much sense they made in a climate like this. November in Chicago was no walk on the beach, but this Minnesota cold snap made Chicago feel balmy. Her usual tolerance for deep freezes seemed to have evaporated, or else she was more nerved up than she'd expected about finally meeting Minna McGrath.

"My mother," she murmured. Amazing, how difficult it still was to say. Mother, not Mom. Mom was taken. But mother . . . she could just about wrap her mind around that word. She could even imagine using it after awhile, if Minna wanted her to. If they liked each other. If they spent any real time together. If her surprise appearance didn't wreck things before they got started.

Sunlight glancing off a glass-sided office tower made her squint as she reached the intersection. A bright yellow cab shot past, just beating the red light. Breathing through her mouth against the smell of exhaust, she crossed the street.

She still wasn't sure what she wanted from Minna. Not a replacement for Mom—no one could ever be that. But . . . some sense of family. Some rootedness that came from belonging. She'd lost her belonging place, and had been floundering ever since. Maybe meeting Minna McGrath would help her get it back.

She slowed as she reached the gallery entrance. Her stomach had shrunk to a fist-sized lump. She passed the doors and ambled down the gallery's long facade, gazing at various items on display. She saw black-and-white photographs of downtown Minneapolis/St. Paul; an oil painting of a bag lady that Mom would charitably have called "naive"; a pair of blown-glass candlesticks that looked like alien plants; a collar-style necklace of gold-washed safety pins; a hand-high sculpture of a leaping rabbit, with a comically elongated body and ears. Like the Trix rabbit by way of Rodin. The thought made her laugh, which gave her a glimmer of courage.

She strolled past the window twice more before the relentless cold drove her inside. The sudden warmth made her cheeks and fingers burn. The air smelled of cedar. Subdued track lighting glinted from the edges of numerous display cases. Jewelry sparkled in several; others held small statues, hand-painted dishes, stained-glass vases and such. Paintings and photographs covered the walls, along with brightly colored tapestries. Rachel drifted toward one of the latter. The base fabric was turquoise, from which a pattern of triangles and diamonds leaped out in magenta, gold and green. The beauty of it entranced her, until she spotted the price tag. *Five hundred dollars. Good God.*

"Hmong work," said a soft voice behind her. "The Hmong are from Laos originally—though the woman who made that lives in the Twin Cities. A lot of them came here after civil war destroyed their homeland. I have others like it, if you're interested—not quite so big, or so expensive."

The speaker was a small, stocky woman in a dove-gray wool suit and matching silk blouse. The lapel pin she wore—a hammered tin flamingo tinted bright pink—shone against her clothes. Stylishly cut brown hair, with a tinge of silver, framed a pleasant, open face. Somewhere in her mid to late fifties, Rachel guessed. The woman looked startled as Rachel met her eyes.

"I'm afraid I didn't come here to buy," Rachel said. "I'm looking for the owner—Rose Mulvihill."

"You've found her." Rose Mulvihill's smile looked shaky. "Excuse me, but can I ask—"

"I'm Rachel Connolly." The words she'd so carefully planned flew out of her head; she could only blurt out the bare facts and hope she didn't come off as rude. "Minna McGrath's daughter."

Understanding crossed Rose's face, along with a hint of sympathy. "I wondered. You look a lot like her." She glanced away, then back. "I wish you'd written first. I—"

"Did she change her mind?" The question tumbled out of Rachel's mouth. "She did, didn't she? I'm sorry, I thought—I hoped—" She clamped her mouth shut and looked at the floor. "It's all right. I'm sure this kind of thing happens all the time. It's my fault, I should have been in touch—"

"Miss Connolly—" Rose put a hand on her shoulder. "Rachel. We need to talk. Come with me—there's a pot of tea in my office."

Rachel followed, numb with uncertainty. They entered a tiny cubby at the back of the gallery, wedged between a storeroom and a closet-sized bathroom. Her mind took refuge in physical details: sunlight streaming through the single small window, a battered metal desk sandwiched between two filing cabinets, the scents of potted marigolds and cinnamon-orange tea. A framed snapshot, in a small clear space on the desk amid a litter of receipts and inventory slips, drew Rachel's eye and held it.

The photo showed a woman of late middle age, laughing at the camera. Several of her short curls had fallen across an eye, and Rachel could just make out a patterned scarf around her neck. Strong nose, pointed chin, dark hair with a reddish tinge. Only the eyes were different—brown to Rachel's blue-gray. Ra-

chel felt suddenly dizzy, as if she'd stared too long at a fun-
house mirror.

"That's Minna." Rose nodded toward the snapshot as she
lifted a teapot from a two-burner hot plate atop the shorter filing cabinet. She snagged a pear-shaped, blue-glazed mug from
a nearby desk corner and filled it, then sat Rachel in the padded
swivel chair and handed the mug to her. "Drink a little; it'll
help."

Rachel sipped and then set the mug down, cradling it with
her fingers. "Help what?"

"Minna passed on six months ago. Melanoma." Rose sagged
against the edge of the desk, arms wrapped across her chest. "It
took me awhile to contact the public-health people in Illinois. I
just couldn't write that letter—it made losing Minna so
concrete. I should have done it sooner, bureaucracy being what
it is . . . but after so long without a word, I guess I thought
Minna's daughter wasn't interested. I'm so sorry."

Her voice sounded very far away. Rachel's throat felt tight,
and a hole gaped where her gut used to be. She found herself
mesmerized by three tiny dents in the edge of the desk, near
where her hands rested. *It's all right,* she wanted to say—a
distancing reply, the way people said "Fine" when they weren't.
She gripped the mug. For a moment, its heat made her clammy
fingers feel even colder.

The warmth seeping into her hands, along with the weight
and feel of a solid object, gradually steadied her. When she
looked at Rose again, she felt just about capable of a coherent
sentence. "Was she ill for long?"

"About eight months. She turned down chemo; a mutual
friend of ours went through that, and Minna couldn't bear the
thought of it. She told them flat out she had no intention of
spending her last year too sick and tired to move, hoping the
cancer would die before she did." Rose's expression softened in

memory. "Minna was like that. Went her own way and took no guff from anyone."

"If I'd done this sooner—if she'd known I was coming . . ." Rachel trailed off, unable to speak through the ache in her throat.

"We can't know that. She chose what she chose. You mustn't blame yourself." Rose's eyes were very bright. "I wish I had better news for you. I know this isn't what you expected."

Suddenly, Rachel wanted to cry. It made no sense, this pang of grief for a woman she'd never met, but she felt it nonetheless. Rose's hand covered hers, cool and smooth as porcelain. She gripped the other woman's fingers.

"This is so silly . . ." Her voice cracked. "She was a name and address on a piece of paper. I didn't even know what she looked like until I saw that photograph."

Rose eased her hand away, patting Rachel's as she stood up. Rachel heard her cross the room, open a file drawer and then walk back to the desk. A blue cardboard folder appeared in Rachel's line of sight. After a moment, she took it.

"I kept these, just in case Minna's girl ever turned up," Rose said. "So at least you'll know something about her."

The folder held two newspaper clippings, an exhibit catalog and something that looked like a letter. On the cover of the catalog was the leaping rabbit Rachel had admired in the gallery window. As she brushed her fingers over the papers, she was dimly aware of Rose leaving, the office door clicking shut behind her.

She unfolded the first clipping—a glowing review of a recent showing at Mulvihill Galleries, complete with a grainy picture of Minna and Rose holding up champagne glasses and grinning. The second was an obituary from the *Minneapolis Star-Tribune*. It listed no surviving family. Minna had been born in Oak Park, Illinois, in 1939; curious that she'd moved to Minnesota, with Chicago's art scene so close to home.

Finally, she picked up the letter. Perhaps Minna had left a few words for the daughter she'd never known, though the paper looked too yellowed to be very recent. Maybe she'd written it years ago, before she knew for certain whether she ever wanted to see her lost child again.

The date across the top—1894—dashed those faint hopes. Rachel almost put the letter down again, but found herself reading the first few lines as if on autopilot.

Dearest Alma, we are all as well as can be expected after yet another frightful winter. I am still trying to persuade Richard to relocate to some warmer clime, or at least a more consistent one—back East to Vermont, for example, where winter is winter and spring is spring and you know when to expect each one. They say Chicago was built on swampland, and after the flooding we have seen in recent weeks, I have no trouble believing it . . .

Rachel skimmed the rest of the page, then the other side. Family gossip, more complaints about weather . . . why had Minna kept this, or wanted her daughter to see it?

. . . happy to say that Baby Duncan has come through a mild bout of croup and is well on the road to recovery. If we never live through another such crisis, I will be a happy woman. His father insists he was never in any real danger, with a good doctor close at hand; but I cannot be so sanguine. Our little boy has brought us such happiness, Alma, as much as if he had been born to us. I wish I knew who his poor mother was, so that I might thank her for this angel child . . .

She set the letter down and reached for her cooling tea. Giving up children appeared to run in the family. Eighteen-ninety-four . . . Minna came along about four decades later. Baby Duncan must be her father, or perhaps a youngish grandfather. Had Minna gone looking for her own roots? Had she found them?

Rose Mulvihill might know. Letter in hand, Rachel hurried from the room.

"I don't know much," Rose said later, over a cup of hot chocolate heaped high with whipped cream. She blew on it twice, then took a cautious sip that left a white streak on her upper lip. She dabbed the streak away with her napkin. "But Minna asked me to tell what she did find out, if her daughter ever came looking. She thought she—you—had a right to know."

They sat in a coffee shop down the street from the gallery, a little place that smelled richly of hot beef sandwiches and grilled onions. Too tense to eat, Rachel had only ordered coffee; now, eyeing Rose's slice of apple pie, she was beginning to reconsider.

"Have something if you want," Rose said. "My treat."

"After we talk, maybe." Rachel's nervous laugh was no more than a puff of air. "I'm sorry. It's been kind of a roller-coaster day."

"I can imagine." Rose gave her a sympathetic look. "All this way, and . . . well." She took a bite of pie. "Minna found the letter in her grandmother Ida's things, after the old lady passed on—years ago, before you were born. Alma, Minna's great-aunt, had passed the year before, and her family sent Ida all the letters her sister had kept. They were very close, those two. Until she read that letter, Minna had no idea her father was adopted; no one had ever told him a blessed thing. They didn't, in those days. He didn't want to know anything about it. Understandable, I suppose. I mean, it's one thing to know all your life that you weren't born to your parents; quite another to find out like Duncan did, so abruptly and after so much time. It must have been a terrible shock. But Minna was interested."

"Did she find anyone?"

"Not living. She did trace a possible grandfather—Joseph, I think the name was, or . . . no, Jonas. I knew it was something Biblical. He was long dead by the time she found him, of course." She sipped her chocolate. "Minna said she didn't get serious about looking until after you came. I didn't know her then; she was still in Chicago, didn't move up here until years later." She looked at Rachel. "I wish I could tell you what she was thinking, or how she felt about giving you up. I got the feeling she regretted it—not that she felt she'd done wrongly, but that she wished things could have been different. She never said why, never told me a thing about your father. But she'd get this wistful look sometimes, whenever we'd see women out with their grown daughters, lunching and whatnot. She wanted that, I think."

"I wish I'd known her. Even for just a little while." Rachel's coffee had gone lukewarm. She signaled a passing waitress for a refill. "What about Jonas—did she find out anything more definite?"

Rose nodded. "He'd been an artist like her, lived in Chicago most of his life. He was born in Minnesota, though. Birch Falls, a little town up in the Iron Range—about forty miles south of Canada, to give you an idea." She ate the last bite of pie. "Minna used to talk about going there, seeing if she could find other family members. Jonas had no children—not legitimate ones, anyway—but there might have been cousins or something. We once thought of going together, but never found the time; it's a long trip. In the end, I guess finding out about Jonas was enough for Minna. She knew where she came from, or thought she did. I think that was all she wanted."

"But you weren't so sure?"

Rose shrugged. "Jonas Schlegel signed an affidavit, saying

he'd found the baby on some church steps. Minna said it was far too clichéd. I had to agree with her there. But even if he lied, that doesn't necessarily make him the father." She took a sip of water. "I think Minna wanted him to be, because of the artist bit, and also because there wasn't much of anywhere else to look. And she wanted family. She didn't have much left by then."

Just like me. Rachel sat back in the cushioned booth. An idea was taking shape in her head. A crazy idea, considering it was damned near winter, but she didn't care. "How far is Birch Falls from here?"

"By car? About five hours. Four if you don't stop to eat and the weather holds. Which is no certain thing this time of year." Rose drained her chocolate. "You're not thinking of going there now, are you?"

"I've already come this far. Why not go a little farther?"

"In November? My dear, you could run into blizzards that far north. And even if you don't, the weather will still be unspeakable. I'm from those parts myself. The Iron Range is no place to visit in the back end of the year, unless you want to drive yourself into galloping depression. At least wait until spring, when there's sunshine and a few flowers to make the place look presentable."

"I'd rather not wait." *Or I might never have the guts to go.*

"All right, but don't say I didn't warn you. I can give you a brochure for the Windy Pines Hotel; Minna and I thought we might stay there, if we ever went. Those chain places are all right as far as they go, but . . . well, you know."

They walked out of the coffee shop into swirling snow. Upon discovering that Rachel had no plans for the evening other than a solitary dinner in the hotel restaurant, Rose invited her over. "Don't be silly, of course it's no trouble. I always make more food than I can eat, and Pyewacket hasn't coped well with leftovers ever since his spot of kidney trouble. I've got him on Science Diet now. We'd be delighted to have you. And I can tell you all about Minna."

Luke Chapman's digitized face had appeared on the early local news as "wanted for questioning in connection with the death of a woman on the North Side." Posters were up in the neighborhood of the S & G, on the off chance that Chapman had holed up close to his quarry. They'd also put out a police all-call, from which Florian expected the best results. In his experience, fellow cops were less likely than civilians to spot imaginary perps. If the all-call netted them something, it was likely to be genuine. Lucky the guy wasn't a serial killer, or they'd have more sightings of him than Elvis.

He hunched over his typewriter, four-fingering his way through a sheaf of paperwork describing the case's progress. Much more of this and his neck would be a chiropractor's nightmare. He finished the last line of the blue form, then indulged in a back-cracking stretch. Outside, the afternoon was fading toward twilight.

He and his partner had spent most of the day talking to proprietors of cheap hotels in the area. None of them recognized Chapman. The guy might've skipped, but Florian doubted it. Chapman wanted the little girl; as long as he thought she was still in the city, he was unlikely to run.

He gazed for a minute at the sunset glow, then reluctantly reached for the next form. Green this time, the color of old mint gum. Mitchell would demand every detail, even though killings of nobody important usually stayed low on the lieutenant's priority list. This was Florian's case, and so Mitchell would make an exception. He had done so for two years, ever since the Leavitt fiasco.

Even now, the thought of Emily Leavitt made his gut feel like lead. It didn't help to tell himself, as he always did, that Mitchell and he had equally failed to take her fear of her ex-husband seriously. Leavitt's death had nearly cost Florian his job, along with what he'd hoped was his future.

"You wouldn't listen," Ruthie had said, her face and voice like stone. "She told you, I told you—how many times? Did you think we were stupid, Jamie? Or crazy? 'You know how they get at that time of the month. All those hormones.' Was that how it went in what passes for your brain? A couple of silly women and their imaginary fears?"

Guilt made him answer more harshly than he'd meant to. "I talked to Mitchell like I promised. And I'm damned lucky he didn't laugh me out of his office. A few phone calls and one yelling match in a restaurant don't cut it, not when the guy's record is clean and his own shrink gave him a pass. He'd never even owned a BB gun, for Christ's sake. What was I supposed to do, read his mind? Tail him all over town in my copious free time? Throw myself in front of the goddamned bullet?!"

His tirade didn't shake her. "You could have talked to Mitchell like you meant it. But you made up your mind there was nothing to it, so that's how you laid it out. Don't blame your boss. You gave him an excuse. And you didn't even do that much for Emily. You didn't do it because you thought it mattered. You did it to keep your nice warm spot in my bed. Well, consider it gone, James Florian. It and me."

Small rats were chomping on his neck muscles. He rolled his head and shoulders, as much to erase the memory as to ease the physical ache. Mitchell would expect everything in writing, on file and in triplicate. Failure to exhaustively document his own and Harper's every move would earn him a barbed lecture, calculated for maximum embarrassment. Which would ordinarily roll right over him without leaving so much as a scuff mark, except that the Chapman case was reminding him too much of Emily Leavitt. It was far too late to save the victim this time. The only thing left was to find the perp and make a solid case.

The paperwork wasn't helping his mood. Nor was the thought of how he'd spend most of the next week—sifting through a slush pile of tips, ninety-five percent of which would be useless. Lots of hours on the phone, talking to people who'd watched too many episodes of *America's Most Wanted* and figured this was their chance to grab a chunk of the limelight. Lots more hours running tips to earth, finding out just how bogus he'd already known they were. And finally, if he was lucky, actually getting somewhere, even if it turned out to be two steps forward and one step back. By that time, of course, Chapman might have discovered that his kid wasn't in Chicago anymore and hit the road. Which would mean a whole new round of publicity, another mountain of tips, another few months' worth of wasted hours. "Story of my life," he muttered as he headed toward the break room for his third cup of coffee.

"Hey, Jim." Detective Maggie Harper straightened up from behind the refrigerator door and gave him a friendly smile. "You got any idea what happened to the half-and-half I bought last week?"

"Mitchell drank it to piss you off." He managed half a smile on his way to the coffeepot. He liked Maggie, and not just because their boss didn't. Blessed with a quirky sense of humor and a sharper mind than half the detectives in the precinct, she was also easy on the eye. And lucky enough to be married to a guy who could take his wife being a cop. He sometimes wondered how they handled that, especially with Maggie looking like a stiff wind could blow her halfway across Lake Michigan. Her scrappy toughness didn't match the fragile packaging—as more than a few people on both sides of the badge had found out, to their regret.

She gave a cry of triumph, muffled by the depths of the refrigerator, and surfaced with a red carton in hand. "At least I don't have to drink this rotgut black, on top of everything else."

"Slow day for you too?"

She made a face that reminded him of an irritated cat. "Don't ask."

As they walked back into the main room, another detective intercepted them. With coffee-colored skin and a build that belonged on an NBA All-Star team, Scott Jamieson was one of the few cops in the precinct who made Florian look short. "Something you might be interested in," he said to them. "Assault at an apartment on West Albany last night."

At the street name, Florian stiffened. Jamieson went on with a questioning look. "Housebreaker. Lady couldn't give much of a description; it happened too fast. So far, we've got Mr. Generic: white guy somewhere around six feet, with lightish hair. Brown, she thought." He shrugged. "She runs a shelter for battered women. So it could be any one of a hundred pissed-off husbands, exes, boyfriends or otherwise significant others. Could also be somebody to do with your Jane Doe."

"What's the vic's name?" Maggie beat Florian to it by a quarter-second.

"Ruth Mason. Runs a shelter on Montrose."

Florian felt the blood leave his face. "How bad?"

"Walking wounded, last I heard. She's home now. Friend of yours?"

"You might say that." He set down his coffee on the nearest desk. "Let's go."

"I don't know if it was him." He could see Ruthie trying not to wince as she talked. Chapman—or whoever—had landed quite a blow, from the size of the bruise on her jaw. Lucky for her he hadn't broken it. Florian's grip tightened on his notepad. "It could have been," Ruthie continued. "It probably was. But I couldn't swear to it."

"And he didn't take anything?" Maggie asked from her place on the loveseat. Florian knew he should join her, but felt too keyed up to sit—especially there, on a piece of furniture he'd last seen two years and a month ago. The brown velveteen was a touch more worn, and one fat arm sported a coffee stain. He wanted to pace, but sensed that his looming frame in the background was making Ruthie tense enough. After their conversation yesterday, he wasn't surprised. On the little round table next to her chair, he spotted a bottle of painkillers the size of horse pills. It looked half gone.

"Nothing that I can tell. And that's what I don't understand." Ruthie paused, then continued in a subdued voice. "He found Grace's bag. I was keeping it for her. He found it, and he left it. I'd have expected . . ."

"What?" Maggie asked as Ruthie trailed off and stood up. The frozen look on Ruthie's face told Florian that whatever had occurred to her, it was bad.

She headed for the kitchen. Following, they saw a brown leather handbag on the corner of the butcher-block table. She rooted through it twice, the second time laying out and inspecting the contents of each pocket. "Damn it. Damn it, damn it, damn it!" She looked through the emptied bag a third time, then snapped it shut with controlled violence. Florian started toward her, then halted with an effort.

"It was him." Her voice sounded stretched, like piano wire. "He took the ticket. Twenty dollars and a bus ticket to Birch Falls. I asked Sophie at work to buy it for Grace; when Grace didn't show at Sally's, I took it in case she turned up here. He couldn't have mistaken it for cash; it was in a separate pocket, and I never took it out of its holder. Those things don't feel remotely like money." She clenched her hands around the top of the handbag and bowed her head. After a moment, Florian realized she was crying.

He couldn't move. Suddenly it was late September, three years back, and he was watching Ruthie grieve for a different woman. He hadn't been able to touch her then, either. With something like envy, he saw Maggie rest a hand on Ruthie's shoulder.

"Where's Birch Falls?" he asked gently, once Ruthie had composed herself. He wanted to hold her and let her cry it all out, but she wouldn't take that kind of help from him. Not now. Probably not ever again.

"Northern Minnesota." Two words, flat and dull, as if neither they nor anything else mattered anymore. "About two hours north of Duluth. Linnie's there. With her grandfather."

They left her with what few words of comfort they could manage. He knew how empty they were and wondered if she would despise him for saying them. His last thought, as they drove back to the precinct house, was how much Lieutenant Mitchell would love this.

Linnet wished she could cry. Anything would feel better than the frozen lump in her chest, as if she'd swallowed a piece of an iceberg. There must be something wrong with her. Or maybe she still just didn't believe it.

When she'd first seen the letter, sitting on top of her pillow, she thought it was the best birthday present she could have asked for. She'd hardly paid attention to the strange handwriting on the envelope as she tore it open and lifted out the single page inside. Then she read the letter, and everything went away except for black ink on white paper.

She remembered sitting down hard on the floor, as if her legs had gone boneless. For close to forever she sat there, staring at the words until they dissolved into meaningless letters. The old man had knocked on her door, called her name a couple of times. Then silence. Nothing but silence, ever again.

She was thirteen today. Mama had talked about going to Zephyr's ice cream parlor and trying to eat their way through the sixty-four-scoop monster sundae. You had to do something special for thirteen. It would never happen now. She would never go home. She looked around the room, as if it belonged to a stranger. This was home. A tiny room in a tiny house brimming over with loneliness.

With an effort, she hauled herself up on her bed. The letter fell from her hand. She buried her face in her pillow, then lifted her head as she felt the hard rectangle beneath it.

She slid Mary Anne's diary out of the pillowcase, rolled on her back and balanced the slim volume on her chest. She ran her fingers over it—the raised spine, the crinkly pattern on the covers, the soft-edged pages. She brought it to her nose and breathed in the scent of old paper. Words would help her not to think. Words written long ago, by a girl who lived in a wonderful house and had everything she could wish for.

CHAPTER EIGHT

1 October, 1892
All ash, all dust, all gone. Except for this one book. Because
he wanted it that way. And my father must always have what
he wants.
I will never forgive him.

Even for the Iron Range, it had been a cold autumn. Mary
Anne's breath dissolved in white puffs as she jogged toward the
mailbox by the side of the road. Two weeks she'd been coming
here, from the very first day she could reasonably have expected
a reply from Northwestern University. Whether the answer was
yes or no, Father mustn't find out. Not until her bags were
packed and she was ready to walk out the door.

She hitched her skirt calf-high, keeping the hem clear of her
shoes as she walked down the last few sloping feet to the road.
Surely an answer would be there today. The waiting was fraying
her nerves. She kicked a pebble out of a nest of frost-tipped
grass; it flew satisfyingly far across the road before landing with
a puff of dust. If Father had only been reasonable this summer,
she wouldn't need to sneak around now. His response to
Northern Lights still made her cheeks burn.

Dear Sir,
Please be advised that my daughter will not be accepting
your offer to publish her literary attempts. She is in no need of
personal funds, being well provided for by her family. On her

behalf, I thank you for your interest, and request that communications from your establishment cease upon receipt of this letter.

Sincerely,
Andrew Jackson Schlegel

Attempts. As if Mr. DuFresne had taken pity on her, like the homely girl that no one asks to dance. As if a publisher would stake good money and his reputation on printing drivel that wasn't worth either. Why had she ever thought Father would change his mind?

The college applications were her only hope now. She'd sent four since June, all for spring admissions. Oberlin had turned her down; two more would not reply until November at the earliest. Northwestern was the one she hoped for most. Near Uncle William, who would surely help her however he could if she needed it. And Jonas wasn't so far away, either.

She fumbled with the mailbox hasp, fingers stiff inside her knit gloves. Father had promised her a new pair of leather ones for Christmas, fur-lined inside for extra warmth. As if a pair of gloves could compensate for having her achievements ignored, an opportunity snatched away. From now on, she would make her own opportunities.

The box fell open. Mary Anne grabbed the slim bundle inside and riffled through it. Ward's holiday supplement, two letters for Father and a stiff, thick envelope. She turned it over. The return address read *Northwestern University, Evanston, Illinois.*

The rest of the mail dropped to the withered grass as she stripped off one glove and tore open the envelope. Unfolded, the letter trembled in her hand.

It is with great pleasure that we inform you of your acceptance to Northwestern University, for admission in the upcoming Spring semester . . .

She read the words again, momentarily unable to believe them.

That girl. Andrew strolled out of his study, the latest Ward's catalog in hand. He would try once more to get a civil answer out of her about what color of glove she preferred; if she snubbed him again, he would order the black ones and be done with it. Clearly, he had left things in the hands of the women for far too long. Julia had done nothing to curb Mary Anne's fantastic notions of writing for money, and he suspected Miss Hanley might actually be encouraging her. He would find out for certain, and then hire another governess. It was high time he took charge.

Halfway up the stairs toward his daughter's room, he glanced out the window and saw her vanishing through the trees toward the main road. Going after the mail again. If he didn't know better, he might have suspected a secret lover, so ardent was she about getting to the box before anyone else. More likely it was simply something to do; the autumn chill and gloom, combined with pique over the Northern Lights affair, had given Mary Anne a galloping case of moodiness. A short daily walk doubtless served as an outlet for her restlessness. He felt sorry for the child, but he'd had no choice. Someday she would understand that.

On impulse, he strode down the stairs and followed her.

It was true. She was going to college, taking the first step on the road out of Birch Falls. The road to a new life, where Mary Anne Schlegel could say and do and think whatever she wanted. She paid scant attention to the grainy snow flurries that swirled around her, spotting the letter and stinging her cheeks. The spring term began in March. Five more months to work out how she might manage tuition and living expenses, with or

105

without Uncle William's aid. Five more months of putting up with Birch Falls. Then, finally, she would be free.

"Why, Mary—you didn't tell me you have a beau!" Father's voice behind her, full of amusement at his own joke. She stiffened. Grass crunched as he walked around to face her. "What does your young man say, my dear? Can you bear to share a bit of it with this old man?"

For a moment she considered lying, but couldn't think of anything plausible. The teasing grin on his face made her stomach clench. She drew the letter close, like a shield. "Northwestern University accepted me. I applied a few months ago."

"Northwestern University," he repeated, as if speaking a foreign tongue.

"Yes. I'll be going there for the spring term."

His jaw clenched. "You will do no such thing."

"Oh, yes I will." His display of temper couldn't cow her this time, not with her own rising to match it. "I'm not Mother, to be shouted into doing your bidding. Northwestern wants me, and I'm going." With crisp, angry motions, she folded up the letter and started to replace it in its envelope.

He snatched it from her and tore it in two, then flung the pieces to the ground. As she stared at the torn paper in shock, he turned and stalked toward the house.

"You can't stop me," she shouted into the wind as she hurried after him. "Tear up a thousand letters, and I'll still go. Do you hear me, Father? I'm leaving here in March. No matter what you say, no matter what you do!"

His strides lengthened, forcing her to run to keep up. He disappeared inside the house. Breathless, she followed.

He was halfway up the stairs as she stumbled through the front door. She flung herself up the staircase and clutched his arm as he opened the door to her bedroom. "That's my room!

You can't—"

He whirled and grabbed her just below the shoulders. She yelped as he marched her across the hallway and up against the far wall, like an inconvenient piece of furniture. Before she could recover her wits, he had vanished into her room and locked the door.

The heavy oak panels muffled his daughter's voice, scarcely audible over her furious pounding. Andrew ignored the faint sounds as he noted every place in the room that might conceivably hide papers. Mary Anne had been corresponding with these college people behind his back for weeks. Heaven knew how many other establishments she'd written to, or what they had sent her. He would find it and burn it, every last scrap. Then a short letter to Northwestern, and anywhere else that might prove necessary, to end this foolishness once and for all.

Her desk drawers held letter paper and envelopes. The upper right-hand drawer was locked. After a brief search, he found the key under a mounded string of pearls in her jewelry box. Julia's voice had joined Mary Anne's outside, but he paid them no heed.

The drawer was full to bursting with letters and circulars from schools in nearby states: Downer Women's College in Wisconsin, Oberlin University in Ohio, Northwestern, the University of Chicago. Jonas had gone to Chicago. One more part of Andrew's life lost to that den of corruption, where the greedy and venal thrived while honest men paid for others' wrongdoing.

He snatched up the pile of papers and slapped it down on the desk. He refused to lose his daughter as he had his son. This time, he would stop things before it was too late.

Below the circulars lay a bulging portfolio. He opened it and cast an eye over the first sheet of paper. Then he reread the first few paragraphs slowly enough to absorb the words. Not more letters, as he'd first thought. Stories. Mary Anne's stories, that had started all the trouble.

Beneath the portfolio he found two small leather-bound books also filled with scribblings. He paged through them, reading lines here and there, while his heart warred with the knowledge of what had to be done. Reluctantly, he added the books and portfolio to the stack of college correspondence. When the drawer was empty of everything save a few blank sheets of stationery, he picked up the pile and turned to leave.

He couldn't help flinching as he shot the bolt back. He shifted the papers to lie more securely in his arms, then walked out to face his wife and daughter.

At the click of the bolt, Mary Anne stepped back. Her father stalked past them without a word, his arms full of paper. He had her portfolio, her diaries. Everything.

"Where are you going?!" she cried as he started down the stairs. "Answer me! Father!"

She grabbed his shoulder. A few sheets of paper fluttered to the floor. He shrugged her off, throwing her backward toward the top of the staircase. The edge of the landing caught the back of her knees. She fell against the newel post and clutched it to keep from rolling downward. With a shocked cry, her mother ran to help her up.

Father's heavy tread seemed to echo up the stairwell. Mother was asking her something, but the only sound that mattered was the downward tramp of her father's feet. She tore herself from her mother's grasp and dashed after him.

A loose hem stitch caught her heel as she reached the ground floor. She went down hard on one knee, saved from sprawling by a quick grab at the nearest doorjamb. Ignoring the pain, she lurched up and stumbled on toward the kitchen.

The fire in the stove, normally banked to a pleasant warmth between the cooking of meals, blazed high and bright. She smelled scorched leather. Her diaries were burning. Even as she watched, the portfolio landed on the pyre.

With a cry, she launched herself toward the stove. Strong hands caught hers before they could reach the flames—Father's hands, large and cruel. She twisted and bucked, desperate to escape before the fire devoured everything. He tightened his grip as she struggled. "No, Mary Anne. You'll burn yourself. Don't—"

She broke free just as the last edge of paper curled into brown ash. She reached toward it, then let her hand fall. Useless now. There was nothing left to save.

Beneath the crackle of the flames, she heard her father clear his throat.

"Don't." Her voice was low and hard. "Don't speak to me. Ever."

They had left her alone at last—Mother and Miss Hanley, with their anxious faces and bitterly inadequate sympathy. Some day, perhaps, she might thank them for trying. Just now, their well-meant words fell on her spirit like cinders.

Cold from the windowpanes chilled her where she sat in the padded window seat. The darkness turned the rose upholstery gray. She looked around her bedroom with dulled eyes. There was no color in it anywhere.

Her father hadn't dared come up all evening. She could imagine what he was doing now: writing to the dean at Northwestern, apologizing for his upstart daughter's presumption and declining admission on her behalf. Northern Lights all over again, only worse. He would watch her every move now. No more walks to the mailbox, no more sending out letters unscrutinized by the paternal eye. He would make a point of knowing everything she did—everything she thought, if he could manage it. Until he felt certain she had no more notions of straying from the life he thought she should have.

She clenched her fists to stop their shaking. They blurred as she stared down at them, two dim whitish shapes against the dark gray of her skirt. Abruptly, she left the window seat and walked to her writing desk.

Her coat lay where she'd dropped it, over the back of the chair. She reached inside the left-hand pocket and drew out a small, leather-bound book. Half its pages were blank; she'd only begun this journal last June. Four months and a lifetime ago.

She took a pencil from a drawer and returned to the window seat. The moonlight was bright enough to see by. Open book propped against her knees, she began to write.

Brown grass crunched under Mary Anne's feet, accompanying the swish of her heavy skirt. The overcast sky gave her no sense of how long she'd been walking. Long enough to feel the chill, even through her thick woolen coat. Not long enough to leave reality behind.

Father had sent Miss Hanley packing last week. Her replacement was due to arrive next Wednesday. Mary Anne hadn't asked the woman's name, or anything about her. That Father had chosen her was knowledge enough. The new governess would teach her French and drawing, and what little else Father might deem appropriate for a respectable young lady. And no doubt had instructions to report her conduct, especially any suspicious amount of writing.

Her journal bumped her thigh as she walked. She carried it with her everywhere, though she couldn't write in it much. Only late at night, or the few times when Father left his office to talk to the mine foreman. Or out here, on one of her rambles to nowhere.

Father allowed her these walks to keep her from brooding, or so he said. More likely because he found it difficult to be in the same room with her for long. He got restless—shifted his feet, moved his chair, constantly adjusted his shirt cuffs or cleared his throat. She took occasional, grim amusement in watching him. Mostly, she stared at her French grammar and composed stories in her head. Sentences and paragraphs, repeated in her mind's ear in the hope of retaining them long enough to write them down. Sometimes it worked. More often, she found herself huddled in the meager shelter of a birch stand, cudgeling her brain and cursing her stiff fingers. The cold had nearly driven her back to the mine office more than once in the past few days, but the thought of spending one more hour in that room made even the worst weather seem preferable. Fortunately, they'd so far been spared the usual October sleet showers. She refused to contemplate what she would do when real winter came.

She looked up at the scudding clouds and sniffed the air. It smelled of pine, old leaves and damp earth. Rhys Powell had once claimed he could smell rain. Snow, too. He'd tried to describe it to her. "Rain smells rich—like the soil right after you've turned it. Or creek mud, where the frogs like to sit." She'd laughed at him, while secretly wondering if he really could smell weather. Rhys was like that—a collection of odd notions and unexpected talents that cropped up at random moments. He didn't fit in Birch Falls, any more than she did.

Would he understand the intolerableness of it all? Or would he see a spoiled rich girl, complaining because her comfortable life wasn't perfect? Back when they were ten years old and had played hooky from school together to go fishing, she'd have known the answer. Now she wasn't sure. She wasn't sure of much anymore, except that she had to get out. But where could she go, with no money of her own and winter coming on? Her father had confiscated her hoard of pocket money, no doubt to prevent it from going toward more application fees. Or a train ticket. She could hope for no help from her mother, who had been paralyzed with indecision since the burning. *The last thing Mother wants is another midnight flight. If that turns out to be my only choice, she'll stop me.*

That sobering thought made her halt beneath a line of birches. She propped an arm on one rough trunk and rested her head against it, fighting the desire to cry.

After awhile, the tightness in her throat receded. She straightened slowly and saw Rhys Powell standing not ten yards away. His back was half turned to her, open sketchbook resting on one arm while his free hand moved over the paper in quick, smooth strokes. He hadn't heard her approach, let alone witnessed her moment of weakness. Her impulse to run faded. Instead, she watched him sketch while debating whether to speak. It would be so nice to talk to someone who might understand, even a little; yet she was reluctant to disturb him.

He ended her silent debate by tucking his pencil over one ear and stretching, which turned him toward her. He closed the sketchbook and gave her a formal nod. "Miss Schlegel."

"Oh, no. Not you, too." The words came out before she thought, making her blush, but she plunged on. "I've been 'Missed' and 'young-ladied' every blessed day since school ended, and I can't tell you how tired I am of it."

He glanced down as if embarrassed. "I wasn't . . . I mean, we didn't talk much this summer. I thought . . . ." He smiled at her. "I'm glad I was wrong."

She felt light inside suddenly, more cheerful than she had in the two weeks since the burning. "Can I see your drawing?"

"It's just scratches." His eager tone belied the words as he flipped open the sketchbook and passed it to her. He'd drawn a squirrel perched on the knob of a bent pine, one cheek bulging with whatever squirrels ate. Swift, clean lines suggested the tree and its occupant, along with just enough shadows to give them dimension and depth. Mary Anne felt a pang of not-quite-jealousy. After months of lessons from her mother, she couldn't draw a ball that looked like one. Yet Rhys could just scratch down a scene with so much life in it that she half-expected the squirrel's tail to twitch.

"You should go to Europe. Jonas went, before settling in Chicago. He said he couldn't even begin to tell me how much he learned there."

Silence made her look up. Rhys was gazing past her at the bent pine, his posture once more stiff and formal. "Not to give offense," he said, "but some of us haven't the money for that sort of thing."

She closed the book. "Neither did Jonas. Studying art wasn't on our father's approved list of expenses."

He took the book from her. "So how did he get there?"

"Worked his way over for passage, then took any odd job that would keep him eating." She smiled, remembering the intermittent letters with postmarks from all sorts of places that had seemed so unimaginably distant. "He didn't share many details. One doesn't, with a six-year-old." She picked up a handful of tiny pinecones and flung them one by one at the nearest gnarled pine trunk.

"I was wondering . . ." Rhys said. "Could I sketch you?"

Surprise made her look at him. "Now? Here?"

"Well . . . I suppose that'd be a start. Sure. I'd like to do more than one, though. Maybe even a real portrait, if that's all right." The words tumbled out, as if he needed to say them all before he lost his nerve. "I've always wanted to. Sketch you, I mean. I need to start drawing people anyway. And I just—well, I've always liked the way you look. You hardly ever have the same face twice." He broke off and folded his arms over his sketchbook. "I sound like a fool."

"Where?"

"Where what?"

"Where do you want to sketch me?" She couldn't quite keep the laughter from her voice. He was behaving so completely like himself—one moment happily swept away, the next squirming in fear of being snickered at. The sheer normality of it delighted her beyond reason. She wanted to match him, gift for gift—and the thought of how much her father would disapprove only added spice to the idea. Not that she had any intention of telling him. "I don't mind posing out of doors for as long as the weather holds, but your fingers will surely give out before I do. And what if the snows come before we're finished?"

"There's storage sheds near the mine head . . ." He trailed off. "No, forget that. No heat. I don't suppose we could find some space at the manse . . . ?"

"I'd have to smuggle you in. Unless we wait until spring, assuming Father hires you on again—"

"Assuming I could steal enough time from work to be worth it." He was hugging the sketchbook again, the way a small child might hug a stuffed toy. "Maybe we should just do it out here, for as many days as we've got left."

Inspiration struck. "The servants' cottage. Down back of our gardens. Miss Hanley was living there, but she's gone. I'm sure Father won't give it to the new one. He'll want her in the main house. Our maids live out, and Mrs. Tomczack—the cook— hates being alone at night." She shoved her hands into her pockets to warm them. "There's a stove in the kitchen. If we keep the fire small, surely we can warm that one room without anyone noticing."

"They'd see the smoke."

"Maybe not. We keep the curtains mostly drawn in winter; cold glass lets in quite a chill, and who wants to look outside when there's nothing to see but snow and gray sky and bare trees? Anyway, it's better than a storage shed."

"And if we're not there for too long . . ." Rhys began to pace. "I can get away most Sunday afternoons. My family's used to me disappearing for awhile. Or Wednesdays—Mr. Nilssen at the grocery gives me a half-day off." He flashed her a smile. "He thinks I ought to go away and make something of myself, not knock around here until the mine sucks me in. Pays me for the half-day anyway, while I go off and sketch or study. Scholarship money, he calls it." He frowned. "Though I don't like lying to him."

"You won't be. You'll be practicing your art." She pursed her lips as another thought struck her. "How are we going to know when to meet?"

"I can see your window from the birches behind the grounds. Hang something there, maybe, whenever you manage to get away. I'll come by every Wednesday and Sunday afternoon; if there's something in the window, I'll know you're waiting for me."

She laughed. "I feel like a heroine in a Gothic novel. Mysterious signals and secret assignations!"

He gave her a sober look. "If you don't feel right about it, we don't have to do it."

"Don't be ridiculous." Unexpected warmth in her cheeks made her speak more sharply than she'd meant. "We're friends. Friends do favors for each other. If you want to sketch me, I don't see any reason why you shouldn't."

"Let's start this Sunday, then." He tucked his sketchbook under one arm, then held out his other hand. "Shake on it?"

She grinned. "Should we spit?"

"Only if you want to."

His palm felt warm against hers despite the cold. For the first time in days, she began to hope that she might survive the winter with her sanity intact.

A green velvet hair ribbon pinned to the outside of her bedroom curtains served admirably as a signal, showing up vividly against the white lace. They managed only one outdoor sketching session before the first cold wave struck, just before All Hallows Eve. Miraculously, the snow held off until the Sunday before Thanksgiving. Despite Rhys' assurances, Mary Anne doubted his family would believe a ramble in search of subject matter in the teeth of a winter storm.

They had limited the first few indoor sessions to an hour, to cut down on the risk of discovery. After a month without incident, they reached an unspoken agreement to stretch the time a little—an extra quarter-hour, half an hour, almost another hour once. Mary Anne took care to keep the kitchen clock well wound, and to position herself where she could see it; when working, Rhys was oblivious to everything else.

She stood by the kitchen table now, gazing at an assortment of fruits and vegetables he'd culled from the barrels at Nilssen's Grocery. Potatoes, a string of onions, four apples that had seen better days. "Minnesota still life," he'd jokingly called it, before settling to the serious business of putting it down on paper. She raised her eyes just enough to watch him without moving her head. He was drawing with fierce concentration, ignoring the swatch of black hair that threatened to cover one eye. A charcoal smutch adorned his left cheek, where he'd scratched an itch with the blunt end of his pencil.

She loved to watch his hands, their movements so graceful and yet so purposeful. Not hands meant to wield a miner's pick. Fingers and palms more slender than her own, oddly delicate for a man despite the calluses that testified to many a summer's hard work. An artist's hands.

116

"I always wondered what it meant, to have an artist's hands," she mused. "Mother used to say that So-and-so had an artist's hands. I never knew whether it was something physical, like the length of the fingers, or just having a certain skill. Now I know."

Rhys made a companionable noise. She was used to their odd half-conversations by now—she chattering on about whatever crossed her mind, he chiming in with the occasional "Mmmmh" just to let her know he was there. Sometimes, when they rested, he would say or ask something that made it clear he'd been listening, though she'd have sworn he was too caught up in his work to have noticed a herd of elephants rumbling by.

The freedom to speak of anything emboldened her. Over several stolen afternoons, she told him things she'd never have dreamed of confiding. About the offer of publication from Northern Lights, and how badly it had ended. About her father's refusal to accept her admission to Northwestern, and the truncated life he'd forced on her ever since. About her dream of leaving Birch Falls to make a life as a writer, and her fear that it might never come true—that she would give it up simply to make her gilded cage more bearable.

She still couldn't speak of the burning. The horror of it had grown with time—as if, when it happened, she'd been too much in shock to recognize the extent of the violation. She wasn't ready to share that pain yet, not even with Rhys in this odd haven they'd created.

A haven for him, too, she thought as she watched him bend lower over the paper. A place where nobody kidded him for his "unmanly" artistic pursuits, or made snide remarks about some people giving themselves airs. Over cups of tea and cookies purloined from the manse larder, Rhys had spoken of things that sounded achingly familiar: wounded pride, the temptation to stop drawing just to quiet the jeers, the fear of then losing his gift through neglect. Worst of all, the loneliness of having no one who understood what he was doing, let alone why he needed to.

He'd turned his pencil sideways to expose a broader surface, and was shading the curve of something in short, neat strokes. She resisted the temptation to crane her neck so she could see the whole drawing. Time enough for that when she called a break, which she planned to do in the next ten minutes. Nearly an hour had passed already, and her feet were starting to ache. As unobtrusively as she could manage, she lifted her toes and stretched her arches. As her toes touched the floor again, Rhys looked at her. Or rather, at her hands, each of which lay cupped around an apple.

"Unbutton your cuffs. They're too neat."

"If only my mother could hear you." One by one, she undid the tiny buttons. "Will this do?"

"Roll them up a little. Looser than that. A little careless . . . here, let me do it." He took each arm in turn and rolled up her sleeves, then set her forearms on the table and shaped her hands around the fruit. One smudged finger traced a line down the inside of her right wrist. "That's what I want. That curve, with no cloth in the way." He sat back down and pulled the sketchbook across his lap with a lopsided grin. "I know. Artists are crazy. You don't have to say a word."

"Welsh artists who've spent their lives drawing ratty old pine trees in the back of beyond are crazy," she retorted as she dropped her gaze to the tabletop. She could feel a blush rising, which made no sense at all.

"So are nice German-Irish girls who pose for them in the dead of winter, just for something to do."

Her head shot up. "Is that why you think I'm here? Because I'm bored?!"

He looked up, startled. "I was joking. I'm sorry."

"So you should be." She clenched her fists, astounded at how near she was to tears. A silly passing remark, no worse than her own quip, and here she was ready to dissolve on the table.

He put the sketchbook down. "Tell me."

"I can't even have my own letter paper. He makes me come to him for it. He counts out the sheets."

"You have your journal."

"It's running out. I haven't pocket money to buy another, assuming I could manage it without getting caught."

He went to her and gently gripped her hands. "We'll manage something. I owe you for the sitting, anyway."

She gave a breathless laugh. "You are *not* proposing to pay me?"

"Not in cash." He glanced at the sketchbook. "But I can generally get paper when I want it."

She threw her arms around him. They stood together for a moment; then he eased away, color high in his cheeks. He managed half a smile before returning to his place, though he couldn't quite look her in the eye. "Are you ready to go on?"

She nodded, taking hold of the apples once more. They felt smooth and cool against her palms. A pleasant combination of colors they made, red and green against the golden-brown of the wooden tabletop. The kitchen felt too warm; her neck itched under the high collar of her blouse. Poor Rhys, she must have embarrassed him dreadfully. She glanced at him, and saw with relief and disappointment that his attention was completely on his work. The past few minutes might never have happened.

She watched him in silence while convincing herself that her emotional display had been a passing aberration. Father's strictures must be getting to her more than she'd realized. Apologizing would only make them both self-conscious. Best to copy Rhys and pretend none of it had occurred.

He put the pencil aside, with a glance at her as if refreshing his memory. Then he brushed a thumb across the paper. Fingers

119

could smudge sharp lines into softness, giving the illusion of depth more effectively than pencil shading. The repetitive motion of his thumb half hypnotized her as he stroked it across her penciled cheekbone. She could almost imagine that light touch on her skin—

The clock chimed the half hour, jarring her like a dash of cold water. "It's time. I have to go." Not bothering to roll down her sleeves, she stumbled past Rhys and snatched her coat off the doorknob.

He started toward her as she shrugged into it. "Are you all right?"

"Just a little headache." She forced herself to look at him, to smile as if everything were normal. "It's half past four. We shouldn't stay."

"I suppose not." He looked as if he wanted to say more, but thought better of it. "See you Sunday, then."

"See you," she repeated, and ducked out the door.

CHAPTER NINE

Eighteen hours in a fucking Greyhound, sandwiched between a fatso with a giant bag and a screaming, stinking baby. Stops in at least a dozen podunk towns, which added five hours to an already too-long trip. Luke staggered off the bus and gulped the freezing but fresh night air. He'd left Chicago at seven that morning; it was one A.M. now. He'd never been able to sleep sitting up, not that the damned baby would've let him. He needed a place to crash. And a drink. And a smoke. Right now, he'd kill for a cigarette.

Bleary-eyed, he looked around the bus depot. A Days Inn sign beckoned from across the macadam. He hitched his duffel bag up on his shoulder and trudged toward it.

The place was clearly used to customers at all hours; the punk-haired girl manning the night desk spared him a single, bored glance as she quoted a room rate, took his cash and handed him the key to Room 106. He mumbled his thanks and headed down the hall, keeping an eye out for a cigarette vending machine. A drink would have to wait until he found a place in town. He couldn't stay here on the outskirts of Birch Falls, dependent on a car to get around. A rental would cost money he didn't have and leave a paper trail. Moving into town would also make finding Linnie easier. He'd worry about quick transport out of here later, when he needed it.

He still wasn't sure of his next move, which didn't help his mood. He didn't have time to waste pissing around. He wanted to get Linnet and take off, which likely would have worked in the city, but probably not in this fleapit excuse for a town. Places like this, everyone knew everyone else's business. If they didn't, they'd die of boredom. There'd be news stories about a missing child, local police swearing up and down they wouldn't rest till they'd found her, all kinds of hell he'd just as soon avoid. He'd have to find a way to get Linnie nice and legal, fast.

A few feet shy of 106, he passed an alcove with vending machines full of snacks, sodas and cigarettes. He dropped his duffel in his room, then bought a pack of Marlboros, a bag of nacho Doritos and a Pepsi. Back behind his own door, he lit up and then sat smoking on the edge of the bed. Nice to be sitting on something softer than scratchy bus-seat upholstery. Even nicer to be somewhere quiet and out of that toilet-stinking air. The room's lingering odor of stale tobacco didn't bother him. Another cigarette or two and he just might manage to sleep.

Checkout time was ten A.M. He'd stay here another night, give himself time to call other places. Then . . . what? He looked around for an ashtray, spotted one on top of the dresser and crushed out his cigarette in it. Legalities. He needed to know how custody law worked up here—what he could use, what might be used against him. Back in his student days, he'd figured on taking the bar in Illinois. He'd meant to practice somewhere in Chicago or the fat-cat suburbs, maybe go into politics where the real money was. Minnesota hadn't even been a blip on his radar. What he knew about its laws could fit on the end of his cigarette and still leave plenty to burn.

He swigged Pepsi. Even this hick town must have a library. If luck was truly smiling on him, he might run into Linnet there. She loved books, used to bring home armloads from the nearest library branch. Smart little thing. Took after him that way. He ate some chips, then carried his Pepsi to the window. The heavy curtains, like the thin comforter on the bed, were the color of dried blood. He fumbled in the curtain folds for the drawstring, then opened them enough to see out. Beyond the bright spill from the little highway strip, a few stars glimmered in the blackness.

He imagined showing them to Linnet, pointing out the constellations. *We'll have a great life together,* he promised her silently. *This time, everything's going to work out.*

Dusk was falling as Rachel left the highway and drove toward the Windy Pines Hotel. Her car, thank God, was still in one piece, if she didn't count the odd grinding noise every time she flipped on the turn signal. She was so tired, she almost missed the turn-off. She swung to the right, then hit the brakes at the unexpectedly steep downward slope into the parking lot. Too exhausted to swear, she crept the rest of the way and claimed a space. Then she turned off the ignition and sat for awhile. She could feel her brain relaxing, like feet after kicking off a too-tight pair of shoes. A five-hour drive from Minneapolis through the bleakest landscape on God's earth, after a night of scant sleep and an emotional morning visiting Minna's favorite haunts, had left her wrung out. Finally, when fatigue threatened to overwhelm her, she opened the door and climbed out of the car.

The hotel was a two-story ranch-style building, with a hacienda-like tile roof. The number of cars in the lot suggested a respectable amount of business. Who came to a tiny town like this in the middle of nowhere on the brink of winter? Too early for diehard snowmobilers, too late for summer visitors. Conventioneers looking for someplace nice but cheap, maybe, who didn't mind driving two hours to Duluth.

She sleepwalked through registration. The fresh-faced blond guy at the front desk insisted on carrying her single suitcase down the short hallway to her room, chatting all the way. He'd wanted to take her laptop too, but she'd balked. Apparently the Windy Pines didn't run to bellhops. She half-listened to his rambling dissertation on local eateries while working out whether or not to tip him. Before she managed to decide, he'd bidden her a cheery good evening and vanished.

She eased the laptop to the floor, slipped off her sneakers and lay back on the bed. It felt marvelously soft. The artwork wasn't bad, either—local landscapes, understated, as if inspired by Japanese prints. The one over the bed—a squirrel in a pine tree, done in varying shades of charcoal—was signed *Powell*. She wondered what Mom would have thought of it. Or Minna, for that matter.

It was so nice to be stretched out instead of folded up in the driver's seat. She shifted around, getting comfortable, and felt a small, hard lump against her thigh. Her coat pocket had gotten underneath her. She tugged it loose and reached inside it.

The lump was a piece of honey-gold wood, a touch smaller than her fist, whittled into the shape of a leaping rabbit. Rachel held it up and stroked its textured curves. Rose had pressed it into her hand just before she'd left the Twin Cities. "Rabbits are lucky, you know. Minna told me that's why she sculpted them. She made three of these, along with the big one you saw at the gallery. I sold two and kept this. Now it's yours."

Rachel hadn't had the heart to refuse. Hadn't wanted to, either. She turned the rabbit to face the squirrel print on the wall. "Mrs. Rabbit, Mr. Squirrel. Mr. Squirrel, Mrs. Rabbit." Silly with fatigue, she made her voice high and squeaky. "Pleased to meet you. Likewise."

Snorting with laughter, she rested the carving on her chest. She felt punch-drunk and too tired to move. She decided to lie still for a little bit longer, then unpack and go see about dinner. Maybe Beaver Cleaver could recommend a nice local spot. Again. With her paying attention this time.

Her eyelids fluttered shut. She drifted off to sleep.

If he never saw a pine tree again, Florian thought, he just might die happy. And these weren't even real pine trees. No dark green Christmas-tree fullness, begging to be adorned with ornaments. Just scrawny trunks, mostly bare, with a scraggly crown of branches near the top. Clumps of them, towering over the birches in their midst as if sucking the life from the smaller trees. He'd seen little else since crossing over Lake Superior into Minnesota around two that afternoon. Now it was near six, and Florian couldn't decide if he felt too tired to eat or too hungry to sleep. That sonofabitch Chapman had better be here, and provably guilty of something. Nothing else could justify this nightmare of a trip.

At least he'd found a decent place to stay, he thought as he glanced around the neat lobby of the Windy Pines Hotel. In an alcove to the left of the doors, a fire crackled in the fireplace. An elderly man was nodding off in front of it, the *Duluth Herald-Times* sliding off the arm of his easy chair. Two similar chairs, empty, invited Florian to sit down—though after all day and then some in a car, he wasn't sure he ever wanted to sit down again. He inquired at the desk about room prices and was pleasantly surprised at the answer. Mitchell would be pleased as well. The less his department spent of the taxpayers' money, the better it made Mitchell look.

The desk clerk, a young man wearing a crisply ironed shirt and a chipper expression, led him upstairs and down the hall to his room, livening up the trip with a nonstop ode to local restaurants. "There's Charlie's, that's a hamburger joint—a nice one, though, not a grease pit. Some people bought it last year, did it up nice like a fifties diner. Good burgers, decent beer on tap. Then there's Valentini's. Italian. They really are—Italian, I mean—so the food's authentic. You want a nice plate of gnocchi in a killer marinara sauce, Valentini's is it." The clerk glanced over his shoulder, apparently to make sure Florian was still following. Thin blond hair flopped over his forehead. Without missing a step, he smoothed it back. "Or you could try Zimmy's. They serve a little of everything. Coconut shrimp, pizza with fresh tomatoes. It's named for Bob Dylan, you know. Zimmy's, Zimmerman—Bobby Zimmerman? Or you want Chinese, there's Wen Ho's—no, wait, they're closed for remodeling—"

"Actually," Florian broke in, "what I'd like at the moment is to stretch out a little. Preferably with something to drink."

The clerk opened the door, then handed him his key. "There's a pop machine down the hall. Turn left just up there; you can't miss it. An ice machine, too." He gave Florian an eager look, like a dog hoping for a walk. "Anything else I can help you with?"

"Maybe." Florian dug out Luke Chapman's sketch. "I'm looking for this guy. Have you seen him around?"

The clerk frowned at the picture. "I don't think so. I'm good with faces; I'd probably remember." He looked up at Florian. "Has he done something wrong?"

"Right now, I just need to talk to him." Florian replaced the sketch in his pocket. "What's your name?"

"Richard. Richard Nilssen. Though most everyone calls me Bogart." He smoothed his hair again, then tweaked an imaginary wrinkle out of his shirt collar. "Rick, you know, and my favorite hat is this great old fedora, brown felt, got it trained just right . . ."

The improbable nickname made Florian want to laugh, but he controlled himself. "If you see this guy around, will you let me know? The Chicago Police Department'll be in your debt."

"Of course." Looking suitably impressed, Bogart nodded and walked away.

Florian ducked into his room. A brief sit-down with a bottle of real Coke, then dinner somewhere from Bogart's extensive list. After that, he'd check in with the local department and find out where else in town Luke Chapman might have gone.

Somewhat refreshed by her brief nap and nursing serious hunger, Rachel left her room in search of information. This time, she found the desk clerk's bouncy chatter enjoyable and the breadth of his culinary knowledge impressive. Italian food sounded good, and Valentini's had the added virtue of being within easy walking distance. The thought of climbing into a car again, even for a short trip, made her shudder.

"You'll like it," the clerk said. His nametag read *Rick*. "Most of our conventioneers do. As good as anything in Duluth or even the Twin Cities, they tell me. Now, breakfast—room service starts at six o'clock. You can leave your request with me, and I'll make sure your breakfast arrives first thing. I know you'll want an early start—"

"That's all right. I'm not here for a convention."

"Oh." He colored faintly. "My mistake. It's just that I've never seen you before, and I know most people with family in town, so . . ."

"Actually, I'm writing a book. About the Iron Range." Why did she say that? It was none of Rick's business why she was in Birch Falls. Though at least it was true . . . sort of. She could just imagine confessing the real reason. *I'm here on the off chance that the birth mother I never met might have left behind some living, breathing family. I don't suppose you know any descendants of Jonas Schlegel?* He'd probably think she was nuts.

It dawned on her that he'd asked a question. "Sorry?"

"History or fiction?"

"A novel. Though it's set in the past." From the corner of her eye, she saw a gangly, dark-haired man approaching the front desk. He had an interesting face, made more so by the obvious break near the bridge of his nose. *Jesus. Not even a month after Nick, and I'm scoping out total strangers. Can you say rebound?* "Which street is Valentini's on again?"

"East Twelfth. You'll see the sign when you turn the corner at the end of this block. Before you go . . ." He rummaged through a drawer just below desk level, then handed her a cream-colored brochure with black scrollwork letters and a sketch of a house. "You'll want to go see Schlegel House for sure, if you're planning any historical research. It's a little drive from here, or a long walk when the weather's fine. Closed for the season, but I'm sure you can make arrangements with the caretaker." He took the paper back and scribbled a phone number on it. "You talk to old Jackson; he'd be thrilled to have the place written up."

Her fingers closed over the brochure. "Schlegel House," she repeated. Sudden, irrational hope surged through her. *Cue burst of theme music as Cosmic Destiny takes a hand . . .*

"Mmhmm. It was built by the town's leading citizen way back when, before Hadleigh Mine got tapped out. A lot of history there, and Jackson knows it all."

"Thanks." She turned away, feeling dazed, and tucked the brochure in her pocket. Her fingers brushed the rabbit carving. She shouldn't get too excited just yet. Schlegel House might have nothing to do with Jonas Schlegel. There were probably dozens of Schlegels in town, and in other towns nearby. The name could be like Smith, shared by countless people with no blood ties whatsoever. German surnames were pretty common in the Upper Midwest. But she would go see the place, chat with Mr. Jackson. At least she'd get some interesting book material.

And if these Schlegels are my family? she wondered as she walked toward Twelfth Street, fingering the slick paper and the rabbit carving. *Are any of them still around, or is this another dead end?*

The smell of marinara was making Luke's mouth water, even though he hadn't felt hungry when he walked into the restaurant. All he'd wanted was enough shots and beers to settle his daylong craving. There were no liquor stores out by the Days Inn, and he hadn't quite dared carry a bottle-shaped brown bag into the public library. None of the abundant local bars opened until seven. Valentini's, with its bar in the front room, had saved his sanity. After two rounds of boilermakers, he was finally starting to relax.

Tomorrow he'd move to the Windy Pines Hotel, just a couple of blocks from this place. Not far from the library, either. Today had been mostly a wash. Wading through paragraphs of family law without even one drink had given him a pounding headache. He lifted his half-empty beer glass and gulped another mouthful. "Better luck tomorrow," he muttered.

Finding Linnie was the other major problem. He stared into his beer, watching the swirly patterns in the foam. He'd counted at least thirty Schlegels in the dog-eared county phone book tucked away in the nightstand drawer. Grace's dad might be any of them. How many doors could he knock on before one of them called the cops? Plus he'd already lost one day to research and was going to lose at least one more. God knew how long it would take him to find an angle. A door-to-door search for Linnie was a last-ditch option. Hell, he'd probably do better roaming the streets. Place this small, he could scout out her few likely haunts besides the library and hope to get lucky.

Which brought him back to the custody issue. He drank more beer, working things out. Grace's dad likely didn't have custody legally. From what little Grace had told him when they were dating, he gathered she didn't have much use for her family.

Sending Linnie here was a panic reaction to his own arrival in Chicago, not a thought-out strategy with the paperwork to back it up. So he might need no more than proof of marriage and paternity, plus a sympathetic judge. Or a good lawyer, assuming the old man knew about him slapping Grace around.

Cold air hit him as the front door opened. He moved down a couple of stools and signaled the bartender for a refill. Most important, he needed to keep buried any connection to Grace's death. Back in Illinois, the right judge might not hold that against him if nothing could be proved. Up here, he wasn't so sure. Maybe he should try to get custody decided in Illinois . . . file a motion, or whatever it took to get things going. He planned to move back there, which should count in his favor.

His stomach was telling him to eat. Dinner might slow his racing mind enough to let him plot out a strategy. He picked up his beer, left money to cover the tab, and walked into the dining room. A few minutes later he was sitting at a corner table, wolfing foccacia while he waited for three-finger cavatelli in bolognese sauce. Two tables away, a couple of oldsters—the man with a beer gut that would have done Luke's father proud—shared a plate of cannoli. A fortyish woman nearby doled out salad to her husband and two sons, while the husband stopped the younger boy from flinging a pepperoncini at his brother. Across from the aborted food fight, a younger woman sipped wine as she read a brochure. Dark hair, nice cut; pale gray turtleneck that clung just enough under a matching cardigan. Worth a closer look, maybe, once he had some food in his stomach to keep the beer from talking.

She glanced up just as he took another mouthful of beer. He choked on the cold liquid, his grip tightening on the glass. The face above the turtleneck was Grace's.

You're dead, he wanted to shout at her, then realized with horror that he'd muttered the words out loud. He cleared his windpipe, then shot a look around. No waiter, no one sitting within earshot. With a napkin, he wiped beer and sweat from his face.

Grace's twin was still looking at him. He shook out the napkin and laid it across his lap, then swigged more beer as casually as he could manage. The last thing he wanted was that woman trotting over and asking what the matter was. *Nothing, lady. Just that you look one helluva lot like my wife, who I beat the shit out of and ended up killing a little while back. Spooked me for a second, that's all. Don't give it another thought.*

Mercifully, she went back to studying her brochure. He looked her over as he drank more beer and his nerves steadied. She didn't really look that much like Grace, he decided. The same color hair and about the same age, that was all. And kind of the same face—pointy chin, big eyes. Hell, most women between twenty-five and forty looked the same, unless they were real hot or real dogs.

He spotted the waiter heading his way, loaded tray in hand. His cavatelli sat between a house salad and a pair of oil and vinegar cruets. Her order? She didn't look like one of those women who only ate rabbit food. A little too much weight on her, in just the right places. You could keep your supermodels; he liked a little hip and tit. She dressed better than Grace had. Even if they could have afforded decent clothes, Grace wouldn't have looked so at home in them.

The waiter set down his pasta, then gave the woman her salad. Luke watched her fork up a mouthful. A southpaw. Like Grace.

He turned to his own food. The cavatelli was terrific. He ate several forkfuls, savoring the rich sauce. Thoughts of Grace receded to the back of his mind.

The rising wind cut straight through Florian's raincoat, heavy lining and all. Hunched inside its meager protection, he hurried toward Twelfth Street. Maybe he should've ordered room service. But he had a taste for Italian, and he wanted to see a little of the town by night.

A stoplight shone through bare branches up ahead. East Twelfth—the main drag. He turned onto it, leaving behind the mostly dark houses and front yards dotted with leaf piles. Red and orange spill from a few bar-front neon signs mingled with dim streetlights and the headlights of passing cars. He could just make out the sign for Valentini's, across Twelfth and two blocks down, its green script glowing against the night sky.

He slowed briefly as he passed a five-story brick building, an oddity amid the stretch of dinky storefronts. Letters carved above its front door read *Sons of Italy, 1886*. One window was boarded up. *Not many Sons of Italy left, I guess.*

Neither the cold nor the sights proved sufficient to distract him from yet another rehash of his recent telephone conversation with Terry Powell. Try as he might, he couldn't find anything that explained the local police chief's behavior. A certain coolness, he'd have understood; nobody liked outsiders on their turf. But Powell's frigid monosyllables . . . either he had a whopping small-town inferiority complex or something was eating him.

The smell of garlic hit him as he reached the corner. One more block to warmth and his second-favorite comfort cuisine. He wondered if there were any Hungarian restaurants in these parts. Bogie would probably know.

Powell was tomorrow's problem. He hurried down the street, eager for a hot meal.

Decent food and cheap, too. Flea-pit towns had their good points. Luke handed the cashier his check and some cash. While waiting for change, he looked back toward the dining room. The woman in gray was just finishing a bowl of gnocchi. As he watched, she set down her fork and rummaged in the pocket of the red coat draped over her chair. He could hang around a little, strike up a conversation when she came to pay. On her own like she was, she might appreciate a little male attention.

The cashier handed him three singles and a couple of quarters. He ambled back to his table and dropped two bucks. As he passed the woman, she reached for the dessert menu. Not leaving anytime soon after all. Her loss. He left the restaurant, feeling better than he had in days. Amazing what food could do.

He looked up as he reached the intersection and spotted a tall man in a trench coat approaching. As the man halted to check for traffic, Luke realized where he'd seen that loose-limbed, hunch-shouldered stride before. The cop at Sally's Place.

The light changed. Luke flipped up his coat collar and crossed the opposite way, obeying gut instinct even as his brain argued with it. It couldn't be the same guy. Tall, dark hair, trench coat—there must be a hundred people who fit that description. *And even if it is him, what's he going to do? Arrest me? For what?*

For assaulting what's-her-name Mason, he realized with a chill. Jesus, what a boneheaded move that had been. She must have told the police about the missing bus ticket; how else would they have known to follow him here? Had they gotten evidence from Mason's place fast enough to send someone after him already . . . ?

But the cop had gone to Sally's Place before Luke hit Mason's apartment. He slowed down, breathing heavily. So if this cop was tracking him for anything, likely it was Grace. He hadn't left much there for anyone to find. His breath began to come easier. Whatever this cop thought he knew, it couldn't be enough to put Luke inside.

He would play it safe, he decided as he turned toward the motel shuttle's downtown stop. Now there was a laugh. Downtown Podunk: three bars, a grocery, a dime store, an abandoned Whatever Lodge and a post office. Still, even the most pathetic dump had a police department. He'd have to stay out of their hands, or he could kiss his prospects in family court goodbye.

The shuttle pulled up as he reached the stop. He boarded it and slung himself into a seat far away from the door. Relaxing in the warmth, he watched downtown Birch Falls recede into the darkness. He imagined Linnie somewhere in it, fobbed off on Grace's dad like a hand-me-down. Lonely and scared, waiting for someone to take her home.

Don't worry, Linnie, he promised her silently. *Daddy's coming for you.*

CHAPTER TEN

At nine A.M., Florian arrived at the Birch Falls police station. The weak morning sunlight, filtered through thin cloud cover, coaxed a warm glow from the worn red brick. Welcoming. Downright homey, in fact.

He walked in the door and up to the reception desk, which was manned by a balding uniformed cop with an impressive beer-and-potato gut. Nothing unusual so far. "Detective James Florian, Chicago PD. I'm here to see Chief Powell."

The desk cop grinned. "Welcome to the Range. The chief's in his office." He nodded over his shoulder. "That door right back there. Can I get you some coffee?"

"No, thanks." He'd already sampled the local brew; boiled lawn shavings would taste better. The desk cop seemed affable enough; maybe things wouldn't go too badly. With a friendly nod, he headed for Powell's sanctum.

Powell was at his desk, staring at a snapshot. He made no sign of acknowledgment when Florian came in. Florian waited a moment, then cleared his throat.

Powell set the photograph face down next to a stack of manila folders. When he looked up, his expression made Florian think of a shuttered window. Black hair, graying in spots, framed his craggy face. Broad in the shoulders, big hands; not the kind of cop you wanted to brawl with. Glasses with thin gold rims straddled his beak of a nose. He looked like a pro wrestler

135

turned librarian. "You'd be Detective Florian. Have a seat."

Two straight-backed chairs stood against the front wall of the office. Florian dragged one over to the desk and sat. Powell watched him silently. Comfortably settled, Florian put on his best "how-can-I-help-you" expression and waited. If he made Powell talk first, maybe the man would give some hint of what ailed him.

The police chief folded his hands. His fingers rested on the photo. He was radiating buried tension. "Tell me what you have against this Chapman so far."

"Nowhere near as much as I'd like." Florian summed up his case. Powell listened as if absorbing the brief recital through his pores. His intensity made Florian uneasy. With a nervous shrug, he concluded his report. "That's it. My next move depends on you."

The chief stayed still a minute longer. One fingertip brushed the snapshot. Then he stood up and snagged a heavy leather jacket from a three-hook tree in the corner behind his desk. "Our next move. We'll discuss it on the way out." He'd gone several steps past the door before it dawned on him that Florian wasn't following. "Coming, Detective?"

Florian shut his mouth on the questions that came boiling up. Maybe police chiefs normally added themselves to investigations in small-town departments. Or maybe Powell didn't think anyone else could handle it. In any case, it wouldn't help matters to challenge the man's first decision.

The strangeness of the situation made him try anyway. "Are you sure about this, sir?" he ventured as he caught up to the chief. "I mean, wouldn't another detective, or a patrol officer—"

"This town is my responsibility. I take that seriously." He

glanced at Florian, face and voice under tight control. "Is that a problem?"

"No, sir." *Not yet.*

The Iron Range had its own stark beauty, Rachel thought as she hiked the mile of open land between the eastern edge of Birch Falls and the grounds of Schlegel House. According to the caretaker, the distance had originally been more than twice that. "Of course, even a little town like this saw its boom times," he'd said over the phone. "Things've got built up a little in the past hundred years."

The local definition of "built up" amused Rachel. Spindly trees covered most of the lots she'd passed; on several, house trailers dressed up with gingerbread trim peeked out from the woods. The occasional lot had a split rail or chain link fence, usually adorned with a sign that read *Private Land—No Snow-mobiles.* She guessed the trailers belonged to local folk, or maybe they were summer getaway places. Minnesota was supposed to be the land of ten thousand lakes. *I bet the fishing's good around here.*

Before long, the wooded lots gave way to a more open landscape. Clumps of birch and pine rose from the reddish earth, the birches gleaming against the gray sky. On a sunny winter day, with fresh snow hiding the brittle brown grass, the pines would look greener and the birches whiter. She could imagine finding it lovely then—or in spring, when wildflowers gave extra color to the new grass and the birches were covered in pale green leaves. Now, in the dead end of autumn, the landscape held the wistful allure of loneliness. An artist would love the starkness of it. Minna likely would have. She touched the wooden rabbit, deep in her coat pocket.

The earth's chill seeped through her shoe soles. A crow flapped upward from a nearby stand of trees, drawing a black arc against the pale clouds. She smelled pine, sharp and green, and beneath it the wet-cotton scent of snow on the way. She shivered. The land felt barren, bleak, alien. Was this really where she'd come from?

No wonder Jonas Schlegel had left for Chicago, even then a sprawling bastion of commerce and opportunity bursting with messy life. Had he gone looking for fame and fortune, or for a more personal reason? And how did his life in Birch Falls tie in with her grandfather Duncan, a foundling adopted in 1893?

Proving Jonas Schlegel's paternity would be the tricky thing, she realized as she ambled up the sloping ground. The few available records of Duncan McGrath's adoption, left by Minna with Rose Mulvihill, didn't include a birth certificate. Apparently Duncan didn't have one—not unusual, in a day and age where a neighbor with a midwife's skill frequently delivered children born in Chicago's poorer areas. All Rachel had was the affidavit, signed by Jonas and the presiding social worker at Hull House, where Jonas had brought the baby. That and Minna's gut feeling—not much of a basis for claiming family ties. And yet, Jonas Schlegel was her only lead. If any record existed of the infant Duncan's mother, Minna hadn't found it. So she might as well try to confirm Minna's hunch.

A line of trees crowned the slope. From Jackson's description, the mansion lay just beyond. She decided not to tell him about the real purpose of her visit. Hearing his full name had startled her: "Don't know who Mr. Jackson might be, miss. I'm Jackson Schlegel. That boy over at the Pines give you only one name, did he?" It would feel so awkward to tell this stranger that she thought they might be kin, but wasn't sure. How would the poor man know how to act? Better stick with the book story for now. No ambiguities there.

She passed the tree line and stopped, caught by the sight of Schlegel House. It loomed over the surrounding land, flanked by ornamental trees. The ubiquitous pine-and-birch stands were absent, as if they didn't dare grow too near their elegant cousins. The house itself was a mid-Victorian folly, at least on the outside. The inside would likely be just as lovingly preserved by whoever ran the place as a local tourist attraction. Why was Jackson Schlegel—surely a descendant of the house's original inhabitants—merely its caretaker and not its owner? There had to be a story in that. Maybe she could get him to tell it.

For the tenth time in as many minutes, Jackson Schlegel looked out the window toward town. A woman appeared through the thin line of trees, stood still a moment, and then started down. He liked her standing still. City stranger she might be, but this Miss Connolly knew a work of art when she saw one. "She likes you," he murmured to the house.

Imagine a writer from Chicago, wanting to hear him chatter on about local history! He wished Linnet were here, to listen and be proud of him. But she'd gone off early, Lord knew where. He still felt shy of laying down the law to her too hard. In a few months, maybe, when she'd had a little more time to adjust.

His thoughts returned to Miss Connolly's visit. He might tell her about his own book. His family history. Maybe she could advise him where to send it. Once it was published, Schlegel House and the man who'd built it would finally get the attention they deserved.

He glanced once more at his reflection in the mirror on the parlor wall. His shirt was clean, the mended spots hidden by his new jacket, which you could hardly tell was secondhand. His glasses, in unbroken silver frames picked up the day before, made him look like a professor at the Agricultural College down the road in Ely. He looked as he imagined an author might: respectable but not flashy, as befit someone who lived a life of the mind. Not like an eccentric old man who frightened little girls.

Satisfied, he walked out to meet his visitor.

From Mary Anne's room, Linnet watched the writer lady walk toward the house. She wasn't what Linnet had expected. Not a bit like Sister Agnes, who taught Language Arts back at St. Teresa's. Sister was thin-lipped and angular, with nose-pinching glasses, a preference for gray suits and a face that said "fun" was a four-letter word. This woman wore clothes like anybody's: jeans, sneakers, a bright red coat with the hood hanging down the back. Her hands were stuffed in her pockets, and she wore no hat. A gust of wind ruffled her hair; when she brushed it out of her eyes, Linnet saw she wasn't wearing gloves, either.

Curiosity satisfied, Linnet started to turn away, then froze as the woman looked up. Though she knew it was impossible from this distance, Linnet had the odd feeling she could see right into the stranger's eyes.

Then she heard the front door open. The writer lady dropped her gaze and walked toward the porch, out of Linnet's sight.

As Rachel reached the porch steps, a smiling Jackson Schlegel came down them to meet her. "Found your way here all right, I see." He reached handshake range and stopped. Surprise flashed over his face. Then he was clasping her cold fingers and smiling once more, leaving her to wonder if she'd imagined his momentary freeze-frame. "Would you like some tea, or coffee? Cold walk from town."

His voice sounded rusty, as if he wasn't accustomed to using it much. The poor man must get lonely out here, especially once the place closed down for the season. She caught herself searching for a resemblance to Minna and closed down that line of thought. Relatives didn't always look alike.

She accepted the offer of a hot drink with thanks. "I'd be happy to tell you whatever I can about the Range," Jackson said as they walked to the front door. "Of course, Birch Falls is the place I know the most about. And this house and its people are what I know best."

"That sounds great," she answered as they entered the huge front hall.

The staircase drew her eye first. Wide enough to accommodate three people, it had the color and gleam of a well-loved violin. The stretch of steps between the landing and the second floor formed part of the ceiling where the hall narrowed into a long corridor that likely led back to the kitchen. Past the upper staircase hung a brass-and-crystal chandelier, just the right size not to be ostentatious. Rachel's gaze traced the curve of the stairs, then the high arc of the ceiling. Even on this overcast day, the gracefully shaped space gave an impression of airiness and light.

On either side of the hall were two sets of double doors. Those on the right were closed. The left-hand pair stood ajar. Rachel moved toward them, drawn by a glimpse of glass rimmed in burnished gold. An ornamental mirror. She loved them. Jackson would surely show her the room if she asked. He was probably dying to show her the whole house.

"A beauty, isn't she?" Jackson murmured. "Want the grand tour?"

"Yes." She turned toward him, and for a moment they shared a delighted grin. "Oh, yes, please."

He led her to the kitchen and fetched coffee from a hotel-sized percolator atop an iron stove, filling two Styrofoam cups three-quarters full. She saw no electrical cord; apparently the percolator was battery-powered. Next came sugar packets, from a cardboard carton tucked away in what once must have been the ice box. "There's no cream. Got Carnation, if you want it."

He gestured around the kitchen, with the pride of an interior decorator showing off his finished creation. "Not a thing's been changed in here since 1874, the year old Andrew Jackson finished building this place. He didn't hold with refrigeration— called it newfangled foolishness just waiting to break down. Wouldn't have it put in."

"Andrew Jackson?"

"My namesake. Andrew Jackson Schlegel. Built this house and this town." He sipped his coffee, taking care not to spill.

Her own cup was taking the chill from her fingers. She dumped liquid Carnation into it, stirred, took a tentative sip and was pleasantly surprised to find it much stronger than the thin, brown paint-water she'd had for breakfast at the Pines. "Was he any relation to Jonas Schlegel—an artist, lived most of his life in Chicago?"

His face lit up. "You know about Jonas?"

"I ran across some of his sketches," she improvised. *God bless wi-fi.* "At the Chicago Historical Society. He did a series of charcoal drawings of the 1893 Exposition."

"Quite a talent, Jonas had." He spoke as if Jonas was a personal friend. "Of course, Andrew Jackson didn't see it that way. There was bad blood between them over it. Long story short, Jonas ran off in 1881. Andrew disowned him the next year, but never really got over it." He faltered, eyes dropping to his cup. "You don't—losing a child."

She wondered who he'd lost, and how recently. As if aware of her thought, he looked up at her. He seemed about to speak, then blinked and took another sip of coffee.

"I'd like to hear Jonas's story." Hoping to draw him out, she improvised again. "I'm basing a character in my novel on him. The main character. A small-town boy, doesn't fit in, goes off into the world to find his art and himself. Anything you can tell me might be useful."

"Come have a look at him first." He drained his coffee, crumpled the cup and put it in the carton. "If you've had enough to warm you, can I ask you to leave that here? Just inside the box will be fine. I know Styrofoam's not supposed to leak, but you can't be too careful."

"Of course." One more swallow; then she set the cup down and followed him into the hallway.

A single step creaked as they climbed the majestic staircase. Upstairs, the second door on the left opened into a bedroom nearly half the size of Rachel's small apartment, furnished in dark wood and deep colors. The only contrasting note came from three prints and a painting on the walls. One print, of Japanese peasants crossing a bridge in the rain, Rachel vaguely recalled from a book on Oriental art. The other two were wildflowers rendered in ink and watercolor. The final piece of artwork, to which Jackson led her, was a portrait of Jonas Schlegel.

He'd have made a lovely girl, was the first irreverent thought that came to mind. She dismissed it as the product of nerves and studied the painting. Dark gray eyes dominated a delicate face, capped by tawny blond hair. The painter had caught his subject's lanky slenderness, along with an impression of pent-up energy. Jonas sat in a shallow wing chair as if unaccustomed to stillness, like a wild thing briefly snared. Not much resemblance to Minna McGrath, but maybe Minna favored a different side of the family.

"Commissioned for his nineteenth birthday." Jackson's comment broke her train of thought. He flicked a handkerchief across the nameplate at the bottom of the heavy gold frame. "He took off about a year later. Some in town claimed he left because of Julia—Mrs. Andrew Jackson the second—but no one could back it up. Not even the worst of the gossips, and they tried."

Here was pay dirt . . . possibly. "What was she—or he—supposed to have done?"

"Tried to seduce him. Or he tried to seduce her, depending on who did the talking—though most people who wanted to believe in a scandal assumed she was the guilty party." Jackson snorted. "As if anybody would've dared step around on Andy Jackson, let alone his own wife and her stepson. But Julia was only ten years older than Jonas, and some people never got over Andrew Jackson marrying his son's teacher not even a year after the first Mrs. Andrew died. Of course, him being the town's leading citizen and employer, no one would speak a word against him. Poor Julia got it instead."

She wondered if Jackson was wrong, if there'd been some truth to the sordid allegation. If so, Julia Schlegel would have had to follow her stepson to Chicago in order for their baby to turn up on the church steps . . . *twelve years later. Which means she waited that long to go after him and then got pregnant, or left Andrew and became Jonas's common-law wife . . . and then abandoned their baby? No. That doesn't wash.* "Why do you think Jonas left?"

He gazed at the painting a few seconds before answering. "Sometimes a child just has to go. Or they think they do." He gave her a small smile. "I think Jonas really did. Hate to say a word against my namesake, but old Andy could be a hard man when he thought he was right. He wanted Jonas to run Hadleigh Mine, look after things when he was gone. Jonas wanted to draw and paint. Both of them were pig-stubborn about it. Situation like that, something's got to give."

"Could he have been running from involvement with someone else?"

"Jonas?" Jackson chuckled. "He never had eyes for anything that wasn't a piece of paper or a canvas. If he took up with anyone, he did it in Chicago. Or in Europe, maybe—he spent some time over there before settling back in the States. Paris, London, Florence. All over the place."

Damn. She'd hoped for a local lover or jilted fiancée who'd followed Jonas to the city. Possible candidates should be few enough to trace easily, especially if relatives still lived in the Birch Falls area. Done-wrong love stories invariably became favorite family tales. She could have gone back to Chicago with a name, maybe even a letter home full of pertinent details to point her toward a more solid connection. But looking for a Jane Doe great-grandmother in the city, or any of three European metropoli . . . "Did any of Jonas's children come back up here, or grandchildren?" Unless Jackson himself was the artist's descendant, in which case he knew of no family stories because there were none. She hoped that wasn't true.

"Jonas had no family. They didn't hear much from him after he left, except for the few letters he wrote to Mary Anne. Julia's daughter, his half-sister." He grinned at her. "Now there's a story for you. The family mystery, in fact. She left home for the big city, too . . . only she never turned up anywhere else, at least not as far as anyone knew. And they looked. Andy Jackson paid them well to. But nobody ever found her."

He led her to another room, a little way down the hall on the opposite side from where they had just been. Rose and white with touches of gold, it clearly belonged to a young girl—the subject, Rachel guessed, of the magnificent picture that hung across from a deep window seat.

Mary Anne Schlegel looked nothing like her half-brother, and yet the two portraits strongly resembled each other. It took Rachel a minute to realize why. Like Jonas in his chair, the slender girl at the escritoire seemed imprisoned. Her calm absorption in the rose she held was an illusion; deep in her eyes, the artist had captured the desperate fury of something caught in a trap.

"She was sixteen when she sat for that." Jackson spoke with the echo of a father's regret for his own lost child. "Andrew had it done as a birthday present. How many times he must have come up here, afterward, and just stared at it . . ." He turned his head to gaze out the window. "She took off in late February. Next he heard anything of her was near a year later, when a Birch Falls police sergeant came knocking on his door asking if she'd come home. That was how he found out his daughter had gone to Chicago. Went off to the Exposition and never came back."

"Eighteen-ninety-three," Rachel murmured. The same year Jonas Schlegel found baby Duncan McGrath on the steps of St. Bartholomew's Catholic Church. She frowned at the painted face of the girl. Mary Anne reminded her of someone.

She turned to ask Jackson a question and saw blank shock in his eyes. Concerned, she stepped toward him, away from the portrait. "Are you all right?"

He blinked. "Fine. Fine. Thanks." The smile he gave her looked forced, but she didn't feel sure enough of herself to push. He gestured toward the hallway. "I'll show you the rest of it."

Master bedroom, schoolroom, upstairs parlor, sewing room and maid's quarters passed in a blur of dark wood, rich colors and late-Victorian clutter. The tour seemed to help Jackson recover his equilibrium. He didn't bring up the odd moment in the bedroom, and she felt awkward about asking. Head bursting with historical trivia, she hung back as they reached the top of the staircase. "Could I take another look at Mary Anne's portrait? Would you mind?"

"Not at all. Go on ahead." He sounded reluctant. Or maybe he was just tired, and her imagination was running away with her.

She returned to Mary Anne's room. There *was* something

familiar in those features—the line of the nose, the curve of the jaw. She studied the portrait, determined to find the connection.

Her shoulder blades prickled, as if eyes were on her. She swung around. "Mr. Schlegel?"

The room was empty.

Another morning damned near gone, and he still hadn't found anything useful. Luke straightened up from the law tome he'd been poring over and stretched his cramped shoulders. Then he pushed back his chair and headed for the men's room upstairs.

A title caught his eye as he passed the paperback racks. *The Hunt for Red October.* He'd always wanted to read that. He loved techno-thrillers, cop stories, anything with good solid action in it. Not like that romance crap Grace used to read. Real grab-the-tissues junk, with swooning women or feathery trees and flowers on the covers. He wondered what the woman in gray from last night read. Artsy stuff, he'd bet. She looked smart, but repressed—dark clothes, not an inch of cleavage showing.

He'd get the Clancy on the way back, give himself a breather from all the legalese. Maybe he could smuggle it out, or charm the checkout girl into thinking he'd lost his card. He was good at charm. *I could get Little Miss Gray out of her turtleneck in nothing flat.* Grinning, he swaggered up the stairs.

Linnet paused, panting, just inside the library's heavy glass doors. It felt good to be out of the wind. The weather guy on the local news kept talking about how unseasonably warm it was. Thirty degrees with a minus-something wind chill. Some warm. Her fingers ached. Maybe she should start wearing mittens.

Bypassing the paperback racks, she headed down the third row of bookcases toward the chair at the opposite end. A few of these, in Day-Glo shades of peeling vinyl, were scattered around both floors, tucked in alcoves behind the crowded bookshelves. She liked the privacy of them, especially when she read the diary. She carried it with her most of the time. Not having it felt funny, like she'd used to feel when she left Ears behind.

She still balked at getting a library card. Doing that meant for sure she'd never leave. She knew she'd have to get used to that idea, just like she'd gotten used to worse things, but nothing said she had to do it soon. In the meantime, she read the diary or sometimes a book off the shelf for variety. It gave her something to look forward to.

From her usual seat, she could see straight down the folklore aisle all the way to the front doors. When she got tired of reading, she people-watched. Not as colorful a bunch as in Chicago, or even back in Minneapolis, but enough to hold her interest for a little while. The only people immediately visible were a pimply-faced girl in front of the Celtic folklore collection and a man with mussed brown hair wearing a greenish-gray jacket.

Jacket Man was bent over a drinking fountain against the far wall. After a minute he straightened up, wiped his chin with his sleeve like Mama had always told her not to, and ambled toward the paperback thrillers. As he came close enough for a clear look, Linnet stopped breathing.

Run, said one part of her mind, even as another insisted it couldn't be her father. Mama had sent her here so he wouldn't find her. He couldn't be in Birch Falls, half a room and a glance away. Then a heavyset woman in a down vest and jeans jostled him as she passed through the paperbacks, and the snarl on his face told her the awful truth.

He had a book in his hand. Maybe he'd leave without seeing her. If he didn't go soon, she'd have to. *It's so unfair,* she thought, before fear swallowed up all other emotions—*I can't be anyplace!* Then she was off the chair and creeping though the stacks, seeking a spot from which to observe unseen.

He was heading across the lobby toward the research room. She watched him walk into it. Time to leave, before he came back out.

The stack of law books remained where he'd left them. Suddenly, he couldn't face them without a break—a real one, not just a five-minute piss. He realized he was hungry. Lunch with a good book—that was what he needed. Then he could focus on the job at hand.

He glanced toward the checkout desk just as a skinny kid in a purple coat flew past it. Honey blonde braids, the right height, about the right age . . . and that coat. Grace had bought Linnet a godawful purple parka at a church rummage sale not too long before they'd both run off.

She was moving so fast, he couldn't be sure. He dropped *Red October* on the nearest piece of furniture and strode after her.

Rachel hit the outskirts of town with a feeling of relief. Normally she enjoyed long rambles through the countryside, but the wind had been picking up for the past quarter-hour. Time to break down and buy a pair of cheap gloves before her fingers fell off.

She thought about Jackson Schlegel as she walked down the street, scanning shop fronts for something like a K-Mart. His strange reaction in Mary Anne's bedroom stuck in her mind, like a wrong note in a familiar tune. That odd moment on the front porch, too—she hadn't imagined it. What had she been doing that might have unsettled him? He'd been coming to shake hands, and he'd just . . . stopped for a second. Like he'd smacked into a window too clean to see. Then upstairs, she'd been standing next to the portrait—

She halted in a small pile of leaves. A sudden gust sent them fluttering around her ankles. *No. I'm so desperate for kin, I'm see-*

ing things that aren't there.

But Mary Anne's face had looked so familiar. The nose, the jaw line. She'd thought of Minna at first, but that didn't quite fit. She began to walk again, her breath coming shallow and fast. The hairstyle, the dress, how young the girl was, had kept her from seeing it at first—but Mary Anne Schlegel's face could almost have been her own, half a lifetime ago.

Laughter bubbled up, with a hysterical edge. *Adoptee Dead Ringer for Long-Lost Girl . . . This is crazy. Things just don't happen that way!*

But Mary Anne Schlegel had left a comfortable home in the dead of winter. No one would do that without a pressing reason. She'd surfaced briefly in Chicago, then vanished in the same year Duncan McGrath was found. How soon before or after that had Mary Anne Schlegel disappeared? Had she gone to Jonas in Chicago, and was Duncan her baby? Hers and who else's?

Too much to think about, too soon to make sense of it. With relief, she spotted a red storefront; its lettering read *Andersen's Five and Dime.* Here was the answer to a question she could handle. They might have cheap gloves, plus full-sized shampoo. The dinky bottle at the hotel had barely served to lather up her hair last night; she wanted one a lot bigger, preferably smelling like something she could identify.

With a quick glance around for traffic, she jaywalked toward the store.

Near the end of the block, Linnet risked a look back at the library. The sidewalk was empty. Then Jacket Man walked out, looked up the street, and started toward her.

The five-and-dime was just ahead. Maybe she could lose him in the aisles. She walked toward Andersen's as fast as she dared.

A peek over her shoulder told her he was gaining.

Panic took over. She ran.

As Rachel reached for the In door, a flying body knocked her aside. Someone thudded to the sidewalk with a whuff of air. Rachel fell hard against the corner mailbox. "What the hell—?"

The tirade died on her lips as she caught sight of her assailant—a waif in a shiny purple parka, with sandy braids and huge gray eyes. The impact had knocked her to the pavement. She started to get up and then froze, staring at Rachel as if in disbelief. One nail-bitten hand clutched the ratty fake fur at her throat. Her chapped red fingers contrasted sharply with her pale face.

What is it with people around here? Rachel knelt beside her. "Are you okay? Are you hurt anywhere?"

The girl shook her head. Color was returning to her cheeks, but fear lingered in her eyes. "Help me," she whispered. "Take me somewhere. Anywhere. Please?"

Two dried-up old bats walked out of the hair salon, cutting off Luke's view of the fleeing girl. Reeking of hairspray, they stood gabbing in the middle of the sidewalk. ". . . On her third husband. Her third! Such a mouse, no one would dance with her at the prom. Thinks she's Liz Taylor now."

"And her poor parents are such nice people! It's a crazy world, Gladys—excuse me! Excuse me, young man!"

Luke ignored them as he shouldered past. Up ahead, a flash of purple over blue jeans vanished around the corner. Next to it, he caught a glimpse of dark hair and a bright red coat. The kid was with someone.

"Crazy," floated after him as he hurried down the street. He turned the corner and stopped. The block ahead was deserted.

CHAPTER ELEVEN

Two doors down from the five-and-dime, Witek's Coffee Shop (Best Crullers in Town) welcomed them with a blast of cinnamon, chocolate and coffee. Rachel breathed deep, then looked at the girl. "You want some hot chocolate or something?"

"Okay." Her answer was barely a whisper.

Rachel walked past checkerboard tables and bentwood chairs to a window booth cushioned in bright red vinyl. She started to sit, then saw that the girl was still standing near the door. "It's all right," Rachel said, beckoning. "I never bite on first acquaintance."

The girl toyed with a braid, tense as a stretched rubber band. "Not by the window," she said.

"Okay." Rachel left the booth. "Pick us a spot."

The girl chose a table deep inside the café, then wadded up her bright coat and sat on it. Rachel thought of a chameleon, changing its color so as not to attract attention. Apparently, whatever she'd been running from was still a threat.

Poor kid. Rachel handed her a menu from the tabletop holder. She took it with a barely audible "thank you" that choked off as if her throat had closed on it. Shoulders hunched, she studied the laminated cardboard. Rachel had the sense she was fighting not to cry. She started to reach out on instinct, then stopped. The girl looked about twelve or thirteen. Too old to accept a consoling touch from a stranger.

"You want to tell me what this is all about?" she asked instead.

The girl shook her head.

"Fair enough." Rachel read her own menu. *Hot cider,* she thought, while the rest of her wondered what was wrong with this kid—and why she cared. Something about the way the girl had looked at her, out there by Andersen's—as if Rachel were the thing she'd always wanted, but forever out of reach. *Another stray.* Nick had once accused her of spending her life picking them up. *First a cat, now a child.*

The girl had laid down her menu and begun looking around. The café's cheerful atmosphere, half old-fashioned ice-cream parlor and half pizza joint, seemed to have a calming effect. Three giant ceiling fans whirred slowly over the scattered tables and booths, despite the chill outside. Watching them turn, the girl made a small sound that might have been a laugh.

Encouraged by this glimmer of humor, Rachel introduced herself. "I'm Rachel Connolly."

"I know. I saw you this morning. At my house."

It took Rachel a moment to realize what she meant. "Schlegel House? I didn't think anyone lived there."

"I don't." The girl met her gaze with a lift of her chin that dared Rachel to challenge her. "But it's mine anyway."

"Nice place."

"Yeah." Whatever the test was, Rachel had passed it; the girl gave her a shy smile. Suddenly, her thin face was beautiful. "I'm Linnet."

Rachel couldn't help grinning back. "Pleased to meet you, Linnet. So what's good here besides the crullers?"

The smile faded. Linnet looked down at her hands. "I'm just visiting. I've never been here before."

Not a chameleon. A hedgehog, curling up with its spikes out whenever it got poked. Looking around the café, Rachel saw a shiny glass-fronted counter near them that held trays full of baked goods. A heavyset waitress in a starched white apron stepped out from behind it and headed their way.

She ordered an elephant ear to go with her cider. Linnet, mouse-quiet again, managed to order hot chocolate. Silence reigned as the waitress bustled away. Rachel busied herself pulling wadded-up cash out of her pocket and straightening the bills. Cider, chocolate, pastry . . . at small-town prices, she'd have plenty left over for shampoo and gloves. "I'm visiting myself," she said, eyes fixed on her task. Her next words took her by surprise. "I'm looking for my family."

"My grandfather said you were writing a book."

"I am." Rachel smoothed the bills against the tabletop. "I didn't tell him about the other thing. It's . . . kind of private."

Their order arrived. Cider mug in one hand, Rachel pushed the plate with the elephant ear to the middle of the table.

"Why are you looking for them?" Linnet asked.

"I guess I want to know if I have any." She broke off a chunk of pastry. It felt good to tell the real story to someone, and Linnet's vulnerable air drew her. "I'm adopted. I thought I'd found my mother, but she died."

Linnet stared into her cocoa. "Mine, too."

Shock made Rachel set down her mug. "I'm—" *I'm so sorry,* she'd been about to say. *The same thing everybody says and nobody means.* Improvising fast, Rachel finished her sentence with the first thing that came to mind. "I liked Schlegel House. It was gorgeous. Lonely, though. A huge empty place like that, still surrounded by wilderness after all these years . . . I think if I lived there, I'd get nervous. Or I'd get a really big dog." Cheeks flaming, she took refuge in her cider mug.

"Sometimes . . ." Linnet began. A splotch of melted whipped cream adorned her upper lip. She wiped it off, then gazed at the foamy streak on her thumb. "Sometimes I pretend I live there for real. It was nice, back when—back in the old days."

"When people lived there?"

Linnet nodded. "When Jonas and Mary Anne were alive."

Rachel ate another piece of elephant ear. The pastry melted on her tongue, full of butter and cinnamon. "I saw their portraits. Mary Anne didn't look much older than you."

"I'm thirteen." Linnet shredded a fragment of pastry. "I wish I'd been her. Sometimes I pretend I am. That I grew up in that house. With everything." She broke off and stared at the pale flakes sticking to her fingers. "I know. It's stupid."

"Sometimes I pretend I'm a character from a favorite book," Rachel said after a pause. "I imagine what they do every day. I have whole conversations in my head with people who don't exist."

Linnet looked up. "You don't really."

"I do really."

"Is that why you write books?"

"How else can a grown-up play let's-pretend and get away with it?"

"Mary Anne wanted to write books. Her father wouldn't let her." Linnet jabbed her spoon into what was left of the whipped cream. "He was a jerk. My grandfather thinks he's God. I think he was mean and stupid. He made her run away." The spoon snapped down on the table as her voice rose. "Why do they do things like that? Don't they know it's wrong to hurt people?"

Her distress made it clear there was more to the question than curiosity about the motives of a long-dead Victorian father. Suddenly uneasy, Rachel wondered how Linnet's mother had died. *Oh, stop it. She could have had cancer, or been hit by a bus.* "I wondered why Mary Anne went away," she said, her tone carefully casual. "Did your grandfather ever tell you?"

"He doesn't talk to me much. I don't think he likes me."

Jesus, this poor kid could use a hug. Better yet, a friend. Rachel glanced toward the window while searching for something innocuous to say. It had begun to snow; she could just make out flurries dancing on puffs of wind like snow fairies. A lone human being passed by on the far side of the street, too distant to put a face to.

Linnet finished her chocolate as if she didn't expect to have more of it anytime soon. Her mug empty, she stood up and shook out her coat. "I have to go. Thanks for the chocolate. And everything."

"I'll come with you." Rachel dug out her neatened roll of bills and started to peel off a few. "Where are you headed?"

"Just back to the library. It's not far." The hedgehog had returned. Linnet zipped up her coat, avoiding Rachel's gaze. Then, for a moment, she looked Rachel in the face. Rachel had the odd sense of a question being asked. Then Linnet turned away.

Cold wind ruffled Rachel's hair as the door banged shut. She watched the small figure pass the window while she tried to work out the meaning of that last, silent interchange. Maybe there wasn't any. Maybe Linnet was just a lonely kid who'd latched onto her, like lonely children sometimes did, and her sense of the dramatic was working overtime. As usual.

She dropped some bills on the table, buttoned her coat and left. Outside, she looked toward the library. No purple parka, only a rotund man in a red-and-black hunter's jacket heading her way. Either Linnet had started running the minute she was out of eyeshot, or she'd changed her mind.

She yanked up her hood, as if blotting out the wind and snow could erase the afternoon's events. She had enough mysteries on her plate just now. She didn't need another one.

Jackson sat back on his heels and contemplated the nearly finished stretch of baseboard. The small brush with which he'd painstakingly applied three coats of varnish dangled from his hand. Ordinarily, the sight of a job well done warmed him inside. Just now, that satisfaction eluded him. He couldn't get Rachel Connolly out of his mind.

A trick of coloring, that's all it was. Or blind coincidence. Didn't everyone have a doppelganger somewhere? Lots of women looked alike on the surface, especially to him. He wasn't much good with faces. She'd reminded him a little of Grace at first, until he watched her move and heard her talk. Mary Anne was sixteen in the portrait; Miss Connolly was thirty if she was a day. How real could any resemblance be with that kind of age span between them?

Their faces—one painted, the other living—rose in his mind. He could visualize the bone structure underlying each. The same lines, the same shapes. Bones didn't lie. Only people did.

His grip tightened on the brush handle. The smell of the varnish made him feel sick. He was thinking like a crazy man. Rachel Connolly didn't know him, or the family, or anything about Mary Anne's lost baby. No one knew about that except him. In a hundred years, the trustees had never discovered that child's birth; it was impossible that Mary Anne's grandchildren or great-grandchildren, if there were any, should turn up now to claim a legacy they couldn't know existed.

A glob of varnish splatted against the newsprint on the floor. Jackson dipped the brush in the can, then scraped off the excess against the inside rim before dotting the thick liquid across the old wood. He should keep his mind on the task at hand, or at least save his worry for a genuine threat. Like Linnet's father. Thompson and Bizal had surely contacted Grace, which meant Luke Chapman might well know his child was a walking gold mine. Jackson felt a chill that had nothing to do with the cold outside. *If he walked up to her on the street, I wouldn't know. I've never even seen his picture.*

He thunked the brush into the can. First thing after dinner, he'd call Terry Powell. Grace's old beau had stayed friendly

157

over the years, and surely a police chief knew a good lawyer willing to wait for his fee. Linnet had come to him, and he meant to keep her.

He smoothed the last drop of varnish, then set down the brush and headed for the attic. A look at Mary Anne's diary would settle his foolish fears about Miss Connolly. Since hearing from the lawyers, he'd been over it dozens of times and had found no clues that could point to the whereabouts of Mary Anne's child. Silly as it was, he needed a reminder that there weren't any to find. Grandfather Randolph had only guessed it, and he'd never told.

"Needs airing out," he muttered at the sight of the attic's dusty clutter. The furniture needed oiling, too. That would be his project for this winter. He opened Mary Anne's trunk and went through the small stack of books inside.

Cold settled in the pit of his stomach. He searched the books again, then emptied the trunk. The diary was missing.

Florian was beginning to wonder if Chapman had vanished into thin air. The punk wannabe desk clerk at the Days Inn by the bus depot had admitted to maybe seeing someone who looked kind of like him; further inquiries to the manager had confirmed Chapman's presence under the name Johnny Walker. He'd checked out that morning, about two hours before the police arrived. Since then, Florian and Powell had spent the day checking out other motels, rooming houses and even the town's sole bed-and-breakfast. Now they were driving back to the Windy Pines, where Florian hoped to find good news from Maggie Harper about her end of the investigation. He could use some.

He glanced at his companion. It felt strange to be chauffeured by the chief of police. "I know my way around. You don't," Powell had said that morning—a remark whose double edge Florian chose to ignore. The chief hadn't said much else since. He rationed words, as if afraid of using up his quota. Just now, he was watching the road like he expected it to try something sneaky. He set Florian's teeth on edge, mainly because Florian couldn't figure him out.

The scene at the Days Inn flashed through his mind. The clerk, sporting molasses-colored hair spikes and a stud through her lower lip, had looked up from her bored slouch as they came in. "Help y'th somethin'?"

As Florian reached for his badge, Powell had flashed his own. The girl straightened up fast. "Man's got a picture to show you," Powell said, chopping every word off short. "Tell us if you've seen him."

On cue, Florian displayed Chapman's sketch. The girl peered at it. She bit her lip, with a nervous glance at Powell. "I don't know. Maybe. I see lots of people."

Once again, Powell beat Florian to it. He leaned over the counter, spreading his big hands against it. "Think harder."

The girl shrank away from him. "How'm I s'posed to remember every jerk comes in here off the bus?!"

Before Florian could say a word, the chief straightened and ran a hand through his hair. When he turned his attention back to the clerk, his face and posture had softened. "Julie, isn't it? Art Sivak's girl?"

Black-painted fingernails toyed with her lip stud. "Yeah."

"We're after a killer, Julie." Powell dropped his voice, inviting confidences. "I know you can help us. Just try."

And she had helped, though not as much as Florian would have liked. Powell's quick-change act had made quite an impression on her. On Florian as well, though he was still sorting out what kind.

The chief had put his armor back on the moment they left the motel lobby. Silence surrounded him like a wall. Florian squelched rising irritation. He was trying to stay professional, but so far all it had earned him was the right to stand around waving his sketch while Powell did all the talking. The guy owed him at least a few words of civil conversation.

He shrugged his shoulders to shed some tension. "Fishing any good around here?"

"Don't fish much." Three syllables, heavy as boulders. A red stoplight on cables glared down at them from the approaching intersection. Powell slowed. The clicking of the turn signal filled the car.

Florian tried again. "Maybe we'll find Chapman at the Pines."

"Maybe. Maybe not." The flatness of Powell's tone said he didn't give a damn. His throttle-grip on the wheel said otherwise.

I'm going to regret this, Florian thought, even as his temper took hold of his tongue. "Would it kill you to talk like a normal person? Maybe even tell me what the hell your problem is? Because I can't do my job if I have to keep ducking the chip on your shoulder. You want this guy caught or not?!"

Powell gunned the car through a yellow, then whipped it onto the gravel that passed for the county highway shoulder. They coasted to a stop. Powell sat stiff at the wheel for several seconds, while Florian unglued his fingers from the door handle and prayed he hadn't set off a lunatic.

The chief reached inside his jacket. For a panicked millisecond, Florian thought he was going for his gun. Instead, he brought out a photograph and handed it over.

The snapshot showed a much younger Powell, teenage-skinny and not quite comfortable in a dark blue suit. Under his arm, fitting as though sculpted there, was an equally young Grace Chapman—or whatever her name had been then. She wore a filmy, rose-colored dress, a white corsage and a bright smile for the camera. Powell's smile was all for her.

"Senior prom," Powell said quietly. "Wasn't too many years

later Grace took off. I'd have married her if she wanted. She didn't want." Vinyl creaked as he shifted his weight. "That answer your question?"

"One of them," Florian said carefully. "The other one is, am I working with you, or for you?"

They locked eyes for a few moments. "Don't know yet," Powell said finally.

Florian nodded. "Okay."

The car crept back onto the road. Florian fingered the corners of the snapshot. Nothing had been resolved, but the air felt clearer. The way things were going, he'd take any improvement he could get.

The road spun out before them, a dark gray ribbon beneath a pale gray sky. Fall in the Range was a miserable season. Lulled by the clean cold of winter and the lazy summer, Powell forgot every year how much he hated autumn—until November rolled around to remind him.

This fall was the worst in years. Too warm for much snow, too cold for rain. Sleet and flurries damned near every morning, wet wind chasing him home every evening. He hadn't bothered to clear the past few days' leaf sludge off his front walk. What was the point? There would only be more by morning. The unsightly build-up would eventually irritate the neighbors, but at the moment he couldn't bring himself to care. Nothing mattered except Grace. Catching her murderer was all he could do for her now.

Bare trees, their branches black with freezing rain, flashed past the car windows. They'd reach the hotel soon. The Chicago cop would be glad to get out. Powell could hear him fidgeting in his seat. He was still holding the photo, balancing it by its edges between narrow fingers. Considerate of him to be so careful. Florian's flare of temper had surprised Powell, but on balance he was glad it happened. He didn't want to treat this man any worse than he had to. But he had to do this himself. For Grace. Could this city stranger understand that? Or would he only see some bumpkin getting in his way?

He swung the car off the highway onto Eleventh Avenue. Florian had mentioned finding Chapman at the Pines—which was possible, but not likely. "Not exactly the place for someone who takes a Greyhound up here," he said, thinking out loud.

"What?"

"The Windy Pines. All the way across town from the bus depot."

"Chapman might see that as an advantage." Florian laid the photo on the dashboard, then tugged at his coat. "He's looking for his little girl."

"Little girl?!" Florian's statement startled Powell into taking his eyes off the road.

"She's in town someplace with her grandfather. A bolt hole close in would make it easier to search."

Powell turned onto Twelfth Street and headed toward Highway 22. The Windy Pines lay just a few blocks away. As neat frame houses rolled by, he debated with himself about how much to say. Florian didn't know where Grace's girl was—but he did. The town grapevine had been abuzz for days over the early-morning arrival of a youngster at the Schlegel place. If he told Florian, would the other man be bound by law to take the child from her only remaining family? Or worse yet, hand her over to her murdering scum of a father?

"Custody dispute gone bad?" he asked, in what he hoped was a casual tone. "Don't suppose they'd let him have her, would they? Assuming we can make a murder case."

Florian scowled. "I hope to hell not. Depends on the judge. Luck of the draw could give us a smart one or an idiot who just wants to clear his docket and save the State of Illinois some pennies. That's assuming the Illinois courts get the case. The Chapmans were living in Minneapolis before Grace took off to Chicago with the kid, so the case might stay here."

They rattled into the Pines parking lot. The squad car needed new shocks. Thinking about that helped Powell keep his anger from showing. As long as there was the slightest chance of Grace's child ending up with that monster, he'd keep his mouth shut.

Cold air laced with sleet smacked Florian in the face as he climbed out of the squad car. Jesus, what a rotten climate. He noted with grim amusement that Powell was keeping a step behind him as they headed for the lobby doors. His temper tantrum seemed to have paid off.

"I still haven't seen him," Bogart said when they reached the front desk and asked after Chapman. "Of course, I don't work the morning shift. Our usual check-in is at one, an hour before I get here." He turned toward the nearest computer terminal. "I can check our records . . . what's the name?"

"Johnny Walker," Florian said. Powell kept quiet. "Or Luke Chapman. Or anything close to either one."

They waited while Bogart played with the keyboard. "Walker . . . ah—no, wait, that's Hiram Walker. Buyer from Duluth, comes up here every year for deer season. Mattie Walker . . . she's here visiting her sister Joanne Witek, who runs a coffee shop in town. Best homemade crullers you ever tasted. Chapman, now . . . nope, not a thing." He frowned at the screen. "There's a Chaplin, David, Room 213, checked in early at eleven this morning. Also a Roger Chiproe, Room 110, checked in at one-thirty, and Lucas Manning, Room 204, about the same time." He looked up. "Does that help?"

"They pay cash, check or charge?"

Bogart tapped more keys. "Chiproe used Visa. Cash for the other two."

Florian turned to Powell. "Ten to one he's paying cash, but—"

"We'll trace the Visa number." With a slight smile, Powell continued. "For now, how about you pick us someone to talk to?"

Chaplin turned out to be sixty-plus and none too pleased at being awakened from his afternoon nap. Chiproe was out. They'd caught Manning in the shower; beads of water glistened on his chocolate-brown skin as he listened with dignity to their apology. They returned to the lobby and commandeered a sofa, from which they tried to plan their next move.

"He's got to be here somewhere, damn it," Florian muttered. "Maybe somebody just has a poor memory for faces. Or he is at the Pines, and pulled a new alias out of the local phone book."

"We could look at everyone who checked in before two yesterday. Not sure it's worth the bother, though." Powell sounded skeptical. "I'm thinking he's holed up in another town. Chisholm, Virginia, Ely . . . those are all pretty close to here."

"Can you get to them by bus?"

Powell nodded. "Milk-run Greyhound stops everyplace."

Florian dug a quarter out of his pocket. "Heads goes to the bus depot to see if our boy bought a ticket today. Tails checks out more names."

This time, Powell's grin almost reached his eyes.

The coin came up tails—Florian's choice. Powell hauled himself off the sofa. "If the depot's a wash, I'll start on car rental places by the highways. Join me when you finish up here."

"Will do."

As Powell headed out, Florian approached the desk. Bogart was on the phone. "Just a moment," the clerk murmured, then turned the receiver against his shoulder. "There's a Detective Harper on the phone for you. Would you like to take it here, or in your room?"

"In my room. Thanks." He made the trip fast, eager to hear his partner's report.

Receiver in hand, he stretched out on the bed. The puffy comforter seemed to draw fatigue from his muscles. "What've you got?"

"Fingerprints." Maggie's voice sounded tight, like it always did when she was excited about something. "Two clean ones and a partial from the swing set in Mountjoy Park, a perfect match for Luke Chapman. We also found Grace Chapman's Minnesota driver's license in the stairwell outside Ruth Mason's apartment building. Fell out of his coat pocket, probably. The evidence techs are checking it for prints as well; I'll let you know as soon as they tell me anything."

Got him, Florian thought. *As soon as we find him*. With a sinking feeling, he wondered what would happen to the little girl.

"Jim? You there?"

He shook himself. "Yeah, sorry. That's great. Good work."

"Everything going OK?"

"Fine," he lied. "Gotta go. I'll check in tomorrow afternoon."

He hung up, then forced himself off the bed and out. He'd pick up a list of names at the front desk and go over it for like-lies, then catch up with Powell and give him an update. As he turned to flick off the entryway light, a flurry of movement caught his eye. Before he could get a good look, a nearby door slammed shut, leaving him alone in the corridor.

Luke sagged against the wall of his room and willed himself to stop shaking. The cop had almost seen him. Next time he might not be so lucky.

Logic, feebly attempting to assert itself as he flung clothes and cigarette packs into his duffel, told him it was stupid to run. Okay, the cop probably knew who he was. The guy must've

ID'd Grace, checked out her background, got hold of the domestic complaints and figured Luke for the type who'd slam his wife into a swing set. But the cop had no proof. He'd made sure to pick up his cigarette butt, checked for other debris, never touched anything except Grace's clothes. You couldn't get prints from cloth, he'd read that in a mystery somewhere. The cop had nothing but a suggestive past, nowhere near enough even to haul him in for a chat. He'd be fine staying. Besides, where could he go?

That thought stopped him cold, with a wadded-up pair of black sweats in his hand. The cop would check every place in town. Maybe he already had. Maybe it was safe to relocate. Or maybe the cop would keep checking back, just to see. Maybe he should stay put.

He threw down the sweatpants, snatched up an open pack of Marlboros and snagged one. He was out of matches. He wrenched open the top drawer of the nighttable, but found only the inevitable Gideon Bible and a small fan of colored brochures for local tourist attractions. As if anyone would come up here for the sights. He was about to slam the drawer when a fragment of print caught his attention. He looked more closely at the brochures, then picked out the cream-colored one and read its front page. *Schlegel House. A national historic landmark. Birch Falls, Minnesota.*

He dropped to the edge of the bed and began to laugh. It was too much. After the day he'd had, it was just too fucking much.

After sobering up, he carefully finished packing. Now he knew where to go, and where to find what he'd come for.

The cold air made Linnet's throat burn as she jogged along the road out of town. If she kept up her pace, she should make it back to the cottage before dark. Not even four yet, and already it was hard to see her breath in the dimming light. In Chicago or Minneapolis, there'd be lights from a thousand signs and shop windows and apartments and houses, plus streetlights and car headlights and people everywhere. Here, there was nothing but ticky-tacky trailers and scraggly trees. And no one but a gruff old man and a big, empty, sad house. Rachel was right. Schlegel House was so lonely it hurt.

A tear made a warm track on one chilled cheek. Angrily, she brushed it away. She was tired of feeling alone and afraid. First her father in the library, then Rachel, who just for a second had looked exactly like Mama. Reminders of everything she didn't want to think about. "It's been a rotten day," she muttered as she ran. "Rotten. Horrible. Putrid. Scrofulous. Pustulent. . . ."

Though she'd half expected it not to, the word game worked its familiar magic. By the time she ran out of synonyms, she felt halfway normal. The birches looked almost pretty against the gray sky, which promised real snow by morning. She wondered how Schlegel House would look surrounded by a carpet of white.

A mild stitch in her side made her slow to a walk. The top edge of the diary dug into her ribs; running must have shifted it some. She unzipped her coat and tugged the book from beneath her thick sweater. Her skin itched where the diary had pressed. She scratched, then stood still and contemplated the little volume.

I'm looking for my family, Rachel had said. And she looked like Mary Anne. A lot more than she looked like Mama, once Linnet recognized it. That had to mean something, didn't it? Plus, Rachel had helped her. Linnet owed her for that.

She stroked the leather cover, then brought the book to her nose. It smelled earthy and old, like the roots of a tree. *Maybe we're Rachel's family—me and Mary Anne.* The thought should have been startling, but instead felt strangely right . . . like a puzzle piece that didn't belong anywhere, but somehow fit perfectly into the last gap.

She tucked the diary back in her waistband and walked on through the dusk.

CHAPTER TWELVE

28 January, 1893

I don't know what to do. I don't know what to tell him. I only know I must—and then we have to go away. To Minneapolis, at least; farther, if we can manage it. And soon.

It's what I wanted, to go away. Only not like this. What we'll do when the time comes, I can't imagine. I can't imagine anything beyond telling him. I can't even imagine the look on his face. I've seen that face a thousand different ways, and now I can't conjure it up even for a moment.

He'll see we have to go. It's what he wants, too, he's said so all winter. Everything will be all right. Surely it will.

The cold nipped at Mary Anne's cheeks above her thick scarf as she plowed through the calf-high snow along the road to town. Wool underclothes, merino dress and heavy coat had so far kept her body warm enough. Something other than the winter chill made her shiver as she walked, slipping a bit when impatience overwhelmed the need to step carefully. Her boots would be soaked through. The wind blew straight and steady, promising more snow before long. Not a blizzard wind, thank God. She'd never have dared this mad trip in a real storm, and heaven only knew when she'd get another chance to slip away.

She wondered what Mr. Nilssen would make of Andrew Jackson Schlegel's daughter warming her toes before the common stove at the grocery, like any housewife venturing out to buy potatoes or soap. He would likely guess why she'd come. Fortunately, he was a miser with words. Mother and Miss French were both down with head colds, and Father was hiding from their illness in the mine office. Fate had handed her a chance to see Rhys just when she most needed it. She chose to take that as a good omen.

It had been cold and snowy that afternoon in early December, the chill crinkling her nose and biting her ears as she walked toward the cottage. She'd taken a roundabout route from the manse that day, so as not to leave telltale footprints. If anyone saw the trail leading away from the back door, they would assume she'd gone on one of her treks. Her parents and Miss French were accustomed to what they termed her mad insistence on walking out in any weather short of a blizzard or a dangerous cold snap. So accustomed, in fact, that Miss French had anxiously inquired about her health when she'd stayed home the previous Sunday. A snowstorm had kept her in on Wednesday, blessedly forestalling any decision about whether or not to meet Rhys for their usual sketching session.

A chunk of snow dropped over her boot cuff, burning cold against her ankle even through her thick wool stocking. The sudden discomfort was a welcome distraction. All too soon, however, her thoughts returned to the same uncomfortable channels in which they'd run for the past ten days. *I want him to hold me again. I want to touch him. What in heaven's name is the matter with me?!*

By the cottage's back door, she shook the snow from her boots and hem, wishing she could as easily shake her inexplicable feelings. She'd known Rhys since they were ten. They'd gone fishing together. How could a girl possibly be falling in love, or anything like it, with a boy she'd seen covered in fish guts?

She couldn't. She wasn't. She was just lonely, half-crazed with boredom most of the time, and the mind did strange things when deprived of sunlight. If she ignored this winter-madness, sooner or later it would pass. In the meantime, they had a drawing to finish.

The kitchen was dark and cold, curtains drawn against the faint afternoon light. Twilight would fall soon. Rhys should arrive before then. She turned on the gaslights, built the usual small fire in the stove and unstiffened her fingers over it, then wound up the clock and set it by her watch. These ordinary actions calmed her. Suddenly, her overwrought emotions seemed ludicrous. She had done right to come. No sense depriving Rhys because her silly brain had confused him with the hero of a romantic penny dreadful. A nice, calm, normal sketching session would surely sort things out.

Rhys had half expected to have slogged all this way through the snow for nothing. To head home once again with anxiety gnawing at him, wondering if Mary Anne were simply ill, or something worse. He never should have touched her like that. But she'd seemed so lonely, he couldn't help it.

He ducked under a snow-bent branch and found himself at the edge of the tree line. The mansion loomed ahead. Careful to stay under the trees, he walked around the house until he saw Mary Anne's window.

The ribbon was there, dark against the white curtain. The sight of it made him happier than Christmas. He half-ran along the top of the rise, speeding up even as he chided himself for being so eager. This session would be the same as every other—lots of drawing, a little tea, some talk. There was no need to run toward it as if meeting a lover . . . Rhys shied away from that thought and ran faster.

He stopped on the back step to knock snow off his boots,

then lingered in the cold and stared at the door. Suddenly, foolishly, he was afraid to open it. What if she'd put up the ribbon just to tell him she didn't want to see him again? She'd acted so odd that last day, bolting off as if he'd frightened her. Maybe he had. Maybe that was why she'd stayed away last Sunday. She'd felt the change in him and didn't like it.

Or she did like it, and she's just as scared as I am.

That was crazy. He knew it. Girls like Mary Anne didn't fall for poor miner's sons who scraped paltry savings stocking groceries and dry goods. And even if they did, nothing came of it. Nor did he want anything to come of it. He was going to be an artist, travel the world, make a name for himself. He'd have gone already, if only his family didn't need quite so much of his wages. It was hard to save what he needed, but he'd manage. Eventually. Once he had enough, he'd bid Birch Falls goodbye. The last thing he needed was to lose his head over a girl. Even a girl like Mary Anne, whose smile could brighten a room and whose slender body fit so perfectly against his own—

He grabbed the doorknob. Enough idiot mooning. He had a still life to finish.

Not quite an hour later, he was no closer to doing so. "I'm sorry," Mary Anne muttered after yet another shift in position. "I don't understand what you want."

She sounded as weary as Rhys felt. He glanced up from his sketchbook and was startled at how limp she looked—like a wrung-out shirt after too many washings. He squinted at the clock.

"Just a little longer," he heard himself saying, as if the words belonged to someone else. He should give her a rest, but he could feel frustration building even as he struggled for calm. He had to accomplish something, or his head would explode. "Ten more minutes. Try turning a little to the right . . . no, right, I said! . . . That's too much. Come back this way."

She was biting her lip as she moved, clearly on the brink of snapping at him. He should let her rest. But he couldn't yet, not with so much time gone and nothing to show for it.

"You come and move me," she said, sounding exhausted beyond patience.

He didn't dare. If he touched her, everything would leave him but the desire to keep touching. He'd frighten her half to death. And he couldn't even tell her, because that would frighten her to death, too. So he was stuck with being a pig, short-tempered and demanding for reasons he couldn't explain. He gritted his teeth and described, as politely as he could manage, the pose he wanted her to take.

Miraculously, she moved into exactly the right position. The curve of her head, her bare neck, the roundness of her shoulder—he wanted those lines, those exact shapes on paper. He began to draw, charcoal pencil flying over a fresh sheet.

Mary Anne listened to the muffled scratch of the pencil, for once not accompanied by grumbling. Scarcely an hour had passed, and it felt like three. Her hopes of a normal afternoon seemed laughable now. Rhys had hardly looked her in the face since his arrival, and had met every attempt at conversation with a growl like a wounded bear. She'd made allowances at first—Lord knew she was no angel of civility when writer's block struck—but this much snapping and snarling presumed on their friendship. If she had any sense, she'd leave. But she knew she would stay. *Miserable as I am right now, it's still better than home. And at least I'm with him.*

How pathetic that was, to find such sour-tempered company preferable to solitude just because it was Rhys. She should ask him straight out what ailed him. She had the funny feeling he wanted to make her angry, to drive her away . . . but that made no sense. If she'd offended him, throwing herself at him that day like she had, he needn't have come. She closed her eyes, wishing she could massage away the headache that was creeping across the bridge of her nose. Puzzling out Rhys's behavior took too much effort. It was hard enough controlling her own feelings, which veered between wanting to snap back and wanting to stroke his hair until his frustration melted away. How could she ever have thought that seeing Rhys again would sort anything out?

A loud curse shattered the silence. Sketchbook and pencil hit the floor, the pencil hard enough to snap its point off. Mary Anne stared at Rhys. He was standing by his chair, breathing like a workhorse, fists clenched so hard his knuckles were white.

Memory struck, overwhelming. *Father's hands, that same white, hurling my stories into the fire. . . .*

She must have made some sound. Rhys looked up. His rage vanished like snow-melt at the sight of her. "I'm sorry . . ."

He was coming toward her, white-faced with worry. She wanted to reach out to him, but remembered fear held her still. He stopped a few steps shy of her, one hand raised as if he wanted to touch her, but didn't dare. *It isn't you,* she tried to say, but the words wouldn't come.

The misery on his face demanded that she speak. "He burned them," she said finally, choking on the words. "My stories. Everything I ever wrote. Father burned them all."

He took her in his arms then. He felt reassuringly warm and solid, his hands gentle as he stroked her hair. Neither of them moved for a long time. The clock chimed the quarter-hour, its delicate notes oddly loud in the stillness.

"I've wanted to hold you all day," he whispered against her hair. *Confession for confession,* she thought. "I wanted to and I knew I shouldn't, and I could hardly stand it . . ."

She shifted just enough to look up at him, then kissed him softly on the mouth. Then again and again, the third time twining her fingers in his hair. Every place she touched felt warm and alive and strange: the dark strands between her fingers, his bare neck, the hard curve of his jaw. She slid her hands downward and touched bare shoulder, a scant inch of it reachable under his shirt collar. *I should stop,* came the dim thought, but she ignored it. Just for once, she would do what she wanted.

He caught her hand as she reached for his shirt buttons, pressed it flat against his chest. And then let it go, to reach around her and unfasten her skirt. The sudden coolness as the wool fell away reminded her how cold the rest of the cottage was . . . *not very comfortable, though, rolling around on the hard kitchen floor! Nor very romantic . . .*

Laughter bubbled up before she could stop it. Rhys pulled away slightly with a questioning look. She took his hands, stepped out of her fallen skirt and led him toward the hallway door. "Come on. I have an idea."

The cold air on her face made a refreshing contrast to the warmth beneath the blankets. Mary Anne burrowed closer to Rhys, who sounded as if he were asleep. She was half-asleep herself, the happy drowse of an early winter morning when there was no need to get out of bed. The vague thought came that she ought to feel guilty. That she didn't was puzzling, but not terribly important. Not nearly as important as the pleasant way Rhys smelled, or the softness where their bare skins touched. She shifted against him, easing a crick in her neck. He made a grumbly, muttering noise, then opened his eyes and smiled at her.

"I thought you were asleep," she murmured.

"Mmh-mmh." His head turned slowly on the pillow. "Thinking."

"About what?"

"Sketching you." One hand moved beneath the covers, tracing a line from neck to waist. "Like this."

He pushed himself up on one arm to look at her, dislodging the blankets. She yelped and pulled them back under her chin. "It's freezing!"

Laughter colored his answer. "I wasn't planning on doing it in here." He sat up, with a gasp at the cold, then tucked the second layer of blankets around her before snatching the top coverlet off the bed and wrapping himself in it. "Come on. Wrap up and grab some pillows."

They took all three thick blankets, the pillows and most of the sofa cushions from the tiny parlor, giggling like children as they shaped their booty into a comfortable nest on the kitchen floor. Rhys wrapped the coverlet around himself Roman-toga style, then sat cross-legged on the last fat cushion and settled his sketchbook and pencil—freshly whittled to sharpness—on his lap. He swept one arm toward the assembled bedding. "Would my lady care to take her place?"

"Why, thank you, kind sir." She sat down, draping her own blanket across her shoulders and upraised knee. "Now what?"

He gave her his artist's look—a long, steady gaze, as if watching her change from a living, breathing person into a collection of shapes and shadows. "Stay like that, but without the blanket. Tell me when you get cold and we'll break off. Lean back a little, with your other arm resting on your knee . . . perfect. Don't move."

Comfortable silence fell, save for the whish of pencil on paper. The pose was easy to hold. Mary Anne drifted, her attention settling briefly on various things: the soft pillows beneath her, the drape of the coverlet across Rhys's chest, the gleam of his hair in the light.

The clock struck six. They jumped, then sat frozen until the last stroke died away.

Rhys dumped the sketchbook off his lap and shot up from

the floor. The coverlet's gold fringe lapped at his calves. "Lord, it's so late, I should be home, they'll be expecting me . . . Why didn't you say something?!" He hauled her off the floor and threw the blanket around her shoulders. "We've got to get dressed." Before she could say a word, he vanished down the cold hall. Minutes later, he reappeared with his arms full of their discarded clothing. He tossed underthings, petticoat and blouse at her, then shook out his trousers and grabbed his shirt. Haste made him miss the sleeve. He fumbled frantically for the opening. For no good reason, Mary Anne began to laugh. She stood holding her underclothes, giggling helplessly as Rhys stumbled into his trousers.

"What's the matter with you? Get dressed! We've got to get out of here before someone comes looking—"

"Like who? My father?" Amusement gave way to annoyance. Who did he think he was, talking to her like that? "No one will come. They'll just think I'm sulking in my room. I keep the door locked so they can't disturb me. You don't have to be so scared." She pulled on her bloomers, then slowly buttoned up her undervest. "We could stay here all night if we wanted to."

Rhys stared at her as if she'd gone mad. "We can't."

"Afraid?"

"Yes. So would you be if you were thinking straight!" He bent and scooped up two sofa cushions, then stalked out of the room.

She watched him go as she slowly finished dressing. By the time he returned for more pillows, she was buttoning her cuffs. They looked at each other for a long moment, he standing still in the doorway. "I'm sorry," he said finally. "I can't help being afraid when there's something to lose."

His honesty made her ashamed of her anger. She held out a hand. He came and took it. She squeezed his fingers in mute apology, then plucked a blanket off the floor and held out one end to him. "Here. Help me fold this."

With all evidence of the afternoon's activities erased, Rhys seemed almost calm. "You'll come Wednesday?" she asked, suddenly anxious herself as they walked out the back door.

The smile he gave her dispelled her fear. "Not even a blizzard could keep me away." A final kiss, firm and possessive; then he disappeared into the darkness.

She lingered on the step, watching the spot where he'd vanished until his kiss faded from her lips.

Since that first time, she'd kept their secret safe. A reputation for moods and sulks had unexpected benefits, she'd discovered—it explained several weeks of intermittent disappearances, for example. Even her father, on the rare occasions when they met on her way out, never asked where she was going. *Because he doesn't think it matters anymore.*

Buildings loomed ahead through a swirl of snowflakes. She was approaching the outskirts of town. Her steps faltered. Since that first day, Rhys hadn't shown open fear—but he watched the time carefully, and she could sense constant tension simmering beneath the surface. In the midst of joy, something in him still feared getting caught. What if he panicked again? What if he bolted in the middle of the night? Or turned away from her, denying everything they'd shared for the past seven weeks?

Anxiety nagged at her as she kept walking. Surely Rhys wouldn't let her down. He loved her. He'd said so often enough. Nothing would make him happier than to go away together and . . . her thoughts ground to a halt. And what? Get married? Have the child, keep it and raise it, while she learned to write and he learned to be an artist? How could she study and be a mother? How could Rhys become an artist if he had to support a family?

She stopped and leaned against a nearby wall. They couldn't

178

do it. She was a fool to think they could. She wanted to run home, throw herself down with her head in her mother's lap and cry until the world went away. Instead, she closed her eyes and bit the inside of her lip until she tasted blood. The pain cleared her head. She looked up and realized she was standing by the train station.

She walked inside to the ticket window. "How much is one-way fare to Chicago, please?"

The agent, whose bewhiskered face she remembered from coming here to meet Uncle William once, smiled at her. "First class, Miss Schlegel?"

"Second, please." She returned the smile. "My father approves of thrift."

"Wise man." The agent opened a thick book and flipped several pages, then quoted her a price that made her wince inside. She would get the money somehow, though. She had to. "You'll need to change train lines in the Twin Cities," the agent continued. "Get off the Great Northern in St. Paul, then take the Chicago, Milwaukee and St. Paul line through Wisconsin down to Illinois." He closed the book and beamed at her. "Family planning a trip?"

The lie sprang to her lips without thought. "We may visit my brother. He's an artist, you know."

"No, I didn't." He chuckled. "Isn't that just like your father, never saying a word about it. Great city, Chicago. Filthy time of year for travel, though. You want my advice, wait until spring. You tell your father I said so."

She promised she would, thanked him and left. The snow was falling more thickly; she would need to start back now if she hoped to make it home. Without seeing Rhys. Or she could go on to Nilssen's as she'd planned, and afterward take refuge in the Windy Pines Hotel. Mrs. Pryce, who ran the place, would gladly give Andrew Schlegel's daughter a room for the night. Of course, she would have to explain to her parents just what whim had seized her so powerfully that she'd set out for town with the snow flying . . . a shade of embroidery thread or a new hat ribbon she simply couldn't live without?

Abruptly, she turned homeward. She couldn't tell Rhys. It wasn't fair to him. Or to her. She didn't want a baby, a husband, a settled life. Whether in Birch Falls or anywhere else, it would be the same—running the house, minding the child, probably doing all the cooking and cleaning as well. They wouldn't have the money to keep servants. And her dream of living by her pen would fade a little every day until it vanished. Worst of all, she might not even notice until it was gone.

The seed of a plan had come to mind at the station. She let it grow and take shape as she strode onward into the rising wind.

CHAPTER THIRTEEN

"You'll make someone a terrific wife someday, Bogie." Sherri Skovic, Bogart's shift partner, swished out of the office. A sheaf of printouts sprouted from one hand, bound for the "Paid in Full" drawer.

Bogart glanced backward at her. "That's just as funny as the last ten times you said it." He grinned to take the sting from his words, but kept gathering loose paperclips. A handful of them pattered into their plastic holder, next to the neatened row of pens.

She came to eye his handiwork. Sherri was so short, she had to stand on tiptoe to see over his shoulder. One thick, blonde braid grazed his collar. "Why do you bother? We'll only mess them up again when things get busy."

"I like things neat. You get like that when you're the oldest of seven kids who are all total slobs."

"Ronnie's not a slob."

Ronnie was his closest brother, and Sherri's devoted swain. "Is so. It'd kill him to hang up a shirt. And I'm not even going to talk about what he does with his underwear."

With a snort of laughter, she went to dump the printouts in the file drawer. "Bathroom run. Back in a second."

Bogart swept up the last of the paperclips, then started neatening the piles of charge slips. Hands occupied, his mind drifted. Detective Florian should find the check-in list helpful. He wasn't sure whether to hope Florian's quarry was here or not. The man must have done something significantly wrong, or they wouldn't have bothered to chase him all the way up to the Range. Exciting, though, to think of a serious criminal being apprehended in Birch Falls. The last real event in town, three years ago January, had been the near-death of Joanne Witek's husband Bill, who'd fallen through a patch of thin lake ice while cutting a fishing hole.

The approach of a customer made him look up. He froze, then managed to force out, "Can I help you?" with what he hoped was a normal smile. The man leaning against the front desk was Luke Chapman.

Chapman wanted to check out. Bogart took his cash and called up his room record, mind racing for an excuse to delay. The detective was in the coffee shop; he had to let Florian know his quarry was about to slip the net.

"I'm sorry." He gave Chapman his best sad-basset look. "I can't find you in the system. It does that sometimes." Pause, punch keys; silly-me smile, shrug. "I can never remember how to get out of this. Won't take me a minute to look it up." Without waiting for Chapman's reply, Bogart ducked into the office and out the other door into the hall.

"You just missed him," the coffee shop manager told him when he arrived, breathless and barely able to say Florian's name. Jessie Lund looked just like a grandmother of six should, and regarded the restaurant as her personal people-watching playground. No matter where she was in the café, she always knew who came in and who went out. "Left about five minutes ago. Didn't say where he was going. Nice tipper."

Bogart clamped his mouth shut over a swear word. Either Florian had gone to join Chief Powell, or else he was knocking on doors elsewhere in the Pines. God knew how long it would take to run him down. "Thanks," Bogart told Jessie, then sprinted off. Maybe he could find out where Chapman was going.

Back in the office, he loitered for precious seconds while his breathing calmed, then plastered a smile on his face and walked out. "Sorry I kept you wait—"

The lobby was empty. Sherri was back, fiddling with the printer that spat out customer receipts. "I took care of that guy for you. Thought maybe he had to take a leak, he was dancing around so much. Where'd you disappear to, anyway?"

Bogart grabbed his hair and counted silently to five. "Did he say where he was going? Did he give any hint?"

"I didn't ask. You OK?"

"No." A half-acknowledged wish for a minute of fame, buried in his mind since Florian's arrival, flared up and died. He glanced at the computer screen, which still showed Chapman's reservation. At least he had a name. That was something.

"Edward Burke," Florian muttered as he stared at the monitor. "Chapman went to school in Chicago. Of course. How the hell did I miss that?"

Behind him, Powell shifted his weight. "Local celebrity?" They'd come back to the Windy Pines empty-handed; neither car rentals nor bus depot had yielded any trace of Luke Chapman. Now they knew why.

"Aldercritter. Big-shot Chicago pol. In the news a few years back for successfully winning legal guardianship of a crack-addicted foster kid." Florian gave a dry laugh. "Our boy's into wishful thinking. Remember any Burkes from the rental places?"

Powell shook his head. Florian sighed, the controlled exhale of a man trying not to throw something. "Back to the motel circuit. Unless you've got a better idea?"

"Split 'em. Cover more ground faster." At Florian's puzzled look, Powell elaborated. "He was here. He left. Must've had a reason. Either something spooked him, or—"

"He found her."

"Could be."

Florian swore. "You take the Days Inn. They'll talk to you out there." Another two minutes' discussion divided the list between them. Armed with a local map from Bogart, Florian stalked in Powell's wake to the parking lot.

From the front seat of his own car, Powell watched the Chicago cop's taillights recede into the darkness. When they were out of sight, he started the car and cranked the heat, then backed out of the parking space. Once out of the hotel lot, he drove as fast as he dared toward Highway 22. The right-hand turnoff led to the Days Inn. He passed it and took the left-hand one, heading eastward out of town.

Baked-on tuna hot dish was a stubborn thing to scrub off. Jackson scraped a thumbnail across the Pyrex, dislodging fragments of crusted cheese. The running water washed them into the drain-catcher, where they made ugly brown blotches against the white-painted metal.

Linnet had hardly eaten a thing. He felt sorry for her, but also annoyed at the waste of his efforts to make a nice meal. He should talk to that child, tell her how things would be from now on. Get her in school. She spent too much time wandering by herself, getting into who knew what. Taking things that didn't belong to her, like Mary Anne's diary.

He rested his arms against the sink edge. Foamy warm water lapped at his wrists. The child must have found the journal on one of her scrounges through the attic and figured he wouldn't miss it. Slowly, he ran the scrubber sponge around the inside rim of the casserole dish. What harm would it do to let her keep it? There was nothing in it to tell anyone, and no one to tell. He only needed to make sure the book stayed here, where it belonged.

He rinsed the dish, then filled it with fresh soapy water to soak. After drying his hands, he headed toward Linnet's room.

The shriek of the doorbell made him jump. He heard it so rarely, he'd almost forgotten what it sounded like. For an awful moment he imagined Linnet's father on the other side, armed with paperwork that would let him take her away. Then he heard a familiar voice: "Jackson? It's Terry. Got to talk to you."

The night air smelled of snow and pine, a welcome contrast to the lingering odor of tuna and cheese. Linnet sat by her cracked-open window and breathed deep. Christmas smells: sharp dark green, distant white. The thought of Christmas brought a dull ache in her stomach, a pain so familiar she could almost ignore it.

The diary lay open across her lap. Squinting at the small handwriting had given her a mild headache. She rolled her head to ease her stiff neck. Muffled voices reached her from the hallway: her grandfather and someone else, unfamiliar and urgent.

She closed the diary, got up and went to the door. No one ever visited here. She pressed her ear to the cool wood. They used drinking glasses in old movies, but she didn't have one. From the tone of the voices, she guessed the old man and whoever would quit talking the minute she stepped out.

"—don't know where yet. We're tracking him now." That was the strange voice, low and clipped. Angry, and something else. Linnet shivered. She knew the sound of buried fear.

"—haven't seen anybody around." Her grandfather's voice, thin and doubtful. "You're sure?"

"I wish I wasn't. You'd best keep the girl close. Did Grace—?" The stranger's voice cracked, then resumed, flatter and tighter.

"Is Linnet yours? Legally?"

"I wanted to talk to you about that . . ." Her grandfather's words trailed off into muffled sounds, accompanied by footsteps. They were heading for the kitchen.

Linnet strained her ears, but caught nothing more. If she snuck out, they'd hear her door open and clam up for sure. She hovered where she was, clenching and unclenching her hands. Then she buried them in her hair, pulling until it hurt. She wouldn't go with her father. Not even if they called the police to make her. She'd run all the way to Canada first.

She lowered her hands and stared across the room, out the window. Moonlight glowed through a break in the scudding clouds. She could just make out part of the manse, a dark mass in the sudden light. As she watched, a shadow flickered across the snow and disappeared against the house.

Two steps took her to the light switch. She snapped it off, then crept to the window and stared until her eyes watered. Nothing moved except the clouds.

A deer, she told herself. *Or a rabbit.*

Her heart pounded against her ribs. Renewed voices and footsteps in the hall made her start. The visitor was leaving.

She waited for the front door to shut, then went out to her grandfather.

Jackson shut the front door and shot the deadbolt. Lived here for more than forty years and he could count on one hand the number of times he'd had to do that. Damn Luke Chapman to hell, and damn Grace for taking up with him. He clenched a fist against the smooth wood, then slowly unclenched it.

He turned to go back down the hall and saw Linnet. She looked as nerved-up as he felt. All stiff-bodied, like she might bolt if he said the wrong thing. He cleared his throat and tried to smile. "Terry Powell. Came by to chat." He glanced away.

"Used to be sweet on your mother."

Linnet tucked her hands in her sweater sleeves. "Did she like him?"

"Not enough." He fiddled with his glasses. What an old fool he was, to feel so nervous talking to his own granddaughter. "You, uh, you want some cocoa or something?"

Surprise crossed her face, then shy warmth. "Yeah. Sure."

She followed him to the kitchen, her footsteps so light he could barely hear them. Her resigned glance at the lumpy chair cushion made him grin. "Take that off if you want. Get comfortable."

He could feel her watching him as he got out a saucepan and the milk bottle, from which he poured two mugs not quite full. "Milk expands when you heat it. Got to leave room at the top, or it'll overflow."

"I never had this kind before. Only Swiss Miss, with hot water."

"This is better." He looked at her over his shoulder. "You like cinnamon?"

"Yeah." She was almost smiling now. All over a simple cup of cocoa. He took extra care measuring and mixing just the right amounts of cocoa powder, sugar and a touch of milk. A little sweeter than usual—after that oversugared, processed stuff, she might not like bittersweet chocolate. He could share that pleasure with her in time. If Luke Chapman gave him the chance.

He didn't want to think of Chapman now. Instead, he described each step of the cocoa-making process as he did it. "First you mix a paste. Then stir in the rest of the milk slow, so it stays smooth. Then a pinch of cinnamon . . ." He sprinkled it across the steaming milk. The rich scent tickled his nostrils. Their cook had made cocoa just like this, before the bad times came and they had to let her go. He remembered watching her in the kitchen of their big house back in Illinois. Near sixty years gone, that memory. Funny to think of it now.

Just before the milk boiled, he turned off the heat and poured the cocoa into mugs. "Careful," he warned as he handed Linnet one. "It's real hot."

"It smells nice." There was that almost-smile again, turning her plain face pretty enough to make his throat hurt. She was Grace's girl, all right.

He watched her sip her cocoa. Her obvious pleasure in it couldn't disguise the strain beneath, or the stiffness of her posture. He wanted to ask what was wrong, but didn't know how. "Thought we might start you in school, come December," he said, then kicked himself for raising what had to be a touchy subject. Even the awful news about Grace hadn't resigned her to living here. The last thing she likely wanted was any reminder that Birch Falls was home.

"That'd be great. I don't want to get too far behind."

He sipped more cocoa to cover his astonishment. "That's settled, then." Relief swept through him at the awkwardness over with, so much more easily than he'd expected. What was prompting this burst of openness, he couldn't guess and didn't want to. Enough for now that Linnet was talking to him. They might learn to be a family yet, if he didn't mess things up.

"Granddad?"

Her use of the word startled him into setting down his cup. She dropped her gaze to her own, while her thumb played across the handle. "If I want to stay here . . . can I? No matter what?"

He blinked sudden moisture from his eyes. "No matter what," he said through a tight throat. Terry Powell knew a lawyer in town who specialized in custody cases and did pro bono work. Jim Kovacs's card was in his back pocket. He'd call first thing in the morning.

Linnet was drinking again, nose and upper lip hidden in her

mug. The overhead light touched the top of her head with gold. He couldn't ask about the diary now and risk breaking this fragile connection. She wouldn't hurt it; in all these weeks, he'd never seen her treat any object carelessly. He could wait.

Chapter Fourteen

Sunlight poured through the kitchen window, coaxing cheer from the dusty linoleum and plain white walls. Linnet carried her bowl to the sink and rinsed it. She'd almost liked the oatmeal this morning. Living here might not be so bad. At least she could stop being afraid all the time.

Her grandfather drained his coffee cup and pushed back his chair. "We'll go into town tomorrow, get you registered for school. Too much to do today." He gathered up his own dishes and stood holding them while he looked at her. "I, uh . . . I'd rather you didn't go off on your own. I know you're used to it, but—"

"It's okay." She didn't want to hear the reason. As long as neither of them actually said it, she could keep it out of her mind. "Can I come to the house with you?"

He looked at her as if the floor had spoken. Suddenly nervous, she kept talking to fill the silence. "I won't hurt anything or get in the way. I promise."

A slow smile spread across his face. "You haven't yet. Come on along."

Suitably dressed for the cold, they left the cottage together. As he locked the door behind them, her grandfather cleared his throat. "If you find anything you want—old books, or . . . or toys, or anything—you can have it awhile. Just tell me what you found, so I know it isn't missing."

"Okay." She wondered if the diary counted. She should probably tell him about it, now that she knew he wouldn't get angry. She didn't want to yet, though. It was her secret; she wanted to keep it awhile longer.

They walked onward a few steps. "Found anything much so far?"

"Old books. Poetry and stuff." She resisted the impulse to look at him, to see if he believed her.

Silence fell again. Halfway to the house, her grandfather stopped. "Forgot something." He fumbled in his pocket, then handed her the keys. "This one's for the back. Go on and let yourself in; leave these on the windowsill by the door. I'll be there in a minute."

He strode back toward the cottage. Clutching the keys, she flew up the path.

Gilded by sunshine, Schlegel House looked almost cozy despite its size. Rachel gazed at it from the tree line. *Home. Once upon a time.* She wanted to believe it so much, it made her heart flutter in her chest. One hand crept to her coat pocket and touched the wooden rabbit.

She saw no one near the mansion, or around the caretaker's cottage where Jackson and Linnet must live. She shifted from foot to foot, hoping to warm her frozen toes. She should have called Jackson before coming. What if he wasn't here? He might have gone into town for groceries, or paint, or furniture polish, or whatever else he used on the job.

She tightened her hood under her chin and strode toward the house. If Jackson was gone or wanted her to wait, she'd happily explore until he was ready for a break . . . which was what she wanted to do anyway, she realized. He'd given her the guidebook tour yesterday. Today she wanted to see Schlegel House through her own eyes.

All last night, she'd thought about Mary Anne Schlegel. Unable to shake the notion between bouts of fitful sleep, by four A.M. she'd convinced herself that Duncan McGrath was Mary Anne's son. This dead-of-night brainstorm, unlike most, had refused to fade in the cool light of morning. Now she needed proof, and knew of nowhere else to find it.

Bogart at the Pines, who seemed to know everything about everyone, had mentioned yesterday that Jackson was writing a family history. Maybe the old man would let her look at it. He must know every Schlegel story, down to the faintest whisper of an illicit romance or unwanted pregnancy. Funny he hadn't mentioned the book to her. His face rose in her mind, the same image that had woken her twice from troubled dreams: the way he'd stared at her in Mary Anne's bedroom, bloodless and blank-eyed, as if grappling with something impossible. Had he made the same connection she had? If so, it clearly upset him. Much more than it should have. Or was she reading too much into a passing moment, and he'd merely been surprised at an unexpected resemblance?

She stopped a few yards from the mansion to shove loose hair back under her hood. She could just make out footprints between the big house and the cottage. Jackson, starting work early. Powdery snow scattered underfoot as she walked toward the mansion.

The creak of floorboards over his head woke Luke from uneasy sleep. He sat halfway up, grabbing the blankets he'd cadged from an upstairs linen closet. Barely breathing, he listened as the footsteps crossed what must be the kitchen floor. Soft sounds—somebody small or awfully light on their feet. The sounds moved away from him, toward the opposite end of the basement.

He wadded up his makeshift bedding, mind working overtime. If Grace's old man came toward the basement stairs, he could duck behind the furnace and hide in its shadows. Unless the old man was coming to fix the furnace. As he eyed the distance between it and the door that led out to the root cellar, the footsteps passed the stairs and receded.

He stuffed the bedding behind a stack of paint cans, then walked soft-footed to the root cellar door. By a miracle, he'd managed not to break anything battering through it last night. He examined the lock and saw why. The metal tongue barely reached across the door's edge. Instead of snapping the lock, his assault had merely made it slip its hold.

Satisfied that no one could spot his break-in, he cautiously headed upstairs. He couldn't stay in the damned basement all day; he might as well watch his father-in-law awhile. The thought of spying on the old man gave him a pleasing rush of power. The tough bit would be getting through the upstairs door. Thank God the old man kept the locks and hinges well oiled. With patience honed from years of stringing marks along, he turned the handle soundlessly and slipped into the kitchen.

Light footfalls from above told him the old man was heading for the second floor. He stuck his head around the entrance to the back stairwell and glimpsed a slight figure—female, parka hood down. A pair of thin braids trailed over her shoulders.

Her name caught in his throat as his brain caught up with his instincts. If he called out to her, she'd probably run. He watched her reach the second floor and start down the hallway, then followed.

The fifth step creaked. He froze, waiting for sounds of flight or of Linnet coming to investigate. After a minute of silence, he allowed himself to breathe again. Old houses made random noises; she must have figured it was one of those. Feeling his way with extra caution, he ascended the staircase and found himself looking down a long, empty corridor. Linnet must have gone behind one of the shut doors.

The first was the linen closet from which he'd stolen his blankets. The second led to a room with an old-fashioned sewing machine, two dressmakers' dummies and assorted pieces of furniture that would have turned a nice dollar in an antique shop. He was about to go try the third door when he heard a woman call out from downstairs. "Hello? Mr. Schlegel? It's Rachel Connolly . . ."

Luke eased inside the sewing room and held the door shut.

Jackson glanced around Linnet's bedroom. No diary. She wasn't likely to come back here soon, with Schlegel House to explore, but work was waiting. Where would he hide a diary, if he were thirteen years old and unsure if it would get him in trouble?

The desk yielded drafts of his own manuscript, his Grandfather Randolph's memory box, a stash of yellowed stationery and the usual flotsam: pencils, pens, paper clips, rubber bands. A quick feel under the blankets and pillowcase likewise turned up empty. Setting aside a guilty twinge, he rifled through Linnet's small suitcase. Nothing. He searched every nook and cranny as methodically as he could manage. The diary was nowhere to be found.

Rachel's voice sounded small and thin in the huge kitchen. Jackson must be around; she couldn't imagine him leaving the back door unlocked otherwise. Yet no one answered, and she heard no activity. Maybe he'd gone to the cottage to get something.

She strolled out to the front hallway and called once more. The answering silence was thick enough to touch. She closed her eyes and breathed deep. The house smelled of old wood and dusty fabric, with a hint of fresh varnish. Somewhere upstairs, a window rattled. The sound died away, leaving a renewed quiet so profound she could almost hear the walls breathing.

Unnerved by her own fancy, she opened her eyes. The huge staircase gleamed in the sunlight. Despite its warm brown glow, the curving banister felt cold. Step by step, she mounted the stairs. She felt as if she'd walked inside *Sleeping Beauty,* as if no one but herself had set foot in this house for a hundred years.

Her feet took her past Jonas Schlegel's room, past the master bedroom and the schoolroom and the upstairs parlor. The door to Mary Anne's room was closed. Hadn't she left it open yesterday? She laid a hand on the doorknob, her heart pounding. Absurd, to be this nervous. She wasn't going to hurt anything. All she wanted was another look at the portrait.

She opened the door and halted on the threshold. Linnet was curled in a corner of the window seat, knees drawn up, hugging a book to her chest.

After a moment, Rachel collected her wits. "I'm sorry. I didn't mean to disturb you."

"I thought you might come up." Linnet's eyes never left hers. One thumb moved back and forth across the book's back cover.

She took a few steps into the room. "Interesting reading?"

"Mary Anne's diary." Linnet looked down at it, loosening her grip just enough to touch the front. "I found it in an old trunk in the attic. Nobody wanted it. They just left it up there." She splayed her hand across the book, as if drawing comfort from its feel. Then she held it out to Rachel.

Slowly, Rachel crossed the room and took the little volume. She sank down on the empty half of the window seat and opened the front cover. *Mary Anne Schlegel. 1892* . . . Her breath caught as she riffled through the book, noting dates here and there. *June, 1892 . . . December . . . January, 1893.* . . .

Half a dozen responses arose in her mind. She looked at Linnet and words died on her lips. The girl was picking at a loose thread on one knee of her jeans, intent as a neurosurgeon removing a brain tumor.

"Thank you," Rachel murmured.

Linnet briefly stopped her picking, but didn't look up. "If you find out who your family is . . . will you tell me?"

The murmur of voices carried through the crack in the sewing-room door, but not clearly enough for Luke to make out words. He snuck into the hallway, getting as close to the voices as he dared. If one of them came out suddenly, they'd walk right into him. But he had to know who this Connolly woman was and what she wanted with his daughter.

". . . not so bad, really. Once you get used to it." Linnet sounded like she was trying to convince herself.

"I bet it's pretty in the summer." Soft voice, good diction. No local accent. From Minneapolis, maybe. He thought about edging close enough for a look. "Come June, I bet those gardens are covered in flowers."

"They'll look nice then." Poor Linnie, she sounded so sad. God knew what bullshit the old man had told her about him. He wondered if she knew about Grace, what whoever told her might have said.

"You know what kind of tree this is?"

Christ, trees and flowers. Why would some strange woman be sitting in a bedroom with his kid, gabbing about stupid shit like that?

The effort to move noiselessly forward made him lose Linnet's answer. He could see them now, through the gap between the hinges. Linnet was visible from the knees down, in faded jeans and battered sneakers. *Damned old bastard's too cheap to buy her boots.* The Connolly woman was wearing a red cloth coat instead of a gray sweater, but he recognized her from Valentini's. What was she doing here?

The red coat bothered him. He'd seen it before. A flash of red around a street corner, next to thin legs in faded jeans and the bottom of a purple parka. Linnie, vanishing from an empty street.

A stone settled in the pit of his stomach. She'd taken Linnie somewhere that day, this woman in red. This out-of-towner who came by looking for Grace's old man and spent time with his own daughter. This stranger who obviously wasn't, if she could just walk into this showplace and hang out like it was her living room. Old Man Schlegel must have called Social Services and gotten himself a watchdog. Rachel Connolly was here to keep Linnet out of Luke's hands.

He wanted to kick the door off its hinges, grab the interfering bitch by the throat and toss her out the window. Instead, he clenched his hands until the nails bit skin. The pain cleared his head long enough to master his outrage. Moving slow and quiet, he retraced his steps to the sewing room. With the door shut behind him, he sat on the nearest overstuffed chair and considered his predicament.

Social Services was in the game. That meant the old man planned to fight. Luke sat back in the chair, fingers drumming on its fat arms as he felt the adrenaline burn. Dad-in-law would get a lot more fight than he wanted—starting with little Miss Do-Gooder down the hall.

CHAPTER FIFTEEN

"Linnet?!" Jackson burst through the mansion's back door. "Linnet!"

The sharpness of his voice pulled him up short. He'd frighten the child half to death if he didn't calm down. Hands clenched in his pockets, he forced himself to walk at a normal pace to the front of the house. "Linnet? You upstairs?"

His pulse hammered in his ears. Thoughts of the missing diary loomed like a symbol from a nightmare, heralding more losses to come. Superstitious claptrap, his good sense told him, but his gut didn't believe it. He wanted that book back in his own hands, the sooner the better.

"Coming . . ." Thin and nervous, Linnet's answer floated down. Up in Mary Anne's room again. He started toward the stairs to meet her. The sound of two sets of footsteps made him halt with one foot on the bottom stair. Who in the name of God could Linnet be with?

When he saw her at the top of the staircase, all the blood in his body seemed to rush toward his heart. He could feel the hard knot of it pressing against his lungs. Rachel Connolly was just behind Linnet, carrying the diary.

As they reached him, he forced a nod for Miss Connolly and a smile for his granddaughter. "Guess I don't have to ask now." He gestured toward the little book. "Noticed yesterday Mary Anne's journal was gone from her trunk. I wanted to make sure Linnet had it safe. The Trust wouldn't like it to go missing."

Lord God, he sounded awful. He might as well have the word
"liar" branded on his forehead. Linnet looked down at her toes.
He could see her shrinking further into herself with every word.
Not an hour ago, she'd wanted his company, and here he was
driving her straight back into her shell. Yet he couldn't stop
talking. "Part of the family history and all—got to be extra careful with things like that." Sweet Jesus, he was babbling now.
Another minute and they'd both think he was crazy.

Miss Connolly touched Linnet's shoulder. "Your granddaughter was kind enough to show me this. If it's all right with
you, I'd like to read it. I'll stay here, if you want. I just—" She
broke off, looking embarrassed. "I'm afraid I wasn't entirely
honest with you the other day, Mr. Schlegel. I am writing a
book, and I was interested in Jonas—but not for the reason I
said." She gave him a hesitant smile. Suddenly, he knew what
was coming. He wanted to clap his hands over his ears, or press
them to her mouth until he forced the words back down her
throat. Instead, he stood numbly and listened.

"I think we may be related. I'm not sure; I don't have all the
pieces yet. I didn't want to say anything without having a clearer
idea. But I have records linking Jonas Schlegel with my maternal
grandfather. He was adopted as a baby. I thought at first Jonas
might be the father, but when you told me about Mary
Anne . . ." She glanced down at the diary. "She wrote this
around the time she ran away. It might tell me whether or not
Mary Anne Schlegel is my great-grandmother . . . or at least
point me in another direction for proof." Her eyes met his, in a
plea he desperately wanted to ignore. "I'm not asking to take it,
or keep it. I just want to know what it has to tell."

He couldn't think how to refuse. Just saying no, with no good
reason he could admit to, would make him look like the hard-
souled old man Linnet had believed he was. For a moment he
hated Rachel Connolly—outsider, disrupting everything, mak-

ing him risk his grandchild's affection along with his dreams for their future. Then a thought, clear and bright as a headlamp, cut through the darkness in his head. *She doesn't know about the money. She can't get what she doesn't know exists.*

He clung to that idea as he answered. "See you take care with it."

"I will. Thank you." Her smile lit up the hallway. Suddenly, shockingly, she kissed him on the cheek. With a short nod, he fled from the gesture and the bright hope in her face. He could sense Linnet watching him as he strode toward the kitchen.

Work would steady him. He hung up his coat and rolled up his shirtsleeves, taking some comfort from the knowledge that at least nothing else could go wrong.

Luke lingered in the sewing room until the receding voices and footfalls told him an escape route was clear. Wired up as a cat on the prowl, he crept down the back stairs and outside. He didn't want to stick around while the old man was there—not until Linnet understood how things were going to be.

In the meantime, he needed to pick up a few things, like food and a hot plate. Who'd have figured the huge pile of house behind him wouldn't have a real stove? The big black thing that passed for one burned wood, for Chrissake. Not much good for heating up soup, or making himself instant coffee on a cold night. He'd have to watch what he bought. He was shorter on cash than he liked, plus he'd need some bucks to deal with Rachel Connolly.

He passed scattered trailers, mostly tin boxes built to look like half-assed knockoffs of houses. Summer places, probably, homes away from home for enthusiastic fishermen and other lovers of the great outdoors. Fools who didn't understand that beer was made to be drunk in the comfort of your own living room, preferably in front of a large-screen TV with a bowl of beer nuts, not bobbing around some pisspot excuse for a lake in a rickety boat pretending to catch dinner while clouds of gnats buzzed around your head. Luke slowed as he pondered the trailers. One or two ought to have something worth swiping, and no sales clerks to remember his face.

Right now, he wanted a decent breakfast. Eggs and bacon, and other things nobody'd keep in a dinky kitchen from summer to winter. He dug a wad of bills from his jacket and counted them as he walked. Meal and a hot plate, no problem. And surely even this hick town had one diner worth the name.

"So that's it." Sitting on the edge of the guest chair in Powell's office, Florian rubbed his thumbs across his eyelids. He hadn't slept well. "Between us we've got three possibles." Forehead resting in his hand, he tangled his fingers in his hair. Frustration made him want to pull it until he yelped, just to have something tangible to be angry at. "You got enough people to stake out three motels until our maybe-Chapmans turn up?"

Powell nodded. Florian watched him pace over to the coffee-maker and top off his cup for the fourth time in an hour. Something was eating the man again; he could see it in the tightness of Powell's movements. He considered provoking another argument to make the chief open up, but felt too discouraged to make the effort. Nothing to do now except watch for his suspects and pray . . . and do a lot of cursing if they all turned out to be somebody else. He clenched a fist against his forehead and thought of Ruthie. Now he knew how she must feel every goddamn day.

He opened his eyes to find Powell staring at him, the way doctors look at the families of dying patients. The taut "What?" came out before he could stop it.

"One more place he might be." Powell's expression grew grimmer.

Do I have to pull it out with your teeth?! "Where?"

"Schlegel House." Powell's shoulders sagged a fraction, as if merely naming the place weighed him down. "Mansion just outside town. Museum piece. Grace's home, in a manner of speaking. Her father takes care of it." He paused, as if gathering his resolve. "She sent her girl to him. Been here about ten days."

Florian straightened in his chair. "You knew. Yesterday. You knew where she was."

Powell cradled his coffee mug in one big hand. "I didn't know what might happen to her if I spoke up. Seemed safer to keep quiet."

The chief's misgivings echoed Florian's own. His initial flash of anger died, replaced by a thrill of hope. Maybe they could finally nail this bastard. "And Chapman would know about Whatsit House?"

"Tourist attraction. Bogie Nilssen at the Pines probably gave him a brochure." He tightened his grip on the mug. "Place closes after Labor Day. There'd be no one out there except Jackson and the girl."

Florian stood up and started buttoning his coat. "How about you and I change that?"

Halfway back to the mansion and the coffee was still warm. Luke sipped, savoring the heat that bled through the Styrofoam and his thin knit gloves. The hot plate in its plastic bag swung from one arm. Buying it had been a risk, but the trailer people were less likely to have one than to have food he could use. Canned stuff, instant coffee, maybe some crackers or chips. He could eat hot soup tonight, a welcome change from packaged chocolate-chip cookies going stale.

The legal research hadn't gone badly, either. Now he knew what to file and how to file it, and also what move Grace's old man would likely make: temporary emergency custody, alleging domestic violence. But he'd never hit Linnet in her life, and smacking Grace across the chops a few times didn't matter a damn under Minnesota law. He'd found that lucky provision all dressed up in legalese, Section 257.825 of the state statutes on parentage: "The court shall not consider conduct of a proposed custodian that does not affect the custodian's relationship to the child." Schlegel's lawyer could argue himself silly over whether slapping Grace around meant Luke would hurt Linnet, while his own side pointed to the total lack of evidence that he'd ever been anything but a loving daddy.

The cop from Chicago might yet manage to make a manslaughter case, but that still didn't make Luke a child abuser—and Minnesota courts weren't allowed to consider just one factor in deciding custody. He had plenty in his favor that would outweigh violence toward his runaway wife. If all else failed, he could file a custody petition in Illinois, then work on Linnet while the two states' courts tossed jurisdiction back and forth. By the time they decided who got to say what, he'd have her begging to live with him—and at thirteen, she was old enough to make the guys in black robes pay attention.

First thing tomorrow, he'd go see Jim Kovacs and get the paperwork rolling. Of the five lawyers in the local phone book, only Kovacs based his practice in Birch Falls. He worked out of his home: a big frame house, well kept, in what passed for the rich part of town. The place had impressed Luke, walking by to check it out. Manicured grass under the thin snow, squared-off evergreens, fresh paint job. Anyone who paid that much attention to detail was his man—plus, it'd be hell getting anywhere else without a rental car in this godforsaken end of Minnesota.

He stepped up on the highway verge and swigged coffee while he surveyed the road. Empty in both directions. The snow posed a problem, but he could always come back with a branch and brush his footprints away. He walked further up the verge, then stepped through the rails of the low wooden fence that marked the boundary of his first target's property.

A loose latch on a back window was an unexpected piece of luck. Luke hefted himself through the opening and into the trailer's tiny kitchen. A cupboard by the refrigerator yielded three cans of soup and two of chili. He dropped his bounty into the bag with his hot plate.

From the next empty trailer, a hundred yards down the road, he took some canned beef stew and a jar of instant coffee. A brief trip to the bathroom suggested a few other items. The plumbing at the old mansion worked fine, and he needed to look decent for the next several days. A bar of soap, some cheap razors, a washcloth and a towel went into the plastic bag. It was starting to bulge. At the next place he'd swipe a garbage bag.

He walked outside and froze at the sound of a car approaching. Keeping well in the trailer's shadow, he watched it go by: a big brown road barge, burning a little oil by the smell. "Chevy Impala," he murmured, tagging its make out of habit. Years back, he'd made a party game out of naming passing cars. No one had ever beaten him at it. He gave the Impala plenty of time to vanish, then headed toward his next stop.

. . . Outside the train window, the world looks frozen in time . . . except for me, rushing through it, bound for an unknown city and a future I can't even guess at. Lord knows what Jonas will say. I wish I'd dared write to him. What will I do if he's gone—off on one of his jaunts to Europe, or across the country?

He won't be. He'll be there.

This is a new beginning. I have to remember that. My new beginning. And my baby's.

Poor Rhys. Will he guess? It seems cruel not to tell him, and equally cruel to do so. Perhaps when the time comes, I'll have a clearer head about it. Just now, it takes all my strength not to admit how scared I am. Please, dear Jonas, be home! I don't want to lose myself in a huge city, where not a living soul knows or cares whether Mary Anne Schlegel lives or dies—

"Jackson? You around?"

Loud and tense, the strange voice roused Rachel from her reading. She dragged her mind back to her present surroundings. Fat-cushioned chair beneath and behind her, smelling of dust; thin sunlight gilding the floorboards and Turkish carpet near the tall front windows; mahogany furniture gleaming darkly against cream-and-gold striped wallpaper. Footsteps in the front hall, heavy and masculine. She closed the diary and walked out to see who it was.

Two men stood by the front door, in long coats but bare-headed despite the cold day. The taller of the two looked familiar: an interesting face, with an ill-healed broken nose. His companion, slightly shorter but built like a mountain, wore a policeman's uniform under his outerwear. "He's cleaning upstairs, I think," she told them.

Mountain-Man gave her a wary look, with more than a hint of surprise in it. "And you'd be?"

She smiled and held out a hand in a gesture calculated to disarm. "Rachel Connolly. Mr. Schlegel knows I'm here; I'm researching for a book."

Some of the tension left the big man as he grasped her hand. "Terry Powell. Chief of police." The last name caught her attention, but he continued before she could speak. "Could you tell me how you got here, and about what time?"

"Around nine-thirty. I walked from town." His manner suggested this wasn't the time to ask if he was related to the Rhys Powell in the diary who might be her great-grandfather. Powell and his partner were clearly on official business. She could track him down for a chat another day.

"Seen anyone around besides Jackson?"

"Just Linnet. His granddaughter." She nodded toward the half-open door to the parlor. "I've been reading in there. Can't say I've paid attention to much else for the past little while."

Powell shot the taller man a look.

"Trip into town, maybe," the other man said.

"Or we bet wrong."

The man smiled without mirth. "How much would you stake on that?"

"Terry?"

All three of them looked up. Jackson, swathed from collar to knee in a heavy cotton apron spattered with wet spots, was coming down the stairs. "There some kind of trouble?"

"Your son-in-law." Powell met him near the bottom of the staircase. "He may be camping out here."

"We'd like to search the house and set up a stakeout," the second man said. "If he came here, he's bound to be back before dark."

Jackson gripped the newel post as if for balance. "You talk to Jim Kovacs yet?" Powell said, more gently.

"Tomorrow." Jackson blinked, apparently dazed by whatever tragedy seemed to be looming. "Got an appointment at eleven."

"Keep it." Powell clasped the old man's shoulder, then glanced at his companion. "We'll start in the cellars."

The policemen moved off, Jackson leading the way. The son-in-law must be Linnet's father. At the coffee shop the other day, Linnet had said her mother was dead. . . . A chill crept down Rachel's spine, which she swiftly shook off. *Family custody disputes almost always get nasty. Linnet's mom probably died when she was three or something.*

She went back to her comfortable chair, opened the diary and propped it on her lap, but found herself gazing at the tight script without reading it. Too many secrets uncovered in too short a time; she was having trouble taking it all in. She flipped through the rest of the pages, all of them crammed with words. As she turned back toward the page where she'd stopped, she caught a glimpse of penciled lines and curves. There was a drawing on the inside front cover. A portrait of a young man, with deep-set eyes, high cheekbones and a pencil stuck behind one ear. The signature at the bottom—R. Powell—looked familiar. Or was it only because she'd been seeing him for half the morning through Mary Anne's eyes?

She peered at the signature again. It *was* familiar . . . from the Windy Pines. She'd last seen it on the squirrel sketch in her room.

Bogart could probably tell her where that sketch had come from. Or maybe Chief Powell could, assuming he was willing to make small talk with an out-of-town civilian. *Good-looking guy, Rhys. I'm not surprised Mary Anne fell for him.* She felt a pang of sympathy for the long-gone young man. He must have guessed the reason behind Mary Anne's flight, and yet he never knew for sure if he had a child. Unless she'd told him after all.

Rachel found herself hoping so. She turned back to her stopping-place and resumed reading.

It was a little early to come back, but Luke was tired of lugging his loot around. He could see Schlegel House through the tree line. The sun had vanished behind creeping clouds; in the gray-tinged light, the mansion looked like a house of shadows.

Caution made him follow the trees closely around the house to the garage—a wide, squat building with half-doors that must have been stables before Birch Falls got the automobile. He could stash his takings there, hide himself if necessary. On a cold day like this, the old man likely wasn't planning to work on his transmission.

The sight of a car next to the stables made him halt. A Chevy Impala, big and brown. He swallowed, mouth gone dry. Probably the old man's car. *Old bastard must've gone to town for something earlier.*

He frowned at the car. He hadn't seen it here this morning, on his quick way out the back. If it was in the garage then, why park it outside now? Unless the old man had more errands to run. He looked around the grounds for a good minute, but saw no one. After dropping the loaded bag behind a gnarled pine tree, he headed toward the Impala.

Another quick look as he reached the vehicle told him he was still safe. He crouched down next to it and peeked in the passenger-side window. Attached to the dashboard was a handset radio. An inert revolving light sat near it, on the ledge between the front seats.

He backed away from the Impala and ran for the trees. His shoulder blades crawled, as if an unseen gun had a bead on him. The fucking cop was here, probably with local backup. He grabbed his bag without breaking stride, not slowing down until a thick screen of trees lay between him and Schlegel House.

Back to the last trailer he'd hit, the one with the rifle by the door. No other trailers lay between it and the mansion, which meant he only had to worry about observers from one direction. With no one around to report a break-in, he ought to be safe there. He gripped the bag tighter as he stumbled onto the road.

CHAPTER SIXTEEN

2 March, 1893

Noise, smoke, steam, crowds. Hordes of people, in fine suits and silk dresses or tatty homespun and ragged shawls. Bells clanging, engines snorting, train wheels screaming, and everywhere the bawling cries: "All aboard!" "Chicago, end of the line!" "Next stop, St. Louis!" or any of a hundred other places even farther away. And I in the midst of this Bedlam, like a strip of bark in a churning creek. The current pushes me where it will. I have no strength to resist it.

Dear Lord, what manner of place have I come to?

Walls and rushing people loomed, ghostlike, through clouds of locomotive smoke. Breathing it, Mary Anne tasted metal. A million sounds echoed from the stone pile that was the Van Buren Street Station: wheezing train brakes, shrieking whistles, voices shouting in a dozen languages, and everywhere the clash of steel on steel.

Knots of men and women bore down on her from five different directions. None of them appeared to notice her, lingering on the platform like a dazed bird fallen from its nest. A family of five in patched woolens—all but the baby chattering in a tongue she'd never heard—sidestepped her without a glance. A well-dressed man in a greatcoat and bowler hat jostled her with his large leather case. She stumbled, then recovered. Drawing breath for an indignant remark, she found herself facing his retreating back. With a weary sigh, she gripped her small valise more firmly and headed deeper into the station. She had no idea where the exit lay, but anything seemed preferable to being bumped and buffeted by the unending stream of people.

The crowds barely thinned as she made her way through the station. Twice she nearly lost her hat, and once something tugged sharply at her bag. A thousand conversations echoed through the cavernous halls, accompanied by a million footfalls and the gradually dimming clangor of the trains. Ahead of her, a gap appeared in the wall of moving bodies. She clapped her free hand over her hat and shot toward it. Spying another clear space, she aimed for it and slipped through just in time to avoid stepping on someone's trailing hem. Jumping the gaps like stones in a stream, she moved forward until she could see doors looming ahead: the street exit at last.

Outside proved no refuge from the noise and bustle. Mary Anne flattened herself against the wall to avoid getting trampled, then edged away from the station doors. On the far side of an ornamental pillar, she finally found space to breathe. She eased her bag to the pavement and rolled her shoulders to relieve a knot. Pain gone, it was easier to keep at bay the fear she'd struggled with ever since her departure. Right now she needed a map, or at least sensible directions to 2425 Taylor Street.

From the clump of people approaching, she chose the likeliest target: a prosperous-looking gentleman in a long black coat and bowler. "Excuse me," she began as he drew even with her. "Can you tell me wh—"

The man brushed past her without breaking stride. So did her next choice, a middle-aged matron in lavender. A nervous-looking younger woman in a ragged straw hat actually sped up as Mary Anne approached her, as if afraid of exchanging a civil word with a stranger. Two men in smutched overalls and flat caps passed by, jabbering in what might have been Czech. The younger one raised his cap to her, but gave an embarrassed shrug when she started to question him. None of the other passersby paid her the slightest notice. She sank against the wall, gripping her valise hard enough to hurt her palms.

A gust of wind whipped around the corner. It cut straight through her coat and gloves. Eyes and cheeks stinging, she huddled closer to the scant shelter of the pillar. She couldn't stay here forever, and she doubted the city authorities would let her sleep in the station. She turned up her coat collar, hefted her bag, and started walking.

Late-afternoon light glanced off the windows of the taller buildings. Her steps slowed as the spectacle of the city center gradually overwhelmed her fear. Before long, she ceased to mind the bumps and jostles of the hurrying crowd. The towering buildings held all her attention. Six stories . . . eight . . . ten . . . fourteen stories! She looked up, shading her eyes with one hand. The nearest giant pile of dark brick seemed about to topple down on her. Dizzy and frightened, she stumbled backward.

A none-too-gentle hand shoved her upright as someone swore in her ear. "Damned off-the-boaters! Watch where you're going!"

The voice was young, female, speaking clear English. Mary Anne clutched the gloved hand on her shoulder. Its owner, in a gray wool coat and matching hat just like the ones in the latest Montgomery Ward catalogue, regarded her with annoyance. "Leave go, willya? I gotta get home!"

"Please!" Mary Anne clasped the strange girl's hand harder, then made herself release it. "How do I get to Taylor Street?"

"Number Ten trolley car." Looking a fraction less irritated, the girl jerked her head leftward. "Stops right over there. West side of the street." She disappeared into the flow of people before Mary Anne could thank her.

Mary Anne looked around and spied a small clump of people on a corner, three sitting on a narrow bench and several more standing. Waiting for the Number Ten trolley, presumably. She hurried to join them, suddenly afraid of missing it.

The Number Ten arrived after almost as many minutes, pulling up to the stop as if drawn by invisible horses. Mary Anne gaped at it as her fellow passengers squeezed themselves into the already substantial crowd aboard. How did it move, with no horse to draw it or train engine to push it? Automatically, she followed the last pair of feet up the short steps and into the overflowing car. A leather strap dangled in front of her. She grabbed it just in time to keep from toppling into an old woman's parcel-filled lap as the car started with a jerk. Metal screeched on metal somewhere beneath the floor. Some kind of pulley, between the car wheels and whatever lay beneath the street.

Buffeted by bodies, assaulted by the odors of sweat and old wool and a nearby passenger's foul cigar, clinging for dear life to a frail leather loop and with no clear notion of where she was heading, Mary Anne found herself grinning. She was riding a marvel, down a busy street in a city boiling over with more people than had probably ever lived in the Iron Range. The first city of America, or soon to be, if anything Jonas had ever written her about Chicago was true. Her city now. Her home.

The car stopped, took on more passengers and started again. The conductor bawled out the fare. Twisting in the press of people, Mary Anne managed to work a coin from an inner coat pocket. She dropped it into an anonymous hand rimmed in a dark blue uniform sleeve, then turned as best she could to stare out the window. As if waiting for her gaze, a row of electric streetlights bloomed to life against the purpling sky. Another marvel. She watched them, wide-eyed as a child on Christmas, while the Number Ten rattled onward into the gathering night.

Almost an hour later, a footsore Mary Anne reached Taylor Street. She'd missed the nearest stop, then gotten disoriented in the dark and wandered down side streets in search of a familiar name. Narrow, two-story townhouses and three-flats with scraps of yards shared the dimly lit blocks with greengrocers, bakeries and taverns. She hurried past these last, frightened by the bursts of drunken singing and occasional loud disputes. Once, a door opened and a burly drinker came flying out to land in the gutter not ten feet from where she'd halted. In the spill of light from the doorway, she caught a glimpse of wild brown curls and beard stubble. The drunk swore, picked himself up, slapped his dusty flat cap on his head and staggered back into the tavern. Mary Anne ran past it, praying to find Taylor Street soon.

The odor of frying garlic eventually led her in the right direction, to a clapboard townhouse two doors down from a small Italian eatery. The scents of fresh bread and coffee, mingled with garlic and tomato, tickled her nose as she passed the little restaurant. She could just recall her last meal: two bites of a ham sandwich, choked down with a cup of thin tea bought from a vendor on the St. Paul train. The rest of the sandwiches had likely gone stale by now. She wondered if Jonas ate here, or if he'd learned to cook for himself. Her stomach rumbled, but her money was running low, and salvation surely lay just a few yards up the street.

Heart hammering in her chest, she approached the townhouse. Light burned in the upper windows. As she mounted the steep front steps, the door opened. A nearby street lamp revealed a lanky man with thinning gold hair and a half-familiar profile, holding a dishpan.

She drew a breath, but couldn't speak. The man shifted the dishpan and closed the door behind him, then saw her. Seconds crawled by as they stared at each other. Then Mary Anne found her voice.

"Jonas?" The quaver, unexpected, embarrassed her. "Can I stay with you awhile?"

Mary Anne set down her pen and flexed her toes. How wonderful to have warm feet free of high-button boots. She stretched her writing hand, easing a mild cramp. Wonderful, too, to be able to write in a heated room, nestled in a comfortable chair drawn up to a table. Much better than propping a book on one's knees, battling the wind and frozen fingers to set down something intelligible. Until now, she'd never properly appreciated such luxuries.

A creak and a mutter drew her attention toward the sofa, where Jonas had thrown himself. His soft gray tweed trousers and plain white shirt stood out against the cushions, striped cream and a faded chocolate-brown. Sketchbook propped against a drawn-up leg, he was murmuring to himself as he scratched his head with the blunt end of a charcoal pencil. The gesture reminded her so much of Rhys that for a moment her throat hurt.

She gripped her journal to banish the pang. The corners dug into her fingers. She was here and Rhys was in Birch Falls, hundreds of miles away. Nothing could change that, or make her decision to leave any less right.

Rather than dwell on painful thoughts, she studied Jonas. The years had changed him less than she'd expected. He still made her think of a child's stick-figure drawing given flesh and a suit of clothes. A penny-sized pink circle peeked through his hair at the crown of his head, and he had laugh lines around his eyes. She could scarcely recall him laughing at home.

A soft chuffing reached them from the apartment's tiny kitchen. The kettle was boiling. Before she could move, Jonas flipped his sketchbook shut and rolled to his feet. With a lopsided grin and a sit-down wave, he vanished down the narrow hall. He moved easily now, lightly. She remembered watching him when she was younger, walking as if his stomach hurt. Whatever else might be said of sprawling, noisy Chicago, the city clearly agreed with Jonas. She resolved it would agree with her, too.

Faint rattling and banging floated down the hallway: Jonas, assembling the tea things. A stuck drawer shrieked, followed by a muffled curse. Mary Anne chuckled softly. It felt good to laugh. Mellowed by warmth, security and the promise of tea, she sank back in her chair and surveyed the small parlor.

The sofa, a faded armchair and her own armless seat shared the room with the table at which she sat. A second low table stood near the room's center; a battered sideboard held two lamps, one made to look like a leaping fish. The far wall was taken up with a trio of overflowing bookcases. A rag rug partly covered the floor; the bare boards beneath, where she could see them, were scuffed with years of shoe marks. Sketches and paintings, many of them Jonas's work, dotted the papered walls. She got up for a closer look at one: a broad-shouldered man with a fox-like face, easy smile half-hidden behind the drooping ends of his thick mustache. He was sitting on the edge of a pier, trousers rolled up to his knees, arms propped on one bent leg while the other dangled just above the water. The picture suggested affection for the subject. The man must be a close friend.

Jonas reappeared, tea tray in both hands. He set it down on the low table and poured two cups. "Last time I saw you, you only drank weak tea for stomach complaints. Take anything?"

"Sugar, if you have it. One lump." She came to sit beside him, accepting the cup he handed her. A flowerlike scent rose from the steaming liquid. She took a cautious sip, then another. It was like drinking perfume.

Jonas raised his own cup. "Jasmine tea. You can get it in Chinatown. Aly likes it, so we keep it on hand."

215

She drank more tea, wondering who Aly was. So far, she'd seen no sign of a woman's presence. Jonas would surely have written her if he'd married or gotten engaged. Perhaps Aly was a mistress. *Not that I'd have any right to be shocked.*

"Thank you again for letting me stay. I'll try not to be more of a disruption than I can help."

"A welcome disruption." The warmth of his smile made her want to cry. "I don't miss much about Birch Falls, but I did miss you. All the letters in the world couldn't show me my little sister, growing up every day."

"Sometimes I lived for your letters."

"Likewise." He sipped, cheeks pinking. "How is Julia?"

Devastated came to mind. "Not terribly happy about me, I expect," she temporized. "Aside from that, well enough. She was helping me with my writing for awhile." She hesitated, unsure whether to say more. "I think she was lonely after you left. She's been lonely for a long time."

Silence fell. Not for the first time since deciding to leave, Mary Anne felt assailed by guilt. *Now it's just Mother and Father. No one to tend to except him, no one to dream for. Nothing to do except tinker with the gardens and keep Father happy. If anyone can. But I couldn't stay, even without the baby. I'd have gone staring mad.*

"Are you going to keep the baby?" Jonas asked.

She shook her head. "I hoped you might know how to place it in a good home." Gently, she spread one hand over the barely visible bulge in her stomach. "I don't want it, but somebody will. I owe my baby that."

Jonas stared into his tea. "I'd take it myself if I could."

She touched his arm. "Not many bachelors would even think of taking on an infant—and you need your freedom, just like I do."

He glanced at her, then away again as he cleared his throat.

"Aly should be home soon."

Not fond of children, his mistress. Or something. Clearly, Aly was a delicate subject. She refilled their teacups and steered the conversation to safer ground. "The baby should come before you leave for Europe. Assuming I've counted right."

He clasped her hand. "Never you worry about that. I'll stay in town as long as you need me."

Tears welled up then, for the first time since leaving home. Jonas pulled her close in a rough hug. They held each other for a few minutes, until self-consciousness made her pull away. She wasn't some sniveling heroine in a penny dreadful. Jonas must think her a complete coward.

From a trouser pocket, he unearthed a creased but clean handkerchief. She took it with a watery laugh and wiped her face. "Now that's over with, I can start thinking about what to do after the baby comes. How does an overeducated rich man's daughter earn a living here?"

"That might not be necessary." Jonas drank tea. "Let me talk to Uncle William. He helped me quite a bit when I first came here, until I could afford to keep myself. He has money enough; I'm sure he'd be willing to part with some on your behalf."

"Not until after the baby comes. Even the most generous uncle may balk at helping a niece who's unmarried and expecting."

They lapsed into silence once more. "Did you tell Rhys?" Jonas asked after awhile.

"No." She didn't want to talk about Rhys just now.

After a long pause, he drained his teacup and set it down. "You might want to reconsider. Sometimes nothing's worse than not knowing for certain."

She traced the handle of her own cup with one finger. "I'll think about it."

"We'll see Uncle William in October, then." He grinned at

her. "Or thereabouts."

She managed a smile. "October."

"You see my problem, Mr. Schlegel." The speaker was a corpulent man in his late fifties, wearing a finely tailored suit as if it were a burlap sack. His watch-chain would likely measure the perimeter of the dining-room table. William wondered sourly just how much of his own money had gone into his creditor's ensemble.

He plastered a smile on his face. "Of course, Mr. Yerkes. A businessman needs to make a profit. I understand that." He leaned back in his chair, brushing his graying beard in a deliberately casual gesture. "And I assure you, you will. Everything I owe you, plus considerable interest. If you could simply wait a short while, until certain other investments come in—"

"Kickbacks," Yerkes said. "I know all about your political 'investments,' Schlegel. I also know how many others you've touched for a bit of ready over the past few years. Even if the aldermen you've bought deliver, how many of us have to fight for a piece of that pie? Your more savory enterprises won't pay off for years, if ever. I can't wait. I've a few investments of my own down in Springfield, which must be tended to or I'll lose them." He eyed his watch. "If that's the best answer you can give me, then we've nothing more to talk about." With effort, he began to heave himself out of his armchair. "I regret the necessity, but you leave me no—"

"I can get you half within the week." William heard, and cursed at, the desperate edge in his voice. "For the rest, you're at the top of my list. I'll put that in writing, if you like."

Yerkes halted halfway to his feet. "Half. Dare I ask from where?"

Susannah would be furious at having her rubies pawned.

Still, it was better than losing the house—or worse, given the nature of Yerkes' associates. He could always buy his wife's jewelry back. "You'll get your money," he said, more sharply than he'd intended. He needed this man, at least until after the next round of elections.

Yerkes chuckled. "Not beaten yet, eh? And you want to make sure I know it. Half will serve my needs. For the moment." He hauled himself upright and gave William a look that made his scalp crawl. "However, this is the last time I will be so understanding. I am, as you said, a businessman."

His departure seemed to suck all the air from the room. William flopped back in his armchair, gasping like a beached fish. Spots hovered near his eyes. He crept to the liquor cabinet and poured himself a straight Scotch. Two, swallowed neat, eased the pounding in his skull. After a third, he thought he just might be able to sleep. Susannah had retired hours ago—another of her sick headaches. Thinking of her brought a flash of anger. If she hadn't insisted on building this brick barn, paying the famous and expensive Daniel Burnham to design it—! "Women," he muttered as he poured a fourth drink.

Susannah, of course, wouldn't see things that way. She regarded the house as her due, considering the fortune she'd brought him. So far, neither she nor any of her family knew how much of it was gone. He gulped his drink, savoring the clean burn of it down his throat. Expensive stuff, like everything else he owned. Once upon a time, he'd easily afforded it. Now . . . *bad luck, costly womenfolk and a son who can't play cards. Not a lucky hand. Not like some people.*

He thought of his brother Andrew through a haze of resentment. Once upon a time, Andrew had owed him everything. It was William's idea to hire on at building sites, William who'd caught Boss Bill McCollum's eye, William to whom the old man had left his construction business after McCollum's only son got roaring drunk and fell into the Chicago River. William himself had made Andrew a junior partner. They'd piled up money, selling lumber and felt and shingles to build housing for the hordes of eager new arrivals. Tenements and cottages, barns and sheds, saloons and storefronts—quick, cheap and plenty. Then came the Great Fire.

He swirled the whiskey against the sides of the glass. They'd have pulled through fine if Andy hadn't lost his nerve. Never did have any guts. All he'd cared about was clearing his own dirty conscience. No thought for his only brother, or William's family. Just Andy the hero, confessing to the Inquiry Board and devil take the consequences for anyone else.

He drained the whiskey in a single toss. Little brother Andy had fallen on his feet in the twenty-odd years since the inquiry hearing. By rights, the hearing should have finished him. He'd kept the books, his name was on the purchase orders, while William carefully confined himself to hunting down new custom. Who'd have guessed Andrew would end up virtually owning a town? And a profitable iron mine, and a sizable chunk of the Great Northern Railway that kept his little bailiwick alive. *The wages of sin, he'd call my difficulties. Sanctimonious jackass.*

If I could get my hands on that property of his . . . he snickered. Fat chance brother Andrew would leave him or his so much as a five-cent piece. He'd once hoped for more through Jonas, but the time was long come and gone for that boy to have worked himself back into his father's good graces. He bolted his liquor and thumped down the glass. *Maybe Jonas will sell a painting for real money someday soon. And maybe my feet will grow wings.*

If he stood here any longer, he would drink the whole bottle and have a killer head in the morning. Drunken binges were best left to his fool of a son. He left the study, snapping off the electric lights as he went. Another indulgence of Susannah's, wiring the entire house. As if gaslights weren't perfectly serviceable. But she had to have everything in the latest fashion. So electric lights it was, and no bothering her head about paying the bills. That was the man's job.

He mounted the stairs slowly, light-headed from delayed nerves and drink. Susannah's jewels were a stopgap. Lord knew how he'd pay Yerkes the rest of his considerable loans if something didn't break his way soon. He could probably keep the man off his back until October or November; with half the debt paid and election season gearing up, Yerkes would be busy buying off state legislators. Before next winter, though, he'd better have a windfall. Otherwise—

He refused to contemplate "otherwise." Something would turn up. It had to.

CHAPTER SEVENTEEN

A low-pitched burble from her stomach reminded Rachel it had been awhile since breakfast. She closed the diary and flexed her shoulders. Her back and neck felt stiff as old paint. From the light outside, it was well past noon.

She rose and stretched, then stood awhile contemplating the book in her hands. Part of her wanted to finish it right now, this minute; the rest was begging for time to absorb it all. She gazed out at the snow-swept landscape, cradling the diary close to her chest. *My great-grandmother's diary. I'm a Schlegel, just like her.*

She looked around the study, as if seeing it for the first time. Mary Anne Schlegel had walked across this floor, sat on that sofa or that ottoman, read the books that lined the far wall. Slowly, Rachel walked to the mirror she'd admired—was it only yesterday?—and gazed at her reflection. For a moment, she saw a face like her own but younger, framed by upswept long hair and chin-high lace. She reached toward it. Her fingers struck cold glass, and the illusion vanished. She shivered and turned away.

Suddenly, sharply, she wanted Mom. She needed some sturdy common sense right about now. But Mom was gone. One hand closed over the tiny wooden rabbit in her coat pocket. What would Minna have thought of all this?

Out in the front hallway, she listened for sounds that might tell her where Jackson Schlegel was. She hadn't exactly promised not to take the diary off the premises, but she could tell he was

222

uneasy about letting it out of his hands. Understandable—the diary belonged to the house. She could no more expect him to let her go off with it than to walk away with a piece of antique china or an embroidered footstool. The murmur of voices from under the floor told her Jackson was in the basement with Chief Powell and his nameless colleague. Recalling the chief's last name made her chuckle. *I bet we're cousins or something. I've got family crawling out of the woodwork!*

She wouldn't bother Jackson now. Whatever the trouble was with Linnet's father, it was clearly quite enough for him to deal with. Linnet could keep the diary safe. Rachel started upstairs.

She didn't find Linnet in Mary Anne's room, or anywhere else on the second floor. A door in what must have been the schoolroom led up to the attic. Rachel climbed the creaking steps, holding tight to the banister. She hated steep stairs, especially ones like these, so narrow you could hardly fit more than your toes on them.

The staircase gave into a small room with a long table and some shelving. Another door in the far wall stood half-open. Rachel poked her head through and gaped. The huge chamber beyond was a pack rat's dream, a smorgasbord of furniture and carpets and old clothes and objets d'art and steamer trunks and boxes, boxes everywhere. And somewhere amid all this flotsam, one small fellow human being. Rachel hovered in the doorway, torn between the desire to find Linnet and hand over the diary, and an unexpected shyness. *This is where she found the diary. It's her place. And I'm invading it.*

The muffled squeak of a drawer opening cut off her train of thought. She looked around and spotted the honey-brown curve of a rolltop desk. Next to it, half-hidden by a small stack of boxes, she could just see the top of a pale blonde head.

She picked her way over to where Linnet was. The girl sat cross-legged in the dust near some open desk drawers. A packet of letters tied with a pink ribbon perched on one knee; a bulging leather-bound folder, like a smaller version of an artist's portfolio, lay next to her. Several other letters were scattered around, some in packets tied with string, others spilling across the floor.

At Rachel's approach, Linnet looked up from the letter she was reading. Rachel held out the diary. "I thought I'd leave this with you, come back and finish it tomorrow. I've read enough for one day, I think."

"So what did you find out?"

The eagerness in her face startled Rachel. Her personal quest seemed to matter a lot to this girl she'd met just a day ago. *My cousin. Or something.* Suddenly, she needed to sit down. She groped across some nearby boxes, found one sturdy enough to take her weight, and sat. Having something solid beneath her made her confusion recede a little. "I'm pretty sure Mary Anne is my great-grandmother."

"Because of the baby."

"Mmmhm." She caught herself searching Linnet's face for a family resemblance and forced herself to stop, before she made Linnet self-conscious.

Linnet eyed the scattered papers. "I was trying to find out what happened to it. I haven't had much luck. Mostly there's stuff about Jonas. Letters Mary Anne's uncle wrote. He used to live in Evanston. I guess he was rich—he sure talks about money a lot." She tapped the packet bound with pink ribbon. "And there's some letters Jonas wrote to his stepmother. I haven't read them yet." She glanced at the portfolio. "That's all legal stuff. I tried to read it, but it gave me a headache. If I ever wrote junk like that, Sister Agnes would make me rewrite it ten times."

"Ah, Catholic school." With a grin, Rachel reached for the nearest desk drawer—short and shallow, in the top right-hand corner. "Sister Mary Ellen was my English teacher in seventh grade. We called her Sister Mary Elephant. She used to circle every spelling error in bright red ink and then make the three kids with the most mistakes write out the misspelled words on the blackboard in front of the whole class. We hated her. But we learned to spell really well."

"Did they laugh at you?"

Rachel nodded. "They weren't supposed to, but you could hear everybody snickering behind their hands. I never felt so embarrassed in my life."

"Wow." Linnet was wide-eyed. "I'm glad no one ever did that to me."

Rachel picked up the drawer's meager contents—a piece of cardboard and some more letters. "Now I'm supposed to tell you it was good for me because it made me learn. Of course, it also made me hate English until I got to high school and discovered creative writing. Lots more fun than 'What I Did on my Summer Vacation.' "

The cardboard had faded writing on it: *William and Andrew, Chicago, 1849.* She turned it over. Two young men, one with a heavy mustache, grinned up at her from an old photograph. Their arms lay over each other's shoulders; behind them was a jerry-built wooden signpost with the words *Kinzie Street* painted across it. They wore dusty work boots and trousers with suspenders. The one without the mustache held a battered cap by his side. Knobby wrists peeked out from his shirtsleeves.

"Look at this." She handed Linnet the photo. "Papa Andrew and Uncle William. Though I'm not sure which is which."

Linnet brushed a finger over Mustache Man. "That's William. My grandfather has this same picture. William was his great-grandfather."

"Wow." Rachel stared at Linnet and did some quick figuring in her head. "That would make you and me . . ." She felt a silly grin spreading across her face. "Fifth cousins. I think."

"Whoa." Linnet's answering smile mirrored her own. They locked eyes for a moment, caught by the wonder of it. Then Rachel glanced down at the first paper in her lap: a letter to Andrew, dated October 1894.

My dear brother, please let me express my condolences on the loss of your daughter . . .

Her stomach dropped to her feet. *The loss . . .* But Mary Anne couldn't have died. Not so soon. Not with a whole new life barely begun.

"What is it?" Her shock must have shown in her face; Linnet sounded anxious. With an effort, Rachel pulled her wits together.

"This." She waved the letter. "From William. Saying how sorry he is about the loss of Mary Anne." She began to read out loud from the point where she'd stopped. " '*I firmly believe she is alive and well—*' okay, that's a relief—'*. . . though sadly I can offer you no proof of my conviction.*' " She looked up. "All right, I'm an idiot. Jackson—your grandfather—told me no one ever knew what happened to her. I should have remembered that."

"Read the rest," Linnet said.

Rachel found her place and resumed. " '*I can only urge you to trust in a benevolent Lord, and tell you I share your sorrow and bewilderment. Should she contact me in future, I will not hesitate to inform you. For the moment, all I can offer is the momentary comfort of renewing our family tie.*' Huh. '*In light of our long estrangement, I realize you may not wish any closeness between us, or trust my motives for this attempt. They are sincere, however. When tragedy strikes, or appears to, I find I can no longer afford the luxury of holding a grudge.*' "

The letter was signed *William*, in a crabbed scrawl that would have made her grade-school nuns blush with shame. She glanced at the photograph, which Linnet had laid on a desktop corner. They looked so close—two brothers challenging the world. What had driven them apart?

Linnet played with one of her braids, looking thoughtful. "I wonder what happened."

"Your grandfather hasn't told you anything?"

She twined her fingers tighter around her hair. "Not much."

Rachel chose not to pry. Between information overload and hunger, she was feeling a little faint. "Hey, you want to go get lunch someplace? My treat. If it's okay with your grandfather."

"I can't." Fear flashed across Linnet's face. "He, ummm . . . he doesn't want me wandering off." She swept together a pile of letters, which seemed to calm her somewhat. "We could make sandwiches. At the cottage. Grandfather won't mind that."

"Sounds great." Rachel kept her tone casual, as if she hadn't noticed Linnet's reaction. Was Jackson such a martinet, or was she afraid of running into her father? "Can we take the letters with?"

"As long as we don't get food on them. He'd be mad."

Rachel helped gather up the yellowed papers. "We'll be careful."

"These are from upstairs." Jackson shook the hand-stitched quilt free of the plaid wool blanket. "They shouldn't be here." He began to fold the quilt, smoothing it after each fold as if handling a work of art. His hands were trembling.

Florian hoped the old man didn't have heart trouble. From the shade he'd turned when they found the crumpled bedding, he might keel over any time. Florian's own nerves felt stretched with adrenaline, like they always did near the end of a chase. "Get many drifters out here?"

Jackson shook his head. "Trailers along the road," Powell said, from the door that led out to the root cellar. "Someone looking for shelter'd go there. More likely to find food." He jiggled the door hasp with a gloved hand. "Lock doesn't set right, Jackson. You'll want to get that fixed."

Florian glanced at Powell. He knew the police chief was thinking the same thing he was. "Cold last night. He was probably wearing gloves."

"Worth checking anyway." Powell resumed his inspection of the door.

Eyeing the floor where the blankets had been, Florian saw a scrap of cellophane no bigger than his pinkie fingernail. Too small to take a print. A fragment of red plastic clung to it. He picked it up and sniffed it. Cigarettes. A sudden desire for one made his mouth go dry. Almost five years now, and the craving still hit him sometimes. He shook himself and pocketed the cellophane. "He'll be back," he said.

The chief nodded and turned to Jackson, who had finished folding the plaid blanket. He stood with the neatened bedding in his arms, looking small and lost and old. "If we could stay . . ." Powell began.

"Do whatever you have to." Jackson's voice rasped like the caw of a crow. "Just keep that bastard away from my girl."

CHAPTER EIGHTEEN

"Listen to this one." Rachel cleared breadcrumbs and bologna from her throat. " *'Dear Andrew, Though you have not yet answered my letter of this Christmas just past, I know you will want to hear how well your son is doing. He has just received a commission to paint Florence Pullman's portrait. I am sure you recall her father, George Pullman, who has become one of Chicago's leading men in the years since you left the city . . .'* " She trailed off and took a sip of milk. "It's dated June tenth, 1887. The sixth one in a row without a reply."

"My grandfather says they had some big misunderstanding." Linnet polished off her sandwich, then snagged two more slices of whole wheat from the bread bag. "The one time we talked about it, he told me Andrew and William were both great men, and it was a shame they couldn't see eye to eye." She coated a butter knife with brown mustard and slathered the bread with it. "He didn't say what they didn't see eye to eye about. Probably figured I wouldn't get it." Two bologna slices covered the mustard, followed by the remaining piece of bread. "Or maybe one of them did something bad to the other, and he doesn't think I should know. He's awful proud of being a Schlegel. He wouldn't want to talk about anything shameful." She bit into the sandwich, then stopped chewing in mid-mouthful and gave Rachel a wide-eyed look. Hastily, she swallowed. "Maybe they committed a crime. One of them robbed a bank, or killed someone, or something."

"And that's why Andrew left Chicago." Rachel finished her own sandwich, then wiped her fingers on a paper napkin. "He did something and ran off to avoid getting caught, or he knew William did something and left because he couldn't deal with it."

"And he wouldn't tell the police because it was his brother." Linnet was getting caught up in the story. "Or Andrew did whatever it was, and William told him to skip town because he didn't want to see his brother in jail even if he deserved it."

"Okay. We've got a theory. Now how do we test it?"

"I guess they wouldn't write each other about it," Linnet said after a moment. "I mean, what if somebody else read their mail? Like Jonas or Mary Anne. Or Andrew's wife."

Rachel frowned in thought. "They might talk about it without talking about it. Little cryptic phrases that only they would understand."

"Then how are we going to understand it?"

"We could ask your grandfather. I bet he knows."

Linnet gave her a "yeah, right" look. "I bet he wouldn't tell you. Especially if you really are family. He wouldn't want you to know the embarrassing bits."

"Okay." Rachel reached for a handful of unread letters. "Let's look at the dates. If we know when Andrew left, we can find out what happened around then. Newspaper archives, the Chicago Historical Society—they're full of murders and robberies and scandals and everything important that ever happened in the city. I bet I could dredge something up on my laptop. At least then we'd have a starting point."

They pushed the remnants of lunch aside and laid out the letters in chronological order. "November 1872," Linnet said. "That's the earliest one." She picked it up for a closer look. "Wow. He sounds mad. '*Andrew, enclosed is a draft for the sum of five hundred dollars. If you have any sense, you will accept it on behalf of your family. Henceforth, please address all correspondence to my place of business. William Henry Schlegel.'* " She looked up. "That's not very much money."

"Back then, it was." Rachel took the letter. "That date is right after the Great Chicago Fire. So is this Andrew's cut of some scam they had going? Or dear Andrew, here's five hundred dollars to keep your mouth shut?"

"Maybe they did rob a bank and they split the money. Only Andrew felt guilty and didn't want his. So William sent it anyway, to remind him he was in it up to his neck and not to talk."

"You've seen a lot of old gangster films, haven't you?"

Linnet shrugged. "Half days in school, the nuns ran old movies in the auditorium. *Treasure of the Sierra Madre, The Maltese Falcon,* all that old forties stuff. A lot of the kids thought they were lame, but I liked them."

"In my day, they showed kid movies. *Robin Hood,* with the fox as Robin and a giant bear as Little John."

"And the hens playing football? I love that part!"

"Me, too." Rachel chuckled, then returned her attention to the letters. "So. A payoff in 1872, then no correspondence at all until . . . 1885. Thirteen years later. I wonder what made him start writing again?"

"There's another gap, too. There's a bunch from 1885 through 1887, and then nothing until 1894. October." Linnet looked at Rachel. "After Mary Anne disappeared." She took the diary from her coat pocket and flipped to the last page. "October 28, 1893. That's when the diary ends."

Rachel picked up the final letter. "And William offers condolences almost exactly a year later. After a seven-year silence. What was going on with these guys?"

Linnet gathered the letters into a neat pile, folded them and pushed them across the table toward Rachel. They shared a look. Then Rachel carefully tucked the letters away in her coat.

"I'm sure Grandfather wouldn't tell you anything," Linnet murmured.

"You're probably right."

As they cleared away the lunch things and put on their coats and boots, Rachel kept touching the letters. They ought to be burning a hole in her pocket. She had no right to take them off the premises, still less to have this child help her do it. But she had to find out—not only why Andrew Schlegel had left Chicago in 1872, but what William might have known about his niece's vanishing act.

Jackson's hands shook as he tucked the blanket and quilt back on the closet shelf. That Chapman bastard had no right to touch them. He clenched his fists, then grabbed the covers back. They needed washing. He wouldn't let Luke Chapman soil anything that belonged to him—not the linens, not Linnet, nothing.

Arms full of fabric, he marched down the hall to Mary Anne's room. Linnet would be there, likely curled up in the window seat with a book in her lap. He needed to look at her, to reassure himself that the morning's incident with Rachel Connolly and the diary hadn't frightened her away from him again.

To make sure she's still here. He shook his head as if to dislodge the thought. Chapman couldn't have gotten in and out without someone hearing him, not with two policemen and the Connolly woman all skulking around. He was a fool to worry. Chapman had gone off earlier, probably to talk to some custody lawyer, and he'd find Birch Falls' finest waiting for him when he got back. Linnet was safe.

No one answered when he called Linnet's name outside the bedroom door. One look at the empty room sent the blankets to the floor and him hurrying to the attic. Silence and more emptiness met him there. He stood in the middle of the room, calling

Linnet as if repeating her name could conjure her out of thin air. Then he began to prowl around, looking behind furniture and box piles.

She'd been here, he was sure. Patches of disturbed dust suggested the prints of smaller shoes than his own. Andrew Schlegel's old desk offered more evidence, its sticky top drawer not quite shut. Jackson jiggled it. The drawer refused to close. He tried again, this time jamming the sticky side.

"Goddammit!" He grabbed the handle and pulled. Wood shrieked. The horrible sound brought him to his senses. He felt the drawer carefully inside and out, terrified that he might have damaged the piece. His fingers passed over a thin cardboard rectangle, then closed around it. Slowly, he drew out the old daguerreotype.

Great-grandfather William had had one just like it—himself and his younger brother, arriving in Chicago ready to set the city on fire. That copy now lay in Jackson's desk. His Grandfather Randolph had kept it in his memory box, along with the sheet music to a drinking song, his college diploma and a hair ribbon of dark green velvet.

"Did Grandma give you this when you fell in love?" he'd asked about the ribbon once, a curious ten-year-old just feeling the first stirrings of liking for the pony-tailed girl who sat two seats away in his fifth-grade class. He'd expected one of the old man's rare smiles, maybe even a laugh, followed by a long story told over a cherry-smelling pipe. He'd gotten a sharp "No," and a shuttered face. "Go away, boy. I'm tired. Go on, get out."

He touched William's sepia cheek, imagining instead a soft scrap of fabric. Grandfather Randolph hadn't let him near the memory box after that. Three years later, when the old man died, the box came to Jackson along with a letter not to be opened until his eighteenth birthday. Visions of a secret fortune, to be his when he came of age, made it easier to cope with too-short Salvation Army pants and holes in his shoes and their cramped new apartment where heat was a passing guest. For five years he'd kept himself afloat on someday-soon dreams: someday soon he'd have so much money that Mother wouldn't have to work, someday soon he'd buy them both a big house like the one he'd been born in, someday soon he'd have shoes that fit and clothes fancy enough to impress a pretty girl. And then someday came, and he read the letter, and he wished he hadn't.

The story it told eventually sent him up north, to the offices of the Schlegel Trust in Duluth. He'd hoped for money, at least enough to buy him a bachelor's degree on his way to becoming an architect. Instead, he found a caretaker's job that needed filling. Years of scraping along had made him handy, and the one year of college he'd managed to afford gave him a background in fine arts that wasn't otherwise likely to pay his rent. Keeping up the Schlegel mansion seemed as close to architecture as he was likely to get—and he'd harbored some hope that the trustees might reward diligence on the job with part or even all of the family inheritance. After just six months in the grand old house, he knew he would never leave it. To spend his days in it was all the inheritance he wanted.

He turned away from the rolltop, with a brittle laugh at his own naiveté. He'd actually been glad not to want the money anymore, as if losing that desire could somehow make up for the sins of the past. Jackson Schlegel, payer of debts and layer of ghosts. And now here he was, caught back up in the greed that had crippled his family, about to lose a fortune again. A real one this time, unless he could keep Linnet. And get rid of inquisitive Rachel Connolly.

He stalked across the attic toward the stairs. He'd take the diary back, for starters. He never should have let her read it. If she found the Schlegel Trust and told them her story, he could lose everything. The diary had to go, and so did she.

As he ducked into the anteroom, he saw two figures walking toward the manse from the caretaker's cottage. Linnet and Rachel, chatting like old friends.

"You should start back before dark, but if you want to look for more stuff, we've got a couple of hours." Linnet hunched her shoulders against a blast of wind.

Rachel sniffed the air. The cold made her nostrils wrinkle. "Make it one hour. Snow's coming."

"You can smell that?"

"Yup."

"Linnet!" Jackson's voice cut through the air. He strode down the back steps toward them. Next to Rachel, Linnet shrank further inside her parka.

"Something must have happened." Remembering the policemen's arrival, Rachel slipped an arm around Linnet's shoulders. "I'm sure everything will be all right."

"Get in the house," Jackson said to Linnet as he reached them, with a curt nod toward the cottage. He ignored Rachel.

Linnet stood frozen for a moment, like a deer in car headlights. Then she slipped out of Rachel's grasp and raced down the path. As the cottage door slammed shut behind her, Rachel turned to Jackson. "What—?"

"You'd best go, Miss Connolly." He sounded like ice. "And I'll thank you not to come back."

Rachel felt as if she'd walked off a cliff. "Wh—I—"

"Linnet lost her mother not long ago. Latching on to strangers is her way of coping. But strangers leave, Miss Connolly. You'll leave, once you've got what you came here for. So it's best you go away and stay away, before she gets hurt."

If rock could be angry, it would look like he did now. Reasonable arguments died in her throat as she took in his closed face, mouth shut tight and eyes like frozen flint. "Could I at least come back to finish the diary?" she faltered. "I won't disturb—"

"Best not. I'm sorry."

He didn't look it. Anger sparked inside her, a slow burn that started in her stomach and spread. "You have no right—"

"I have every right. This is private property." He held out a hand. "I'll take the diary now."

"I gave it back to Linnet. She found it."

"Then you'll be going."

"We're family," she said desperately. "I found out that much. Doesn't that mean anything to you?"

"What you make of a teenage girl's ramblings is your business. I have a house to mind. Afternoon, Miss Connolly." He turned and stalked away.

She stared after him until his blurring figure vanished through the kitchen door. Not until a tear trailed its wet warmth down her cold cheek did she realize she was crying. She dashed it away, then slipped her gloves on and started walking. The gloves weren't enough against the biting cold, so she shoved her hands in her pockets. Her knuckles brushed Minna's rabbit. The feel of it gave her courage. The trail couldn't end here, with the words of an angry old man. She'd come back whether Jackson Schlegel liked it or not.

Brisk walking calmed her down. By the time she reached the road, she was thinking of other steps to take. Like talking to Terry Powell, who likely knew Rhys's story. And William's letters—she could read them at her leisure, maybe piece together some clue to Mary Anne's disappearance.

The sound of running footsteps made her turn. Linnet was pounding along the pavement several yards behind, braids flapping against her sweater. What had she done with her coat? "You'll catch your death," she said as Linnet reached her.

Linnet held out the diary. Her breath made white puffs

against the backdrop of the pine trees. "Here. Take it."

"I can't," she protested as her fingers closed over it.

Still winded, Linnet shot her an impatient look. "I found it," she said when she could speak again. "So it's mine. Now it's yours."

"But your grandfather—"

"I don't care." Linnet hugged herself against the cold. "He's mean. I thought he wasn't, but I was wrong."

"Linnet . . ." Rachel trailed off. She had no idea what to say, how to begin patching the rift it seemed she'd caused.

Another gust rattled the trees. Linnet shivered. "I have to go."

Rachel stripped off her gloves, then loosened her hood enough to slip off her wool hat. She handed over the gloves and pulled the hat down snugly on Linnet's head. "I'm staying at the Windy Pines. Bring these back if you can."

CHAPTER NINETEEN

The light was fading by the time Rachel reached the Windy Pines, even though it was barely four o'clock. She blew into the lobby with a gust of wind. The cheerful crackle of a fire in the fireplace reminded her that other things existed in the world besides odd old men who took sudden, irrational dislikes to people. She hovered near the flames awhile, warming her hands. When they'd thawed out enough, she unbuttoned her coat and looked around for Bogart.

He was just finishing with a customer as she approached the front desk. "I won't ask if it's cold enough for you," he said with a sympathetic look. "Those fingers and that nose say it all. When will you folks from down south learn to dress for real winter?"

"I'm from Chicago."

"That's down south."

She leaned against the counter. "I wanted to ask about the artwork in my room. Do you know who the artist is?"

"Was," he corrected. "Terry Powell—that's our police chief—donated them to the Pines when the new owners remodeled it a few years back. His great-grandfather did them. You've probably never heard of Rhys Powell unless you're a birdwatcher, but local publishers used his wildlife sketches in nature guides for almost twenty years. That kind of thing didn't happen much to poor miners' sons in the early nineteen hundreds. I guess you could call him a local celebrity. Anyway, Terry had a trunk full of loose sketches rattling around in his attic. He gave the hotel the ones in the best condition. Much better than the usual junk they hang on the walls, aren't they?"

"Definitely." She could feel herself grinning like an idiot. She wanted to laugh out loud, kiss Bogart on his well-shaped lips, grab the snoozing businessman out of his armchair by the fire and waltz him around the lobby. *I have a family again,* she felt like shouting. Instead, she thanked Bogart and headed toward her room. A steaming shower would drive the cold from her bones and let her come to grips with the shocks of the day, joyous and otherwise. William's letters could wait.

She considered ordering room service to avoid going back out in the deep freeze, but decided she wanted the distraction of other people. Something to slow her down in case her brain threatened to explode. She swiped the key through the lock and opened her door. She could manage the two blocks to Valentini's once she'd thawed out.

Smooth as a baby's ass, or whatever the ad says. In the trailer's closet-sized bathroom, Luke ran a hand over his chin. If he were a woman, he'd like what he saw. Smelled, too. Whoever lived here had aftershave he liked—clean, fresh, not overpowering. Most of that crap left you smelling like a rose garden or rubbing alcohol. Neither would do tonight. Tonight, he was out for conquest.

Valentini's seemed like as good a spot as any to start looking for Rachel Connolly. He'd get a good meal whether or not she showed. Plus, their wines were the good-but-cheap stuff. Nothing like a glass or two of Chianti to get a woman to open up. And he wanted her to open up. He wanted to know everything about her. Most women loved that. Center of his attention, axis of his universe—she'd lap it up like a dog drinking water. And who knew what bit of knowledge might come in handy?

He thought of Grace's old man and smirked at his reflection as he shrugged into a borrowed sport shirt and sweater. Not too flashy, not too dull. Classy. Old Man Schlegel'd keel over when he realized Luke had seduced his own social worker out from under him. With luck he'd die of a heart attack. Problem solved.

A borrowed parka and his hat and gloves completed his outfit. He was stuck with his own scuffed shoes, but they'd add to the portrait of the noncustodial daddy forced to shell out to a bitch of an ex who wouldn't even let him see his beloved kid. His date would find all that out later, of course. A good con was like good sex—it took time. Tonight, he'd let her do most of the talking.

The night air made his ears burn. He pulled his hat lower and headed toward the road. He wondered if Connolly was a decent lay. A lot of the repressed ones were, once you got past their defenses. He might end up enjoying this a lot more than he'd thought.

The highway was a dark strip between banks of moonlit, powdery snow. Beyond the verge, the trees melted into solid blackness. Luke stared at the darkness, half enthralled and half afraid. *You could hide a body in there for months. Find a fallen tree trunk, cover it with pine needles . . . nobody'd walk through until spring. June, probably, up here. There'd be nothing but bones by then. Even harder to see.*

He took a deep breath and moved on. Why the hell was he thinking like that? He didn't want to hurt anybody. He just wanted his daughter and what belonged to both of them.

Valentini's front bar was less crowded than the other night. The cold must be keeping some of the regulars home by the fire. Rachel halted halfway through the long room and eyed the chalkboard drinks list on the wall over the bar, looking for hard cider. She deserved a little extra celebration tonight.

"Hornsby's Dark and Dry," she told the bartender as she perched on a barstool. Not quite the thing with Italian food, but what the hell. She glanced around, noting with amusement the pockmarked dartboard, girlie calendar and television tuned to the inevitable sports station. Two tiny, glowing figures in snappy suits and hair helmets were bantering about football, while names and numbers flashed by on the bottom of the screen.

She couldn't remember the last time she'd been out to a bar on her own. Mostly she went with girlfriends, to discourage the pond slime from getting too friendly. Nick had hated the bar scene; fancy wine-and-cheese parties were more his speed. She snickered at the memory of the oh-God-no look on his face the one time she'd dragged him to the Abbey Pub for some decent drink and an Altan concert. He'd spent the whole time failing to look interested and keeping an eye out for roaches. As if there'd have been any. "Snobby bastard, weren't you, Nicky?"

" 'Scuse me?" The bartender, a craggy-faced man somewhere between sixty and dead, set down her drink with a startled look.

She laughed as warmth crept down her cheeks. "Sorry. Ode to an old boyfriend."

His grin revealed a missing upper incisor. "I hear a lotta those. Better luck next time, huh?"

"Oh, yeah." She raised her cold bottle toward his departing back. The cider tasted tart and sharp, with a hint of sweetness. Just what she needed to put a capper on an incredible day.

Cold shot down the bar as the door opened and another patron blew in. Rachel glanced over her shoulder. Male, young-ish but no kid, just about tall enough to play for the Bulls. His navy knit hat, pulled low on his head, clashed with his brown parka. She smiled into her cider. Either he was single or the woman in his life was fashion-impaired.

The new arrival took a seat two stools down from her,

comfortably distant without being insulting. She dismissed him from her mind and fished the diary out of her coat. After sopping up a few water beads with a convenient napkin, she laid the book down, opened it and studied the sketch inside the front cover. Hard to see any resemblance to the local cop she'd met earlier. Maybe Terry Powell took after his great-grandmother's side. She hoped he'd give her a friendlier reception than Jackson Schlegel had.

Thinking of Jackson made her fidget. The suddenness of the old man's attitude change bothered her almost more than the change itself. *You'd think he'd be delighted to find a relative, or at least a little friendly. It's not as if I'm claiming to be his long-lost illegitimate daughter. He doesn't like me being family. And I'm damned if I know why.*

She closed the diary and stroked its cover. Linnet had told her how proud he was of his family name. Maybe, in his mind, the taint of Mary Anne's bastard son carried down to her. That might explain why he hadn't wanted her to read Mary Anne's journal in the first place. His grudging permission should have warned her, she supposed. She tossed back more cider, feeling defiant. No more asking permission. Private property or not, Jackson Schlegel had no moral right to bar her from finding out who she was. And if the answer made him uncomfortable, that was his tough luck.

"Excuse me," said a voice from down the bar.

She looked up. The man in the parka was standing by his bar stool, coat folded over one arm, looking shyly her way.

"I, uh—" He gave a nervous chuckle, glanced at his scuffed shoes and smiled gamely. "This is a rude question, I guess, but . . . are you on your own?"

Good God, a come-on already. Though he was somewhat more attractive than the usual pond scum, with sandy brown hair falling boyishly over one eye. Nice build, too—and not too badly dressed, with his coat and hat off. She gave him a thanks-but-no-thanks smile. "I'm waiting for a friend."

"Oh." He looked crestfallen. "Sorry I bothered you. It's just I hate eating alone, and I was kind of hoping . . ." He was blushing now, so hard she felt sorry for him. "Never mind. Thanks anyway." He turned away, shoulders hunched in a seeming attempt to look shorter, and started to pull on his coat.

"Wait a minute." *God, did I just say that?*

He stopped with one arm in a parka sleeve. The hopeful-scared look was back, at higher wattage than before. She couldn't tell him no now. And he seemed so embarrassed by his own pickup attempt—not like most bar-crawlers, who came on like they were God's gift to the other half of the human race. Ninety minutes of conversation over a good meal should be easy enough to get through. She might even enjoy it. "I could join you until my friend gets here. If that's all right."

The smile he gave her transformed his plain-vanilla face. Suddenly, he looked twice as handsome as Nick ever had. "That'd be great." With awkward haste, he slipped off his coat and folded it over his arm again. He held out his other hand to her as he approached. "Lucas Walker. Luke to my friends."

"Rachel Connolly." He had a firm handshake, no sweaty palms. Maybe she hadn't made a blunder after all.

They moved into the dining room, where the smiling hostess seated them. Rachel draped her own coat over the chair back and glanced at Lucas. He looked like somebody she knew, or maybe she'd seen him somewhere before.

He handed her a menu. "You're not regretting this already, are you?"

He looked so nervous, she hastened to reassure him. "Not at all. It's just that you seem familiar, only I can't think from where."

"Don't tell me—I remind you of your second cousin Bill.

The one who works in insurance."

She laughed. "I don't think I have one. But I could be wrong."

"Now that remark sounds like there's a story behind it."

"Oh, there is." Though she wasn't sure she wanted to tell it, even to this unexpectedly engaging stranger. Seeking a change of subject, she pounced on the wine list. "Would you like to share something, or are you not a wine drinker?"

"The house Chianti's pretty good. Or so I hear. This is only my second visit; I haven't been in town long."

Memory clicked into place. "You were here the other night. The choker."

"Tried to breathe my beer." Suddenly, he looked shy. "I saw you then, actually. You seemed like a nice, quiet kind of person. I was thinking of asking you to join me, but then I started hacking, and I thought that made a pretty rotten first impression."

"So you decided to give it another try."

"Do you mind?"

"I think I'm flattered. Just try not to breathe any liquid tonight, okay?"

"Deal." Humor sparkled in his eyes, which were gray leaning toward green. Odd color. Attractive. Definitely attractive. Rachel shook herself. The cider was getting to her. Maybe she shouldn't have any Chianti.

Lucas suggested splitting a house salad, to which she agreed while weighing the merits of four-cheese rotini versus pasta alla puttanesca. A basket of piping hot foccacia heralded the arrival of their waiter, who rattled off the night's specials and then took their orders. "We could split a half-carafe of Chianti, if you want," Lucas suggested.

Why not? She could handle a glass and a half. And it felt nice to be sitting in a restaurant, drinking wine in pleasant company. Especially after the bizarre unpleasantness earlier in the afternoon. "So you're from out of town?" she asked as the waiter departed.

He nodded. "My daughter's up here." His wistful tone suggested it wasn't by his choice.

She could guess the rest of the story from his dusty parka and worn shoes. No need to press for details. She snagged a chunk of bread and drizzled olive oil on her plate. "I'm from Chicago, myself."

"Visiting family too?"

"You might say that." The bread was delicious, studded with pungent sun-dried tomatoes and flecks of fresh basil. "Try some. It's terrific."

He took a piece. With a small inward sigh, she noticed the nicotine stains on his fingers. "You don't want to talk about it. That's okay. They make you crazy, huh?"

"Crazy isn't the word."

The Chianti arrived; she poured him a generous glass, then one for herself. The taste of it, smooth and fruity, relaxed her. She looked at Lucas over the rim of her glass. Just an ordinary guy, with a nice smile and a loneliness that made him reach out to strangers in the hope they'd be kind. She could tell him the whole wild story, get it off her chest. Likely she'd never see him again, so it wouldn't matter if he thought she was flaky. "I'm adopted," she began, while trailing oil across her third piece of foccacia. "I came up here looking for my family, only now that I've found them, they don't want to have anything to do with me."

Between bites of bread, she gave him an edited version of her search so far and then told him about Jackson Schlegel's strange reactions—first with the portrait, then with the diary, and finally that afternoon. "I thought I was imagining it the first time he weirded out on me. And I figured he was just being anal about the diary—not wanting some stranger's grubby fingerprints all over a piece of his history. I can understand that. But today—I couldn't believe it. He warned me off Linnet—that's his grand-daughter—like I was a plague carrier or something. I only met her yesterday. Bumped into her on the sidewalk, literally." She broke off and sipped wine. "She seems like a great kid. Thoughtful, bright, imaginative . . . lonely. There's nobody in that museum of a place but her and old Jackson. She could probably use a friend. And I'm a relation. I'm not just some stranger off the street. I mean, I know it's awkward, but she seems to like me, and I like her, so . . . I'm babbling. I must be boring you silly."

"No, you're not." He looked enthralled, lounging in his chair and cradling his wine glass. "I've got to say, I've never heard anything quite like this."

She laughed at that. "Sounds like a Regency romance, updated for the twenty-first century. Wait, you're a guy—you wouldn't know." The waiter was approaching with a loaded tray. Anticipating food, she poured herself a touch more wine. "If this was a Regency romance, there'd be a whacking huge family fortune involved, to which I'd be the sole legitimate heir. Too bad there's only a giant Victorian house in the back end of beyond."

"I don't know." He attacked his rotolo like a starving man. "At least you don't have to look out for fortune hunters."

"True." She forked up a bite of her own pasta. The puttanesca sauce had just the right kick. She must thank Bogart for pointing her toward the best Italian restaurant she'd been to outside Little Italy.

"So where are you staying? If that's not too personal a question . . ."

"The Windy Pines. It's nice." A remnant of common sense kept her from mentioning how close it was to Valentini's. She was enjoying herself, but not so much as to prompt the suggestion of a nightcap. Certainly not with a divorced dad about whom she knew nothing except that he dressed with taste on a budget, had gorgeous eyes, listened well and looked terrific when he smiled. "You?"

He shrugged. "Day's Inn for me. I haven't got a lot of extra cash to throw around these days." Abruptly, he looked embarrassed. "I'm sorry. That sounds terrible. I can pay for dinner. For both of us. I insist."

They dickered politely over it, ultimately agreeing to go Dutch. The conversation moved to other channels—favorite ethnic eateries, comparisons of winter in Chicago and Minneapolis, mystery novels and TV cop shows. Lucas had been a lawyer—"I got out when I couldn't take the rat race anymore—" and spoke approvingly of *Law & Order.* "They get most of the details right, or at least pretty close. A lot of those shows don't bother."

"Which doesn't matter to the layman like me. We just want a good story." Rachel nibbled at her cannoli, successor to the pasta and salad. She hadn't enjoyed an evening this much since the first time she'd gone out with Nick. A good sign, or a warning?

"Still. You want a cappuccino or something?"

"I'll be up half the night. No, thanks."

They finished their desserts and paid the bill. Rachel left a generous tip. Lucas helped her with her coat, then stood awkwardly beside her with his hands in his trouser pockets. "Listen, uh . . . oh, hell, I stink at nice speeches. I just want to say I really enjoyed tonight, and I'm sorry I probably won't see you again."

"You never know," she said, aware that she was blushing. "It's a small town."

He smiled and stuck out a hand. "I'll hope for good luck, then. Good night."

Later, sprawling on his borrowed bed in the trailer, Luke reviewed the evening with satisfaction. Hook, line and a handful of sinkers. He could still work the magic, make a woman dance like a puppet on the end of his string. Of course, he hadn't expected her to turn out to be a relation. It wasn't Linnet she could take from him, but a chunk of the money. He'd have to figure out just how much of a threat she posed, and decide what to do from there. Still, it could be useful getting her to fall for him.

He pushed himself up on his elbows and reached for the coffee mug on the bedside table. He cupped the mug in his hands, dreaming of all the ways his life seemed finally set to change. His and Linnet's.

Funny to think of Rachel Connolly as a relative. It explained why she looked a little like Grace. They must be cousins or something. A sudden thought sent him off the bed and over to his duffel bag, from which he dug his wadded-up jacket. The letter from the Duluth attorneys was still in the inside pocket. He took it out and read it over, frowning. . . . *the heirs and assigns of William Henry Schlegel . . .*

The Connolly woman had said her great-grandma was some girl named Mary Anne, who'd disappeared a hundred-some years ago. Who was also, she'd told him, the daughter of Andrew Schlegel, the old guy who'd salted away all the family money. Which meant . . . what?

Letter in hand, he paced across the tiny bedroom. Was William Andy's son, or a brother or nephew or something? Did it matter? If Rachel wasn't directly related to William Henry, did she get nothing? Or did being related to Andrew's daughter mean she got everything?

That last possibility turned him cold where he stood. He had to find out the terms of the old guy's will—whether everything went to Billy boy's descendants regardless, or if they only got the bucks because the daughter was gone. He strode to the bed, snatched his cigarettes off the nighttable and lit one. If the news turned out to be bad, he'd have to keep Rachel Connolly from proving who she was. One way or another.

For you, Linnie, he thought as he smoked. *Whatever happens, it's all for you.*

CHAPTER TWENTY

24 September, 1893

My baby is gone. Gone with nothing from me. Not even a name.

I wanted this. I chose it. Yet my arms feel empty.

I won't think of that. He'll be well and happy, my little son. And I . . . I can get on with my life now. The life I want. The life I've paid for.

I'll make it worth the price.

Fatigue made Jonas's eyes burn. He blinked several times, then picked up Mary Anne's hairbrush. It felt heavy in his hand, almost too heavy to lift. At Aly's urging, he'd tried to nap on the sofa around midnight, but Mary Anne's screams had made that impossible. He shuddered at the memory, feeling chilled despite the pleasant warmth of the early morning air. First a cold snap, now Indian summer. In all his life, he'd never known a more unsettled September.

Neither Aly nor the midwife had taken his sister's agony as anything unusual. They had simply done their work, Aly bringing the midwife clean linens and cool water to bathe Mary Anne's face when necessary. All he could do was hover in the parlor, trying to keep out of the way, yet unable to desert Mary Anne in so much pain.

He lifted the brush again and drew it through her hair. Combed free of sweat, the dark locks shone against the pillow.

The portion he was brushing felt as he imagined clouds must, soft and insubstantial. He pulled it gently straight, working out the last tangles. The ends curled over his fingertips, their reddish highlights gleaming in the pale light of dawn.

He patted the last lock of hair into place, then set the brush down next to Mary Anne's diary. He knew she'd want it when she woke up. Mary Anne slept on, oblivious. She lay on her side, curled under two blankets and a cotton quilt. He and Aly had changed the soiled sheets and dug out a clean nightshirt, while the midwife washed and swaddled the baby. The newborn boy nestled in the crook of Mary Anne's arm now, swathed in a pale blue baby blanket Jonas hadn't been able to resist buying. He could do little enough for his nephew: see him well placed with loving parents and try to ensure no one knew who the child's mother was. He'd promised Mary Anne that.

"I want my baby free," she'd said, wrapped in a shawl against an early autumn chill, a cup of jasmine tea clenched in her fingers. God, was it only five days ago? Her face above the cherry-colored wool looked as grimly set as their father's ever had. "Father knows which university accepted me. It won't take him long to guess where I've gone. I'm my own woman now; if he finds me, I can tell him to go to blazes. But if he guesses why else I left—"

"He'd still have to find the baby. That'll take time. Time enough for the adoption to be finalized." Jonas refilled his own cup. The action helped him keep his temper, which was the only way he could hope to win this argument. Anger simply made his little sister more stubborn. "The child has a right to know where it came from. It may want to, someday."

"I can't take the chance." The hardness in her eyes chilled him. "Who knows what the law allows the grandparent of a foundling? He could claim my baby like a lost parcel, bring it up in that miserable little town to be exactly what he wants it to be. No chance of it ever choosing its own life. But if Father can't get his hands on it, it won't grow up to be a puppet, or have to run away like we did."

For a moment he was thirteen again, back and legs trembling under the sharp blows of a birch cane. Father had caught him drawing in the shadow of the servants' cottage. He felt a phantom twinge in his wrist, where Father's big hand had hauled him off the ground. He remembered the stark sound of paper tearing, the snap of his charcoal pencil. Dirt and dead pine needles spattering the two halves of his mother's face. To this day, he couldn't recall how she'd looked before her illness. Only her final months, huge eyes gleaming at him in a face that had shrunk to little more than bones.

He shook off the memory. "What about Rhys?"

The hardness fled. She looked down at her cup. "I won't have my child become our father's creature. Not even for him."

"I'll bring the baby to Hull House," he said after a long pause. "I'll say I found it somewhere. I know someone who'll help."

She sank back in the sofa corner, as if relieved of a tremendous weight. "It's best, Jonas. You'll see."

A footstep roused him from his memories. Aloysius stood in the doorway, his sweat-stained shirt replaced with a clean one. He hadn't managed to fix his hair yet. Reddish thatch stood out in several directions around his head. In his eyes, Jonas saw a mixture of affection and sadness. "She's here."

"Already." He glanced once more at his sleeping sister, then hauled himself off the edge of the bed and walked around to the other side. Gently, he lifted the baby. The small blue bundle squirmed. Startled, he clutched the tiny boy closer. The infant's eyes opened, two slits in his tiny face. Then they fluttered shut, accompanied by a small sound between a burble and a snore.

"I made tea," Aly murmured as Jonas reached him. A callused hand brushed Jonas's shoulder as he passed with his small burden. The infant seemed to get heavier with every step down the short hallway. He felt almost weepy with gratitude toward Aly, for not saying what they both knew. Two bachelors sharing an apartment for as long as they had was oddity enough; two men and a child would surely raise dangerous questions. They couldn't keep the boy; it was foolish even to think such a thing. And it would break his promise, besides.

As they walked in, Laura Hastings rose from the edge of the sofa. A full teacup sat on the table in front of her. This morning especially, her narrow face and angular build made Jonas think of a stork. The aptness of the image made him smile, though with little mirth. He saw her start forward as if to console him with a touch, then check herself in midstep.

"I brought the affidavit," she said. "You're sure you want to do this?"

"I promised." He handed the infant to Aly, who cradled him as easily as he held a sick cat or a wounded pigeon. The paper Jonas was to sign lay next to the teapot. Without reading it, he bent and scrawled his name at the bottom.

Laura took the pen from him, pressing his fingers in mute sympathy. She added her own signature in silence, then folded the affidavit and tucked it into her handbag. "I may have found a family already. Irish, fairly well off. The woman had a miscarriage last year. They're about your age, very tender with each other from what I saw. And they desperately want a child."

"That's good." Mechanically, he poured himself tea. "Don't tell me any more."

She looked as if she wanted to say something, but knew it would be futile. He dredged up a thin smile. "I'm sorry. I'm not taking this too well."

"You don't have to lose touch entirely. You can—"

"No, I can't." He sounded harsher than he'd meant to and hated himself for it. "How happy would this Irish couple be, for their new son to have a relation who lives with another man and scratches out a living painting society portraits?"

"The latter being the worst, of course." A gentle joke, delivered with the warm sympathy that had once drawn him to her. Before he met Aly and realized what he truly was.

Ashamed of his momentary bitterness, he clasped her hand. "You'll keep an eye on him?"

"I'll let you know how he's doing." She took the baby from Aly with practiced ease. "And if you ever want to know their name, just tell me."

Aly walked her down to the street. Jonas lay back on the sofa and listened to their receding footsteps, followed by the muffled bang of the downstairs door. Several minutes later, Aly returned. Illogically, Jonas peered behind him for a glimpse of Laura and the child he knew he would never see again.

"Stop it," Aly said gently as he sat down beside Jonas. Two warm, strong hands began to knead Jonas's shoulders, easing knots he hadn't known were there. "It's done, and it's what Mary Anne wants. Laura will see things right."

"I miss him." He bowed his head under Aly's ministrations. "Ridiculous, isn't it? Our paths crossed for a few hours, most of which he slept through. But I miss him."

"You didn't grow up with three younger sisters and twin baby brothers." Aly's hands moved down his back, tracing firm circles under his shoulder blades. "The noise, the smell, the worry . . . I don't know how my mother stood it until my older sister and I got big enough to help out."

"I want a son," Jonas whispered.

Aly gave him a gentle squeeze. "Come on. Sleep. You'll feel better."

Overwhelmed by fatigue, Jonas let himself be led toward their small second bedroom. At the door of the larger one, he stopped and looked in. Mary Anne hadn't moved. He peered closer to see if her chest was still moving. "Should she be sleeping so deeply? Maybe we should get a doctor . . ."

Aly nudged him down the hall. "She's all right. I've watched two sisters and I don't know how many maternity patients go through this. Mrs. Sanders did a good job, and Mary Anne's strong and healthy. Right now sleep is the best thing for her."

"Uncle William." God, he was tired; his mind was jumping from track to track like a train possessed by imps. "She'll want to see him as soon as she can." He started to turn around. "I should write a note—"

"Later." Aly steered him into the bedroom and sat him on the bed. "Rest now."

"You didn't tell him anything?" Mary Anne held tight to her brother's arm as they walked into the Palmer House hotel. She still felt shaky on her feet sometimes, but she looked well enough, and she was done with waiting. Her son had gone to his new life almost three weeks ago. It was time to embark on her own.

"Just that you're visiting and that you'd like to see him." Jonas patted her gloved hand. "From which he'll surely guess something's up, seeing as you're here on your own. But I left it for you to say."

She looked around the opulent lobby, trying not to gawk like a farm girl. Rose-streaked marble fought for notice with gilded leaves and wheat ears and the slender, twisted columns that framed intermittent floor-to-ceiling mirrors. The sight of her reflection embarrassed her: short and dumpy, in a desperately unfashionable dress and with far too much color in her cheeks. They were so red, she looked like a painted woman. Not rouge, but rampant nerves. She cursed silently, a string of words picked up from occasional loud altercations that floated up to Jonas's flat from the street. It seemed to help. "I only met Uncle William once. I scarcely remember what he looks like."

"He may be in the restaurant already. They know him here; he has his own table." Together, they walked toward the hotel dining room. "It'll go all right. You'll see."

The maitre d', in an elegant coat, regarded them warily until Jonas mentioned Uncle William's name. Suddenly all deference, he beckoned to a white-jacketed Negro. Mary Anne tried not to stare. The young man's skin was the shade of strong coffee. "Ezra, show these people to Mr. Schlegel's table."

"Yessir." Ezra turned toward them. "Right this way, sir, miss."

He moved as if someone had taught him to dance, leading them smoothly around the scattered tables. Mary Anne caught glimpses of more dark faces, some framed by loaded silver trays the waiters seemed to carry with amazing ease. She saw glittering chandeliers, snowy linen tablecloths lapping at bright silk skirts, well-fed men in dark suits, light glancing off gold-rimmed china. Snatches of talk struck her ear like a foreign language: "—on Kansas wheat, one tick up." "—ward alderman'll turn the troops out, never you worry . . ." "—city in the world, I'm telling you. Why, the White Palace alone—" "—Little Cheyenne, ask for Mary Hastings. But don't say I sent you!"

Then their guide was halting by a square table set for four. The table's sole occupant looked up from a folded newspaper he was reading. A moment's dizzy confusion made Mary Anne clutch the back of the nearest chair—*Father?*—before good sense reasserted itself. Father would never wear a silver-paisley waistcoat. And the man's mustache, almost the same silvery shade, flowed into a well-trimmed beard.

"My dear." The smile he gave her shattered the illusion. Father's smiles had never held that suggestion of merry mischief, even when she was a little girl. He rose, took her hand and bowed over it. "You've become quite the young lady since we last met."

"Uncle William." She smiled shyly back, warmed by his welcome but skittish with the knowledge of what lay ahead. "I'm glad to see you again."

"And I you, my dear." He pulled out a chair and set her in it, then shook Jonas's hand. "Good to see you too, my boy. We mustn't let so many months go by."

"My fault, I'm afraid. I was traveling." Jonas sat down and draped a napkin across his lap. "I'll be off again later this month, now that I've finished the Exposition sketches. Europe this time. I've a mind to go back to Florence."

"Don't bother with those," Uncle William said as Jonas started to pick up a menu. He glanced at Mary Anne. "I know what's best here—if you're willing to trust me?"

The humor in his eyes was contagious. Her nervousness gave way to a sudden giggly feeling. "I wouldn't know what to order if my life depended on it," she answered gaily. "I've never eaten in a restaurant before."

"Then we'll make this an experience to remember." Uncle William beckoned a passing waiter over. "We'll have the prime rib, medium rare—two regular, one lady's cut. And three baked potatoes and creamed spinach, with a Palmer House salad to start." He glanced at Mary Anne. "Will you take a little wine, Mary?"

She'd never had that before, either. "Yes, please." Jonas gave her a dubious look, which she ignored. She would only have half a glass or so. What was the use of coming all this way without doing something a little daring?

"A bottle of the Chateau St. Court Beaujolais, then, and three glasses." The waiter nodded and moved off. William leaned back in his chair. "You wait until you see the pastry cart, my dear. More delicious confections than you've likely ever imagined." He shook his head. "Such a shame my brother left Chicago. This is just the kind of place where a lovely young woman should grow up, with all the world before her."

"I agree." She sipped water from the gold-rimmed goblet nearest her, to keep back the instinctive sharp comment about the so-called virtues of small-town life. Uncle William might well sympathize, but it was wiser not to take the risk. Her job this evening was to charm him, which she seemed well on her way to doing. Displays of wit could wait until she knew him better.

The graceful Ezra deposited a basket of hot rolls on their table and departed. William offered her the basket, then took a roll himself and broke it in two. Steam rose from each half as he tore off a smaller piece and buttered it. "So, my boy, where have you been lately?"

"San Francisco." Jonas buttered his own bread. "I'm planning a series of oils for my next gallery exhibition. Immigrants, from as many different lands as I can find."

William popped a fragment of roll into his mouth. "You needn't have gone traipsing off to California for that. You can find every nation under the sun inside the Chicago city limits."

Jonas shrugged. "I like to move around. People are different in different places."

"You think so? I find them much the same. Which, I suppose, is why you're the artist and I'm the businessman." He tore off another chunk of bread, his eyes going dreamy. "I went to San Francisco once. By Pullman car, with Susannah and the children. A wonderful trip. I recall an exquisite fish restaurant, on the Wharf . . ."

Mary Anne sipped water and listened as the two men talked of eateries and inns and sights in a city she'd never seen. She hadn't known Jonas could lie so well. Uncle William would never guess that he'd actually spent most of this year waiting for her son to be born. She certainly wasn't going to tell. She lounged in her seat, watching other diners while the conversation flew past her and her churning emotions steadied. Jonas was right. Everything was going to go perfectly.

"—are your parents? Keeping well, I hope?"

She blinked, startled out of her reverie. "Very well, thank you, Uncle William." A half-full wine glass stood by her water goblet. It must have come while she was people-gazing. She took a cautious sip, then a larger and more appreciative one. "This is very good."

"It ought to be. We pay enough for it." William sipped his own wine. "Though I oughtn't to say things like that. My wife says a lady never bothers about what something costs. We gentlemen take on that task."

Here was the opening she wanted. Her fingers tightened around the stem of her glass. "Then I'm afraid I'm not entirely a lady, Uncle William. Because I'd like to talk to you about the cost of something very important. Something I hope you'll help me with, for I can't manage it on my own."

He set down his wine, his face suddenly serious. "Go on."

"Jonas told you I was visiting. He hasn't told you why." She drew in a breath, then plunged ahead. "I've left home. For good. I can't see any other way to get a college education. Father—" She pressed her lips together to squelch the bitter edge that was creeping into her voice. "My father saw no point in educating me beyond a certain . . . ornamental finishing. I have other ideas. I want to be a writer, earn my own way with my words. I can't do that in Birch Falls, and I can't do it elsewhere without more learning than I've got."

He hadn't said no yet. She chose to take that as an encouraging sign. "I applied to Northwestern this summer." Reapplied, actually, filling out the form and scribbling another essay while Aly cleaned house around her. "They offered me a place for the spring term. Only I need tuition money, and a place to stay." Another sip of wine steeled her nerves. She put the glass down and faced her uncle in direct appeal. "Jonas told me how much you helped him when he first came to Chicago. I know it's a lot to ask, but I'd be grateful for any similar help you can give me."

"Well, now." He picked up his wine glass and swirled it. Mary Anne could hear her heart beating madly in the silence. Seemingly absorbed in the movement of the liquor, Uncle William continued. "This will take some thought."

"Of course." He was going to refuse. She could read it in his carefully neutral expression. Her nose stung, and for an awful moment she feared she might cry. Out of sight beneath the table, she dug her fingernails into her palm. "I can earn my way, if I have to. If you know of some job I might take, or someone I might talk to . . ."

"I'm not sure you recognize the difficulties involved in that kind of scheme." His tone was gentle, the voice parents use to tell their children the dog died. "The kinds of positions you're most likely qualified for don't pay top wages. Certainly not enough for Northwestern's fees, let alone room and board."

"Then I'll find some other way." Her eyes felt hot. She took refuge from impending tears in her wine glass. "I'm sorry I troubled you. I didn't mean—"

"Oh, dear." Suddenly he sounded rattled. Then he was pressing a napkin into her hand and patting her fingers closed over it. She raised it to her cheek and felt moisture seeping through the cloth. "I've given you completely the wrong idea," Uncle William went on. "Of course I'll do what I can, as far as my finances will allow. There's no need for you to turn shopgirl, or bury yourself in a cheap tenement in a rough neighborhood. You come and stay with us. I'll talk to my banker and see what can be done."

She blinked at him over the napkin. Then she set it down, clenching both hands in it. "I—I don't—" The giddy feeling was back. A laugh bubbled up, then another. She clamped her mouth shut on a third, knowing that if she let go, she would dissolve in giggles or tears. Uncle William would swiftly repent his generosity to such an obviously crazed young woman.

"Don't say a word." William smiled as he refilled her wine glass. "A toast, my dear girl. To the first novel or story you publish. You'll mention your old uncle in the dedication, won't you?"

William drove them home, thankful for the darkness that hid the worn patches in the brougham's leather seats. His niece was primed to believe him capable of miracles just now, but Jonas might notice and wonder. He didn't need anyone wondering about his means, not when he'd finally spotted a possible way out of the debt trap.

The night's chill invigorated him as the horses trotted northward. Cold made the stars glitter like diamonds. For a moment he fancied them smiling at him. He'd fallen on his feet again. Through Andrew's girl. How fitting.

Mary Anne was the key to his freedom from the crushing weight of money troubles. She seemed to have Andrew's headstrong streak, but he could be quite persuasive. So could Susannah when she really wanted something. He should have no trouble convincing his wife how important it was that Mary Anne Schlegel go back to her father. Against the two of them, what young girl could possibly stand her ground?

Jonas's note had arrived on a particularly bad afternoon. Randolph, the young idiot, had managed to run up yet another mountain of gambling debt. Stomach cramping from dyspepsia, William had glared at the trembling boy from the depths of his favorite armchair. "I could tell you I'm not made of money, but I doubt that would make much of an impression. Perhaps a good working-over by your friends in the gambling halls will teach you what I can't."

Randolph went as white as a virgin on her wedding night. "You wouldn't!"

"Tell me why not." His son's spinelessness suddenly angered him as much as the lost money. "Go ahead. Give me a single good reason why I shouldn't leave you to the mercy of those sharks you play with. Make it good enough and I'll bail you out. For the last time!"

"Whatever I say, it won't be good enough." Randolph sounded petulant, as always. "It never is. Why should I try anymore?"

"Because otherwise your friends may leave you dead in a gutter. And good riddance!"

Color rushed into Randolph's cheeks. "You old bastard," he said through gritted teeth. His voice had an edge William had never heard before. "You want me to die for my sins? Then on your head be it!" He whirled and stalked out. The tail of his jacket caught the edge of a scalloped wine-table as he passed it, knocking a small china bird to the floor. Oblivious to the shattering noise it made, he slammed the study door behind him.

From across the room, William stared at the shards. They made a gleaming rosette against the varnished floorboards. He'd waited years for a flare of defiance like that, attempted to provoke it on several occasions. Yet now it unsettled him. He stood up and went to pour himself a whiskey.

The creak of the door made him turn. Not a white-faced Randolph stammering apologies, but Susannah. Her expression could have frosted a live coal.

"Congratulations on another civilized discussion with your son. You're so very good at them." Her gaze traveled to the glass in his hand. "Especially when you've been drinking."

"Shut up." He tossed the whiskey back, then poured himself another.

She watched him drink it in frigid silence. "I have no more

262

jewelry to pawn," she said when he set the empty glass down. "You'll have to think of something else."

"And so I did," he said as he drove, as if Susannah still stood in front of him. His bark of a laugh echoed in the night air. He'd racked his brains after Susannah withdrew, and come up empty. Until the note from Jonas came, with its glimpse of trouble in brother Andrew's paradise.

He turned the brougham onto Lake Shore Drive. The ring of hooves blended with the crashing surf. Andrew never would have let his daughter come to Chicago alone. Indeed, he'd vowed never to let any of his family set foot there. Her arrival on her half-brother's doorstep suggested deep trouble between father and child. The cause of it, he could only determine by getting to know the girl. For the moment, it didn't matter. What mattered was that any rift between Andrew and Mary Anne might be turned to his advantage.

So he'd invited his young relations to dinner at the Palmer House, seen his niece and taken her measure. Her desire for wider horizons seemed sincere, though he would have bet every penny he'd once possessed that something more serious had played a part in her flight. For flight it was, and no mistake. The girl had said as much. Left home for good. *Not if I have anything to say about it, my dear.*

A gust of wind brought the smell of horse sweat. He breathed it in, feeling lighter of heart than he had for months. Young Mary Anne would come to Evanston, make herself at home with her dear uncle and his family. And then he'd start to work on her. Point out the hardships of independence for a woman, the likelihood of her starving slowly in a garret. The pain her poor mother must be suffering, bereft of her only daughter. How much she would miss the comforts of the life she'd left behind. By the time he finished with her, she'd be begging for a train ticket back home.

Andrew might even be grateful. Especially after his little darling told him how well Uncle William had explained the way the world worked. Grateful or not, his pride would force him to pay William back somehow, to balance the scales between them . . . for example, by lending William money to pay Randolph's gambling debts. The funds would go to more pressing things, of course, until William cadged another loan. He smiled. Between the embers of Andrew's family feeling and his fierce desire not to owe his brother anything, William could string this out for months—maybe even a year or two. By that time, one or another of his enterprises would surely show returns.

He thought of his niece, half-crying with joy at his promise of help. *Oh, I'll help you, my dear. As much as you'll help me.*

CHAPTER TWENTY-ONE

A fierce neck cramp woke Florian from uneasy sleep. Close by, he smelled coffee. His eyelids felt gummy. He pried them open and saw Powell sitting on a Spackle barrel, sipping from a Styrofoam cup. The basement glowed with the grayish light of early morning.

"Coffee's upstairs." Powell sounded wrung out. The bags under his eyes looked like giant bruises. "I checked with the men at the cottage. Nobody showed."

"God damn it." Florian swore without energy. After a night of catnaps, with only a thin quilt and pillow between him and the cold cement floor, he felt twice his forty years. He threw off his borrowed blanket and creaked to his feet, bones protesting like an arthritic old man's. "He made us. He knew we were here."

"Or he's paranoid. Days Inn, Windy Pines—could be he likes to move around."

Memory nagged at Florian, of a hotel-room door hastily slammed shut. "No. That bastard knows me. Must have spotted me back in the city." Outside Ruthie's apartment, maybe, skulking around to see who turned up. It hardly mattered. What mattered was that his own presence at the Windy Pines had spooked Chapman badly enough to keep him on the move. So they were back to the guessing game, against a quarry who knew they were hunting him.

He tottered upstairs to the nearest bathroom, then found the industrial-sized percolator on a counter in the vast kitchen. Options for lightening the thick, dark brew were powder or heavily preserved liquid in dinky plastic cuplets. He dumped two cuplets of creamer into his coffee, swirled it around to mix it and headed back down.

"The trailers," he said to Powell after a healthy swig. He could feel the caffeine burning into his brain stem, kicking his slumbering instincts awake. "Which ones are empty, and who lives nearby?"

"Not many folks in them this time of year." Powell rubbed his eyes. The coffee had brought some color to his cheeks, though he still looked like a hangover victim. "There's Paul Olmsted about half a mile down the road—snowmobiler, comes up for the end of deer season and stays through March. Frank and Lucy Harrison—they run a Christmas tree farm halfway to town. Bill and Joanne Witek have a cabin close by. Joanne runs a coffee shop in town. Bill goes ice-fishing. The rest are summer places." He drained his cup. "Addresses are in my office."

Florian gulped his own coffee. "Let's go."

"A large hot cider and an elephant ear, please," Rachel told the counter girl at Witek's Coffee Shop. Probably not much older than Linnet, she was stockier and bustier, with braces on her teeth and a pea-sized zit in the middle of her chin. Her sullen face said she hated her looks, her job, Rachel and every one of the other three customers in the place.

Rachel swallowed a manic chuckle. Half-empty quiet was what she needed right now, along with a nice blood-sugar hit. Maybe then she'd stop feeling like a character in a Victoria Holt novel. Clementine would love this whole crazy story, once Rachel got back into town. She paid for the food, then carried her hot mug and full plate to a window table. She could watch the passersby, few though they were. Maybe she'd spot Lucas

Walker. The urge to laugh came back. *If I told him what I've been doing this morning, he'd probably think I was bonkers.*

She still couldn't believe it. A cautious sip of cider, tangy-sweet and hot enough to boil an egg, steadied her a little. She gazed at the street without seeing it, instead recalling the morning's conversation in Terry Powell's office. *Cousin Terry. I never had cousins before. Now I've got at least two I know of, and I've only been up here four days!*

She almost hadn't talked to him, busy as he was. The cop who'd been with him at the mansion was there, both of them bent over a legal pad on which Chief Powell was writing. Neither man had shaved, and Powell's hair stuck out in wisps. She'd started to turn away and stumbled over a badly placed chair. The cops looked up then, and she knew she'd never forgive herself if she walked away. The worst Powell could do was tell her to come back later.

He hadn't. In fact, he seemed to welcome the distraction. The second cop, introduced as Detective Florian, tore the written-on page from the pad and ducked out right after her arrival. She wondered if they'd found Linnet's father, but swiftly dismissed the question as none of her business. She had something else to talk about.

As Powell sat down with a politely interested look, she took out the diary, opened the cover, and slid the book across his desk. "Bogart Nilssen at the Windy Pines tells me this is your great-grandfather. He appears to be mine as well."

For the rest of her life, she would cherish the joy in his face when he saw Rhys Powell's self-portrait. A comforting contrast to Jackson, who had frozen her out the minute he learned she was family. Powell touched the penciled face in the diary as if brushing a real cheek. "Granddaddy Rhys. He died when I was six. Taught me to draw." His eyes went soft with memory. "My Grandpa David went about a year later. Grandma said he

---

missed his father too much to stay. He was Granddaddy Rhys' favorite son. Where did you find this?"

"At Schlegel House." Powell didn't need to know the circumstances. "Actually, Mr. Schlegel's granddaughter found it. Buried in a trunk in the attic."

"Schlegel House." She glimpsed a shadow in his eyes, beneath the warmth and the wonder. "So it was true."

Over cups of coffee that had sat too long on the burner, he related Rhys Powell's side of Mary Anne Schlegel's long-ago romance. "My father told me that story when I turned fifteen. Fell in love with my first girl that year. Jackson's daughter." The shadow deepened. "After she left, I wondered if he'd been trying to warn me: Don't fall for one of them, those Schlegel women have wandering feet." He topped off his coffee with a reflective look. "He always wondered, my Granddaddy Rhys did—whether Mary Anne was pregnant when she left. Never heard from her, though. After word went round that she'd disappeared in Chicago, he raved about going there. Swore he'd find her and bring her home. Their child too, if there was one. But he never went." He gave her a crooked smile. "Afraid of what he might find, I guess. Every town gossip had a theory—she'd been slugged and rolled and lost her memory, killed for pocket money, shanghaied into the bordello life. Granddaddy Rhys hated them for it. Dad told me Rhys once threatened Adeline Pryce with a libel suit for printing some of the juicier stories in a pamphlet guide to town. Addy ran the Windy Pines back in the forties—the old inn. It burned down in 1968."

"She thought about telling him." Rachel nodded toward the diary. "That's her journal. You might want to read it. She loved Rhys—she talks about him a lot."

"Just not enough to stay." Again, some memory seemed to weigh him down. She watched him shake it off with an effort. "Poor old Andrew Schlegel. He was right but never knew it."

"About . . . ?"

"After Mary Anne disappeared, he put everything in trust for her or her descendants. Never gave up hope that some might turn up one day." He looked puzzled. "Jackson didn't tell you?"

"We haven't had much chance to talk." Unease sparked in the back of her mind. "Is there anything left after all this time? There's the house, I assume." Her coffee was going cold. She toyed with the idea of a warm-up. It tasted like distilled tar, but she felt fidgety; she needed to move around.

"Shares in the railroad, too. If nobody sold them off, they'd be worth a good chunk by now. Hadleigh Mine's been tapped out since the seventies, but the family trust likely made other investments over the years."

The spark became a flare. She set down her cup on the edge of the desk, between the In box and a stack of green forms. "There's money? How much?"

He shrugged. "Enough to keep the house up. Maybe more." A frown crossed his face. "The Schlegel Trust owns the mansion. Jackson told me the law firm that manages it, just the other night. Bizal, that was one name. Slovenian. Those always stick in my mind. The other was English . . . like that actress, the one in *Howard's End* awhile back."

She must have looked surprised. He grinned wryly. "Small-town cops like good movies, too. Sometimes we even read the book first."

She blushed. "I'm sorry. What a snob."

"Thompson. That's it. Thompson and Bizal. Not local. Duluth, I think. Could be Minneapolis. Might be worth dropping them a line."

Which she'd done not half an hour ago, her mind veering between delighted and uneasy speculation. The words taking shape on her laptop seemed surreal even as she scanned them for spelling errors before printing.

Dear Sirs,

In seeking my family roots, I recently discovered that I am a direct descendant of your deceased client, Andrew Jackson Schlegel, through his daughter, Mary Anne. I understand that my newfound connection, if proved, entitles me to claim a long-held bequest, and I would greatly appreciate any information you can give me in this matter. I enclose a SASE for your reply . . .

She'd wondered, as she dropped her letter into the corner mailbox, what its recipients would make of it. *Wouldn't it be something if there really is a fortune?* She slammed the door on darker thoughts. She didn't want to wonder anymore why Jackson had kept silent about it.

She nibbled her elephant ear, washing down the morsel with cooling cider. There couldn't be much money, of course. Not after all this time. Yet the thrilling possibility refused to be squelched. She could feel a smile creeping across her face. A small boy, passing by outside in his mother's wake, caught the look and grinned back. She watched him until he was out of sight, feeling misty-eyed. What a wonderful place this drab little northern town was turning out to be.

"You look like you just won the lottery," a half-familiar voice said in her ear. Lucas Walker was standing by her table, wearing the brown parka and a smile that turned shy when she looked at him. "I saw you across the street. Thought I'd say hello. May I join you?"

"Sure." Her giddy mood made her ridiculously glad to see him. "Pull up a chair. Have something. My treat. The elephant ears are terrific."

He dropped his coat on an empty seat and headed toward the counter, returning a few minutes later with his own elephant ear and a cup of black coffee. "Feel like sharing the good news? I could use some."

"I'm sorry things aren't going well."

He shrugged. "It happens. Worst thing's the kid, caught in the middle. I try not to put her there, but . . ."

He blew on his coffee as if blowing glass. Clearly, he didn't want to talk about it. Poor Lucas, he needed a distraction . . . and she had a doozy. She leaned across the table toward him. "I've had the most amazing morning. You won't believe it. I'm still not sure I do myself."

A corner of his mouth crooked upward. "From that smile, I kind of figured."

"You remember me kidding around about being the sole heiress to a family fortune?" She waited for him to swallow before dropping her bombshell. "Well, there really is one. Or there might be. And I get it. I think."

His stunned look delighted her. She broke off a chunk of elephant ear and sat back. "Isn't that wild? I can hardly believe this is happening to me. I never win raffles. I have to cheat at solitaire. I've never once found a parking space right in front of where I wanted to go. But now this falls in my lap. All because my great-whatever-granddad was the stubbornest man alive. He left everything to his daughter or her children. Or their children, and so on. All the way down to me. Isn't that the craziest thing?"

"That's some story." He let out a long breath. "You trust the source?"

"The local police chief. He didn't tell me how he knew it—though he did say he was in love with Jackson's daughter once. Maybe she told him." Through a bite of elephant ear, she continued. "Linnet found a folder full of legal stuff in Andrew Schlegel's old desk. I thought I'd head out there, see if there's a copy of the will."

Carefully, he tore a piece from his own pastry. "You said there might be money. I hate to be a killjoy, but—"

"Oh, I know. There might just be that big house and a pittance to keep it going." She licked buttery pastry flakes off her fingers. "Terry—that's the police chief—told me who handles the estate, though. I sent them a letter this morning. I couldn't quite bring myself to call them; it's not real enough yet. If I don't hear something after a week, maybe I'll work up the nerve to phone."

"If there is any money, they'll want proof." He was shredding his elephant ear, a shocking waste of good pastry. "Got any you can use?"

She patted her coat, which lay across a spare chair. "Mary Anne Schlegel's diary. I photocopied the important pages. They ought to be enough to get me a letter or a phone call back, at least."

"Is there more?" He looked like Quincy tracking a moth. The lawyer in him must be scenting a case.

She nodded. "An affidavit, connecting Mary Anne's brother Jonas to the baby who grew up to be my grandfather. Plus all the records from there to me. And whatever else I find at the mansion." She drained her cider, then threw him an apologetic look. "I'd invite you along, but I'm on Jackson's enemy list right now. If he spots me trespassing, he might have me thrown in jail. Lord knows how he'd react if I turn up with company."

"I've got things to do anyway." He traced a circle in the crumbs on his plate. "I'm dying to know how this turns out, though. Would you have dinner with me tonight? Tell me all about it? I can pick you up. In the lobby, if you'd rather."

"That'd be great."

The skinny busboy had long since cleared his plate with its mountain of pastry shreds. Luke nursed his third cup of coffee while unpleasant thoughts scurried like rats in his head. One minute he owned the universe; the next, it came crashing in on him. Why had he ever thought his luck would change?

The coffee tasted like swill. He fought the impulse to whip

his mug at the wall. His chair shot back, scraping the floorboards as he lurched up toward the counter.

The counter girl gaped as he slammed the mug down hard enough to slop liquid over one side. "I want a refill. Fresh. I'm going to watch you make it."

"S-sure. Okay." She picked up the cup as if it might explode.

"Dump it and rinse it." His rage eased a fraction as she did what he'd told her. He loitered by the counter until the fresh pot was full. Watching it drip kept him from thinking. The way his thoughts were turning just now, he'd punch a hole in the counter glass, and then the little twit on the other side would call the cops. He didn't need that kind of trouble. Rachel Connolly had dumped enough on his head.

Eyes on her shoes, the girl pushed a fresh cup toward him. He sipped it on the way back to his table. Better. Not much, but as good as he could expect. It was hot, and drinking it gave him something to do. Steadied him down a little so he could figure out his next move. No wonder the old man had looked sick, running into him earlier at Kovacs' place. A bitter chuckle escaped him. So much for Kovacs checking the will. Might as well tell him not to bother.

He ripped open a sugar packet and poured it out on the table. A Sweet 'N' Low packet followed. Damned nosy bitch— why couldn't she mind her own fucking business? The minute that letter hit their offices, the attorneys would hold everything while they checked Rachel Connolly out. Too much to hope she wasn't legit; she obviously thought she had proof, and she hadn't struck him as stupid. He picked up a fork and pricked little patterns in the hill of white dust. Why did she have to start asking questions about Grace's family pile?

He gouged the fork into the tabletop. He'd probably win the custody fight, for all the good it would do him. What kind of life could he offer Linnet on a barman's salary plus tips? Only the kind he'd hated—eating macaroni and oatmeal because they stretched, living in a shitbox with gang-bangers on every corner, never having a few dollars to call his own. The edge of the fork bit into his hand. That dumpy little bitch with Grace's face was going to cost him everything. Christ, but somebody up there hated him. Though not as much as he hated Rachel Connolly right now.

The image of pine trees, deep and dark, rose in his mind. He set down the fork. It had left two red streaks behind, deep and angry. One of them was purpling in the center. He massaged the marks. The slow motion of his fingers helped ward off sudden terror. Along with it came exhilaration, which frightened him even more.

I can't do this. I don't know how. I'll slip up. Around went his fingertips, slow circles against his flesh.

I didn't slip up before. Left that cop chasing shadows.

She'd said she was going to the mansion. He glanced at his watch. More than an hour gone while he stewed and moaned. She was probably there by now. He gulped coffee while his mind raced. Head out and nail her on her way back? Or keep their dinner date and find out what she'd managed to get her hands on, so he could bury it nice and deep?

The laugh prompted by that last thought had a ragged edge. He stood up, threw some bills on the table and walked out into skin-tingling cold.

The paper in her hand, yellow and brittle, was barely readable in the fading daylight. Rachel squinted at the faint type.

I, Andrew Jackson Schlegel, being of sound mind and disposition, do on this third of September, 1904, declare this to be my last will and testament . . .

She rubbed her eyes and wished for a flashlight. Dusk came

early this far north, especially with snow threatening. She hadn't intended to stay so long, but the fragments of family history in the old rolltop were too compelling to resist. Julia Schlegel's letters to her stepson, full of the loneliness she couldn't express; Jonas's replies, terse at first, then less guarded and dotted with sketches of life along Taylor Street; Jonas's letters to Mary Anne, getting longer and more sophisticated as their recipient grew older. The words gave her pieces of the past, small bright jewels from the hearts of her forbears. People she hadn't known existed a month ago, who now lived as vividly in her mind as Terry Powell or Bogart Nilssen. She felt a sudden, sharp sympathy for Jackson. Why not live in the past when it was all you had?

The letters sat in neat stacks beside her on the long table in the attic anteroom. Linnet's folder "full of legal stuff" lay open on her lap. She'd found Andrew's will halfway through the pile, sandwiched between an 1872 deed to Hadleigh Mine and William's never-cashed bank draft dated the same year. The will's legalese, combined with the fading print and poor light, made it rough going to read. She skimmed over a paragraph of boiler-plate, then stopped at the name *William Henry Schlegel*.

Paying careful attention, she reread the paragraph aloud. " 'In the absence of any such descendants, I bequeath all my monies and possessions save those previously noted to the heirs and assigns of my brother, William Henry Schlegel. This disbursement shall take place one hundred years after the date of my death. As befits their actions toward me and mine, neither my brother nor his son shall in any way benefit from this my final will. Let them instead reflect upon the wages of sin, and consider those wages well earned.' "

She stared into space while her mind circled warily around the words she had just read. *William. His heirs. Jackson.* Sudden agitation made her fumble as she flipped pages. She found the number she sought near the top of page four. *Seventy-five thousand dollars. Jesus.*

The will drifted to her lap. She'd read Laura Ingalls Wilder as a girl; young Laura had earned nine dollars sewing shirts in the 1880s, then a fantastic sum. How much would seventy-five thousand then be worth by now?

Enough for Jackson to keep his mouth shut when someone showed up who could take it. Her mouth felt dry. She slid off the table in a flurry of motion, clutching the will in both hands. *How do I know there's anything left? Nineteen-twenty-nine, the Depression, two world wars—that's a lot for a legacy to survive.*

For no good reason, she felt a surge of relief. She set the will down on top of Andrew and Julia's marriage license and Mary Anne's birth certificate. She would photocopy the documents tomorrow, as keepsakes if nothing else. Beyond that, she'd wait for the lawyers. Wild conjectures only gave her stomach trouble.

The rest of the folder held several thick sheaves of paper. A cover letter attached to the first one was addressed to Mr. Jonas Schlegel in Birch Falls. Not Chicago. Puzzled, she looked at the date.

October 30, 1907

> *Dear Mr. Schlegel, please accept our condolences on the recent death of your father. He was among our most esteemed clients, and we are confident that his son will prove a capable executor of his estate . . .*

She pushed the letter aside and skimmed the pages that followed. They appeared to be a financial report summing up Andrew's investments. A similar report lay beneath, and a third, and a fourth. She riffled through the rest of the folder until she found the report with the latest date: June 20, 1942. Curious, she hunted through columns of financial jargon for the total. The figure jumped out at her: three hundred thousand dollars.

The jittery feeling came back with the force of a hurricane. *That's more than sixty years ago. It may not mean anything.* She closed the folder and dropped it on the table. Across the wide backyard, she could make out the caretaker's cottage in the gathering gloom. The windows resembled empty eye sockets, blank and dark.

Several tense minutes went by while she argued with herself. Then she scooped up the papers she wanted to keep and headed for the stairs. She'd spotted a standing work lamp in the basement when she'd briefly looked there for Jackson, as well as a shelving unit loaded with supplies. Batteries would surely be among them. The cottage couldn't have much storage space; it wasn't unreasonable to assume Jackson might keep his own important papers here.

Halfway down to the first floor, she glanced out the window toward the tree line. The highway lay beyond it. No way to see if anyone was coming. She hurried down the steps and through the house, anxious to be finished before Jackson came back.

CHAPTER TWENTY-TWO

October 28, 1893

The sun has shone almost every day since I arrived in Evanston to take up my life again. Dare I regard that as an omen? Uncle William advises me not to trust the good weather, that it will change faster than a woman's mind over which hat to wear to church. I forbore to tell him that some of us have only one hat, and prefer it that way. Or to mention how long he took the other night choosing which tie pin to show off at the Auditorium. For all he is giving me, enduring the occasional joke at womanhood's expense seems a small price to pay.

My own clouds have lifted as well, a little more every day. My very first Sunday here, someone's infant started wailing in church, and I nearly dissolved in tears. Aunt Susannah came up later that evening with a cup of chamomile for my nerves. She thought I was homesick. Better that than the truth.

The wait for spring promises to be comfortable, long and dull. I miss Taylor Street: factory girls jabbering in Russian and Polish, stinking stockyard men passing through en route to Packingtown, stout Italian mamas calling their children, old men drinking grappa on the front stoop and arguing half the night. Here, virtually everyone I've met wears the same clothes and talks of the same things in the same language, with the same accent. It's a beautiful town, though. And there is Northwestern, my Jerusalem. November, December, January, February . . . four more months. Uncle William and Aunt Susannah are kind-

ness itself, but I can't help counting the days.

I wish I could tell Rhys. I wonder if he would be happy for me.

Today, at any rate, I shall have my fill of variety. Cousin Randolph is squiring me to the World's Columbian Exposition. A year late to commemorate Columbus' journey to the New World, but I gather the wait was worth it. Chicago seems to do nothing by halves. I can hardly wait to see it.

I love the city. I can feel its heartbeat in my own chest. Greedy, bustling, happily grabbing for everything like a three-year-old rooting through candy barrels. I don't want to leave it. Ever.

The lake breeze, made pleasantly warm by Indian summer, ruffled Mary Anne's hair as the steamer chuffed toward its destination. She leaned as far out over the deck rail as she dared, attempting to peer around a herd of top-hatted, capped and bonneted heads for a glimpse of the fabled White City. Every resident of Chicago, its suburbs and the entire body of surrounding states seemed to have chosen to ride this particular boat to the Exposition's closing day. She could see snatches of buildings through the crush: a portico between two sets of burly shoulders, the point of a Greek-style pediment over a cluster of tulle-swathed hats. The scent of Lake Michigan, clean and damp, reached her on a puff of wind. She grinned and settled back on her heels. Let someone else get a look at the fairgrounds. For the moment, she felt content with the sparkle of sunlight on water and the cheerful buzz of a hundred conversations. The city's music, Chicago itself given voice by a chattering choir.

She turned to Randolph, beside her on the deck. "Isn't it glorious?"

His attempt at a smile didn't reach his eyes. "It's pretty enough, I guess."

She patted his hand, which lay near her own on the railing.

Though nearly thirty, he seemed less sure of himself than a child of ten. Especially around his father. When Uncle William had joined them in the breakfast room that morning, poor Randolph could barely sit still. He'd gotten up for more eggs, then more fried potatoes, neither of which he ate. Then he dropped a fork and needed a clean one, after that a fresh napkin. After ten minutes, he left the room, so rattled by his father's presence that he stuck a butter knife in his pocket. Uncle William appeared not to notice.

Randolph was fidgeting beside her now, toying with something in his trouser pocket. Not the butter knife, she hoped. He was probably bored to death, escorting a youngster like her around a fair he'd doubtless seen several times since its May opening. She wondered if he'd planned to meet a lady, then chuckled at her own fancy. Thin-faced, slope-shouldered Randolph made an unlikely romantic hero.

She missed Jonas and Aly, with a sudden fierceness that made her throat hurt. They would have laughed at the women's outrageous hats, made up funny stories about the visiting farmers in their scratchy Sunday suits, pretended to watch for whales in the lake. Randolph wasn't even up to ordinary conversation. She clenched her hands on the rail and stared across the water. A thin swatch of clouds drifted over the sun, turning the bright wavelets a cold gray-blue. Almost the same color as her baby's eyes, the one glimpse she'd gotten of them before plummeting into sleep. She blinked hard, then craned her neck again for a sight of the approaching fairgrounds.

Randolph cleared his throat. "Are . . . are you all right?"

Surprise made her flustered. "Oh, yes. Fine." She summoned up a bright smile. "I'm not used to boats. I'll be all right once we land."

Looking relieved, he nodded toward the shoreline. "Nearly there now. Where shall we go first?"

They began with the Court of Honor, following the crowd from the boat dock through the water-gate to the huge, walkway-bounded lagoon. Around the shimmering square rose the exhibit halls, colonnaded cliffs of blazing white with cooler gray shadows beneath. Straight ahead of them, the vast gold dome that topped another structure shed light of its own like a second sun. Mary Anne circled in place, head tilted back in a futile effort to take in the whole panorama. The crowd flowed around her like water. Against the turquoise sky with its wisps of cloud, colored pennants fluttered. The quickening breeze brought the smell of the lake, a passing woman's perfume and a far-off scent of grilling onions. She could hear the strains of an orchestra quarreling with a distant calliope.

She breathed deep of the city air, then turned laughing to Randolph. "You pick a building. I can't!"

"That one." He pointed over his left shoulder, long-faced as ever. What ailed the man, that a place this gorgeous couldn't lift his spirits for one minute? Shaking her head, she followed him through the court and down a prettily landscaped canal bank toward their destination. Small boats whizzed by, packed with sightseers. Ahead of her, Randolph slowed, watching the boats.

"Electric power," he said when she reached him. His expression had lightened a little, from thunderheads to mere overcast. "That's how they run so fast. Tamed lightning in their innards. You wouldn't believe what we can do with it nowadays." His eyes followed the speeding boats as another man's might have followed a pretty woman.

Sudden sympathy warmed her reply. "I never saw electric lights until I came here, let alone electric boats."

"Want to see some more?" Almost smiling now, he offered her his arm. She took it, and they walked the remaining yards together to the Electricity Building.

They spent the next hour marveling at electric brushes for

281

soothing headaches, electric calculating machines, even an electric kitchen that would have sent Mrs. Tomczack into sputtering fits of delighted Czech. Randolph eased up enough to start explaining how electricity worked, though she begged him to stop halfway through. "My brain aches. I'll need one of those brush things in a minute."

He looked embarrassed. "I guess I didn't explain it very well."

"You did as well as anyone could. I simply haven't the right spaces in my head to fit all that into. Shall we have lunch?"

He took her to a beer garden atop the Manufactures and Liberal Arts Building, from which they could see a sweeping segment of the White City. It floated on the huge, man-made lagoon the way she imagined Venice must, domes and spires drawing elegant lines between the glittering water and the sky. More electric boats buzzed around the lagoon, or flitted beneath the bridge that marked the edge of the Court of Honor. Mary Anne watched them for awhile, then looked farther south where a gigantic wheel towered over the long strip of the Midway. "What is that?! It must be a mile high!"

"Ferris wheel," Randolph said. "You can't see them from here, but it has little cars attached." He picked up his foaming beer glass, his grin the ghost of Uncle William's. "Care for a ride?"

Her face said yes for her.

A short while later, comfortably full of Thuringer sausage, sauerkraut and German potato salad, they paid the bill and set off across the fairgrounds for the Midway. The line by the Ferris wheel stretched nearly the length of a city block. Anticipating a long wait, Mary Anne unwrapped her handkerchief, which contained four sweet cardamom cookies snagged from their dessert plate. Looking amused, Randolph took one. She did likewise, nibbling its crumbly edges more for something to do than because she was hungry. After a meal like that, she might never need to eat again. She watched the Ferris wheel make its majestic circles high up in the clear air. "Should we be on that contraption so soon after eating?"

He laughed, looking unburdened for the first time since she'd met him. "It moves too slowly to make us sick. The fun of it is in seeing for miles and miles. At the very top, you can almost see clear to Springfield."

"You can not."

"All right, I'm exaggerating. Some." He bit into his cookie. "But you can see an awfully long way."

All the way to Minnesota? She thought of Rhys and caught her breath. He would have loved the Ferris wheel's ponderous grace, the ageless elegance of the huge exhibit halls, all the fair's color and noise and life. She could see him sketching it, or trying to, then giving up as the spectacle overwhelmed him. She swallowed hard and pressed her lips together.

Behind her, Randolph shifted his weight. The crowd stirred, shuffled and inched ahead. She followed. By the time they stopped moving, she had recovered her poise. The huge wheel was closer now, its curving steel ribs throwing shadows on the ground like the web of a mechanical spider.

"You miss home?" Randolph asked.

"This is home. From now on." Putting the idea into words made it real for the first time since her arrival on Jonas's doorstep. *Goodbye, Rhys. May you be as happy someday as I expect to be.* Propelled by a sudden sense of lightness, she followed the crowd forward again. They stopped almost under the Ferris wheel. She and Randolph would be among the next to board.

Two by two, lucky riders passed the red velvet rope that marked the gateway to their adventure. The concessionaire, in a straw boater and striped jacket that didn't quite button over his ample stomach, took each couple's fifty-cent fare. Randolph fumbled in his pocket for coins. As he pulled out a silver dollar, two objects clattered to the ground: the butter knife and a small silver earring-box she'd seen on Aunt Susannah's dressing table.

She started to ask what on earth he was doing with them, then saw his face and closed her mouth. Randolph bent to pick up the fallen items, fierce color flooding his neck above his shirt and jacket collar. He stuffed them back in his pocket, pushed roughly past her and dropped the dollar in the concessionaire's outstretched hand. Silent, she followed him into the car.

The door clanged shut behind them. The car lurched, then rose a few feet before stopping. Below them, Mary Anne saw the concessionaire closing other doors on cars full of excited customers. Randolph was staring over the city, away from the fairgrounds and the lakefront. He sat still as a statue, eyes empty except for a tiny spark of fear.

She kept her voice low, so as not to carry to nearby cars. "You're in trouble, aren't you?"

"Yes." One word, clipped and sharp, warning her to stop.

Her next words surprised her. "Can I help?"

A succession of emotions passed over his face, from amazement to wild hope to bitter resignation. "No one can." One hand went into his pocket, his arm tightening as if he'd clenched a fist around the contents.

They rode the Ferris wheel in silence. Mary Anne enjoyed the marvelous view as best she could, while trying to make sense of what was going on. Her cousin had stolen the knife and his mother's earring-box. He had brought them to the fair, which he clearly had not been enjoying until they started talking about the boats and other electric gadgets. The cloud around him had never fully lifted, she realized—only thinned enough to let a little light through. Whatever the trouble was, it was going to break over him soon. And he knew it.

He was looking toward the stockyards and Packingtown, surely the least pleasant portion of the panorama around them.

Some kind of business setback? She had no idea what Randolph did for a living. He must do something; he was nearly thirty. He left the house almost every day, though at different times, and his attendance at meals was erratic. What kind of business could a man be engaged in with such irregular hours? Come to that, what business calamity could possibly be staved off with a silver butter knife and a lady's expensive trinket?

She let out a sharp, irritated breath. He turned at the sound, looking as if he wanted to apologize, then shifted in his seat until he nearly had his back to her. She gazed back out across the city, trying to lose herself in the grandeur of the huge, flat landscape.

As the giant wheel slowed, Randolph stirred just enough to check his watch. They climbed stiffly out of the car, he offering her a steadying hand as she hitched her long skirts away from her heels. She kept hold of him as her feet touched solid ground. "Randolph, if you'll only tell me—"

"I can't." He snatched his hand away. "Leave it, for God's sake." He tossed the words over his shoulder as he strode down the Midway, so fast she had to run to keep up.

"You could at least slow down so I don't break my neck," she called after him. He stopped, but didn't turn. When she reached him, he looked so miserable that she regretted her sharpness. They walked onward, back toward the exhibit halls and pavilions.

They stopped outside a teashop on the outskirts of the Midway, near the multicolored Transportation Building. Randolph fished in his pocket and came up with two more dollars. "I have to meet someone. Stay here, have a pot of tea. I shouldn't be long—"

"I'll come with you." She turned away from the teashop entrance, only to be stopped by Randolph's grip on her arm.

"You can't. Don't you understand that? You can't help. You

can only get hurt. I'd never forgive myself if I let that happen."

"This . . . person you're going to meet." She didn't look at him, concentrating instead on smoothing her sleeve where he'd grabbed it. "Is he threatening you?"

"Don't you listen?!" His voice cracked. He clenched a hand in his hair, then took her arm again. "If you want to help me, stay here and enjoy yourself. Keep out of trouble."

A uniformed guard, one of the Exposition's own patrolmen, strolled past them. Mary Anne allowed Randolph to guide her into the teashop. "Why not go to the police? Isn't that what they're there for?"

His bitter laugh was loud enough to turn heads at nearby tables. He lowered his voice, but spoke with a similar edge. "Half the police force around here works for the people I owe money to. The rest wish they did. Do you understand now? Even a little?"

"But surely—"

He pressed the money into her hand. "I have to go. I'll come back in an hour." He turned and strode out, past the waiter who was just approaching their table.

The waiter stared after him. Then he clothed his face in polite inquiry and opened his order-book. "What can I get for you, miss?"

She ordered a pot of tea and a slice of apple pie, neither of which she wanted. Randolph had disappeared into the crowd, heading west back down the Midway. Minutes passed while curiosity and anger warred with sneaking fear. Anger won. Randolph's tormentors shouldn't be allowed to harm a kind and decent man. If she hurried, she might still catch up with him and persuade him to get help.

She left twenty-five cents on the table for the waiter and hurried out.

★　★　★　★　★

Forty-seventh and Halsted. Forty-seventh and Halsted. The words tumbled through Randolph's mind in time with his rushing feet. Strange, to be racing toward doom instead of dragging his steps. Sometime during the afternoon, he had ceased wishing to avoid the inevitable. Now he wanted it over with. He thought of his young cousin's smile, her innocent joy in this snake pit she saw as a place of wonders. He might have been that innocent once. He didn't remember anymore.

His mother's earring-box clinked against the butter knife in his pocket. These, his own best pair of wrist studs set with small emeralds, and a forty-carat cigarette case he'd won in his only successful game of cards were all he had to offer. That and yet another IOU, the latest embodiment of a desperate promise to pay up that he had scant hope of keeping. He knew it. So did they.

He stopped dead on the Midway, in the shadow of the gate that marked it off from the surrounding streets. A stout man in a checked coat bumped into him and swore. Randolph scarcely heard him. What was he thinking, offering up penny trifles to Chicago's gambling king? A man who could buy a mayor, half the police force and most of the Democratic Party had no use for a paltry fifty dollars—the best Randolph could hope to get from any pawnbroker, all of whom could smell desperation like sweat. But he had no alternative. Except to skulk home like a whipped dog and wait for them to come get him. Even the worst beating was better than that. So long as he owed them money, they weren't likely to kill him.

He hurried onward, leaving the Exposition behind. The noise of the crowd receded until he lost it in the thunk of his shoes on the damp wooden sidewalk. Last evening's early rain had dried out everywhere but here, where nothing ever vanished completely. Rainwater, mud, the stink of the bottle, the hopelessness of a losing streak—they all lingered, stubborn as the smell of blood from nearby Packingtown. He walked and turned and walked some more, past squalid tenements interrupted by taverns that sold cheap beer. Salvation in a glass or a bottle. Courage for the coward. Luck for the man who'd been born without any. The taste of Irish whiskey came alive in his mouth, smooth and smoky. He averted his gaze from the tavern signs and picked up his pace.

A streetcar rumbled, shockingly close. Someone shouted: "Out of the street, you crazy bastard!" Startled, he halted. The car nearly flattened his toes as it flashed by. Its wake threw grit in his eyes. He blinked to clear them and looked around with cold dread. On the opposite corner stood a gambling den he knew. They would meet him on its far side, out of plain sight.

He gazed after the departing streetcar, wishing he'd had the nerve to throw himself in front of it. Then he stepped into the street.

Drat this skirt. Mary Anne held it as high as she dared, wishing in vain for a pair of bloomers. Even with the hem safely far from her shoes, walking felt as slow as wading through a snowbank. At least she was out of the crowds. The few pedestrians, mostly hurrying about their business, allowed her a clear view of Randolph far ahead. She'd lost him twice on the Midway, then again away from the fair when he turned two corners in quick succession. The city streets, bewildering enough near Jonas's flat, were a maze designed by a madman hereabouts. They crossed and crisscrossed, slanting sharply and sometimes running in tandem. They halted at the river, or became stinking alleys washed by menacing shadows. She had long since ceased to wonder how Randolph knew his way around so well. She didn't care to know.

She passed a tenement of soot-stained brick, one story taller than its neighbors. A whip-thin youth loitered in the doorway. He eyed her as if adding up the value of her clothing and handbag. She hurried past him. Pedestrians were almost non-existent now. She hadn't seen a blue uniform since leaving the fairgrounds. Only low buildings with blank windows, rotting planks over thick dark mud, and occasional people passing with their heads bowed, as if wary of seeing too much. For the first time since leaving the teashop, she felt afraid.

She glanced over her shoulder and was glad to see empty sidewalk behind her. The young tough in the apartment-house doorway seemed not to consider her worth robbing. She could try to go back, though that meant passing the tough again. She slowed to catch her breath, then realized with a sinking stomach that she had no notion where she was.

Motion and a shout up ahead caught her attention. A slender figure, tall, dressed in a gray suit, jumped back out of the path of a streetcar. From the way he moved, she recognized Randolph.

He could escort her out of here, or at least tell her the way. She started toward him just as he crossed the street a block ahead. He passed a seedy-looking corner tavern and vanished around its far side. She lifted her skirts knee-high and ran after him.

King Mike's bully boys were waiting when he arrived. Randolph's gut churned at the sight of them. Mickey, red-headed and burly, leaning on a baseball bat; Crazy Macaulay, grinning with broken teeth as he swung a length of thick chain doubtless cadged from the slaughterhouses; and two men he didn't recognize, both holding pipe sections wrapped in bed sheets. The shirt studs, knife and earring-box dropped from nerveless fingers as Mickey straightened up and came toward him.

"Well, now," Mickey said, in a brogue as thick and rolling as if he'd just come off the boat. The wolf's gleam in his eye made Randolph shudder. "Let's be discussing your debt, Randy-boy, shall we?"

The dull thuds and choking cries carried around the tavern wall. Heart pounding, Mary Anne ran toward the sounds. They were coming from a narrow alley behind the building.

At the alley's mouth, she froze. Her cousin crouched on all fours a few yards down, head and mouth bleeding. Three men were beating him with cudgels and a chain. A fourth man, shorter but thick-built, lounged against the tavern wall cradling a baseball bat. Lazily as a cat stretching, he pushed away from the wall and swung his weapon. It struck Randolph high in the ribs. Randolph dropped over sideways and curled into a whimpering ball.

A small, frightened sound crawled out of her throat. The fourth man looked up. He grinned like a feral cat, dropped his bat and started toward her.

Randolph raised his muddied, bloodied head and choked out something that might have been her name. The sound broke through her fear. She grabbed her skirt and turned to run.

Runnels of blood and sweat made Randolph's eyes sting. He blinked them away in time to see Mickey grab Mary Anne's shoulder and whip her around. She screamed and battered at him, twisting and flailing. One hand connected in an audible slap. Mickey grabbed her wrist and slammed her into the tavern wall. Arms immobilized, she kicked out wildly. Mickey howled and doubled over. Mary Anne stumbled past his staggering form toward the dubious safety of the street.

As Mickey began to straighten, Crazy Macaulay snickered.

Mary Anne staggered as her foot caught in her skirt. In five steps, Mickey was on her. One beefy arm hooked around her neck, half throwing her off her feet. The other clenched fist struck under her jaw. She crumpled to the mud. Mickey turned to face his boys. The short blade in his hand gleamed red and wet.

"What the hell, Mickey?" A deep voice, close, thick Bohemian accent. One of the men with pipes. "Not supposed to be no killing!"

Randolph's stomach heaved. Half-digested sausage and potatoes spattered the speaker's shoes. With a yell of disgust, the big man backed away. Mickey's reply dissolved into meaningless noise as Randolph scrabbled toward Mary Anne. His ribs shrieked; blood dripped from his torn mouth. Somewhere very far away, Crazy Macaulay was laughing harder.

Gravel in the mud dug into his knees. His hand plunged into a puddle made by a horse's hoofprint. When he lifted it out, thin pinkish streams ran down his fingers.

He stared at his hand. Mary Anne lay mere feet away. One arm had fallen across her face. Above it he could see an eye, open and unblinking. A thickening streak of dark red crept toward him across the pale wooden walkway, then vanished in the mud.

". . . get the ring off her finger." Mickey's voice, fading in and out. Heavy shoes squelched in the muck. ". . . something to wrap her in. Go take care of it . . ."

His gut heaved again. Two broken ribs ground together with a sickening noise. The pain shot red sparks across his eyes, then faded into blackness.

CHAPTER TWENTY-THREE

Jackson gripped the steering wheel as if it were his anchor to sanity. He locked his gaze on the road, a dark streak surrounded by white. Next to him, he felt Linnet edge closer to the door.

He cleared his throat. "Got more work to do. You can stay with me, where I can see you, or in the cottage with the doors locked." The girl knew her father was sniffing around; he'd told her about the cellar break-in last night, to excuse his earlier harshness. It hadn't helped much. He had the feeling she wanted to trust him, but didn't dare risk it again. Damn her worthless father to hell for making her so afraid.

He glanced at her. Head bowed, she was fiddling with a pair of black knit gloves in her lap. "Did you hear me?"

"Yes." She balled the gloves in her hands. "I'll stay in my room."

"Don't let anyone in."

"I won't." She stared out the side window. Her face seemed wiped of emotion. He wanted to stop the pickup, grab her and hold her until they both broke down and cried. The road blurred in front of him. He blinked moisture from his eyes and drove on. The scattered clumps of birch and pine were thickening into woods. They'd be home soon.

The sun, bright when they'd left for town that morning, had long since sunk behind banks of fast-moving gray clouds. Snow by nightfall for sure. Panic shot through his chest. What if it was so heavy, she didn't come? He couldn't afford to wait long.

Every day that passed was one more for Rachel Connolly to track down the lawyers and set the paperwork in motion that would take his dream away. His knuckles whitened on the steering wheel. It might be too late already.

He swung the pickup around a curve. Something thumped against the cab: a can of paint, or the new shovel he'd bought. The road straightened ahead of the pickup, long and empty. Nothing to distract him from a memory he didn't want to recall.

He'd left Linnet at the public library with strict instructions to stay there, or run the few blocks to the police station if Chapman approached her. The last place he'd expected to see the man was strolling down Jim Kovacs's front walk.

"Well." The sandy-haired stranger in the worn brown parka smirked at the sight of him. "If it isn't dear old Dad. Don't mind me calling you that, do you?"

It took him a minute to realize who this man must be. Sudden rage warred with panic in his gut. "What are you doing here?"

"Getting my kid. See you in court." Luke Chapman sauntered past, then stopped and turned. "You know, you should've been nicer to Rachel. She's a lot better fuck than Grace. Too bad you missed your chance." With a flippant half-salute, he strode on down the street.

Jackson's breakfast threatened to climb up his throat. By the time he fought it down, Chapman was out of sight. That last, ugly remark wouldn't leave his mind as he walked up to the lawyer's front door. He tried not to follow where it led, but his inner terror refused to be silenced. Chapman and Rachel Connolly knew each other. Intimately. And now Chapman was talking to a custody lawyer, while the Connolly woman circled around Linnet. Deliberately befriended a vulnerable child, conned her out of the diary with its valuable secret. The fading shriek of the doorbell scraped across his nerves; his breath came short and fast, as if he'd just run a mile through knee-high snow. Keeping control with immense effort, he followed the lawyer's secretary down the short hall to Kovacs's office.

He'd barely started talking when Kovacs interrupted. "I'm sorry, Mr. Schlegel. I can't help you. Your son-in-law got here first."

The lawyer looked genuinely regretful, though that was scant comfort. Jackson sagged against the nearest chair. Through a dull roaring in his ears, he heard Kovacs rattling on while rifling through a Rolodex. "I can give you a couple of names and numbers, good people I know. The closest is in Ely. I don't suppose there's any way you and Mr. Chapman can work out this issue amicably?"

"No." The word came out like a falling rock, heavy and cold. His tone made Kovacs raise an eyebrow, but he felt too dulled by shock to care.

Kovacs handed him a scrap of yellow paper. Without looking at it, he crumpled it in his fist. "That's the best I can do," the lawyer said. "Tell Terry Powell I said hello, will you?"

He didn't remember answering. He didn't recall leaving the study, or the house. He simply found himself outside, long strides eating up the pavement toward the hardware store. Why was he going there? Oh yes, paint. The kitchen needed touching up. And more varnish for the baseboards. He slowed as he passed the library and caught sight of himself in its glass doors. Face white, eyes staring as if he'd looked straight into hell. He spun away and half-ran toward the street corner. Linnet mustn't see him like this. Yesterday was bad enough. One look at his crazy face and she'd crawl so far back into her shell, she'd never come out.

He found the paint and varnish, then bought two new tarpaulins. Handy things. You could never have enough of them. Next he drifted toward the garden tools, where he spent several minutes staring at an assortment of heavy shovels.

No, said a small voice deep inside.

He chose a square turf-cutting spade and hefted it. Its edges gleamed in the fluorescent light. As if in a vivid dream, he took the spade and the rest to the checkout counter.

It was wrapped in the tarps now, in the back of the truck. He heard a dull thump as the pickup started up the last rise. Schlegel House loomed on the far side of the crest, a black monolith against the darkening sky. Night was coming on early.

A swift search of the basement for documents had yielded nothing but crumpled blankets and dirty coffee cups. She'd had no better luck anywhere else in the mansion. Rachel lugged the work lamp up the last few twisting stairs and manhandled it into the attic. Switched on, it blazed with a bluish edge and threw jagged shadows against the walls. She stood near it and surveyed the crammed room.

The rolltop held nothing more. Any later papers must be elsewhere. She picked her way around old furniture and stacks of boxes, reading their labels as best she could. *Linens. Dresses, 1880s. Dresses, 1890s. Books. Personal library, AJS. Correspondence.*

She halted in front of that last—one of a five-box stack in the northeast corner, behind a dressmaker's dummy and several carpets. More family letters? Mine records? Anything that could tell her more about Andrew Schlegel's fortune since 1942?

She reached up and hefted the first box down.

Jackson locked the garden shed behind him, concentrating on each movement so he wouldn't have to think. Work would help. It always did. When Dorothy died, when Grace left. Decades ago, when he'd spent hours fixing leaky pipes and window-frame gaps in a succession of cheap apartments, manual labor had kept him out of trouble. It soothed him like a security blanket. With all his attention focused on a job, there was no room in his mind for anything else. Only a comforting blankness, thoughts suspended while his body worked.

His boots crunched across the fresh snow toward the manse. A few flakes swept his cheeks, landed in his hair. Harbingers of a storm to come. After so many years up here, he knew the signs. He could feel them in his ankle bones. Not a blizzard wind, but a big blow for all that.

He stopped just inside the kitchen door, alert as a doe to the crack of a twig. The house was wrapped in darkness and silence. He took the flashlight from his coat pocket, switched it on and played the thin beam across the room. Nothing was out of place, no trace of occupation. The air still smelled of coffee, made by Terry early that morning. No other scents that might have meant people: perfume, cigarette smoke. Still uneasy, he started down the basement steps.

His work lamp was gone, along with a pack of batteries. Jackson stared at the gap on the supply shelves, then strode toward the staircase. As he barreled into the kitchen, a dark shape moved toward him. He raised the flashlight. A youthful face, large ears poking through orange curls beneath a patrolman's hat, squinted back at him. "Mr. Schlegel?"

Relief made him sway on his feet. Jake Zimmerman. Zimmy to half the town. Terry called him "the kid," joked about him having been a terrier in a former life. Jackson had seen him in town off and on, eating crullers in Witek's or ticketing the odd car left parked too long. A nice boy, smiled at everyone. No one to be afraid of.

Zimmerman offered him a supporting hand. "Sorry. Did I startle you? The chief sent me out here in case Chapman showed up. Said you wouldn't mind."

"No." His racing heart began to slow. "No, I don't mind at all."

"Your writer friend's upstairs," Zimmerman continued. "Said she wanted to talk to you. Other than her, I haven't seen anyone all afternoon."

"That's—that's good." His voice sounded unnaturally loud. He shifted his grip on the flashlight, feeling every ridge in the metal under his fingers.

"You going to work some?"

He nodded.

"Miss Connolly's got your lamp upstairs. Didn't need any help moving it, even all that way." The youngster's grin made him think of Terry at eighteen. Zimmerman didn't look much older. He swallowed past a tightness in his throat as the young man chattered on. "I'll be getting back to my newspaper. Got one of those reading lights, battery operated. So small you can take them anywhere. You ever consider wiring this place, Mr. Schlegel? Be easier to work after dark."

"I don't do it much."

Zimmerman chuckled. "I guess not. See you around."

He turned to leave. Jackson swung the flashlight. It hit the base of the officer's skull. Zimmerman dropped like a brained steer.

He stepped around the fallen man, looking for breathing motions. The small of Zimmerman's back rose and fell, slow and rhythmic. He didn't know when the youngster might wake. The flashlight beam caught Zimmerman's gun. Jackson reached for it, then stopped. Linnet would hear the shots. And there would be blood to clean up.

Hadleigh Mine. He pocketed the policeman's gun, then headed back out to the garden shed.

Two shells snicked into place. The chunk of the shotgun closing seemed to echo through the trailer's tiny kitchen. Luke stuffed a handful of additional shells into each coat pocket and tried not to think about the risk he was taking. His palms were sweating under his gloves and his mouth felt dry. He could smell the craving for booze on his skin. Blind instinct made him reach for the bottle on the counter. His fingers closed around its neck. He'd started to unscrew the cap before he came to his senses. Taut with the effort, he set the bottle down untouched.

He could do this. He gulped stale air. Out to the big house, make sure she was there, follow her to just the right spot when she left and pull the trigger. Then ditch the gun with the body and erase all traces of his stay in this tin box. The trailer's owner wouldn't be here to report the stolen shotgun until summer. By the time they found it, and Rachel, he and Linnet would be long gone to new lives—a con man's stock in trade.

He hefted the shotgun. It felt alive in his hand. He'd lost out all his life—to assholes screwing him over, to plain bad luck. He wouldn't lose out again.

He pulled the back door shut and struck out through the swirling snow.

Rachel sat back on her heels and blew hair out of her eyes. Her forehead itched. She scratched it with dusty fingers. All five boxes and she'd found nothing. She quailed at the thought of breaking into Jackson's cottage, but it was looking like she had no alternative. *Some family reunion this is turning out to be.*

Stiff joints protested as she stood up. A glance at her watch startled her; it was nearly five. What could Jackson still be doing in town? Unless he was back already. The thought made her nerves creep. The stable-turned-garage lay on the far side of the manse, near the cottage. With the anteroom window shut and a wall intervening, she wouldn't have heard Jackson's car.

A muffled creak on the stairs made her jump. Footsteps reached the landing and crossed the floor. The anteroom door opened and Jackson stepped through. One hand held a flashlight, the heavy-duty silver kind. The other held a gun.

He squinted in the glare of the work lamp, but didn't turn the flashlight off. "I'm sorry," he said, flat-voiced and blank-faced. "You have to come with me."

"Mr. Schlegel—" The words came out in a dry croak.

He raised the gun half an inch. A thread of emotion colored his voice—anger or fear, or both. "I don't want to do this here. But I will if I have to."

He held himself as if he might shatter. That and his tone convinced her to move. The lamp was too far away to knock over. She thought of disarming him once she got close, but he kept distance between them as she neared the door. Shaking from her innards, she preceded him down the twisting stairs. Where the hell was the deputy she'd met earlier, that friendly kid Zimmy with the carrot hair? Had Jackson shot him? God, no. Surely she'd have heard that. She dragged her feet down the sweeping front staircase and through the house. She could feel the gun trained on her like a malevolent third eye.

They emerged into darkness shot with thickly falling snow. Jackson herded her toward his battered pickup, parked outside the garage. As they neared it, she spotted a pair of heavy shoes attached to a human-shaped lump in a tarpaulin. Zimmy. Alive? Dead? *My fault.* Her throat closed. She looked away and kept walking. *This can't be real. It* is *real. Jesus, what do I do? Calm down, dammit! Think of something!*

Jackson gestured with the gun toward the driver's side. "Get in. Keys are in the ignition."

She opened the door and climbed into the driver's seat. A quick swallow moistened her dry mouth and loosened her throat enough to talk. "Why are you doing this?" she asked, in the calmest tone she could muster.

He got in beside her, gun barrel dead steady. "Drive. I'll tell you where."

Cold and fear made her clumsy. She managed to turn the engine over on the third try. The truck lurched backward, not enough to throw him off balance. Cursing silently, she put the thing in gear and pointed it toward the access road. The tires slipped on the fresh snow; then the chains bit and the pickup stabilized. Rachel eyed the fat flakes tumbling across the windshield. The snow had gotten heavier since her arrival at Schlegel House. Two inches had fallen already. Maybe the truck would bog down before they got to wherever they were going, and she could make a break for it.

Zimmy, though. Her hands tightened on the wheel. If he was alive, she couldn't abandon him.

"Left at the highway," Jackson ordered. The flat tone was back, the glimmer of emotion gone as if it had never existed. She had to dig it out again, find a way into his psyche, talk him down. Nothing else had a prayer of working.

The manse and the cottage dwindled in the rearview mirror. For a moment she thought she saw movement, a flicker swiftly gone in the blowing snow. Wishful thinking; no one had been there except herself, the deputy and Jackson. And Linnet, somewhere in the cottage.

Dear God, what did this crazy man do with her?

She fought down nausea and threw the pickup into a left turn. Jackson braced himself against the seat. The gun didn't waver. "Where's Linnet?" she asked, as if inquiring whether or not he liked his coffee black.

Something unreadable flashed in his eyes. "None of your business. Drive."

Linnet slapped her book shut and threw it across the room. It hit the far wall with a satisfying thunk. She couldn't stay here another minute, feeling like a caged mouse waiting for the hungry cat. She had to get out before she went crazy.

Rachel's hat and gloves made a black woolly lump on the corner of the desk. She stuffed them into her parka and pulled it on. Even in the dark, she could follow the highway to town. And if her grandfather found her gone, too bad for him. He'd been scaring her all day. Let him find out what it felt like!

She paused in the doorway, then went back to the desk. Her grandfather kept his family history in here somewhere. Rachel might like to look at it. She opened the top right-hand drawer and sifted through a stack of blank paper, some sheets that looked like order forms, and a few envelopes. Her fingers brushed smooth wood, sharp-cornered. A box, reddish brown with a tiny gold hasp in front. No lock. She set it on the desktop and opened it.

It held a swatch of green velvet ribbon, yellowed sheet music, a diploma, a thick envelope made of heavy paper, and a single, folded sheet through which she could just make out typewritten letters. The letterhead, thick and black even on the sheet's backside, read *Thompson and Bizal, Attorneys.*

She read it with a funny feeling, which grew stronger the further she got.

As a direct descendant of William Henry Schlegel . . . you and any dependent children may be entitled . . . bequest made by said Andrew Jackson Schlegel . . . to be disbursed one hundred years after the date of said Andrew Jackson Schlegel's death . . . Please contact this office within ninety days of the disbursement date, October 30, 2007, with adequate proof of identity . . .

She could feel her heartbeat in her fingertips. Slowly, she folded the letter and stuffed it into her jeans pocket. Then she picked up the envelope. *Jackson* was written across it, in flowing script that reminded her of signatures on the Declaration of Independence.

The envelope held a wad of papers, mostly handwritten pages. *My dear grandson,* the first page began. *I apologize for passing my burden on to you, but no other of my relations has ever cared for the past. That respect for your heritage leads me to hope I may confess to you a piece of it, and that through you I may finally atone for the terrible crime I have kept secret all these years.*

In late October of 1893, I murdered my cousin, Mary Anne Schlegel.

Linnet stopped reading. The word *murdered* swam in front of her. She blinked several times and then re-read the sentence, as if doing so could make it say something different.

"He knew." Until the whispered words sounded in her ears, she didn't know she'd spoken. He'd known Mary Anne was dead all the time. *He told us both a lie.*

Cold shivers crawled up her body. Outside, the pickup's engine coughed. She clenched her muscles to stop them shaking, pocketed the confession and left the cottage.

A blast of cold air, wet with snowflakes, stopped her just outside the door. The pickup was pulling away down the access road. Schlegel House loomed in the dark. From where she stood, no light shone in the windows.

The rolltop. She ducked back into the cottage long enough to fetch a flashlight. The big silver one was gone. She snatched up a spare and hurried out.

CHAPTER TWENTY-FOUR

October 28, 1893

His left wrist was soaking wet. And cold. So were his fingers. Wet and aching with the chill, as if bathed for hours in ice-water. Other aches crept into Randolph's awareness: little licking flames where his ribs should be, the sharp burn of a torn lip, the dull heaviness of his head. He moved it a fraction and gasped as a wave of pain threatened to blow his skull bones apart. An eternity later, he pried open his eyelids.

Bumps and lumps, black mud mixed with gray gravel and the dull sheen of dirty water. Something limp and weedy trailing across the wet earth. His hand lay in a puddle; the hard ridge of the plank walkway pressed against a hipbone. He lifted his head again, bracing himself against the pain, and spat out mud mixed with grit. Then he raised himself on his elbows, clenching his teeth to keep back a scream. The slight elevation gave him a better view of the weedy strip: dark green and nubbly, no wider than a finger. A hair ribbon.

Memory brought up bile that threatened to choke him. He dropped his head into his bruised hands and whimpered like a whipped dog. Mary Anne. Mickey. A blood-covered blade in a thick fist, a slender body slumping to the dirty ground. An open eye, staring and empty.

They had taken her body, God knew where. The river, most likely, a dumping ground for refuse of all kinds. He swallowed hard, shivering from more than the wind. It had shifted while he lay in the muck, from the warm southwest to the cold northeast. Indian summer was over.

He managed to sit up, though the hot agony in his ribcage made him regret the effort. He loathed the thought of moving any more, but he couldn't stay out here all night. In his thin broadcloth suit, spattered with water and mud and blood, the dropping temperature would give him pneumonia. He thought longingly of his own bed, soft and warm and smelling of clean cotton. His room, his books, a pipe full of cherry tobacco, a stiff whiskey purloined from the decanter in his father's study—

Father. Father would blame him. Randolph could hear his voice, knife-edged with fury. *"You damned fool. A young woman is dead because you didn't know when to toss down your cards. You're a murderer, Randolph. I should let you swing."*

He clapped his hands over his ears and rocked like a child until the worst of the terror receded. He would have to go home. Confess. Take his punishment like a man. Would the police arrest him, try him as an accomplice? He deserved that. It was his fault she'd come here.

He struggled to his feet and wavered over to the tavern wall. The jaunty trickle of ragtime carried through the rough planks, along with raucous voices calling for beer and whiskey and bourbon. Dooley's was doing good business. When he felt strong enough to attempt a step without crumpling, he pushed away from the wall. Then he stopped and looked back where he had lain. Step by painful step, he staggered over to the spot. He squatted carefully, plucked the ribbon out of the mud and stuffed it in his pocket, then stumbled off in search of a streetcar.

"You damned fool." William spat the words at his pathetic excuse for a son. Randolph stood in the middle of the room, drooping like a puppet with its strings cut. His suit was fit for the rag bin, his face and hands all cuts and bruises. An overwhelming desire to add to them made William's palms itch. Instead, he channeled his rage into words. "What were you thinking, taking her *there?* The worst street in the Levee would have been safer!"

"I told you, she followed—"

"Shut up!" He could feel a fist clenching, arm muscles trembling with the need to strike. "It's too late for excuses. She's dead and you've ruined us. I should wring your neck!"

"Go ahead." Randolph sounded hollow, as if the day's events had carved out of him what little life he possessed. His tone brought William up short. A quick glance showed a similar emptiness in his face, even through the fist-sized purpling bruise around one swollen eye. In his present state, the boy might do anything. Or nothing.

He gentled his tone a fraction, the best he could manage under the circumstances. "You look disgraceful. Wash yourself up, put on some decent clothes and come back here. We need to talk about what happens next."

"The police come. We tell them what happened. I go to prison. You drink to celebrate. What is there to talk about?"

"Do as you're told!" Fear, an alien emotion when it came to his son, brought William close to losing control. "Go on, get out. I need to think." He turned his back on Randolph and paced along the edge of the carpet. Its colors made him dizzy. He heard Randolph's dragging steps toward the door, followed by the grumble of hinges. The minute the door clicked shut, he dove for the whiskey.

Randolph reached the top of the stairs. His room was just down the hall. He should strip down to his undershirt, then go sponge off all the grime and blood and sweat. All traces of the beating he'd endured. Except for the pain, of course. That would never go away.

With no memory of walking there, he found himself at the open door to Mary Anne's room. Neatly made bed, violet-patterned coverlet turned down by the maid. Nighttable, white-painted and gilded. Two books and a pair of lace gloves on it, the gloves tossed there as if their owner expected to come back later and put them away.

He took one step into the room, then another. Then another, until he was close enough to read the book spines. The top one bore no title. Bound in dark red leather, it had a familiar look. After a moment's thought, he recognized it. Mary Anne's diary. He'd seen her writing in it dozens of times in the short while she'd lived here.

He picked it up and took it to his room.

The first glass of liquor burned a path down William's throat. He poured a second and then a third in a desperate quest for clarity. There would be no brotherly gratitude to play on now, no prideful itch to balance the scales. Mary Anne was dead, and with her his only hope of tapping Andrew's riches soon enough to matter. Unless he could turn this setback to his advantage.

He poured a fourth whiskey, which he sipped as he paced. Water rattled distantly through pipes; Randolph, washing up. The boy took orders well—his only virtue.

He reached the end of the carpet, turned and paced the other way. Andrew mustn't know how or where Mary Anne had died. Any whisper of the circumstances and the rift with his brother would become a glacial crevasse. Better, in fact, that Andrew know nothing at all. Even without the unfortunate details, he would no doubt assume William had played a part in the girl's murder. William gave a bitter laugh. After more than twenty years and despite several overtures, Andrew still preferred to think him corrupt to the core. "God save us all from reformed sinners," he muttered into his drink. The futility of it washed

over him then, in a wave of something like pain. What hope did
he have of regaining Andrew's trust, even grudgingly, with the
history between them?

He clenched his hand around the glass. He could mend the
breach or lose everything. There were no other choices.

Their history was the key. The life he and Andrew had shared
until October 1871, when a hot, dry autumn and a stray spark
had conspired against them both. Without the Fire and the
deaths, no one would have cared what the damned houses were
made of. Shoddier construction went up all the time, most of it
financed by wealthier men than they were. But Andrew couldn't
see that. All he saw was a guilt he couldn't live with. *Meat to the
wolves, that's what we were. What he made us.*

Hammering at the front door and shouting in the hall had
warned him what was coming that day, even before Andrew
charged into the study brandishing a thin, brown ledger. The
sight of it had made William sit up in his armchair and set
down the whiskey he'd been sipping to mask the taste of smoke
in the air. Almost a week after the Fire, and the stench of the
burning still lingered. With a curious sense of distance, like a
spectator at a melodrama, he'd watched Andrew stride toward
him.

"You lied to me!" Andrew stabbed a finger at him. "You said
we'd build to code. You swore it. DeKoven bought metal
shingles. I sold him metal. But you sold him tar paper. I don't
know how you went behind my back, but—"

William laughed. The fish-eyed shock on Andrew's face only
made it funnier. "Bravo, Andy. Well played. Now climb off your
high horse and we'll talk about this like grown men." He went
to refill his glass. "Whiskey?"

"I went to Conley's Patch." Andrew's voice turned low and
dangerous. "To the tenements on Kibbert Street. I found tar
patches. Scorched and stinking. Not a metal shingle in sight.

Then I went to the office. And found this." He slapped the ledger down next to the whiskey decanter, hard enough to shake William's tumbler. "You knew fire was a hazard. Any fool building here does. All that pine wasn't risk enough? A metal roof might have kept the buildings from catching. But you sold De-Koven tar paper because it's cheaper. Flammable, flimsy junk. For what?! So you could brag a little sooner about how much you're worth? Or were you trying to one-up your wife's dowry?!"

William tensed. "You leave my family out of this."

"What about my family?" Andrew's voice cracked. He paced around the room like a tiger in a cage. "We're ruined, do you realize that? Has it sunk in yet? People are dead because you cut corners. They've launched an inquiry—the police, the Fire Department. They'll talk to DeKoven, and we'll pay—"

"Not if you keep your head." William locked his gaze on his brother's face. "DeKoven will blame the contractor. He paid for metal and that's what we gave him." He laid a hand on the ledger. "Who's going to say different?"

Andrew stared at the slim book. Seconds crawled by.

"I will." His answer was a hoarse whisper.

Shock flooded through William then, colder than Lake Michigan in March. "You won't," he barked. "You're in this, too. You signed those purchase orders. You inspected the shipments. Why didn't you look in the crates, Andy? Why didn't you make sure? I'll tell you why. Because you knew our profits were too good to be true and you didn't want to ask questions. You're as guilty as I am."

"No."

"Isn't that why you came here? To play the righteous hero, confronting the villain? To salve your conscience?" Abruptly, the blaze of anger left William. He poured a second whiskey. Andrew would need it to calm down. "Let's stop pretending either of us is innocent. The important thing is to save the company. The only way to do that is to keep our story straight."

Andrew knocked the proffered whiskey from his hand hard enough to send him stumbling against a chair. He heard the glass shatter. "To hell with your story!" Andrew shouted. "And to hell with you!"

The door slammed shut as Andrew left. Alone in the sudden silence, William checked his shins for bruises, then walked to the bell-pull. One of the maids could clean up the puddle full of broken glass. It was up to him to clean up the bigger mess.

He knew where Andrew was going. To the Inquiry Board. He glanced across the room at the ledger, forgotten on the side table. Then he snatched it up, ripped out the pages and threw them on the embers in the fireplace.

The snap of burning coal brought William back to the present. He watched a flaming lump fall off the larger piece and the whole glowing mass settle backward. Crumbling, like everything he'd worked for. *You made me do it, Andy. You made me blame you. Telling the Inquiry Board it was all my doing. I couldn't let them think that. I couldn't let you ruin us both for what richer men got away with daily. So I gave them the scapegoat they needed. And for more than twenty years, you've hated me for it.*

Suddenly, bitterly, he wanted his youth back. He and Andrew had traveled the same road once: two brothers against the world, determined to make it sit up and take notice of the name Schlegel. How had it all gone so wrong?

He shook off the pang and forced himself to think about the dilemma at hand. He had to reach that younger Andrew, the one who'd tagged after him to the fishing hole and inherited his clothes and followed him to a future they both could scarcely articulate. That one would listen when he asked for money. That one might be persuaded to bail out the poor young nephew, sinking amid the city's nefarious temptations. Requests on his own behalf could come later, if and as needed. Right now, William merely needed to sink the first hook.

He drained his glass and set it down. He could still hear water running. He left the room and headed upstairs. What he had to do shouldn't take long.

The wind bit through Randolph's heavy wool coat and stole the white puffs of his breath. The temperature had dropped steadily since his wild ride homeward, with his fellow streetcar passengers vying to get farthest away from him. He welcomed the discomfort. At least he could still feel something.

Beside him, his father slapped the horses to a faster pace. The brougham wheels jolted over uneven ground. Randolph clutched the small suitcase tight against his body. It smelled of violets, the scent Mary Anne wore. Spring-like, fresh, young. She would stay forever young now, he thought, and fought down a hysterical laugh. Forever young, while he had aged a hundred years in a single afternoon.

He imagined pitching the suitcase into the street, grabbing the reins and driving to the nearest police station. He would confess everything, including his father's attempt at deception. They would be jailed, the house sold or shut up, his mother . . . at the thought of her, his fantasy shriveled and died. He bit his tongue to keep back the whimper. How pathetic he was. Too frightened to tell the truth. Too frightened to make Father do his own dirty work. *Yes, Father. Of course, Father. Please love me for two minutes, Father.* His eyes stung as they sped down Lake Shore Drive. To his horror, he realized he was weeping.

"Stop sniveling." William's voice cut more sharply than the wind. "Fall to pieces on me, and you'll live to regret it. Do you understand?"

He nodded once, then swiped the tears away and shut his eyes. The horses' hooves echoed in the cold. He filled his world with the sound. The brougham turned away from the lakeshore, nosing deeper into the city.

He smelled the Chicago River before they reached it. Eyes open again, he watched Fullerton Avenue sweep past. Wood-frame houses and brick two-flats gradually gave way to three- and four-story tenements and increasingly rundown rooming houses. A gap in the line heralded the Ashland Avenue Bridge.

His father stopped the horses just shy of it, climbed down and tied them to a nearby spindly tree. "Get down."

Moving stiffly, Randolph complied. His shoes crunched on gravel like the grinding of bones. He closed his mind to the sound, walked to the center of the bridge and dropped the suitcase over the side. Weighted by stones from the rockery in their garden, it sank in the black, stinking water. He watched it go and considered throwing himself after it. There would be a kind of justice in that. Or was that another coward's way out, to keep from having to go through with the rest of his father's charade?

"Come on." Father's voice, inches behind him. As if he'd read Randolph's fleeting intent and moved to scotch it. Randolph felt a dull, sick ache in his temples. *You won't even let me kill myself. Not so long as I have some use.* Exhaustion blunted his anger to a damp squib. He couldn't even muster a sharp rejoinder. Dumb with fatigue and his roiling emotions, he followed his father back to the brougham. Father backed the horses around and they set off toward the lakefront.

"What was in the suitcase?" Randolph heard himself ask.

His father shot him an irritated glance. "Clothes. What do you think?"

"Which clothes?"

"Why in the name of God are you asking me such a thing?" Slap, went the reins against the horses' sweating backs. "What does it matter?"

"I'd like to know." Far beneath the exhaustion and shock and grief, a fragment of his soul rejoiced at the sight of his father squirming.

"A brown dress, a flowered one, a blue one, a gray skirt and jacket, some underthings and a pair of shoes," William snapped. "And violet water, three handkerchiefs and a book of Tennyson's poems. Does that satisfy your curiosity?"

He didn't answer, merely slouched in his seat and watched the night go by. Father didn't know he'd taken the diary. Probably didn't know it existed. He could keep it.

The horses' rhythm and the creaking of the carriage blurred the passage of time, until suddenly they were pulling up in front of the brick pile he called home. He chuckled grimly at the notion. *I have no home as long as that man is alive.*

With a contemptuous look, his father clambered off the driver's seat. "I'll see to the horses. You're fit for nothing but a stiff drink and bed. And don't take any of my whiskey." Harness jingled as he unhitched the pair and led them away.

Feeling half-drunk on no liquor at all, Randolph wandered inside. The front hall looked strange to him. He caught a glimpse of his face in the gilt-rimmed mirror and wondered who that battered man was. Not Randolph Schlegel, surely. Not the only son of one of Evanston's finest, an honest man of business and as rock-ribbed a Republican as ever you could find. He grinned at the monster in the mirror. The gesture split one end of his torn lip. The pain struck him as funny. He began to laugh, softly at first and then louder.

The sound roused his mother, who strode out of the front parlor and stopped dead at the sight of him. "Randolph! God in Heaven, what happened to you?"

"Rough night." The words slipped out amid chuckles. Her obvious shock, laced with offense at his flippancy, only made him laugh harder.

She strode over and grabbed his shoulders. The unexpected

gesture stopped his laughter like a cork in a bottle. "Don't you want to know what's happened?"

The tension in her face registered then, the fear in her eyes. "What?" he said, not quite managing to suppress a final chuckle.

She loosened her grip. Her hands flew together, fingers wrapping around each other as if she might otherwise fall apart. "Mayor Harrison has been assassinated. Someone shot him not three hours ago."

CHAPTER TWENTY-FIVE

Jake Zimmerman woke slowly to the feel of his body jouncing against cold metal. He smelled exhaust with a hint of burning oil. The spot where his head met his neck was a pulsing ball of pain. Rough fabric, weighted by snow, seemed to be the only thing between him and the freezing wind. Whatever it was didn't offer much warmth; he was shivering hard, each spasm tying his shoulders in knots. He spent several dazed seconds trying to work out why, and finally realized someone had tied his hands behind his back. A familiar weight against his left hip was missing. Someone had stolen his gun.

Squinting against the swirling snowflakes, he tried to eyeball his surroundings without moving his pounding head. Low metal walls, sky above. Flat metal floor, broken by the bulge of wheel wells, two plastic barrels and a scattering of paint cans. He was lying in somebody's pickup, trussed like a chicken. No, that was wrong. Chickens had their feet tied. His were free. *Jesus. Somebody must've hit me pretty hard.*

Jackson Schlegel. He'd been talking with the old man, something about lights. He'd turned to leave the drafty kitchen. Then thunder had exploded behind his eyes. *He whacked me one. Why the hell—?*

Voices trickled into his consciousness: a woman and a man, mostly the woman. It dawned on him that he'd been hearing them for awhile. As best he could with his arms immobilized, he hitched himself closer to the truck's small cab and listened, careful to stay below the sightline of the rearview mirror.

"—are we going?" Silence. "All right. You don't have to tell me. Let's talk about something else. Let's talk about Linnet."

"Don't say her name. Drive." Jackson Schlegel's voice.

Silence for several heartbeats. Zimmy gazed longingly at his sheltering fabric, which had slipped to his waist. He wished he could pull it up with his teeth. The wind felt colder, though it couldn't get too frigid so long as the snow fell.

"What are you going to tell her?" The woman again, too calm to be natural. Like someone who'd gone clear through terror-stricken and out the other side. Where had he heard that voice before?

"Turn right up at the crossroads."

The pickup jolted over a pothole. "She's going to ask about me, Jackson. She'll wonder where I am. I bet she's a champ at spotting lies. What are you going to say?"

Silence again. Then Jackson, low and tense: "Shut up."

In the brief pause, Zimmy raised his head enough to peek through the back window. Jackson, profile outlined in the headlight glare off the surrounding snow, was holding a gun on a dark-haired woman. Zimmy's gun. The hair and a snatch of red hood told him who Jackson's hostage was: Rachel Connolly, the writer from Chicago.

Zimmy ducked down again and shifted his bound wrists. One index finger found the knot, small and tight against the opposite wristbone. He wriggled his hands, wincing as the rope chafed, until he could pinch the knot between the tips of two fingers. He started to pick at it.

"It won't work, Jackson." Matter-of-fact on the surface, Rachel's voice held a desperate edge. "You must know that. Someone will find out, and then Linnet won't have anyone."

"There's no choice. Don't you see that?" Jackson's sudden anguish caught Zimmy by surprise. "You can take everything I have just by existing. That'd be bad enough, even if you weren't with him."

"Him . . . ?"

"Linnet's father. Luke. Short for Lucifer. I read that once. Suits him. He killed my daughter. Turn left here."

Rachel went quiet for a long time. The knot was refusing to give. Zimmy cursed under his breath. With his hands still tied, he couldn't hope to disarm Jackson. Not that his odds of doing that looked good anyway. To reach the old man's gun arm through the pickup's side window, he'd have to be a contortionist—and that was assuming he could move fast enough to prevent an accidental discharge. Breaking through the back window posed the same risk of a reflex shot. Either way, Rachel Connolly would be just as dead. He relaxed his aching arms as much as he could and surveyed the road, trying to make out where he was.

The pickup followed a gentle curve past a solitary clump of birches. A pine tree rose in the midst of the bare white trunks, straight for half a foot, then bending abruptly like the back of an arthritic witch. A few yards to either side of the clump, the trees thickened into impenetrable blackness. Zimmy straightened, ignoring the twinge in his upper arms. The bent pine marked the last quarter-mile to the best ice-fishing lake in the county. Since his high school days, he'd lugged tackle and heat packs past it through deep snowdrifts in pursuit of his favorite sport. Bill Witek, seventy years old last summer and still a gung-ho fishing buddy, had a winter cabin not far away. If he could just get out of this damned truck—

"Turn right at the next gap." Jackson again. Zimmy's heart fluttered. The rightward fork off this road led to the old mine works, a scrap heap for the past thirty-odd years. During his junior year, two other kids had gone there to neck in the tunnels and died when a section of roof collapsed. There'd been talk about fencing the place off after that, but neither Birch Falls nor the surrounding county had ever come up with the money.

He wriggled across the pickup bed as quietly as he could manage, until he lay flat against the back hatch. The latch rattled as the pickup jounced along. It sounded loose, which would make this a lot easier. The upcoming turn should give him momentum. Jackson and his hostage would take some time yet getting to the mine. The snow would slow them down. He just might manage to reach the Witek place soon enough to make a difference.

The pickup slowed as it reached the fork. As it swung into the turn, Zimmy hurled himself against the hatch. It dropped open, dumping him face-first into fresh snow.

He rolled on his side, spat out a snowball, and struggled to a sitting position. The knot felt looser, but he still couldn't slip it. He rocked to his feet, miraculously staying upright. Careful placement of each foot was the key, unless he wanted to eat snow every other step all the way to Bill's.

The truck's taillights vanished amid the trees. Zimmy tore his gaze away and set off toward Bill's cabin.

The anteroom door was open, a work lamp blazing in the attic. Linnet halted just past the threshold. "Rachel?"

No one answered. She walked further in, feeling like the heroine in a horror movie. Except that she had no intention of screaming the house down the second she brushed past a cobweb. "Hello?"

Open boxes lay scattered in the lamp's wide circle of light. Someone had pulled them from a nearby pile and pawed through their contents. Papers, manila folders, portfolios, even a stack of ledgers like the ones on the anteroom shelves. Had Rachel come looking for more clues? Or had her grandfather come to destroy them?

She left the scattered heaps and strode to the rolltop. The folder she wanted was in the second drawer on the right. She opened it and stared at the empty space. The mountain of legal junk was gone.

She glanced around, as if some attic gnome might have fetched the old papers and helpfully left them nearby. The stuffed brown folder was nowhere to be seen. Had Rachel taken it? She couldn't imagine her grandfather leaving the work lamp burning. But Rachel might have.

Whatever. She wasn't going to find the papers loitering around here. She thumbed her flashlight back on and went to turn the work lamp off.

Heavy footsteps sounded from the anteroom, too close for her own to mask them. Sudden fear froze her in place. "Rachel . . . ?"

Her father stalked through the anteroom door, a huge shotgun pointed ahead of him. For a moment, he looked as startled as she. Then he lowered the gun and grinned at her. "Hey, Linnie. I'm here to take you home."

Pounding at the front door roused Bill Witek from a comfortable half-doze by the dying fire. The new heating ducts he'd put in last fall worked a treat, but there was something about the crackle of burning wood and the smell of cedar logs. The best furnace in the world couldn't beat that for comfort. He snorted awake, nearly knocking over his half-drunk decaf. "Who in—!"

He struggled out of his chair, swigged coffee to clear his head, grimaced at the taste of it cold and headed toward the door. "Hold your horses! I'm coming!"

Angry words boiled up as he flung the door open. Then he saw who it was. Zimmy stumbled inside, covered in snow. As the young man pitched to his knees, Billy saw rope around his wrists.

For a second he could only stand and gape. Shivering like a wet dog, Zimmy looked up at him. "Evening, Bill," he said through chattering teeth. "Can I use your phone?"

Her father started toward her. Blind panic surged through Linnet. She kicked over the work lamp and dove sideways as it hit the floor. Over the sound of shattering glass, she heard Luke curse. Rainbow colors danced before her eyes in the sudden darkness. She stretched out a hand until it met something solid. Cardboard, cool and smooth. She'd landed behind some boxes. She pulled her legs up until she was crouching, then reached out again into the blackness. Empty space for at least an arm's length. Heart pounding in her ears, she edged toward the nothingness.

Her father's swearing drowned out the shuffle of her sneakers on the floor. "Goddammit, Linnie, what'd you do that for? You get over here right now!" She heard the scrape of his heavy shoes, followed by a thunk as he stumbled over something. "Fuck!" His voice came from lower down, as if he'd fallen.

Linnet's fingers found soft plush, dusty-smelling. Rolled-up carpet. She remembered at least three piles of those. The thick dark made her brain go funny. Which way was the door from here? She strained to see, even though it was useless. Fighting down panic, she crawled forward. Another stack of boxes barred her way. She felt around it for free space and kept going.

Luke had fallen silent. Her coat rustled, an impossibly loud noise. She froze, her whole body listening for pursuit.

"I don't know what that Mason lady told you." Calm on top but rough underneath, her father's voice sounded frighteningly near. "But it's not true, Linnie. Your mom and me, we had some differences. But I'd never hurt you. You know that."

She choked down a whimper. He couldn't be as close as he seemed. She'd hear him breathing, or his clothes when he moved. She knew this attic a lot better than he did. All she had to do was keep her head. Which way were the stupid stairs? Out came one hand again, this time finding the smooth curve of a trunk lid. Next to it rose a thin metal pole. A standing lamp. She gripped the lamp and pulled herself up, then felt with her toes for the next patch of bare floor. A memory surfaced of a long-gone summer ballet class. She clutched it close, conjuring up every detail as a bulwark against fear. A wall of gleaming mirrors, the polished wooden barre, the smell of talc and sweaty tights. *Point my toes, relevé, sloooow plié* . . . Noiselessly, she shifted her weight until she was standing on the lamp's far side.

Floorboards muttered somewhere behind her. Then came a muffled thump and a thunderous crash as her father blundered into a box pile. Something clattered to the floor, accompanied by a stream of swear words. This time, she heard pain in them. "This isn't funny, Linnet. You fucking hear me? You tell me where you are. Right fucking now!"

She edged away from the lamp, both arms outstretched. One hand brushed the thin edge of a table. Cold, metal. Wrought iron. The sewing table. The dressmaker's dummy should be right nearby. Which meant the doorway and freedom weren't far away.

Another crash startled her. She heard china smash; Luke had knocked over a table lamp. Wood shrieked as he shoved the table aside. She heard several heavy thumps, as if he were swinging something around. The gun. He must be clearing a path with it, smashing everything that got in his way. "I'm done playing your stupid-ass game, kid, you got it?! You and me are getting the hell out. You want to be smart, don't make me chase you. Understand?!"

He was close now, so close he could grab her if he reached in the right direction. Terror made her grip the table hard. Three fingers hooked over the edges of a small, circular well in the tabletop. A shallow well with buttons in it. She scooped them out and flung them away from her as hard as she could.

The buttons fell near the far side of the attic. She heard her father turn toward the noise with a growl of fury. Crashing and banging, he headed away from her. She used the noise to cover her own inchings around the remaining obstacles in her path. Beyond a stack of empty picture frames, she felt emptiness. A wild surge of joy almost made her laugh out loud. The door was just a few feet ahead.

Her father grunted and cursed, striking out with the gun and probably his arms. She heard a chair fall over and dashed forward. Her palms met wood that gave under her hand. No longer caring for silence, she sprinted through the door and down the steep stairs.

More curses from behind, then heavy footfalls. She couldn't tell how close he was. She dashed through the schoolroom and turned right, then plunged down the narrow back stairs as fast as she dared. The back door had only one lock. She scrabbled at it. It shot back just as her father reached the top of the staircase. She yanked the door open and stumbled outside, then slipped to one knee in the deepening snow.

A swift look up showed her father barreling through the door. Terror jolted her upright and shot her across the ground through an ankle-deep blanket of white. Tire tracks half-filled with fresh fall pointed to the access road and the highway. She stumbled toward them, slipping and sliding but somehow managing not to fall. A few yards behind, her father hit the ground with a grunt. Calves aching, she plunged on.

The thin wail of a siren made her look up. Headlights bobbed over the crest of the highway, car after car like glowing beads on a string. Police. She pushed forward, slipped, fell on her hands and knees, struggled up and kept going. The lights were closing in on the access road. Just a few more minutes and she'd be safe.

A hand grabbed her arm and pulled her around. "You stupid little cow. You think this is fun, don't you?"

She could smell her father's sour breath. He shifted his grip higher, fingers pressing hard enough to leave bruises. "Don't make me hurt you, Linnie. Be a smart little girl." He turned away from the oncoming cars, yanking her along with him. "Come on. We're leaving."

She locked her knees and leaned backward. The snow kept her from digging in her heels. He stopped, as she knew he'd have to. "Goddammit, move!"

You got it. Exhilaration born of blinding fear kicked her brain into overdrive. Her free hand scrabbled in the snow, closed over a handful, and threw it in his face. Sputtering, he jerked back. She braced her feet and twisted hard, trying to break his grip.

He dropped his gun, grabbed her free arm and pulled her forward. She threw her weight back and lost her footing. They fell in a tangle of arms and legs, her father landing face down.

Way back in fourth-grade gym class, she'd been a champion crab-walker. Old skills came back to her as she floundered in the slippery wet. She gathered her limbs under her and scrabbled backward as her father sat up. He grabbed her left ankle. She rolled half over and thrust out her right foot. It struck bone. Luke howled and his hand fell away. She kept crawling until she collided with a pair of legs. Above her loomed a tall man in a flapping coat, his wild black hair frosted with snowflakes. He was pointing a big handgun toward the spot where her father lay.

"Luke Chapman?" the man asked.

Luke sat up and spat snow at the man's feet. "Fuck you."

The man jerked his head. Two uniformed policemen started

toward Luke. In the wash of red and blue light from the police cars, Linnet caught the gleam of handcuffs. "Luke Chapman, you are under arrest for the murder of Grace Chapman. You have the right to remain silent . . ."

The rest of the words blurred into meaningless noise. Shivering, Linnet bent her head. She wished she could cry. She wished she could feel something besides so terribly tired. The legs moved away from her, and she almost toppled over. A pair of large hands caught her and held her upright.

"My name's Florian. You okay, honey? Did he hurt you?" The tall man crouched down next to her, his gun back wherever he usually put it. He had nice eyes, soft and warm like Rachel's. She couldn't answer him. Her exhausted brain wouldn't make words. She drooped against him, craving warmth.

He lifted her up with him as he stood. She heard him calling to someone, something about blankets. Then he was murmuring in her ear. "Everything's going to be okay, hon. Don't worry."

Linnet hid her face in the crook of his neck and began to cry.

CHAPTER TWENTY-SIX

"Out." The pistol barrel tilted briefly toward the driver's-side door. Stiff with cold and fear, Rachel cut the engine. "Leave the keys," Jackson ordered. So much for palming them as a weapon.

She stepped out of the pickup into snow well over her ankles. Four inches. Enough to make running a feat of gymnastics. She wouldn't get anywhere very fast in this. Before she could try, Jackson rounded the front of the pickup. He had a clear line of fire again, no huge hunk of metal barring his way. Her mind felt like a trapped bird batting against the bars of its cage. Flight would likely get her killed. So would going for the gun. He was keeping just enough distance between them to give himself a clear shot if she rushed him.

"Where are—?" Her voice died as they passed the rear of the truck. The snow-soaked tarpaulin was empty. She recalled a muffled thud as they'd turned off the county highway, and her heart leaped. The deputy had gotten away. He was out there somewhere, maybe calling for rescue while she stood here and shivered. Or maybe blundering through the snowstorm, miles from anything approaching civilization. Her elation vanished as swiftly as it had come.

Jackson had halted, too briefly to do her any good. He looked away from the empty truck bed and gestured forward with his flashlight. "Walk till I say stop."

The dim glow of the whitened ground gave enough light to see by, even without the thin flashlight beam. Rachel slogged through the snow, for the first time taking note of her surroundings. A cluster of low buildings, sheds and what looked like a small house, huddled several yards off like sheep in a gale. Not far ahead, the silhouette of a melted Eiffel Tower crossed with a Ferris wheel and a wishing well rose dead black against the sky. Her subconscious tossed up a fragment of memory: Katherine Hepburn on television, striding up a Welsh hillside toward a similar contraption. *How Green Was My Valley.* They were walking toward the headworks of Hadleigh Mine.

"Keep moving." Jackson was right behind her. He sounded nerved up. She started forward again, desperately searching for words.

"Have you ever killed anything, Jackson? You go deer hunting? I bet not. You don't seem like the type. Blood and guts and bone and brains all over everywhere . . . not your kind of thing, is it? You like old woodwork and antique mirrors and china so fine you can practically see through it. You care about that house. You care about your granddaughter. I won't take them away from you."

A dry laugh. "Nope. You won't."

Damn it! She was too frightened to scream, not that anyone was around to hear her. Just clumps of woodland dotting the landscape like a bad haircut. They were approaching the base of the headworks. She was running out of time. "Is it the money you want? I'll give it to you. I don't want it. I didn't even know about it. I just wanted to find my family. We can still be that, if you'll stop this now." They couldn't, of course. But it was all the inducement she could think of.

His bark of laughter held bitter pain. "You'll give me the money. The Schlegel fortune. You and him. Sure."

"Him? What are you talking about?" Her voice cracked. They'd reached the structure's front. Plank walls rose on three sides around a giant elevator car with windows. They were going down the main shaft, she realized with sick horror. Down into the dark tunnels, where no one would ever find her dead body.

She almost broke and ran then, but the dread of a bullet tearing through her back kept her moving slowly. The wooden rabbit in her coat pocket bumped against her leg. *Lucky rabbit. Lucky Rachel. Lucky, lucky.* She couldn't even control her own crazed thoughts. At Jackson's order, she forced her stiff fingers to turn the handle, her shaking arms to shove open the heavy doors. Maybe in the elevator's confines, she could knock him down and grab the gun. Or knock the flashlight out of his hand and run for it once they reached the bottom. Assuming he didn't shoot her in the elevator car.

Jackson followed her inside. He kept the gun muzzle pointed at her midriff as he hauled the doors shut and pressed a button on a panel in the wall. With a shriek like a tortured soul, the ancient machinery started up. The gray squares of glass in the doors shrank and then vanished as the car sank into blackness.

The demented wail of long-disused gears made Terry Powell snap his head up like a pointer dog as he climbed out of the patrol car. They'd run out to Hadleigh silent, not wanting to panic Jackson with the sirens. He raised his voice to carry as two more officers spilled out of the second patrol car. "They're going down the mine." He turned and loped toward the headworks, trying not to think of Rachel Connolly. Since Zimmy's call, he hadn't been able to stop seeing her. Smiling over the picture of Granddaddy Rhys. Standing in the front hall of Schlegel House, a leather-bound book making a dark rectangle against her pale corduroys. Dead and half buried in the snow.

The heavy cables were still rippling off giant cogs as he reached the machinery. He played his flashlight around, looking for some way to stop the elevator car. A switch, a lever, anything.

All he saw were cables and pulleys and the black iron frame that held them. He thought wildly of throwing himself over the edge, landing on the car and battering through its roof. Then the screaming of metal stopped. The elevator had hit bottom.

Ears ringing in the abrupt silence, he strained to hear a shot.

The narrow yellow beam hit her square in the eyes. She could just see Jackson in his corner, shining the flashlight at her. "Open the doors and get out." The light moved away, glancing off glass before descending halfway down one door. Through a dazzle of after-images, Rachel saw the curve of the thick metal handle. She stumbled toward it. A rustle of parka told her Jackson was coming up beside her.

She moved her head just enough to spot the flashlight in his near hand. She would have preferred the gun. Still, the flashlight looked heavy enough to hit him with. Muscles tensing, she threw the handle and shoved the doors apart.

A voice echoed through the roof grille, freezing them both where they stood. "Jackson? It's Terry. You and Rachel want to come up so we can talk?"

Jackson stared upward, caught like a rabbit in headlights. Rachel slammed into him. The impact sent him sprawling. Gun and flashlight spun away across the floor. The flashlight skittered to a stop between the threshold and the rock outside. Its beam picked out the gun in the opposite corner.

Rachel dove for it. Her hand closed around cold, smooth metal. She spun and pointed it at Jackson. Please God he wouldn't see how hard she was shaking. "How do we get this thing moving?"

He didn't answer. On his hands and knees, breathing hard like a beaten fighter, he suddenly looked pathetic. Her arms ached. She wanted to drop the gun, and also to smash him across the head with it. Then he looked up at her, and the slack despair in his face drove most of her anger away.

"It's cold down here," she said. "Let's go where it's warmer, okay?"

He sagged into a sitting position, caved in on himself. Finally, he spoke. "Red button. There."

As he hauled himself slowly upright against the wall, Rachel drew a shaky breath. "Terry? We're coming up."

CHAPTER TWENTY-SEVEN

Rachel set down Linnet's suitcase and pulled the cottage door shut behind her. Schlegel House looked smaller against the dirty-cotton clouds, shrunken by the absence of its faithful servant. Linnet's boots had stitched holes in the snow between the cottage and the manse.

By the time Rachel reached the back steps, her jeans were wet to the knees. She knocked the clinging white clumps off her boots and made a half-hearted attempt to clean her pants, then gave up and went in.

Her heels echoed as she walked toward the front of the house. It felt emptier, if that were possible. Mary Anne's diary, pocketed in her hotel room when they went to the Pines to fetch her car, bumped against her hip. She reached the front hall and gazed up at the majestic sweep of the staircase. Emotions seethed inside her: anger at Jackson for his blind greed, pity for the lonely old man she'd first met. Baffled annoyance at the mysteries that remained. Most of all, bewilderment over the hell she'd gone through for a legacy she'd never suspected and didn't especially want. And beyond all that, an aching sadness for Linnet.

The county social worker who'd dropped by that morning saw little hope of Jackson getting custody of his granddaughter. "Chief Powell tells me you declined to press charges, but I don't see that girl wanting to stay with him even if a court says she should. He's hardly up to handling a teenager in his current mental state." The padded shoulders of her suit jacket barely moved when she shrugged. "Here's hoping she has other family members willing to take her in. The courts'll probably give them a look. Otherwise she comes with me to Duluth day after tomorrow." Her professional detachment slipped as she glanced toward the closed living-room door. "Poor kid."

Linnet's father was on his way back to Chicago, under Detective James Florian's watchful eye. "Killed her mother," Terry had told Rachel last night, over cups of hot mint tea. She'd wandered out of his guest room at one A.M., unable to sleep as soundly as Linnet despite crushing fatigue, and found her host puttering in his kitchen. "Maybe murder, maybe manslaughter. I'd rather the former."

The sternness of his profile as he dipped honey into his tea warned her not to follow that dangling subject thread. She simply let him keep talking. Only half-listening to his rumbly voice, she'd almost missed a familiar name: ". . . Johnny Walker. Then at the Pines, he called himself after some Chicago politician. We were running in circles looking for Chapman, Walker, Luke, Lucas, any variation we could think of—"

She choked down a mouthful of tea. "Lucas Walker. God."

"What?"

"Never mind." She huddled deeper in the armchair, grateful he couldn't see her face in the dim light of the fire. No wonder Jackson had said some of the things he'd said. He must have seen them together at Witek's that day. Or Lucas—*Luke Chapman*—had told him something. Her stomach clenched. She could guess what.

The creeping chill from beneath the mansion's front doors made the hallway cold enough to see her breath. She pushed aside her gloomy reflections and started up the stairs.

Linnet was in Mary Anne's room, curled up in the window seat. She didn't turn around when Rachel entered. She looked closed-off, body hunched, wrapped around her inner pain. Rachel's eyes stung. She took refuge in banalities. "I left your things downstairs," she said. "We can go back to Terry's any time."

Linnet shrugged. Rachel crossed the room and sat next to her. Nose pressed to the window, the girl was staring down at the snow-covered dogwood. "Is it dead?"

"No. Snow doesn't hurt them. They're used to this climate."

Thin winter sun coaxed light from Linnet's hair. Memory came to Rachel: Mom stroking her hair after Dad died, her fingers warm and strong and sure. She raised a hand toward Linnet, then halted. Fumbling, she pulled out the diary. "Here."

Linnet turned her head. Her eyes widened at the sight of the book. "Don't you want it?"

Her shrunken tone made Rachel's stomach hurt. She managed a smile. "Like you said before, you found it. I figure that makes it yours."

After a moment, Linnet took it. Then she dug in her coat pocket. A bulging envelope came out, with Jackson's name written across it.

The envelope held a sheaf of heavy, cream-colored stationery. The writing on it was elegant but shaky, as if the author were very old or very nervous. As she began to read, everything else receded into the distance.

. . . In late October of 1893, I murdered my cousin, Mary Anne Schlegel. My hand struck no blow, but the deed is mine all the same. I was in bad company, from which she sought to extricate me. Instead, they killed her. I watched it happen. I did nothing. Afterward, I helped my father conceal her death.

My father did not wish the circumstances known, for fear my uncle would blame him and widen the breach between them. He wished to siphon money from Uncle Andrew, to pay off his own and my less savory debts. To that end, he concocted a tale of

Mary Anne's disappearance and attempted through her loss to worm our family back into my uncle's good graces. The scheme did not succeed. Not only were no loans forthcoming, but my uncle left all he possessed in trust for my "vanished" cousin or her offspring.

Though my cousin did not speak of it in the days before her death, certain behavior made me suspect that she might, indeed, have had a child. Reading her diary confirmed that this was true. I have since made several attempts to discover the child's whereabouts. I found the person I sought in 1924—Duncan McGrath, a promising architect. I engineered an acquaintance, with the object of telling him his true history. However, I found myself unable to do so. He spoke so admiringly of the parents who had raised him, and clearly believed they were his. I could not tell him otherwise, nor could I bear to relate the circumstances of my cousin's death. Cowardice prevented me from doing what was right. So I ask you, Jackson, to reveal the truth I could not.

I have kept track of Duncan since; his address is at the end of this letter. He may have moved again by the time you read this, but a few short years should prove no great obstacle. Find him, go to him and give him what is his by right: knowledge of his family and the legacy they left him.

The signature—*Randolph William Schlegel*—was a scrawl halfway down the last sheet. Rachel let the confession drift to her lap. Dead all this time, and no one knew. *Because of the goddamned money.*

Linnet picked at her thumbnail, as if nothing mattered except peeling off a perfectly curved strip. "He knew all the time."

Rachel closed her eyes against the ache in the girl's voice. "He didn't hurt me," she said eventually. "He wanted to for awhile, because he was scared. But he couldn't."

Linnet let out a breath. Rachel had a sense of weight beginning to lift from her. Nowhere near gone, but lightened a fraction.

She reached into her coat pocket and cupped Minna's rabbit in one hand. The other rested on her knee. She cleared her throat. "I talked to Terry last night. He knows a lawyer . . ." The necessary words evaporated from her brain. Face flaming, she stumbled on. "There's papers to file and people to talk to, and of course there are no guarantees, but if you think you could stand to live with me . . ."

She trailed off. Linnet turned to look at her, half afraid and half hopeful. One small hand crept over to touch hers, fingertip to fingertip.

She turned her hand palm upward and clasped Linnet's. The girl's fingers were as cold as her own, but she felt the promise of warmth somewhere deep beneath the skin.

ABOUT THE AUTHOR

D. M. Pirrone is the nom de plume of Diane Piron-Gelman, a freelance writer and editor with nearly twenty years' experience. Recent publishing credits include "She Kindly Stopped For Me," in the fantasy-horror anthology *Lucifer's Shadow* (White Wolf Publishing, 2002) and *Handbook: Major Periphery States* (Catalyst Game Labs, 2009), a novel-length fictional history for the *BattleTech*™ role-playing game.

Ms. Piron-Gelman is a Chicago native, history buff, and avid mystery reader. She is also an adoptee, with personal experience of the desire to find one's roots. She lives on Chicago's Northwest Side with her husband Stephen and two sons, David and Isaac.